COLLECTIVE RETRIBUTION
RISE OF THE
FAITHFUL

Collective Retribution Rise of the Faithful

Copyright ©2016 by Storehouse Entertainment

Storehouse Entertainment Group
P.O. Box 1902
Prineville, Oregon 97754

COLLECTIVE RETRIBUTION
RISE OF THE FAITHFUL

D.S. EDWARDS

STOREHOUSE
Entertainment Group

ACKNOWLEDGEMENTS

I would like to thank God first and foremost for placing the desire to create within me.

My best friend, the bride of my youth Velyn. You continue to sacrifice for the sake of my dreams.

To my editor Jim. You make me look good my friend.

Thank you Rhonda, my childhood friend, for your help and opinions.

Thank you, every lover of fiction as you continue purchasing tickets to the theater of my mind's eye.

Thank you Americas Founding Fathers, who through divine providence, created a nation of free people.

THE CATALYST

A T THE START of the twenty-first century, the United States of America was arguably the greatest country mankind had ever created. Its people had the best of everything, thanks to a level of technology no age had seen before. Cars that practically drove themselves. Smart homes that automatically controlled temperature, lighting, security, and entertainment. A cellular telephone in everyone's hands. The wealth of mankind's knowledge just one click away. A central government linked by computers, so strong and powerful that everyone's basic needs were met. Everyone and everything was connected, interwoven by a network of silicon and data. What man had built seemed eternal, indestructible. America's citizens looked at the rest of the world and scoffed. They shook their collective fists in the air and shouted, "Who can ascend the hill of America? No one can topple our shining empire, the envy of the world!"

They were wrong.

On September 11, 2001, terrorist strikes across the country shook the nation. Americans resolved to never let anything so destructive happen again. The nation's leadership called its sons and daughters to the front lines of the War on Terror while everyone cheered them on with pride in their hearts, patriotism bursting forth in every corner of the land, from sea to shining sea. But they were soon reminded of the real cost of war. Many children of the homeland gave their limbs in the great sandbox of Iraq; many others gave their lives. America soon grew weary of war. For the sake of popularity and political power, the nation's elected leaders decided to leave before the job was finished. With a noble yearning for peace and understanding, they opened the homeland to the innocent victims of the horror they had helped fuel. Refugees poured in, seeking the promise of freedom and a life away from the ravages of war. They didn't come alone.

On a cold November day not so many years after that first terrorist strike on U.S. soil, ten men from a land without religious diversity or freedom of speech, men driven solely by hate, walked across America's southern border. They brought nuclear weapons with them.

The nation's foundation of liberty and self-governance, once as solid as granite, had been replaced by self-indulgence and complacency. The change had been driven by technology and the convenience of the internet. The silicon computer chip had enticed people down a path that led to destruction. America had built her house on sand, and she would pay the ultimate price.

In the blink of an eye and a blinding flash of light, all modern electronic technology was destroyed. The country was in crisis.

Those in power at the time of the collapse tried to rebuild. They saw it as an opportunity to change America, to mold her into their idea of utopia. They decided to throw away all that she stood for and turn her into something wicked. The people of rural America who survived the collapse found their strength in the remembrance of what the nation was meant to be. They fought back. The struggle was epic, but the resistance prevailed. The evil that had tried to devour everything good and pure about America was nearly stamped out—nearly, but not quite.

When the survivors in rural America were working together once again to control their destinies, the evil returned in full force.

Those in urban America suffered the most. Resources ran out. As the desperation and hunger of the people grew, the strong consumed the weak. Only those who had weaponry and the will to live survived. The once great cities filled with entertainment, art, and everything man desired turned into devastated neighborhoods ruled by independent dictators and the gangs that had once roamed their ghetto streets. These warlords soon collected all available resources and killed or enslaved the remaining population. Hatred and racism flourished. The wrong color of skin was a death sentence.

Nearly three years after America was attacked, the gangs' resources ran dry. With no knowledge of how to produce food, obtain water, or live independently, they began raiding the countryside to take from those who did, throwing urban and rural America into a violent battle for survival. The gangs took food, water, and clothing, and the youngest and strongest as slaves. At first it seemed easy to get what they needed. Some people protested, but they were outgunned. The gangs controlled the people through intimidation and sheer brutality.

As time went on, a new resistance slowly grew. Finally, those left in the countryside found the courage to push back.

CHAPTER 1

Amish Country
Lancaster County, Pennsylvania
2:00 P.M., Monday, July 28

SARAH BEILER INCHED her way forward, belly crawling through black Pennsylvania mud, carefully choosing her path to avoid twigs, leaves, acorns, and anything else that could give away her position. The seventeen-year-old's long, gray dress was caked with mud, and her greasy, strawberry-blonde hair had begun to fall out of her bonnet. With each movement, she paused long enough to shift her granddaddy's double-barrel shotgun an arm's length in front of her. The stench of decaying vegetation filled her nostrils. Sweat dripped from her head, a bead occasionally snaking down her temple and into the corner of an eye. It stung like peroxide dumped into an open wound.

In the distance, a hen turkey yelped. It was answered immediately by several sharp peeps from its young. Sarah paused, raised her head slowly, and looked over her right shoulder. The field's grass, eight inches high, swayed gently in the breeze. Sarah pulled a turkey wing bone call from the pocket of her dress and gave a short series of hen yelps. She was answered by turkey sounds from fifty yards away. Sarah crawled another ten feet before pausing at the edge of the shallow draw in front of her. She slowly parted the grass and looked intently up and down the path that wound its way through the twists and turns of the canyon. She watched and listened for several minutes, then sent another signal with her turkey wing bone.

A minute later, a young man on the other side of the draw rose up on his elbows, removed a backpack, and placed it on the ground in front of him. He rested his beat-up model 94 .30-.30 on the pack, its barrel pointing up the canyon.

Sarah placed her granddaddy's shotgun on the ground in front of her and waited. Her breathing was steady in spite of the talons of fear clawing at her stomach. Sarah shut her eyes tight and prayed. She wasn't sure if God would forgive her for what she had done, or what she was about to do. Dark memories swirled in her mind. Blood, so much blood. Cold, lifeless eyes staring blankly up at her as dirt was thrown over them. The smell of stomach acid and half-digested roast beef as it gushed from her mouth. The ear-piercing moans of anguish, *her* moans of anguish, echoing through the oak trees.

Sarah opened her eyes, and the memories scurried back into the dark places of her subconscious. A man's voice floated down the canyon.

"Hurry up!" he shouted. "I thought you Amish was stronger than this. If you can't handle the load, then we don't need ya. Maybe we should just cap ya n' haul it ourselves. " Sarah's friend Kevin Hummel, eighteen years old, his sister Naomi, only thirteen, and two men came into view. Kevin was harnessed up like a mule, pulling a cart loaded with raw vegetables, home-canned foods, and two large slabs of beef. Naomi walked at his heels. The two strangers walked ten feet behind, their rifles trained on their captives. They were seventy yards away and moving closer.

Kevin's boot caught on a rock. He fell to his knees. Naomi bent down to help him. One of the men, a red scar running down the full length of his face, rushed forward, grabbed her by the hair, and jerked her backwards. The other man came forward and raised his hand to slap her. His companion caught his arm just before it made contact.

2

"Not in the face, Hanson! If we bring her in all marked up, Randy gonna cap us both!"

Hanson withdrew his hand. Scarface grabbed Naomi by the hair again and dragged her out of the way. Hanson took a step forward and kicked Kevin in the ribs. Kevin doubled over and curled up on the ground in a ball.

Sarah gritted her teeth and fought the urge to jump up and shoot Hanson in the face. They were too far away. If she acted too soon, there was a chance one of them could escape and bring more men than she and her companion could handle.

Usually, when the bad men came to the village, they took what they wanted and quickly left. This time they had stayed four days, lounging around and eating as much as they could. They had also raped three of Sarah's friends.

The extra time had strengthened her hate. Now that hate was starting to consume her. The only way to feed it was to focus it on these men.

Scarface bent down and yelled in Kevin's ear: "Get up!"

Kevin moaned and made no effort to get up.

"We have orders to bring this n' your pretty lil' sister, with no marks." Scarface walked back, grabbed Naomi by the forearm, dragged her next to Kevin, and threw her on the ground.

"Our orders said no marks. Randy didn't say nothin' bout a little trainin'. Maybe we can just wait here for a while. You can catch your breath, n' I can have a lil' fun with sissy. Maybe break her in a little. " Scarface tore open the front of Naomi's dress, exposing her breasts. Naomi screamed and tried to crawl away. He grabbed her by the ankle and dragged her back. He pinned her arms down with his knees, then grabbed a handful of breast with dirty fingers.

"I'm up!" Kevin shouted as he got to his feet. "I'm up."

Kevin's muscles strained and he grunted as he pushed forward, dragging the heavy cart down the path. Scarface let Naomi up. Red faced and sobbing, she held the front of her dress closed and trotted after her brother.

"That's what I'm talkin' 'bout!" Scarface said and the two men followed, laughing, twenty yards behind.

When the foursome was still forty yards from Sarah, Scarface stopped them to take a rest. Kevin let the harness fall from his sagging shoulders and sat down hard in the dirt. Naomi sat beside him and buried her face in the folds of his shirt.

Sarah slipped her finger into the trigger guard of her shotgun and placed her other hand under the forestock. She could hear her blood pounding in her ears. Her breathing, steady just minutes before, now came in short, ragged gasps. A sliver of doubt wedged into her thoughts. Could she go through this again? She knew what she was about to do was wrong. She knew it as sure as she knew it would condemn her to the fires of Hell. Why had God allowed the world to become so dark and violent? Why didn't he protect his people from the anguish and torment? Life had been so simple, so innocent, before the bad people began invading their home, taking what they pleased by force. She just wanted to go back. Back to the way it used to be.

Sarah closed her eyes. Her mind drifted to an afternoon just a month before. She was standing with her father, mother, sister Amity, Grandpa Vernon, and Grandma Grace in the Yoders' barn on a warm morning. Her father held *The Ausbund* hymnal open as they all leaned in close to read the words. The voices of her family and friends rang out loud and in perfect harmony as they sang "Lob Lied." Soft breezes carried the scent of horse manure and Summersweet bushes through the open doors of the barn.

Sarah glanced over her shoulder and caught the deep blue eyes of Jakob Miller staring back at her from the back bench. He really was quite handsome—six feet two inches tall, with coarse, brick-red hair, his boyish face and a smattering of freckles on his cheekbones making him look younger than his nineteen years. The rest of him, though, was definitely all grown up: broad, well-muscled shoulders and long, sinewy arms hardened by many hours behind a plow and from swinging a heavy sickle.

When Jakob grinned and winked, impure thoughts nearly overwhelmed Sarah. She quickly averted her eyes. Her mother caught the exchange out of the corner of her eye, smiled at Sarah, and tilted her head toward Sarah's father. Sarah mustered the most innocent look she could and smiled back at her mother. Sarah had always been a daddy's girl. In her eyes he was the greatest man alive. But her mother understood her and had been her best friend as long as she could remember.

After the weekly service ended, Sarah joined her friends just outside and waited for the women of the village to transform the barn from a church into a meal and fellowship hall. There was much talking and laughing among the girls, but Sarah paid little attention. Instead, she positioned herself near the small doorway so she could watch Jakob visit with the rest of the village men. After the men finished their meal, Sarah got in line with the other women and girls to dish up her own food.

Suddenly, the double barn doors burst open. Four men in tattered clothing ran inside. Three of them pointed rifles at the village men. They swept the muzzles of the rifles side to side, sometimes stopping for a few seconds in front of a bearded face. Children scrambled under the dresses of their mothers, who also cowered in fear.

The man in charge of the group shouted out orders, then walked through the barn, studying the faces of the young men. Sarah tried to keep her head down like the rest of her people, but she couldn't help glancing up. The leader of the invaders was at least six feet tall, his head shaved. Sarah thought he was ugly. He walked with a limp and had thin, red lips set below a gaunt face. Despite the circumstances, part of Sarah felt sorry for him—he obviously hadn't been eating well. She had never known true hunger and had always taken it for granted that her people would have all they needed.

Sarah's father squared his shoulders, walked to the middle of the barn, and addressed everyone in his deep, commanding voice: "Everyone stay calm. These people have come to us for help once again. Let's all cooperate with them and share what God has provided."

Sarah trembled with a mixture of fear and anger. She knew she was supposed to turn the other cheek and forgive these men for all they had done and would possibly do in the future. She'd done it each time they'd come, but every time it got harder.

When the leader stopped in front of Jakob, Sarah's heart stopped. She screamed, knowing what was about to happen, and started to rush forward. Her father grabbed her around the waist, clamping a hand over her mouth. Sarah kicked, clawed at her father's hands, and screamed against his palm as Jakob was led outside. Before she knew it, he was gone.

Half an hour later, Sarah was still shaking and sobbing. Her father had carried her to their house and laid her in her bed. He'd spent a half an hour praying with her, then walked out gently, closing the door behind him.

Sarah sat up in bed, wiped her eyes, and bit her lip, drawing blood. Oh, Jakob! How could her father do nothing? Why did he allow these men to keep tormenting them? Her mind kept replaying the image of Jakob's strong back disappearing as the evil men led him away.

A hen turkey call interrupted Sarah's anguish. She opened her eyes. Kevin and Naomi had already passed by. Scarface was now directly below her. If she'd daydreamed any longer, these men would have been gone and she would have never seen her friend Naomi again.

In one motion, Sarah rose to a knee, slammed the butt of the shotgun to her shoulder, took a bead on Scarface's forehead, and squeezed both triggers. Flames shot from the barrels. The top of the man's head peeled back and came to rest on the back of his neck, hair side down. He stood stiff-legged for a moment, a look of surprise on his face, then crumpled to the ground.

Hanson dropped his gun, dove to the dirt, and began crawling toward the brush just off the trail. To Sarah's right, a young man's .30-.30 barked. Hanson screamed in pain as the .30-caliber bullet tore through the middle of his back and blew out his spine. He clawed the mud desperately, trying to pull himself into the brush, dragging his lifeless legs behind him and moaning in terror. The young man slid down the bank and slowly walked toward Hanson. Ten feet from the man, he raised his rifle, shoved the barrel against Hanson's skull, and fired again.

Sarah half ran, half slid down the side of the draw. Dirt filled her shoes and stickers poked holes in her black tights. Jakob Miller stood over the man he'd just killed. Sarah slipped up beside him and took his hand in hers.

"It doesn't get any easier," he said. "I don't know if I can do this anymore."

Sarah raised a trembling hand and cupped Jakob's chin, turning his face toward hers. His eyes were red, his face twisted up. A single tear slid down his cheek.

Sarah had loved this boy since she was a child. Seeing him in so much anguish tore at her insides.

"We had no choice," she whispered. "We can't let those that serve the Devil hurt our people. It's not right to stand by and do nothing while our friends, neighbors, and even family are taken from us to be enslaved or killed. I'm sorry, but I think the elders are wrong to not fight back. I know in my heart that we're doing the only thing we can to stop this. Is it wrong? Probably. No. It *is* wrong. It's just...we have no choice."

"But we're killing people, Sarah." Jakob protested. "The Almighty commands us to not kill. That is nonnegotiable according to the Ten Commandments."

Sarah let go of Jakob's hand. Flecks of spittle sprayed from between her lips as she hissed her response.

"It also says in the commandments, 'Thou shalt not bow down thyself to them, nor serve them.' In **Psalm 82:4,** *it tells us to* 'Rescue the weak and needy; Deliver them out of the hand of the wicked.' I'm not going to get in an argument with you about the finer points of God's Word," she said. "But I want you to look at them."

Sarah grabbed Jakob's chin and jerked his head toward the two young people they'd just rescued. Naomi sat in the dirt, her knees pulled up under her chin, her head rocking back and forth. Kevin knelt next to his sister, his arms wrapped tightly around her. Both were crying.

"That's why we do this!" Sarah snapped. "We do it for them, and everyone who is like them. We do it for their families. We do it so no one else has to die at the hands of evil. As long as I have breath in me, I will continue to do that." Sarah gestured toward the man she had killed. "I know this will not be the last time I take a life. I know it, just as sure as I know I will be damned for what I have done. I also know that if I don't do what needs to be done, more of our friends and family will die."

Before Jakob could protest again, Sarah walked behind him, reached into his backpack, took out a small folding shovel, and pushed him hard between the shoulders. She turned and walked off the trail, into the thick trees.

She chose a clear spot surrounded by dense brush and began to dig. After a few minutes, Jakob joined her with the second shovel. Silently, they tore into the soft, rich soil. In thirty minutes, they dug two holes, each four feet by eight feet and four feet deep. They retrieved Scarface's body and dropped it into the first fresh grave. Before the body was covered, Kevin and Naomi joined them, dragging the other gangster. No one spoke as they covered the last body and hid the freshly disturbed earth with brush and leaves. Sarah couldn't stop wondering if the men's blood was crying out from the ground to God's ears as Abel's blood had when Cain slew him.

When the task was completed, they gathered around the food cart. Kevin broke the silence.

"I'm glad they're dead. I know I shouldn't be. I know how I'm expected to feel and act, turn the other cheek and all, but I am glad. If I could have, I would have done it myself for what they did to Naomi. May God forgive me for my sinful thoughts, but I would have."

Naomi began to cry again. Kevin held her close.

Now it was Sarah's turn to speak. "You know you can't tell anyone what happened here today. No one in the village must ever fin—"

"You can't expect us to lie," Naomi interrupted, a squeak in her voice. "People will want to know how we escaped, and how we got the food and supplies back. I can't lie to them, especially Papa."

"I can't force you to lie, Naomi." Sarah said. "But you need to decide right now whether or not what you just went through is something you want anyone else to have to face. What if the next time it's your little sister? If the elders find out what we're doing, they will try to stop us. When these wicked men come to the village again—and mark my words, they will come—there will be no one to stand up to them. How would you feel if you are the reason the next girl gets raped or killed? Can you live with that?"

Naomi looked stunned. Sarah could see the inner struggle reflected in her eyes. She felt guilty for putting Naomi in that position, but it was the same position she'd been in the first time she had fought back. Over time, Sarah had justified what she was doing by telling herself it was for the good of her people. She hoped Naomi would agree with her thinking.

"Maybe you don't lie," said Sarah. "Maybe you just don't tell them anything. Maybe the events of today are too painful for you to speak about. Maybe you tell them that. I doubt if they will push you into saying something that would cause you further pain."

Naomi wiped her eyes. "How long have you been...I mean, how many times have you..." Her words trailed off. She gestured toward the woods where they had just buried the men.

Sarah took a deep breath and stared at the trees around the graves before answering. "When Carla didn't come back after the first raid, I cried. I cried for days. I was angry at Bishop Springer, and every other man in the village, including my father. They just stood there and did nothing while she was drug away, being groped and pawed at by animals. The only thing the braaave men of our village did is bow their heads in prayer."

Sarah bit her lip. "My Father, the deacon, protector of our people, just stood there with his hands at his sides. We could still hear Carla's screams as they took her away. I was so angry. No one made a move to go after her."

Sarah clenched her fists at her sides before continuing. "The second time they came, Isaac and Julia were the ones to be dragged off. Sacrificed by the cowards in charge of our village. The time after that, Jakob was drug away."

Sarah paused, looked at Jakob, and swallowed hard.

"Later that evening, I grabbed Granddaddy's shotgun, and slipped out of the village while everyone slept. I followed them for two days. I watched them kick, punch, and nearly kill him the entire journey. When we got close to Pittsburgh, I decided I would let them go no further. I ran through the woods and got in front of them. I hid behind an old rotten log and waited. Just as the sun went down, they came into view. Jakob could hardly walk. He was bruised and bleeding from cuts on his face. I imagined the men were deer, and I was hunting. I slowly parted the brush in front of the log and placed the barrel through the opening. When they came into range, I froze. I couldn't bring myself to do anything. No matter how hard I tried, I just couldn't stand the thought of taking a life. I just watched them pass by no more than fifteen feet away.

"Then they stopped. One of the men laughed at Jakob. He said they were nearly through with him, and told Jakob that he wasn't going to go home. He spit on him, cussed at him, called him a worthless cracker, and cursed the name of God. The anger exploded inside of me. Before I knew what was happening, I was spinning around, the barrel of the shotgun was coming up, and my finger was on the front trigger. It was like I was watching myself from a distance. I had no control over my body. The next memory I have is of Jakob holding me and somebody screaming. I realized it was me."

Sarah couldn't hold back her emotions anymore. Tears streamed down her face. She turned away from the group. A gentle hand on her shoulder turned her around. She looked into the face of Naomi, and the two embraced. Their tears mixed as their cheeks pressed together.

"I'm so sorry," Naomi sobbed.

They held each other for several minutes before Sarah pushed her away.

"I have to do this," whispered Sarah. "There is no other option. Like it or not, our world has changed. We can no longer hide away. We've always had to make sacrifices and put up with hurts from the Englishmen's world in order to live out our faith. But the days of the biggest hurt being someone pointing at us and laughing or saying mean things are over. This is life or death, and I choose to live. I'm not ready to go before the Father and face judgment. I want to have children. I want to be loved by someone, and know what it's like to lay in the arms of the one I love and feel his skin on my skin." Sarah glanced at Jakob. He averted his eyes and his cheeks turned bright red.

Sarah turned back to Naomi and set her jaw. "You need to choose right now, Naomi. Do you want to live? Will evil win and rob you of the life God has planned for you?"

Naomi didn't answer, but Sarah could see resolve in her eyes. She knew she might not decide right away, but she was certain now that Naomi would fight alongside her and Jakob.

Sarah and her companions moved back up the trail. By this time the sun's shadows were growing long. Sarah knew there was no way they would make it back to the warmth and comfort of Amish life that day. Kevin and Naomi were both exhausted and battered from their captivity.

The best thing they could do was find a secluded spot off the trail, warm themselves by a roaring fire, and rest up for the remainder of the journey.

"I am so tired," Sarah said, doing her best to keep Naomi and Kevin from feeling bad about slowing them down. "And for the last mile I have been practically drooling, thinking about cracking open that jar of Mrs. Bontrager's apricot preserves and eating it like pudding."

Naomi smiled up at Sarah.

"I swear, Sarah Beiler," Jakob said. "I ain't never met a girl that could eat like you. You put every boy I know to shame."

Half an hour later, they were all seated around a large campfire. Their bellies were full, and they reminisced about their childhoods and growing up Amish.

"Wait! Wait! I got one," Naomi said. "You guys remember when Mark Yoder ran into the middle of supper after the Lengachers' barn raising, all covered with skunk juice?"

Sarah laughed heartily. She looked at Jakob, who had again turned a dark shade of crimson. "If I remember correctly," she said, "that whole thing was your fault, Jakob."

He shrugged his shoulders and forced an innocent smile. "It wasn't my fault. Mark should've known better than to crawl headfirst into a brush pile just because I told him to. The fact that me and Elmer Stoltzfus had just chased the foul creature in there is completely irrelevant."

This time they all laughed. Sarah understood that they needed the distraction from the world they now found themselves in, a world that had drifted away from the one they'd known before.

The temporary levity was shattered by Naomi's next words: "I really miss Mark."

Silence blanketed the small camp as each of them stared into the firelight and recalled the day Mark was taken from them. It was the same day they lost Julia.

The gang had rushed into the village without warning and begun randomly shooting at farmhouses. Mark's father came out of his house and tried to reason with them, but all he managed was to make them angry. They cracked him over the head with a gun barrel and kicked him up and down his body until he quit moving. Mark ran from the house toward his beaten father. They shot him in the head before he cleared the front porch. Sarah could hear the screams of his mother and sister as he lay bleeding out on the whitewashed stairs.

Sarah closed her eyes tightly and shook her head, trying to dislodge the memory. With each shake of her head, a happy memory rushed into her mind: barn raisings, Christmas dinners at her grandmother's table, afternoons spent leaning over her needlepoint, late summer evenings watching her father as he milked the cows and fed the hogs, family prayers and devotions. Amish life was hard, but it was a way of life she truly loved. She had learned to love peace, and to be charitable above all else. Now, in this new world, those lessons no longer seemed to apply.

"I don't know about the rest of you," Sarah said, "but I'm beat down. If we want to get started early in the morning, we should probably get some sleep."

She lay on her side, settled into a pile of leaves, and stared into the dying flames of the fire. As long as she could remember, she had never needed anything from the outside world. But when the Englishmen's world came crumbling down, it seemed the Heavenly Father had removed his hand of divine providence from her life, and their corrupt world had spilled into hers. Now she was torn between both worlds. She still believed in the Father and the strength of tradition, but she was being dragged into the violence and death that had once been America. It filled her with fear. Would she have to choose between the worlds one day? If anyone from her village found out what she had done, she knew that choice would be made for her.

CHAPTER 2

Silent Run Road
Pittsburgh
8:30 A.M., Thursday, July 31

FOURTEEN-YEAR-OLD JULIA LAPP positioned the stainless steel bucket under the cow's udders and began to pull and squeeze on the teats in a steady rhythm. With each pull, a stream of milk squirted into the bucket and a sharp pain shot from Julia's ribs.

Randy had been especially rough on her the night before when the two men he had sent out for supplies didn't return when expected. Every time something didn't go exactly the way he thought it should, he took out his frustrations by knocking her around. Then he raped her. When his stress was relieved, he usually fell asleep, and Julia would carefully slip out of bed and retreat to her small bedroom in the basement of the huge Fox Chapel mansion. But last night, Randy had not been asleep. He'd flown into a rage when she attempted to get out of bed. He grabbed her by the hair with his left hand, jerked her head back, and slapped her cheek with the other hand. He threw her back onto the bed, knelt over her, and worked his way down her ninety-five-pound frame with his

13

fists. When he had exhausted his rage, he tossed her to the floor, kicked her once in the ribs, and walked over to the gilded liquor cabinet. He pulled a bottle of sixty-year-old Speyside single malt whiskey from a shelf, took a long hard pull from the bottle, and walked out, leaving her to cry on the cold marble floor.

Julia finished milking the cow and carried the bucket to the concrete pool shed where she would let it cool while the cream rose to the top. The outside temperature had been rising steadily since the middle of May and now reached into the nineties most days. The heat mixed with the high humidity made doing the daily chores early in the morning a necessity. Most afternoons, Julia was free to lay in the shade and secretly write in her journal, or explore the twenty-five-acre estate before fixing lunch for Randy and the guards. She had made a mental map of every square inch of the grounds and had searched without success for a weak spot in the wall surrounding the property. There were a few places she could hide away from the guards without worrying about them finding her and directing their lust toward her, but so far she hadn't found a way to get beyond the border of the fortress and escape.

The first time one of the guards had caught her alone in the garden shed and raped her, she had told Randy. Randy had killed the man and hung him on a pole just outside the guesthouse that had been converted into the guard's quarters. From that day forward, it was understood among the men that Julia was the exclusive property of Randy and no one else was to touch her. After the first guard was killed, she promised herself and God that if it happened again, she would not tell anyone. She did not want to be the reason for someone else's death. Even though the men brought other girls to the Fox Chapel house to satisfy their whims, most of these were black or Hispanic. Apparently, the temptation to lay with a girl with cream-colored skin was at times impossible for them to resist. Julia had learned from one of the Latina girls that there had been a few white girls brought to the house just after the city collapsed, but most of them had been killed on orders from Randy. According to him, white people were the cause of all the world's problems, and the city would be better off if they didn't exist.

Soon after Julia was brought to the mansion, Randy's position on how to treat the white girls evolved. It was okay to let a few survive for entertainment purposes, but only a few. Any other white people found within the city were to be shot on sight. It was also okay to use the Amish men and boys from the villages to bring supplies into the city, but as soon as the task was finished, they were to be killed. Occasionally another Amish girl would be brought to Randy, but Julia was never allowed to interact with them. They would keep her locked in her room until Randy was done with the newcomer. When he was finished, the girl would be taken away. Julia wasn't sure where they were taken, but they were never brought back a second time.

Julia returned to the mansion to freshen up, change clothes, and get her journal out of its hiding place behind the big mirror on the dresser. She had a limited wardrobe, but had been provided with a few outfits after her traditional Amish dress and bonnet had been taken from her. She chose a light, flowered dress. It was far too fancy and short to have ever been worn in her village, but it made her feel pretty, like a woman, not like the little girl she had been just a few short months earlier. She stood in front of the mirror studying her reflection before putting it on. Her jet black hair had lightened up considerably since her capture, making the shade more of a dark brown. She reached up and twirled a handful of bangs. Her face had grown a little darker, and had started to lose some of the freckles that had always dotted her creamy white skin. She turned sideways and studied her profile. Her breasts had grown a little larger, and her stomach a little flatter. She gently touched the small bruises on the sides of her breasts, then touched the big purple bruise on her rib cage. She winced and drew in a hissing breath through clenched teeth. This was the worst beating she'd had in quite a while, but she refused to allow Randy the satisfaction of her pain. She would act, say, and do what she did every day. She would cook his meals, tend the garden, clean the house, and crawl into his foul-smelling bed in the evening. She would watch and wait until her opportunity came to escape. Then she would run and never look back.

Julia wasn't sure how she could go back to her home now that she would be considered unclean, but it didn't matter. If her family wouldn't take her back, she would head west and try to assimilate into the Englishmen's world. She had overheard the guards talking about how places out west in Oregon and Washington had been able to get electricity restored. She had never used modern electrical conveniences, had never ridden in an automobile, never seen a movie or watched a television. She was at least three years away from the age where she could have engaged in rumspringa, the time in every Amish youth's life where they lived in and experienced the Englishmen's world. They would decide afterwards whether or not they would stay in that world full of sin and offense to God or return to their family and the church. If they returned, they would then be fully baptized into the faith.

Julia turned sideways in front of the mirror. She winked one green eye and tried her best to look seductively at herself over her shoulder. She pursed her lips in a kissing motion, felt a stab of guilt, and quickly pushed it aside. She decided that the old traditions didn't matter now. She had been defiled, forever changed. The rules she had been raised by were no longer relevant. She was no longer a child.

She slipped on her dress, put her hair in a ponytail, and applied a little makeup to her face. Makeup had been strictly forbidden in her childhood home. Upon arriving at the mansion, she was provided with large amounts of the stuff, and given orders by Randy to wear it whenever she was in the house. The first time she had tried to put some on, she had ended up looking like a clown. Randy had laughed at her until tears poured from his eyes, then proceeded to beat her with his nylon belt. Soon after, she had found an old magazine called *Cosmopolitan* in the library. She had poured through it, studying the faces of the beautiful women on the pages. After several hours, and several scrubbings of her face to the point of her skin becoming raw, she had mostly succeeded in making herself look like the girls in the pictures.

Julia looked at the windup alarm clock next to the bed. It read 10:45. She had at least forty-five minutes to write in her journal before she needed to be in the kitchen preparing lunch. Writing in her journal had become as important to her as breathing or eating. In this dark and violent world, it was the one place she could release her thoughts and hold on to a little sanity.

She reached behind the mirror to retrieve her journal. Her heart stopped—where was it? She held her breath while frantically feeling around and finding nothing but empty space. She dropped to her knees and crawled under the vanity. Maybe the notebook had fallen behind somehow. But no, it was gone. Terror tore at her mind.

Did Randy find it?

If Randy had the journal, she was in for a serious beating, or worse. Her panic grew. She had the sudden urge to run away now, even if she wasn't ready. She'd likely be caught, in which case she would also be beaten or killed. Either way, things were about to get very bad.

"Randy must have found it," she muttered. He didn't allow anyone else to enter her room. Everyone around Randy was in a constant state of fear. What he said was law, no discussion permitted. He had killed men for something as simple as falling asleep on duty. No guard would dare go against Randy's word.

"Whatchya lookin for?"

Julia jerked up, banging her head on the underside of the vanity. She crawled out backwards, rubbed the top of her head, and turned slowly to meet the gaze of Willie Marshall.

"I said, 'Whatchya lookin' for?'" Willie asked again, an evil grin on his face.

He waved her journal in front of him and shook his head while making clicking sounds with his tongue.

"Tsk tsk tsk," he said. "Somebody been naughty. I don't think Randy would like his number one pet writin' things 'bout him. "

Julia didn't know what to say. She was sure she knew where this meeting was headed, but she had no idea how to stop it.

Willie opened the journal and began reading out loud. His voice cracked and squeaked as he did his best impersonation of her.

"March 29. I had to lay with Randy twice yesterday. It was all I could do to keep from throwing up. He smells worse than a plow horse after a day in the fields. His hands are rough and his breath makes my eyes sting. He told me that tomorrow a milk cow is being brought, and that I would be allowed outside the house to care for it, and milk it every morning. I am excited, and as strange as it may seem a little grateful to him for my small taste of freedom. I will be sure to try and learn the surroundings beyond the walls of the house. There may be a way I can escape soon."

Willie closed the journal and stared at Julia. He licked his lips and smiled, revealing his stained front teeth. A small shiver started at the small of her back and travelled up to the back of her neck.

"Ain't no reason Randy have all the fun," Willie said as he started forward.

Julia backed toward the bedroom door with her hands raised, never taking her eyes from his.

"No, Willie!" Julia shouted. "I'm going to scream. Randy will hear. He'll kill you."

"Randy gone," Willie said as he slowly moved toward her, removing his shirt. "He left to take care of some problems. No one here but me, you, and my boys outside. Randy ain't gonna know, lus you say somethin'. You ain't gonna say nothin' are ya? You do, I'll make sure Randy reads this here book."

With those last words, Willie squinted, bared his teeth, and lunged forward. In almost one motion, Julia sidestepped and rushed past him and out of the bedroom, slamming the door in his face. As she ran up the stairs to the main floor, she heard the bedroom door swing open and slam against the wall. From the top step, she heard Willie's feet starting to stomp up the staircase behind her. She struggled to make her feet move faster as terror weaved its way through her mind.

Julia sprinted across the living room and careened off an antique end table, knocking it to the floor. She flew across the foyer and reached for the door handle just as Willie caught her. She held onto the door handle while he tackled her at the ankles, pulling her to the floor. Her hand slipped off the handle just as the door flew open. Willie pulled her toward him across the cold marble floor and rolled her over. He straddled her, pinned her arms behind her, and kicked her legs apart. Drops of rancid-smelling spittle flew from his mouth as he yelled in her face, "You gonna like this, girl!" Her scream echoed off the walls as he leaned down, trying to kiss her.

When his face nearly touched hers, she tilted her chin down, then thrust her head forward and hard, catching Willie in the nose with her forehead. He groaned, let go of her arms, and put his hands over his freshly broken nose. Blood began to pour out. Julia rolled over, kicked her legs free, and pushed herself up. She scrambled out the doorway, got to her feet, and ran across the lawn.

"You gonna pay for that, ho!" Willie screamed after her.

Julia aimed for the garden shed, thinking, *If I can just get inside the door, I can get to the rake or shovel.*

Then her foot caught on a stubby tree root. She fell. She tried to get up, but Willie was already there. He grabbed her right leg and dragged her across the gravel driveway toward the house. Her head bounced up and down over sharp rocks. Julia screamed and kicked at Willie with her free leg. She missed. He turned and kicked her between the legs. Julia cried out in pain, the wind knocked out of her. She lay helpless as he began dragging again.

Ten feet from the front door, Willie stopped and released his grip. The world grew silent. All Julia could hear was her own ragged breathing. Willie stiffened, momentarily stood motionless, then his legs collapsed under him at the same moment a small red hole began to trickle blood down the middle of his sweaty back.

Julia lay on the ground, trying to catch her breath. The back of her head throbbed. What had just happened? A few seconds earlier she was being hauled toward the house by this foul-smelling monster. Now he was on the ground three feet away, a hole in his back, dead. Flies were already beginning to gather around the body. She watched as if she were in a dream. A bright-green fly landed in the sticky blood and began rubbing its feet together. Julia felt groggy. She let her eyelids slip down and settle over her bloodshot eyes. She needed to rest for just a minute, even though her mind screamed, "Go! Now's your chance to get away! Get up!"

Julia tried to obey her mind's insistent plea but she could not make her body cooperate. She was unable to even open her eyes, let alone stand up and run toward freedom.

She heard a distant squeak, the estate's front gate moving on rusty hinges, then the sound of a motor and tires crunching on gravel. She tried again to open her eyes, to roll over and push herself off the ground. She managed to get her arms underneath her chest before her mind slid into darkness.

CHAPTER 3

Silent Run Road
11:00 A.M.

Tom Dixon took his time driving the Polaris Ranger Utility Task Vehicle up the long driveway. His eyes scanned the tree line on both sides of him, and the rock wall that surrounded the estate. He had seen Jackson leave with most of his men earlier in the day. As far as he knew, only Willie and two others had stayed behind to guard the property. He had taken out the two others soon after Jackson left, and he was pretty sure Willie wouldn't cause him any more trouble.

Tom had watched the property from a ridge a quarter mile away for three days. He'd been living on deer jerky and water. The only time he took his eyes off the grounds was to relieve himself or catch an occasional power nap. He had known the warlord of the gang that controlled the Hilltop area of Pittsburgh was running things from here for quite some time, but until today he'd never had the right opportunity to disrupt his operation. After today, Randy Jackson would find himself without a home.

Fox Chapel was an area Tom had been to only once or twice in his lifetime. It was within the Pittsburgh city limits, but felt more like a rural community. Each home was built on a minimum of ten acres and was landscaped beautifully. It had always been a status symbol to live and play in Fox Chapel. The residents looked down on anyone who couldn't afford a slice of the hill. Now that Tom was again amongst the extravagant homes, he remembered why he didn't like coming to this part of the city.

Tom smiled at the memory of his father talking about the people on Silent Run. "Snob Chapel is what it should be called," he'd say.

"I guess your money and status don't mean much now, do they?" Tom said into the summer air.

He pulled the UTV up to the girl on the ground next to Willie Marshall. Tom was very familiar with Mr. Marshall. He had arrested him several times while working in the intelligence division of the Central Investigations unit of the Pittsburgh Police Department. The last time he arrested Willie, it was on an armed robbery and distribution charge. His public defender, some smarmy, do-good champion of the poor, oppressed minorities, had pulled some slick maneuvering and gotten the armed robbery charge dropped. Willie was convicted of distribution of narcotics and served eleven months before President Hartley commuted the sentences of every "nonviolent" offender in the American prison system.

The idea that if you were black and grew up in the projects, you were destined to live in oppression and turn to a life of crime had always irritated Tom. He was the antithesis of that line of thinking. He was black and had grown up on Lexington Avenue, surrounded by violence and hatred. But his childhood and life of poverty had not defined him. Tom's father worked at a steel mill and was away six days a week providing for Tom, his mother, and his three brothers. Most of his childhood friends didn't know their fathers and grew up on the streets. Their mothers all loved them and did the best they could to provide for them, but in the end, most of them had turned to the gangs. Fathers were replaced by gang leaders. Tom and his brothers had gotten away from the hell of their neighborhoods as soon as each turned eighteen. Shortly after his youngest brother left to attend college, his parents moved away from the old neighborhood. Without four extra mouths to feed, they could finally afford to settle in the suburbs.

Tom went to college on a scholarship and studied criminal science. He graduated near the top of his class and enrolled in the police academy. He was a beat cop for two years, but had caught the eye of the director of the intelligence division and was offered a position. Tom jumped at the chance to work in his old neighborhood. His mother hated the idea, and cried for two days when he told her his plans. His dad was also worried, but Tom knew he would never show it. He had put his hand on Tom's shoulder, looked him in the eye, and told him how proud he was of him.

Tom climbed from the UTV, dropped to one knee, and raised his .300 Blackout to his shoulder, sweeping his field of vision back and forth. Satisfied that there were no hidden thugs with guns trained on him, he lowered his weapon and cautiously approached Willie's body. He rolled him over with his foot. Willie's lifeless eyes stared up at him.

He knelt next to the young girl, placed his rifle on the ground, and checked her pulse. She was alive, but unconscious. He tried to ascertain the extent of her injuries. If she was injured too badly, he would have to leave her behind. It struck Tom just how cold and callous this world had made him. He felt a stab of remorse at the thought of just leaving someone to suffer and die, but quickly pushed it away. The reality was that there was no way he could care for major injuries. He knew basic field first aid, but beyond that his skills were limited. There wasn't a doctor left in the city—at least, he hadn't come across one since the collapse. Sure, they had a nurse at his compound, and he had seen her tend to some pretty serious trauma in the last few months. But if this girl's injuries were so severe that she likely wouldn't make it back to the care of Nurse Nicole, then Tom would leave her behind.

Tom reached behind the girl's head. Her blood oozed between his fingers. He took off his tactical vest and made a makeshift pillow. He gently rolled her over and set her forehead on the pillow before examining the back of her skull. He tried to brush her hair out of the way enough to see the wound that was bleeding profusely, but the dirty brown strands were too matted and stuck together. He unsheathed the knife at his side and cut away a good portion of her locks. The gash on her head was deep and bleeding heavily. He returned to the UTV, retrieved his water bottle, and did his best to wash the wound. He reached again under her head, found the front pocket of his vest, and drew out a small sewing kit and a roll of bandage material. He worked quickly, sewing the wound shut and covering it with a bandage. Then he carried her to the passenger side of the Ranger and strapped her in the seat.

After retrieving his weapon and vest, Tom cautiously approached the house. He peeked carefully from cover, then eased his way inside the front door. The house was palatial. He stood on marble floors in a gigantic foyer under twenty-foot ceilings. A brass railing ran up and along a grand spiral staircase leading up to two additional floors. Tom's breath caught. He had seen the houses on Silent Run from the outside, but this was the first time he'd been in one.

Man, he thought, *Dad was right. What a waste of money.*

He carefully searched the house. There was plenty here he could make use of, but he didn't have the time to gather it all. He wasn't sure when Jackson would return and didn't want to be around when he did. If it wasn't for the injured girl waiting in his vehicle, he would have staked himself just outside the property and waited for an opportunity to end Randy Jackson's life. After today, he wasn't sure where Jackson and his gang would end up, or when he'd have another chance at him. The thought of leaving the girl behind crossed his mind again, but he quickly rejected it.

In a side bedroom on the third floor, he found a treasure trove of weapons, ammunition, and explosives. Hundreds of rifles lined the walls. Handguns were scattered across a California king-sized bed and all over the Berber carpet. At least fifty cases of dynamite were stacked in one corner, along with several crates of grenades. In the opposite corner of the room, next to a large bay window, was a stack of ammunition boxes of nearly every common caliber.

Tom smiled and tore the quilt comforter from the bed. He laid it on the floor and grabbed several of the military-issue rifles and handguns. He threw as much matching ammunition as he could carry and a few grenades on top of the pile. He then rolled it all up in the quilt and slung it over his shoulder. His leg muscles burned as he worked his way down the stairs and out the front door. Tom put the bundle into the cargo bed of the Ranger, grabbed a road flare from the jockey box, and went back into the mansion. In the main living room, he opened a gilded liquor cabinet and began throwing bottles of Scotch, brandy, vodka, tequila, and whiskey into what became a pile of broken glass and multicolored alcohol. He emptied nearly all the booze from the cabinet and added it to the pile, except for a couple of choice bottles he saved for himself.

Tom walked over to the puddle of spirits, struck his road flare, and threw it into the pile. The alcohol ignited instantly and a little more violently than he'd expected, singeing his eyebrows and burning his lungs. He walked out of the house, leaving the front door open. By the time he'd stashed his newly acquired treats in the UTV, started the rig, and began motoring down the driveway, the house was almost fully engulfed. Flames shot out the front door as several ground floor windows broke. By the time he turned off of Silent Run Road and headed toward the Allegheny River, the fire had reached the remaining ammunition and explosives stash. The sound of the blast thundered over the noise of the engine and the ground rumbled under his tires. Tom began to laugh.

He was still laughing as he approached Interstate 76 and the bridge across the Allegheny. He slowed down as he neared the bridge. Until now he had only crossed under the cover of darkness. He would be exposed if he crossed in the daylight, but he needed to get this girl back to his people and the safety of his ridge. He studied his back trail and scanned the riverbank on both sides before easing onto the span. He crossed without incident.

Tom turned up Barking Drive and followed the river. Before the collapse, Barking Drive had been a well-used gravel road. Now the roadway was barely discernable through the vegetation that had begun to reclaim the soil under the gravel. As he drove, Tom wondered about the girl strapped into the passenger seat. His mirth was replaced with a mixture of anger and sadness as he recalled the first time he'd seen her. It had been nearly two months earlier, on one of his many surveys of Jackson's fortress. He had assumed she was from one of the Amish villages due to the fact that she was white, and because of the way she'd been dressed when she arrived. Tom had seen other Amish girls brought into the compound, but they lasted a few days at most. They would be inside the main house for a day or two, then be taken to the guards' quarters. When the guards had their fill of fun, they led the bruised and battered girls out the front gate and up the road to a small farm. Once there, they made them kneel in a field and shot them in the back of the head.

Those, Tom thought, were the lucky ones. A few times the guards apparently got a little too rough. Some girls died inside the chamber of horrors and were thrown into a field. Tom had been surprised when this girl hadn't emerged from the house for over two weeks, then one day walked out on her own, trailed by two guards. She had been led to a maintenance shed, given a shovel, rake, and hoe, and begun the task of clearing a spot, tilling the earth, and establishing a garden. Each morning, she tended her garden. After a few weeks, she was no longer escorted. Tom's smile returned as he remembered his admiration for her as she learned her way around the entire estate. She covered every inch of the grounds, as if she were mapping the layout. The daily drama had become Tom's personal reality show, like the ones his wife used to watch. Tom briefly grinned at the memory of his wife in front of the TV, screaming at the characters on *Jersey Shore* as if they could hear her advice.

Tom cut across Coxcomb Road and continued cross country toward the safety of his ridge west of Logans Ferry Heights at the end of Farneth Road. The farm he had chosen wasn't fancy or large, but the location made it defensible. Situated on top of a wooded ridge, he and his companions had a view of the Allegheny River on one side and several miles of hardwood forest on the other. They had a perfect escape route if the need ever arose.

A half mile from the outer perimeter of the farm, Tom emerged from the thick trees and stopped the UTV in the middle of Browntown Road. He and his team, some of whom were avid bow hunters, had set up platform tree stands at different locations around the farm. There was no way to approach the property without being spotted. Each member of his team was armed with a high-caliber, scoped hunting rifle. Some of the bow hunters that drew guard duty took their bows into the stands with them. Occasionally a deer would wander by and they would shoot it, then call for someone from the main house to come dress and retrieve it. With a lot of mouths to feed, an extra deer once in a while helped ease that burden.

The locations of the stands were well placed. One or maybe two well-camouflaged people with stealth skills could get past the first few tree stands, but it was highly unlikely. And by the time they were inside the perimeter they would be spotted by another guard. A large force would never go unnoticed.

Tom pulled a walkie talkie from the jockey box and spoke softly into the mic: "This is Tom, I'm coming in. Please acknowledge."

"Stand one. I see you."

"Stand two clear."

One by one, the tree stands checked in all the way to the main tower on the ridgetop.

"Main tower. You are clear all the way in."

"Watch my six, main tower," Tom said into the radio. "I don't think I was followed, but keep your eyes open."

The radio crackled as the response came back: "Acknowledged."

In a few short minutes, Tom crested the ridge and pulled up in front of the main farmhouse. When he got out of the Ranger, a short, fit, red-headed woman rushed up to Tom, wrapped her arms tightly around his neck, and pressed her lips to his. Tom kissed Mary Parlin back. Then, feeling self-conscious and a little embarrassed, he pulled back, gently pushing her away. Tom still struggled with feelings for his wife. On the night of the nuclear attack, Johnna had become frightened. She left their home with his eight-year-old daughter and two-year-old son, trying to reach the precinct house where she thought she and their children would be safe. Johnna made it only two blocks before she and their children were beaten and trampled to death under the feet of the violent mob that formed when the power went out. Tom found their bodies on his way home to protect them. Even now, his emotions were raw, a mixture of helplessness, anguish, terror, and anger at Johnna for leaving their home. Sometimes the hurt felt as fresh as it had the day they were taken.

Mary looked a little annoyed at being rejected, but quickly turned her attention to the newcomer. "What happened to her?" she asked.

"She came from Randy Jackson's on Silent Run," Tom said. "She was beaten up pretty bad by one of his goons, and she's got a nasty cut on the back of her head. I stitched her up but she may have a concussion. She's been unconscious since we left."

Mary turned to a plump, white-haired, middle-aged woman who'd come out of the house.

"Let's get her inside, Chandra." Mary said. "She can have my room, and I can bunk with you for a few days until she's back on her feet."

As Mary and Chandra carried the girl inside, Tom called after them: "Could you send a couple of guys out to unload the back of the Ranger for me? I need them to take some things to the armory."

Mary nodded. Tom could tell she was upset with him. He really couldn't blame her. She had been there for him through much of his grief.

Tom leaned on the side of the UTV, closed his eyes, and thought back to when he'd met Mary a few months after his family was killed. They'd both taken shelter in the semi-hidden basement of Carl's Tavern off William Penn Highway. Carl's was a favorite hangout for a lot of the guys from his precinct, and Tom had gotten to know the owner well. He and some of the other officers had helped Carl clean up and remodel the place after a fire nearly burned it to the ground. Mary had just gotten a job at Carl's a week before the collapse, and managed to stash food from the kitchen and several cases of water in the space.

They'd stayed hidden there for several weeks, venturing out only to relieve themselves or to scavenge for food and water after Mary's stash ran out. With nothing to occupy their time for days on end, they talked. "They" wasn't quite right—Mary did most of the talking. It took Tom a long time to let her into his world. He was attracted to her physically the first time he saw her, but those desires were the source of much guilt. He resisted them for a long time. The first physical contact between them was only because Mary initiated it. One minute they had been sitting on milk crates across the room from each other, talking about their childhoods. The next, Mary had knelt in front of him and, without a word, grabbed his face in her hands and kissed him. Tom had been shocked and tried to pull away. The harder he resisted, the more forceful she became. Finally he gave in and fell headlong into the passion.

Tom refiled the memory, opened his eyes, grabbed the expensive booze from the Ranger, and walked up the hill toward the main tower. His face was marked by the faint trace of a smile.

CHAPTER 4

Amish Country
Lancaster County
8:30 A.M., Friday, August 1

RANDY JACKSON AND seven of his men walked slowly up the narrow trail, carefully scanning the thick trees around them. They were looking for anything unusual or out of place. The two men Randy had sent to the Amish village were five days overdue, and food was running low in Pittsburgh. For this reason alone, Randy had decided to step out of his comfort zone and the safety of his city streets, to find the men and, more importantly, the food they were supposed to be bringing back. He had only been to the village himself one other time. The trip had been so miserable that he swore he would not go back. Yet here he was again, surrounded by trees, bugs, and the suffocation of wide open space.

Randy had spent most of his life inside Pittsburgh and the comfort of urban life. It was a part of him. He moved through the streets with ease and confidence. The noise and what seemed chaos was like a carefully orchestrated play to him. Everything moved and functioned with precision, and his was the leading role. Two years before the collapse,

31

Pittsburgh's mayor and city council had declared the city a gun free zone. While the rest of the population gave up their weapons, Randy armed his men. It made him the emperor of Lexington Avenue. The only person he'd answered to before the collapse was the leader of the Hilltop Boys, locked up in State Correctional Institute Chester. Now that everything had fallen, Randy was top dog. He could do what he wished.

For several months, Randy and his gang of sixty men had survived on the food and water they'd taken from others, but eventually that supply ran out. They'd resorted to butchering and eating anyone who had survived. Soon, word had spread among survivors what was happening. The people hid, coming out only at night, or they left the city altogether. Randy's desperation and hunger grew. He instituted a lottery system among his crew. Once a month, everyone's name was placed inside a hat and one name was drawn. The lucky winner was butchered to feed the rest. Of course, Randy's name was never part of the lottery. He was, after all, King of Pittsburgh. When he'd first initiated the lottery, some on his crew protested, and some tried to flee. Those who'd rebelled or were caught running away were the first inventory of meat.

But the lottery system proved to be inefficient. As his crew dwindled, Randy realized he'd eventually be left alone in an empty city. He decreased the frequency of butchering dates, and his hunger and frustration began to build. What was his next step? Would he leave Pittsburgh and take his chances in the country or would he butcher what remained of his crew and last as long as he could? He was leaning toward the country when Willie Marshall rolled into town on a bicycle, towing a trailer filled with fresh vegetables, smoked meat, and bottles of homemade root beer. Willie had been one of the first of the crew to flee when Randy started the lottery. Randy never expected to see him again.

Willie and Randy had grown up in the same neighborhood and had been initiated into the Hilltop Boys at the same time. When Willie came back, Randy's first impulse was to shoot him as an example for the rest. Instead of killing him, however, he had him beaten and tied up, then forced him to watch the rest of them feast on the supplies he'd brought. Randy almost liked Willie, but the main reason he hadn't killed Willie outright was that he had to know where those supplies came from and if there were more to be had. When Willie told him about the Amish and their almost unlimited resources, Randy wanted more. He was more than a little disappointed in himself for not thinking of the Amish, but he knew little about them. He'd seen them on a few occasions before the collapse, riding in their little black buggies, but never gave them much thought.

Willie explained that the Amish had everything they needed: meat, milk, butter, cheeses, fresh vegetables, and clothing they made themselves. They were willing to share with those who came in need, but they weren't willing to send resources outside their village. After living with the Amish for several months, Willie had killed a young boy who'd been on his way to the local market, where the villagers traded goods every Friday, and took the goods back to the city.

A week after Willie's return, the gang began its raids on the Amish village. In the first raid, Randy and his crew stormed into the village on a Sunday morning and found all of the homes abandoned. They went from house to house and took what they could carry. They couldn't find a single bicycle with a trailer, and the one Willie had stolen a week earlier could only carry part of their supplies, so they carried the rest in quilts they had taken off the beds. The next few raids were a little more difficult, but Randy enjoyed them so much more. The Amish protested, and Randy shot those who protested the most. He recalled the cries and screams of the women and children as he lined up several men on their knees in the dirt and executed them. He could still smell the burning gunpowder and blood in the air as he put a pistol to each head and happily pulled the trigger. Even though Randy had gained great pleasure from the raids on the Amish farms, he decided after the first few that he'd stay in the city and delegate the task to his crew. In spite of the fun, the fact that he had to travel outside of the city made his mind up for him. That discomfort alone outweighed the adrenaline rush of killing weak white people.

Randy was taken away from his happy memory by the shout of one of his men in the trees next to the trail. "Randy! I got somethin'!"

Randy trotted into the trees. One of his men was kneeling next to some freshly dug dirt. "Look like somebody been digging," the man said.

Randy knelt down and started scooping aside handfuls of fresh, moist dirt. He dug for several minutes, until his fingernails scraped against something solid. He carefully brushed a little more dirt away and found himself staring into the cold, lifeless eyes of Malik Hanson. Hanson had a fist-sized, jagged hole in his forehead. His nose and mouth were filled with dirt and dried blood. Randy swore loudly and stood.

"Cover him up!" he shouted.

When the task was finished, the band of seven Hilltop Boys and their leader moved back up the trail. They hadn't gone a hundred yards before they came upon deep ruts that Randy assumed had been made by an Amish pull cart. There were two sets of ruts side by side. and several footprints in the soft mud of the trail. Randy couldn't tell how many had made the tracks or how long ago they'd been there. He was completely out of his element. But it didn't matter. The cart ruts clearly came up the trail, turned around, and returned.

They moved a little quicker now, the rush of the hunt pulsating through them. It didn't matter whether they were people who had never lived outside of city streets or the most grizzled of mountain men from olden days. They were human, and primal instincts were the same in the urban jungle or the real one.

After three hours of jogging up the trail toward the Amish village, the pace caught up with Randy. Facing sheer exhaustion, he ordered everyone to stop. The sun had nearly set, shadows were beginning to grow long, and dark rainclouds were rolling toward them. There was a clammy chill in the air. Randy realized they wouldn't reach the village until the next day. Even though he hated the idea, he knew they would need to leave the trail and find someplace out of the coming rain to sleep for the night.

They walked into the trees and underbrush, looking for someplace to take shelter. After fifteen minutes of searching, one of Randy's men found a giant oak tree that had blown down. They all crawled under the root wad to wait out the night.

A couple of hours after dark, the rain began to fall. It was a slow drizzle at first, but halfway through the night it turned into a downpour. Lightning flashed in the sky all around them, lighting up the landscape and casting ominous shadows. Randy had always thought he was pretty tough, unafraid of anything. But out there, in this weather, with no solid concrete under his feet, he was terrified.

Randy soon realized they had other problems. The spot they had chosen protected them well from the falling rain, but their hole under the roots began to fill with water and mud. When the water became ankle deep, they crawled out and stood shivering in the wet night air. None of them had worn enough clothing to block out the chill, and no one had thought to bring anything to light a fire with. They were definitely not where they wanted to be. Randy ordered them all under a live oak tree. They stood shoulder to shoulder around the trunk and waited out the night.

By morning they were all shivering, their teeth were chattering, and some of the men's skin had turned ashen. They were hungry and thirsty. They hadn't expected to spend the night in the forest, or to have been away from the safety of their streets for more than a few hours. Randy knew they would need to find water soon or be forced to go back. If they went back, they might never catch those responsible for killing his boys.

"Let's go," Randy said, walking with his arms folded across his chest to warm them up. They hiked for nearly an hour before Randy realized they should have reached the trail already. "We goin the right way?" he asked no one in particular.

"Don't think so," answered one of his men. "It's that way." He pointed to his left.

"No," said another. "That way." He pointed back the way they had come.

Soon, everyone was talking and pointing in a different direction.

"All right!" Randy shouted, quieting the group. "Spread out. We'll go in groups of two, each going a separate direction. Walk in a straight line. One of us should come to the trail. If you find a stream, get a drink and remember where it is. We can all get a drink once we meet back up.

When you find the trail, shoot in the air, wait a few minutes and shoot again. The rest of us will come to you. Danny, you're with me."

They split up and each team walked into the brush. Randy tried to project calm and confidence, but panic was starting to grab hold and squeeze. He had never been lost before. Never been someplace so unfamiliar, so hostile.

After twenty minutes of pushing his way through the tangle of underbrush, Randy and his companion's clothes were torn, their skin was scratched in several places, and they were sweating profusely. Thirst, hunger, and sheer desperation were starting to take their toll.

"We shoulda hit the trail by now. We weren't that far from it last night," Randy whined. "It must be here somewhere."

Randy stopped walking and looked around. The landscape looked the same in every direction. He wasn't even sure they'd been traveling in a straight line. If they would have walked along the highway, it would have been better than following the trail. At least the highway was bigger and harder to lose than the little trail the Amish had led them on the first time they'd captured one. The problem with the highway was that they'd be exposed. With so much open ground, they would be vulnerable to attack. But it didn't matter to Randy anymore. If they got out of their current situation, they would use the highway to travel between the Amish country and his beloved Pittsburgh.

"We've got to keep moving," Randy said. He strode through the thick underbrush again. His stomach was cramping, his muscles ached, and his throat felt as though he'd been swallowing gravel. He hoped they found the trail soon and got to the Amish village before dark. He knew they could take the food and water they needed without much resistance. Randy decided that if they didn't find the trail before nightfall, he would turn back toward Pittsburgh, regroup, and head back out to find those who had killed his men a few days later. If he headed back out at all. Randy wasn't sure it was worth going through this journey again. He had lost two more men, which would make things more difficult and would make him more vulnerable at home. Was it worth losing more to settle a score?

The threat of Tom Dixon made Randy even more uneasy. The

ex-Pittsburgh gang cop had always hated Randy and done his best to put him in a cage. Even after the collapse, Dixon had attacked him and his men on several occasions, and had taken a few of them out. Randy wished more than anything else that the falling city would have killed Uncle Tom Dixon—the name fit—but Dixon had survived and was waging a one man war against the Hilltop Boys. This war was the main reason Randy had chosen the Silent Run location to live. The property was surrounded by high walls and situated on top of a hill. The 360-degree view made sneaking up on them a difficult task.

It disgusted Randy that another black man would turn against his own people and fight alongside the white scumbags. It disgusted Randy even more that Dixon had grown up in the same neighborhood, and thought he was better than Randy because he'd moved out and supposedly made a better life. The most irritating thing of all was the fact that Dixon had married a white girl. Randy would have his fun with white girls, but it ended there. They were great playthings, but he would never actually care for one. He had absolutely no respect for any white person, even the Amish ho at his house. He enjoyed his time with her in his bed, and he really enjoyed the stress release she provided for his fists, but it ended there and always would. He was already growing tired of her and had been bringing in more girls lately. The variety excited him more than the same old thing every night. Randy decided that as soon as he got back to Pittsburgh, he would have his men dispose of the girl and bring in another on their next raid.

Randy stopped walking and sat down under a towering tree to take a break. He was about to lie back in the grass and close his eyes for a few minutes when he heard a distant shot. He jumped to his feet and strained his ears, listening for a second shot. When it came, Randy turned in the direction it'd come from—directly behind him, and from the faintness of the sound, a long ways away. He'd been walking the opposite direction from the trail the whole time! Panic crept into the corners of his mind again. How could he have gone so far from where he needed to be?

Randy jogged toward the shot, forgetting all about Danny. Even more panicked now, he ran faster. Tree limbs dug chunks out of his arms and face. By the time he broke onto the trail, he was bleeding, and his breath came in short, raspy gasps. His companion emerged from the brush a minute later. Randy could see he wasn't in any better shape than Randy was. His shirt was ripped to shreds, revealing nicks and cuts the full length of his upper body.

A moment later, two more of Randy's men rounded a bend in the trail.

"Anybody see the others?" Randy asked. His men just shrugged their shoulders and looked at each other. "All right," he said. "We'll wait a few minutes, and if they don't show up, we're heading back to the city."

"Which way is the city?" one asked.

One of the men pointed one way up the trail. Danny pointed in the opposite direction. Randy felt a stab of panic again. He looked down and studied the dirt in the trail. There were no deep cart ruts where they stood. He looked up the trail one way and down the other. He couldn't see tracks.

"Let's split up again," Randy said.

One of his men frowned. Danny swallowed and kicked the dirt.

"Look," Randy said, "don't leave the trail and you won't get lost. If you come to the wagon ruts we saw earlier, shoot twice like before, then wait fifteen minutes and start walking back. That's the direction we need to go anyway. We can find each other, and the rest of us that haven't shown up will hopefully be able to find us. Walk for no more than a half hour, and if you don't find the ruts by then, turn around and head back. Unless you hear the two shots, stay where you are then and wait for the rest of us to show up."

Randy and Danny walked up the trail while the other two went the opposite direction. After a few hundred yards, Randy found the wagon ruts and the place where they'd discovered the graves the day before. He was relieved to at least know for sure where he was and which direction Pittsburgh was. But now he had to turn around and start walking again. He was also frustrated that he wasn't going to find out who had killed his men.

Randy took out his pistol and shot it into the air. He waited a few seconds, then fired again. After fifteen minutes, the sun was dipping beneath the treetops. He and Danny started walking away from the ruts and back towards Pittsburgh. After another fifteen minutes, Danny stopped. The sky was growing darker. They would need to spend another night in the woods, with no food, no water, and no shelter. Randy cussed and grumbled to himself, and continued walking down the trail to find his companions.

CHAPTER 5

Amish Country
Lancaster County
7:45 P.M., Saturday, August 2

SARAH BEILER STOPPED in the middle of the trail, removed the harness from her shoulders, and reached with both hands under the neck of her dress to rub the raw, swollen welts that had formed on her once-smooth skin. Jakob walked behind her, took his backpack off, and placed it on the ground. She had thought they'd be home by now, but Naomi and her brother had moved slower than expected. It was looking like they would need to either spend another night in the woods or move slow and steady through the night in order to make it in time for her mother's biscuits and gravy.

"You doing all right?" Jakob asked.

His voice startled Sarah. She quickly removed her hands from under her dress and turned around. Her cheeks were hot when she answered.

"I'm fine," she said. "This is the first time I've been behind one of these things. I didn't expect it to be so hard."

Sarah had relieved Jakob an hour earlier to give him a break. He had protested of course and said he was fine, but Sarah had glared at him and forced him into submission. Kevin wasn't able to help after his ordeal with his captors, and Naomi wasn't strong enough to take on the burden. So when they had started for home, it was decided that Sarah and Jakob would take turns pulling the load. Kevin was exhausted and unable to moves as fast as Sarah, even though she was harnessed to the cart. Sarah and Jakob moved up the trail at their own pace, pausing periodically to rest and allow Kevin and Naomi to catch up.

"I think you need to let me take back over," Jakob said as he placed his hand on her shoulder. Sarah winced in pain. Jakob quickly removed his hand and used it to gently brush away a strand of hair that had fallen from her bonnet and over her eyes.

"You are amazing," he whispered.

Sarah's cheeks went red again. She turned to hide her embarrassment. Jakob took her by the elbow, gently turned her back around, and pulled her toward him. He leaned down and looked into her eyes.

Sarah's breath quickened and she closed her eyes. Her skin tingled, and a warmth spread from the center of her heart to her arms and legs. Jakob leaned closer. His lips gently brushed against the point of her chin and slowly rose, his rough beard scraping across her bare neck. Soft lips came to rest on her bottom lip. His warm breath slid across her cheek, sending a shiver up her spine. When he softly kissed her, a slight moan escaped her throat. Sarah reached for and found his calloused hands. She locked her fingers with his, squeezed tightly, and kissed him back forcefully. Jakob pulled a hand away from hers and cupped the back of her head, sliding his fingers under her bonnet and touching her soft hair. He grabbed a handful of greasy blonde locks, pulled her head back, leaned in again, and gently kissed her neck.

Sarah jerked her hand from his and jumped back. Her breaths came quickly and barely filled her lungs. She had never felt such desire, such longing, and such torment. She wanted desperately to move back in and taste his lips. She wanted to be enveloped by his strong arms and feel the skin of his bare chest on hers. She wanted this more than she had ever wanted anything, but she knew it was wrong. She knew it was too soon. They were not married, and these feelings and impulses were not supposed to exist outside of the marriage covenant. Yet here they were. She couldn't stop herself from imagining what he looked like under his clothes. She could see the curvature of the muscles on his chest. She pictured what it would be like if he picked her up, gently cradled her in his arms, and carried her to their bedroom.

"We can't do this," Sarah barely managed to whisper. "We aren't married or even betrothed. You haven't talked to my Father. We haven't even talked about the rest of our lives. I have loved you nearly my whole life, and I have had impure, sinful thoughts about you, but I just can't bring myself to act on those impulses. Every time I have lust in my heart, I am sinning."

"It's not lust," Jakob protested. "If you love someone and want to be with them forever, it's love. I have loved you too, from a distance, and I have had..."

Jakob paused, hung his head, and kicked the dirt with the toe of his boot.

"I too have had thoughts about being with you," he whispered. "Sometimes all I can think about is what it would be like to take you in my arms and feel the warmth of your bare skin beneath me. I want to..."

Jakob paused again, then looked up and locked eyes with Sarah. She felt as though his eyes were burning into hers, that he could somehow see the images that were playing out in her mind. He took a tentative step toward her. She put her hands up.

"We just can't," Sarah said flatly. "We may be able to be with one another and completely know each other one day, but for now we must not give in to lust and fleshly desire."

Jakob looked like he was about to argue again and explain his case more fervently. Then Kevin and Naomi came into view down the trail, rescuing Sarah from further embarrassment.

Naomi walked beside her brother with her arm around his waist, helping support his weight. They both looked exhausted. When the pair finally reached Sarah and Jakob, Sarah knew it was probably time to make camp and regain their strength for the rest of their journey the next day. They were only seven or eight miles from home. Sarah had no doubt that she and Jakob could make it without stopping, but Kevin needed the rest.

"I think we need to stop for the night," Sarah said. She looked up and scanned the thin clouds dotting the deep blue sky. "I'm pretty sure it's not going to rain again tonight, so we can probably just camp here on the trail without making a shelter. Jakob and I will gather some wood. I think you should just rest, Kevin, and if Naomi could get something ready for dinner, that would be good. I have a pan in my pack in the cart, as well as a knife and some utensils."

Sarah and Jakob walked into the brush to begin gathering firewood. Sarah had her first full armload when Jakob walked up and stood in front of her. She pretended not to notice him as she brushed past and headed back toward the cart.

"Sarah, wait." Jakob called after her. "I think we should finish our talk."

Sarah stopped and slowly turned around. "There's really nothing else to say right now. Until we have more solid plans in place, I think we should avoid placing ourselves in situations that—"

CRACK!

The sound of a distant shot burst through the canopy of oak trees. Sarah dropped her armload of wood. The round had come from the direction of where they'd rescued Kevin and Naomi the day before. They'd heard two shots earlier in the day, but Sarah assumed it was someone out hunting. Now, the fact that it was so close to evening and that this shot came from nearly the same place made her wonder. Sarah started jogging toward the trail. "Come on!" she yelled over her shoulder.

A minute later, Sarah and Jakob reached the cart and Kevin and Naomi, who were looking intently down the trail.

"Did you see anything?" Sarah asked.

"No," Kevin said. "But the shot came from that way."

Sarah grabbed her backpack. The pain of the pack straps on her raw shoulders brought a tear to one eye. She reached into the cart, grabbed her shotgun, and broke open the action to check the load.

"I'm going to go check that out." She pointed up the trail. "Go back and get the wood ready for a fire, but don't light it until I get back. We probably don't want smoke in the air right now. I'll be back soon and we can eat."

"I'm going with you," Jakob said. He grabbed his pack and .30-.30.

Sarah walked over to him and placed a gentle hand on his shoulder. "I'll go alone. Kevin and Naomi need someone to stay with them."

Jakob glared at her and started to protest.

"There's no reason for both of us to go!" Sarah said. "Wait here. I won't be gone long. I just want to see who else is in these woods. If I'm not back by morning, then you need to get them back to the village."

Jakob sighed and finally nodded his surrender.

Sarah trotted into the trees and moved toward the shot, paralleling the trail thirty yards into the cover. She had gone at least a mile when a second shot broke the evening stillness. This one sounded quite a bit closer, which meant she would need to slow down and move quietly.

She scurried from tree to tree, pausing for twenty to thirty seconds at each tree to study her surroundings and listen for voices, snapping twigs, or other human-caused noises. Sarah made it to the place they had buried the evil men the day before, slowed her pace, and crouched next to an oak tree. She'd had no intention of ever being this close to the shallow graves again, yet here she was, thirty feet away. She fought the urge to look at the graves, but as she removed her backpack, she scanned the spot and beyond, her eyes coming to rest on the trail.

Sarah's head snapped back toward the graves and froze. The dirt and leaves they'd used to hide the disturbed soil had been moved. The graves had been found.

Her mind raced. What if someone from the village had found the graves? What if it was her father? What if when they found out what she and Jakob had done, they banished them? What if the gang had found the graves, and was watching, waiting for the person who dug them to return? What if they were watching her *now*?

Sarah lay flat on the ground. The break had allowed her breathing to slow and even out, but now she felt it becoming rapid and shallow again.

She lay on the ground for several minutes, until it was almost completely dark. Satisfied that no one had been watching her, she decided that the best way to find out who had discovered her sin was to examine the tracks in the trail. She held her shotgun in front of her with both hands, ready to shoot, and inched her way out of the brush toward the trail. In the middle of the path, she knelt down and studied the tracks in the soft black mud. There were several different footprints. She wasn't sure how many, but there were more than she and her companions had made the day before. She followed the tracks that went the way of the wagon ruts. After a couple hundred yards the only tracks that remained were hers and those of her companions. Whoever had found the graves had not come from the direction of her village.

She made her way back to her backpack. As sat next to the oak tree and downed a snack of jerky and water, she contemplated what she should do.

If there are others members of the gang in my woods, it would be fairly easy to sneak up on them and rid us of future conflicts. But would that be the right thing to do? What if they intend to never come back? What if finding the graves has scared them off? I've killed, but that was to rescue friends, to save lives. If I track these men down and kill some or all of them, that would be murder. Or would it?

Sarah wasn't sure how many others there were. She wasn't sure she could get to any of them without being discovered.

What if they see me before I see them? They're usually well armed. There's a chance, even though a small one, that they'll shoot me. Or worse, capture me, and do unspeakable, horrible things.

Sarah waited near the graves until it was completely dark, then slowly made her way onto the trail again. She'd decided she would at least try to catch up to whoever was out here. Then she'd figure out what to do. She jogged down the trail, slowing and then stopping before each corner to listen. She wasn't certain what faced her or if she could catch up to the travelers, but knew she needed to be cautious.

After two hours of jogging, Sarah's muscles ached. She slowed before yet another sharp corner.

"There has got to be a stream or something to get a drink. We can look again as soon as it's daylight."

The voice came from somewhere ahead on the trail. Sarah jumped off the trail and crawled quietly into the brush. The first voice was shortly answered by a second.

"I don't think it's a good idea to leave the trail again. We lost a whole day wandering around these woods trying to find it. I think we need to move out when the sun's up and not stop until we get back."

Sarah removed her pack and crawled forward, staying behind cover. She stopped just beyond the corner and scanned the area where the trail straightened out again. There was no moon, and the faint starlight was barely enough to make out the shapes of four men sitting back to back in the middle of the path, thirty to forty yards away. She slowly raised her shotgun, resting her finger lightly on the side of the trigger guard. If she fired, she might be able to get them all with the first shot. The pattern would be tight enough at that distance to not miss, yet spread out enough to fill each one with .00 buckshot. If she didn't get them all with one shot, they'd have a chance to fire back before she could run away. If only she was fifteen or twenty yards closer.

Another thought pushed all others away. *What if these men aren't part of the gangs? What if they're people from the city who just wandered out here looking for food?* She needed to get closer.

Sarah crept forward six inches at a time, pausing periodically to rest and keep her breathing steady.

One of the men stood and stretched. "I gotta pee," he said.

The man walked toward Sarah's hiding place. As he neared, she could make out his features in the dim moonlight. He was a black man, with a rough beard, tall and well muscled. Unlike the other men from the gangs she'd killed, he looked like he hadn't missed many meals.

She froze, not even breathing, as the man stepped within five feet of her and relieved himself. She could smell the pungent urine as it splattered on the trail. If he'd come any closer, she would have been discovered.

"Are you sure you want to go back tomorrow, Randy?" one of the men said. "What if we're closer to the Amish than we are to the city? They'll have food and water."

"I thought about it," the man answered in a surprisingly articulate voice. "Not knowing how far the village is, and not knowing if they grew a spine and are ready to fight back, I think it's best to get back to the city. We'll get more of the boys to come out before we go to the village."

Randy walked back to the group and took a seat again. There was no longer any doubt in Sarah's mind that these men were part of the gang that had been terrorizing her village. She had heard the men that captured Kevin and Naomi mention somebody named Randy. She wasn't sure if Randy was the leader, but he must have some authority. If she killed him now, it might stop the raids on their village. Still, it was most assuredly murder if she shot these men when they weren't directly threatening her or someone else. She decided she would get closer. If nothing else, she would be close enough at that point to get them all with the first shot if she decided to commit the ultimate sin.

Sarah crept forward, keeping her shotgun in front of her. After ten minutes, she could make out their faces. She was also close enough to smell their body odor. She slowly moved the shotgun to her shoulder in the prone position, and once again rested her finger next to the trigger. She fought her nerves and the panic that began to choke her, and slipped her finger inside the trigger guard. Her thumb slowly slid the safety off. She took several deep breaths.

This was it. She was going to kill—no, murder—these men. Once she pulled that trigger, there would not be any doubt that she had committed the ultimate sin, and that she was without a doubt destined for the fires of hell.

At the sound of a faint turkey call, Sarah twitched and nearly pulled the trigger. The men in front of her jumped up and looked around. They were now separated enough that one shot would only get one or two of them.

"What was that?" one asked.

"Shhh!" another hissed.

"Which way did that come from?" one whispered.

"I think it was that way," said the man closest to Sarah. He pointed down the trail toward where Sarah had left her companions.

Sarah was angry. The turkey call was probably Jakob. She'd told him to wait for her, but he obviously hadn't. Now these men knew there were others out here. They might decide to abandon their plans to return to the city and continue searching for them. Jakob may have just gotten more innocent people killed—or worse. She knew she shouldn't shoot now that these men were alert and she was so close. She wouldn't have time to get off a shot and run away before they aimed the weapons they were now holding in her direction. There was also no way for her to slip out back the way she'd come, now that they were alert. They would surely see or hear her. But if she didn't do something, Jakob might walk right into them. She had to warn him. Her only option was to shoot and hope the surprise would be enough to cause them men to dive for cover, giving her a few seconds to flee before they could fire back.

Sarah's muscles tightened and her breathing quickened. She would shoot only one barrel. She might need the second shot later. The moon had just started to cast a dim glow on the horizon. Soon the faint shadows would be replaced with silver light. It was now or never. She lined up the front bead on the nearest man's chest, slowly put pressure on the front trigger, and prayed for forgiveness.

The shotgun blast caught the man exactly where Sarah had hoped, in the center of his body. He screamed and grabbed for his chest as the force knocked him off his feet. The other three men dove to the ground and covered their heads. In one motion, Sarah jumped up and began running. Not bothering to skirt the thicker tangles of brush, she reached her backpack and scooped it up, never breaking stride. She was going to make it. She would be around the corner and out of sight of the men before they could shoot. She jumped into the trail and sprinted for the corner. She had just started into the curve when a white-hot pain ripped into her side. She stumbled, dropped her shotgun, and grabbed at her kidney, as she fell to the ground at Jakob's feet. He exchanged several shots with the men, but Sarah couldn't tell how many. The sound of someone crying out in pain drifted into her ears. The shots subsided.

"Sarah, come on, we have to move! Sarah?"

The voice was distant, a whisper carried on a breeze. She had the sensation of floating, of being disconnected from reality. Then even the whispers were gone.

CHAPTER 6

Amish Country
Lancaster County
10:55 P.M.

JAKOB STUMBLED DOWN the trail as fast as he could run. Sarah was slung over his right shoulder like a sack of grain. She'd quit screaming and now wasn't even talking. He hoped she was okay. Jakob knew she'd been hit by one of the gang's bullets, but he had no idea where she was injured. He would stop once he got back to Kevin and Naomi and they were safely off the trail. He knew he needed to get Sarah back to the village for medical attention, but he had to make sure they weren't being followed and weren't in any more immediate danger.

By the time Jakob got back to the food cart, his shirt was soaked with a mixture of perspiration and Sarah's warm blood. "Kevin!" he hissed into the night. "Naomi. Where are you?"

Neither one was at the cart. He wondered if they had run off the trail and hidden themselves in the brush, or if they had fled to the village when the shooting started. He hoped they hadn't moved toward the shots. Neither of them was armed. The thought of having to rescue them while Sarah lay helpless and possibly bleeding to death frightened him.

Jakob removed a light jacket from his pack, walked just off the trail, and gently laid Sarah on top of the jacket. He looked her over and found her dress blood-soaked and sticking to her side just above her right kidney. He retrieved a knife from his pack. His fingers trembled slightly as his hand hovered over the wound. He wasn't supposed to see her bare body at all unless they were married, even if it was just a small area on her side. He shook his head and clumsily cut the fabric of the dress away. The wound was small, but thick blood was oozing out and running down her side, puddling on the jacket under her. He knew he needed to stop the bleeding. He ran back to his pack in the cart and dug around for the bundle of bandages he'd packed, as well as the needle and thread Sarah had suggested he bring. He wasn't skilled at sewing like Sarah and most Amish girls, so he would need to learn quickly.

"Jakob."

Jakob's heart skipped a beat when he heard Naomi's whisper. He jerked his head around in time to see her and Kevin tip-toe out of the brush.

"Where's Sarah?" Kevin asked.

Jakob pointed toward the brush across the trail. "She's been shot." Even in the dim moonlight, Jakob could see Naomi's face turn white.

"Where is she?" Naomi asked.

Jakob plowed back into the brush with Naomi and Kevin on his heels. "We need to stop the bleeding," Jakob said. "I was going to try and sew it closed, but I'm not a seamstress."

Jakob handed Naomi the bandages, needle, and thread. She quickly got to work. Jakob hurried back to the cart to grab his rifle. By the time he returned to Sarah's side, Naomi had cleaned the wound the best she could and had begun to sew it closed.

"I need to make sure we aren't being followed by the rest of them," Jakob said. "I'm going back to check. When you get her taken care of, put her in the cart. I'll be back soon and we can head for home."

Without waiting for an answer, Jakob ran down the trail. When he was within thirty yards of the spot he'd picked Sarah up, he slipped into the brush. The moon was up enough now that he could see to avoid the more noisy tangles of brush and dried leaves.

Jakob stopped where Sarah had run out of the brush and knelt. He concentrated on slowing his breathing and listened intently. As far as he could tell, the other men had left and he was completely alone. He needed to know which way they went. If they'd stayed on the trail and were headed back toward the city, they would be out of danger for now. They'd probably return to the village to take more supplies, but at least he and the others would be safe until then, giving Sarah time to recover.

Jakob tiptoed onto the trail, rifle raised, and scanned the brush on either side of him. Up ahead, a man lay still in the trail. Jakob eased up to the man, knelt down, and checked for a pulse. He was definitely dead. His thin cotton T-shirt was shredded across his back where several buckshot pellets had exited after blowing through him. Jakob rolled the body over. Milky, lifeless eyes stared up at him. The mouth was frozen in a near grin and moonlight reflected off yellow teeth. Normally, Jakob would bury anyone they'd killed, but tonight there wasn't time. They needed to get Sarah back to the village for medical help, soon.

Jakob walked slowly down the trail, his eyes focused on the tracks in the dirt. Three sets of shoeprints in the center of the trail pointed back toward Pittsburgh. By the way the tracks were dug deep into the soft mud, several feet apart, he could tell the people who'd made them had been running away. He followed the tracks for a quarter mile, until the distance between them got shorter. The people had slowed and begun walking again. They were still steadily heading toward Pittsburgh. Jakob quit following, turned around, and jogged back toward his companions a little less carefully, stopping only to pick up Sarah's shotgun.

By the time Jakob reached the cart and his friends, Kevin and Naomi had unloaded the majority of food, tucked Sarah into some leaves in the cart, and covered her with their extra clothing. Kevin had already put the harness on and was ready to pull it toward home. Jakob argued with him briefly, but he was exhausted. He gave in and agreed to let Kevin pull the cart for a while before they switched.

Just as the first rays of the sun started to touch the familiar barns, homes, and countryside, the trio hauling Sarah walked into their village. At Sarah's farm, her father sat on their front porch sipping a glass of apple cider. Jakob stopped the cart just outside the front gate. Sarah's father rushed down the steps.

Jakob swallowed the dry lump that had formed in his throat and addressed Abram Beiler, a man who had always intimidated him. "Sarah's hurt," he said. "She, she, um, she's been shot, sir."

Sarah moaned slightly as Abram carefully picked up his daughter and headed for the house. He stopped at the front door, turned around, and addressed Jakob in a calm voice: "If you would go and get the doctor for me Mr. Miller, I would appreciate it."

Jakob ran toward Dr. Wittmer's house. A jumble of thoughts and fears swirled through his mind. What if Sarah died? There was no way he could ever be happy again if he lost her. His life was going to change from that day forward regardless of what happened. His father would likely banish him, which he knew would break his mother's heart. Once the elders got together and discussed what he and Sarah had been doing, there was no way they'd be allowed to stay in the village. If they were forced to leave, who would protect his loved ones from the brutality of the new world? What if the gang came for his sister the next time? What if now that they had fought back, the bad men decided to come to the village and kill several of them as retribution? What if they took the entire season's harvest and left the people with nothing to survive the long cold winter that was coming? It would be their fault. History would remember them as the ones who were responsible for bringing an end to their village and way of life.

Just as the name Samuel Mullet was now spoken in hushed tones, if spoken at all, their names would be as a curse to God. Mullet had caused a rift in his village when he had misinterpreted the scriptures and had instituted a way of life that was contradictory to tradition and the Word of God. Those who spoke out against him were beaten, and the men had their beards shaved off. The shaving of a beard after marriage was one of the most shaming things that could happen to an Amish man. When the smoke had cleared, and the Englishmen's court had sentenced Mullet and those who were with him to prison, most Amish tried to forget the name Mullet and the shame he had brought to their entire faith. If Mullet was treated like this for changing a few traditions and misinterpreting some scriptures, the punishment for what Jakob and Sarah had done would surely be worse.

No matter what happened once everything they had done came to light, Jakob knew that the only way to assure his family's future safety was to end the attacks from the gang once and for all. After he faced his punishment, he would travel to Pittsburgh, he would hunt down every one of the gang members, and he would kill them all. There was no other option.

By the time Jakob returned to Sarah's farm with the doctor, her father was waiting in the dining room with six of the elders from the village, including his father. They sat around the table. Jakob's heart sank. A feeling of dread closed around his midsection and squeezed. He knew that everything he and Sarah had done would be known to everyone soon. His father motioned for him to sit.

Sarah's father, Deacon Beiler, spoke first: "You need to tell us exactly where you and my daughter have been for the last three days, and you need to tell us exactly what you have been doing."

Jakob started at the beginning. He told them about the day he had been rescued by Sarah after being taken away by the gang. He left nothing out, including how he had struggled with the guilt and shame each time he had taken a life. He tried to justify his actions to them the same way he had justified them to himself, but none of them looked like they agreed with what had been done. When he had finished laying everything out in the open, Dr. Wittmer came out of Sarah's room. Everyone turned toward him as he approached the table.

"She's going to be fine," he said. "She was shot through the right kidney, but the bullet passed clear through. She lost a great deal of blood, but her companions stopped the bleeding in time. If they hadn't sewn her up, she would have bled to death. I have fixed her kidney and reclosed the wound, but she will need to rest for a few days."

Jakob released the breath he hadn't realized he'd been holding, slumped in his chair, and began to cry. It wasn't manly to cry, and he was ashamed of his cowardly display of emotion, but he couldn't stop himself. All of the feelings that had built up in him and filled his every waking moment were released in a flood of tears.

All of the men but his father and Abram Beiler got up from the table and left the house with Dr. Wittmer. Sarah's father stood and walked over next to Jakob. He gently placed a hand on his shoulder.

"Thank you for bringing Sarah back to me," he said. "You should go home with your father now. We will speak about what you have told me as soon as Sarah is well enough to join in the conversation."

Jakob wiped his eyes and nose with a bloodstained sleeve and looked into Abram Beiler's eyes. "I love her," he managed to choke out. "I want to marry her, and take care of her. More than I've ever wanted anything, sir. I know what we did was wrong, and I know we will answer to God for it. But I will not be able to go on unless I can make Sarah my wife."

Abram Beiler's hand squeezed Jakob's shoulder a little tighter. Then he stepped back. "We will speak of this later."

Jakob and his father left the Beiler farm and headed for home. Neither one spoke. Jakob looked down at his feet as they walked down the road. He knew that there was a punishment coming and he knew it was not going to be pleasant. In spite of the dread and uncertainty pushing down on him, he felt as if a large weight had been lifted from his shoulders. The guilt and shame of his actions were his greatest burden. Hiding his sin had nearly overwhelmed him. For better or worse, it was all out in the open now.

CHAPTER 7

Silent Run Road
7:00 A.M., Sunday, August 3

RANDY JACKSON STRUGGLED to walk up the last stretch of road before his mansion would come into view. He and the two other members of his crew that had survived the terror in the forest had walked most of the previous day and all night in order to reach the safety of their hilltop. They hadn't eaten or drank since the day they'd left to go after their missing men. Randy felt nauseated. His muscles screamed for relief. Several times during their journey, he had fought the urge to just give up and lie down.

They rounded the last corner and were greeted by an empty skyline where their home was supposed to be. The thick smell of burned plastic hung in the air. They stopped in the middle of the road and stared, none of them speaking. Randy felt like someone had kicked him in the nuts. After everything they had just gone through, finding their home gone was the last straw.

The trio walked the last two hundred yards and through the open gate of the property. The house was completely leveled. Randy knew there would be nothing left of the weapons and supplies that had been stored there. With no extra weapons and supplies, they would need to be sparing with the little ammunition they still carried.

A distinct set of tire tracks led away from the property. The only vehicle of any kind Randy had seen after the collapse was the little buggy driven by Tom Dixon. Randy swore. He should've killed Dixon when he had the chance. The only thing that had prevented it was the possibility that it would start a war with the entire police force. Randy would have thoroughly enjoyed a war with them. He hated them all and enjoyed killing cops. But a full-scale war would've disrupted his business, making him vulnerable to rival gangs.

Randy walked to the edge of the smoldering debris that had been his home and nearly tripped over the charred body that had once been Willie Marshall. Randy stood over the body, almost wishing that he was Willie. How could he survive now that everything was gone? There were no supplies in any of the surrounding houses. Randy and his crew had cleaned them all out after the collapse. There was no one left in the city he could go to for help. He had killed all of the white people that hadn't fled after the collapse. All of the black people that had survived had joined him or also fled.

Randy sat on the gravel next to Marshall. His body was nearly to the point of completely shutting down. His legs were cramped, his arms felt heavy, and the bile he'd been heaving up had scorched his throat. He sent one of the men to the pool shed to get him a bucket of water from the cow trough. While he waited, he lay on the gravel and closed his eyes. He just needed to rest for a minute. Then he would decide what to do.

When the water arrived, Randy drank nearly a full gallon of the murky green soup. The liquid hit his empty stomach like a rock, causing him to double over with cramps. When he could straighten up again, he pulled a knife from his pocket and began to butcher Willie Marshall. He needed to eat, and this feast had been literally laid at his feet, already cooked. He sliced thick steaks from Willie's butt and slurped loudly as he chewed the tender meat. When he had eaten his fill, he let his men take some while he walked over to the shade of an elm tree, carved a toothpick from a stick laying on the ground, and lay back in the cool grass to pick pieces of Willie and remnants of charred blue jean from between his rotting teeth.

For the next three days, Randy and the last two members of the Hilltop Boys stayed on the property, resting at night in the garden shed and consuming more of Willie. By the morning of the fourth day, Willie's meat had turned rancid and maggots had taken it over, so the trio made several trips into the heart of Pittsburgh to look for supplies. There was no food to be found. They located a few weapons and a small amount of ammunition in the glove box of a wrecked pickup truck, but were still too short on bullets to risk shooting at the few stray dogs and cats that scurried under houses or into the brush when they came upon them.

Randy knew he would need to eat again soon. The milk cow was still tied up on Silent Run, but he would wait until there was no other choice before butchering it. He tried to use the bucket and milk it as the Amish ho had done, but he was clumsy and unskilled in the art of cow milking and produced only a small amount. Finally his hunger got the better of him and he butchered the cow. They had no way of starting a fire, so they consumed as much raw meat as their stomachs would hold. After a few days, the old milk cow also became maggot infested and unfit to eat, so the trio was back to square one.

Soon tempers started to flare. Randy could feel that his control over his crew was failing. If he didn't find a way to feed all three of them, it was just a matter of time before they would try to kill and eat him. Their only choice for survival was to go back into the vicious countryside and take from the Amish again.

"We're going back to the Amish," Randy said to his two remaining men, Danny and Julian. "This time we may stay."

The two crew members glanced at each other. Then Julian Carter frowned at Randy. Julian had been part of the Hilltop Boys nearly as long as Randy. He'd competed with Randy to lead the gang but hadn't had the necessary toughness. Randy sensed that Julian had always resented his leadership.

"Are you sure we need to go back?" Julian asked. "Travelling to the country hasn't worked out so good."

Randy was enraged at Julian's insubordination. He moved in close until he towered over Julian, his chin nearly touching the other man's forehead.

"Are you questioning me?" Randy growled.

Julian swallowed and stared into Randy's eyes. "I think I am," he said. "So far things haven't been—"

Randy's fist shot forward. He felt the bones of Julian's nose give way and crack under the surface of his knuckles. He punched him several more times, until Julian collapsed on the ground, then drew his leg back and kicked him a few times in the ribs and stomach. Now fully exhausted and breathing heavily, Randy turned to look at Danny, the only remaining member of his crew that was not dead or beaten close to death.

"How 'bout you?" Randy asked. "You got a problem with my plan?"

Danny shook his head.

The three of them spent the next few days getting ready for the journey. Julian was a little slow in his tasks, but he never complained. They picked through the charred remains of the house, found several empty whiskey bottles, and filled them with water from the trough. They searched houses in the city and were able to find coats and other warm clothing for the journey, as well as a lighter in case they needed a fire.

Exactly eighteen days after they had been attacked in the woods and run back to the city, the last of the Hilltop Boys started out again for the unforgiving countryside. Randy knew they would need to eat in order to have enough strength for the journey, so they grudgingly used one bullet and shot a stray dog on their way out of the city. They ate their fill, then sliced up several thin strips and put them in their pockets. Randy knew the meat would spoil, but thought it would take longer if they kept the flies from getting to it.

They reached the edge of the city halfway through the first day. By the time evening came, they were only a few miles from the village. Randy had decided to take the highway this time because he thought the walking would be easier, and he was terrified of the remote trail. If they got lost again, he wasn't sure they would survive. At least on the highways, there were comforting reminders of people and technology. Taking the highway proved to be faster. They camped under a semitrailer in the middle of I-376. After a restless night of light sleep, they moved out before daylight.

Despite their desperate situation, Randy was excited about the prospects at the Amish village. He knew there would be food, young girls he could enjoy, and the possibility of resistance from those who had attacked them in the forest. He knew they would have the advantage of surprise. If they moved quickly and acted without mercy, they would succeed.

Randy smiled as he thought about the joy he would get in killing again. He was made for killing, after all. It was only when he was denied that pleasure that life was a miserable existence.

CHAPTER 8

Amish Country
Lancaster County
9:00 P.M., Thursday, August 21

JAKOB MILLER SAT on a straw bale just outside the door of his barn, waiting for his turn in front of the church elders. Sarah had been in with her father the deacon and the others for forty-five minutes. Today, Sarah and Jakob's fate would be decided. Would they be allowed to stay a part of the church and be married, or would they be banished to a life in the fallen Englishmen's world?

Jakob had known a few people who had been banished, but their names were no longer spoken. The shame of the banished was swept under the rug so as not to infect the purity of their faith. Sometimes he secretly thought about the banished and wondered about their lives outside of the Amish. He even envied them a little. When Jakob had been younger, he'd dreamed of one day living as an Englishman, even if it was just temporary for rumspringa. But the allure of the Englishmen's world had died with their technology. The things that had most excited him were cars, electricity, cell phones, computers. Now that those items no longer existed, he wanted nothing more from life than to marry Sarah and raise a family within the church. His people had everything they needed, and always had. The fall of the Englishmen's empire had not affected the Amish, with the exception of those he had been trying to protect his people from. The elders had to understand that what he and Sarah did, they did for them all. Even in God's Word, there were many places where his people had been forced to commit violence to survive. Surely the elders would understand that there had been no other choice.

The door to the barn opened. Sarah walked out, her face red and her eyes puffy. He moved toward her and reached for her hand. She quickly pulled her hand back, averted her eyes, and ran from him, sobbing. Jakob took a step to go after her but stopped at the sound of Abram Beiler's voice.

"Let her go," he said. "We would like to speak to you now."

Jakob nearly ignored him to run after his beloved, but he knew if there was any chance for them to stay in the village, he would ruin it by being more disobedient to the church leaders. He reluctantly turned and followed the deacon into the dimly lit barn.

Six chairs sat in a circle around one empty seat in the middle. Five of the six members of the council were seated. They looked up, expressionless, as he came in. The deacon motioned for Jakob to take the seat in the middle, then sat in the sixth chair.

"We have come to a decision," Abram Beiler said flatly. "We have decided to let you stay."

Jakob's heart skipped a beat. He fought the smile that screamed to come out and settle on his face.

The deacon continued. "We have heard from Sarah about all that has taken place recently. And we understand now that it was she who led you down this path. You may have been blinded by your love for her. We understand that love can cause a man to sin. Just as the first woman led man to sin in the Garden of Eden, this young girl has caused you to ignore one of Gods commandments and kill."

The joy Jakob had felt moments before was suddenly gone, replaced by dread, sadness, and anger. They were blaming everything on Sarah. It was as if he hadn't done any of the killing and had just been an innocent bystander.

"Furthermore," the deacon continued, "it is the judgement of the elders that Sarah Beiler be banished, and that her name no longer be spoken in the family of God."

"But it's not all her fault!" Jakob protested. "I was just as angry as she was that you all did nothing as our people were killed, tortured, and kidnapped by the outsiders. All you would've had to do was fight back the first time they came and it would've ended there. Instead, you stood by and let them get away with it. That alone gave them the boldness to do it over and over again. You can't banish her for something that you had a hand in creating. It was my choice to do the things I've done. You can't punish her for my sins. If it all happened—"

"Enough!" Abram Beiler shouted. He held his hand up, stopping Jakob's protests. "It has been decided, and the council has spoken. If you will agree to abide by our laws from now on and pay a penance for your sins, you will be allowed to stay. If you do not agree to our terms and to be subject to God's law, you will be banished as well."

Jakob stood, knocking his chair over. "You're all cowards!" he shouted. "I looked up to all of you my whole life. I admired your strength. But it was all a lie."

Jakob looked into the eyes of Abram Beiler and pointed toward the door of the barn. "That is your *daughter!* You may as well be sentencing her to die by banishing her. Don't you love your own daughter? If she goes, I'm going with her. I don't ever want to be part of a church that would choose the lives of evil men over their own people. I banish myself!"

Jakob's face burned hot and his fists shook with rage. He rushed the deacon and shoved him hard, knocking him and his chair to the dirt. The other elders jumped up and shrank back. Jakob drew his foot back and kicked Abram Beiler once in the ribs before turning from the group and running out the door.

A few minutes later, his anger slightly cooled, Jakob found Sarah sitting on the childhood swing set his grandfather had built for him and his brothers. He sat in the empty swing next to her and reached out his hand. She locked her fingers in his, looked up, and gave him a half smile.

"I was banished too," he said.

"But I thought... they said... I thought if they knew it was my fault, they would let you stay."

Jakob jerked his hand away and stood.

"I don't want to stay. All of these so-called men are cowards. You have more courage and goodness in your little finger than all the men of our village put together. We will be fine, and we will be together. No matter what the outside world throws at us, we will always face it together."

Sarah jumped from the swing and rushed over to him, wrapping her arms tightly around his neck. They both burst into tears and held each other tightly until Jakob broke their embrace and gently pulled away.

"We need to get some things together," he said, "and be ready to leave in the morning. You should go to your house, gather your things, and say goodbye to your mother and sisters before your father gets back. I will do the same, and we'll meet at the sale barn when we're finished. We can spend the night there and leave first thing in the morning."

They separated and walked toward their houses. Despite his confident words, Jakob was frightened. He felt as though his entire life had been meaningless. Everything he had loved and been taught to respect had been proven a lie. Yet what awaited them on the outside scared him. The Amish way of life was all he knew. Even though the stability he had always felt had now proven to be shallow, it was still stability. How could he handle the responsibility of caring for Sarah and himself with no support structure?

Jakob went into his home and broke the news to his family. His father turned his back on his son and walked out of the house, but his mother hugged him tightly and cried into his shoulder. She begged him to reconsider and to ask the elders if he could stay. But Jakob's mind was made up. There was nothing here for him if Sarah left.

He spent the next hour packing what he would need for his journey to wherever it was they were going. Should they go to Pittsburgh and kill the gang leader? There was no one here he cared about now but his family, but they were reason enough. With the threat of the gangs gone, he wouldn't worry about his family as he made a new life with Sarah. There really were no other options. If he didn't kill the gang leader, his family would never truly be safe. He hoped he wouldn't need to work too hard to convince Sarah his plan was the right one. She had after all been the first to fight back and spill blood. He knew she hated the gang members.

By the time Jakob had gathered his supplies and got to the sale barn, Sarah was already there. She had a lantern burning and had prepared supper for them both. While they ate, Jakob laid out his plan to go to Pittsburgh and deal with the gang. Sarah had protested at first, but hadn't tried all that hard. Even though she wouldn't admit it, Jakob knew her desire for closure and even a little vengeance drove her to agree with him. It was really the gang's fault that she was now banished. They had brought their hate and violence to the Amish, and it had infected Sarah. Jakob knew that their evil had somehow taken hold of her, and just as a wintertime cold is passed around, it had spread to him. The only way to stop it from spreading more was to kill it.

When supper was finished and they had talked in the flickering light of the lantern for a while, they awkwardly crawled into the hay loft to sleep. Sarah made a show of bedding down several feet from him. Jakob could feel that there was more than a few feet of hay separating them. Ever since their moment of passion and desire in the woods, Sarah had mostly kept him at arm's length.

Jakob lay fifteen feet away from Sarah, listening to her slow and steady breathing. He knew he would have to talk to her about what he was feeling, but he wasn't sure how to bring it up. He lay in the dark thinking about what awaited them and wondering how their lives would turn out. Even though he was frightened, he was also excited at the prospect of new adventure and seeing the world outside of their village. He had known others that had been banished or who had decided not to return after rumspringa. They were supposed to cut off contact with those who left, but someone always seemed to go against tradition and managed to keep tabs on them. All of the stories he heard of life in the Englishmen's world were filled with wonder and freedom. Jakob knew that life after the Amish was going to be wonderful. He couldn't wait to start living it.

Yet he also felt guilty about striking Sarah's father in anger. He knew that in spite of being banished and shunned by the man who had given her life, she still loved him. The relationship between an Amish girl and her father and an Amish boy and his father was vastly different. As soon as an Amish boy was able to walk and feed himself, he was expected to work hard and embrace his traditional male role of provider and nurturer of the Amish women. Women were not considered as strong as men. They were to be treated and treasured, as a gift from God to man. As a helpmate, but never equal.

As Jakob lay in the dark feeling sleep overtake him, he knew he could never think of Sarah as anything but an equal. In a lot of ways, she was stronger than him, and more of a fighter. Maybe, Jakob thought. I don't have what it takes to be Amish after all.

Either way, it no longer mattered. As soon as the sun came up, he was an Englishman.

CHAPTER 9

Amish Country
Lancaster County
6:00 A.M., Friday, August 22

SARAH OPENED HER eyes to pitch blackness. At first she couldn't remember where she was or why she was lying in a pile of hay. As she stretched and rubbed her eyes, the events of the previous evening began to come into focus. Everyone and everything she had known her whole life, she would never see again. It terrified her and filled her with overwhelming sadness. Jakob seemed excited at the possibilities of the new life they were starting, but she did not share his enthusiasm. She also was not ready to fully surrender to her feelings for Jakob. It was true, she was no longer bound by Amish ways, and there would be no consequences from her father or the elders if she engaged in inappropriate behavior with the man she loved. Yet even though they were now outside the Amish way of life, she was not ready to throw away that part of who she was. She would hold on to morality and the behaviors she had been taught as long as she could. She knew that if she let go of her personal constraints, it was highly possible that the person she was would die. What terrified her most was the thought that she could be replaced by something ugly and twisted.

Sarah wanted more than anything to give herself fully to Jakob, but she knew that couldn't happen yet. She had lain awake many nights fantasizing about knowing him as only two lovers could know one another. Recently her burning ache for him had risen to the point of physical manifestations. She could actually feel him touching her, and feel the pleasure of their union. Before she gave in, she vowed, she would be married to him. If she could not be married in the Amish tradition, she would find a pastor in the Englishmen's world that would perform the ceremony. Only then would she be right before God.

Sarah got up from the hay and lit her lantern. She dug into her pack and got an apple and some dried beef for breakfast. Jakob stirred, rolled over, and looked up at her with his big blue eyes.

"Good morning," he said. "You sleep okay?"

Sarah flashed him a weak smile and tossed him the apple. "We probably should get going soon," she said. "Everyone will be getting up soon for morning prayer and study time, and I'd like to be gone by then."

They started out of the village just as the sky began to grow gray around the edges. A few of the houses they passed already had flickering candlelight coming from the windows. The smell of wood smoke, frying eggs, and baking bread floated across the breeze.

When they got to the dirt track that led off through the woods toward the city, Sarah stopped to take her last look at the life she would never see again. A single tear rolled from one eye and slowly slid down her cheek. Jakob came up next to her, reached a rough finger up to her cheek, and wiped it away. Sarah pulled back, turned away, and walked into the growing light, leaving Jakob standing by himself.

Soon he had caught up with her, and they began moving down the trail at a brisk pace. After twenty minutes, Sarah slowed, adjusted her seventy-five-pound pack, and took a deep breath. The weight of leaving the Amish had lightened with every footstep, and a sliver of excitement and anticipation began to wedge its way into her thoughts. How their new life turned out was totally up to her. She could move forward relying on hope and new adventure, or she could move forward with one eye continually on her past, pulling her back like an anchor. She turned toward Jakob and smiled. She would break the chain of her history. They would make a happy new life.

A burst of automatic gunfire echoed through the trees, quieting the birds that had been singing their praises to the morning and stopping Sarah and Jakob in their tracks. The shots had come from the village.

Sarah turned and began running back toward her family, Jakob right behind her. They slowed as they entered the open ground and stopped near the first farmhouse. They crouched in an irrigation ditch just off the road that wound its way through the village, and waited. The shots had definitely come from a fully automatic weapon. No one in the village had such a weapon. This meant that the gang was back among her people.

Anna Graber and her five children ran past them and disappeared into the tree line. Soon, several other groups of women ran past with their children.

Sarah and Jakob jogged toward the center of the village, crouched low in the ditch. As they neared her family's home, several shouts of anger greeted them. Sarah stopped running and crawled to the top of the ditch bank to peek over. Three men with rifles stood facing her house. Two of the elders lay dead at their feet. Several more Amish men were kneeling in the dirt.

"We just want the ones who attacked us in the woods!" the man in the middle shouted. Sarah recognized him as the leader, Randy, from their encounter on the trail. "These men told us they lived here, so unless you want to join them, you will send out the murderers. Once we have them, we will take enough supplies to last us awhile, and we will leave. If we don't have them in the next few minutes, we will kill one of them"—he gestured toward the men cowering in fear—"and another every five minutes until they stand before us."

Sarah started to climb from the ditch, but Jakob grabbed her by the ankles, roughly dragged her back down, and clamped his hand over her mouth. "No!" he hissed. "You can't. They'll kill you. We wait. When the timing is right, I promise you we will finish this, but for now we must wait until we can get closer. Your shotgun won't work from here, and I could only get one of them. By the time I lined up for another shot, they'd be on us."

Sarah knew he was right, but if they didn't do something, these men would kill her family. She was sure of it. They needed to get the men away from her house and force them into a place where an ambush would be easier. If they could be lured in front of the sale barn, they would have their best chance. They could hide in the hayloft and have a clear view of the open ground in front. This would give them time to shoot two at once, and hopefully be able to turn on the third before he could fire back.

Sarah shared her thoughts with Jakob as the leader began counting down: "Two minutes left."

They moved up the ditch and past her house, stopping in front of the sale barn. Sarah peeked over the bank and gazed back toward her house. They were at least a hundred and fifty yards away, and had twenty yards of open ground to get across before they could slip into the sale barn. Once inside, they would need to get the men's attention without giving away their exact position.

Sarah crawled over the edge of the ditch bank and belly crawled across the road and into the barn. Once inside, she ran up the stairs two at a time to the loft. She took a position to the side of the upper door and signaled Jakob. He repeated her movements and took a position on the other side of the door, just as the gang leader reached zero and shot the next elder in the back of the head.

Sarah took several deep breaths. She slowly put the barrel of her shotgun out the window and pointed it in the air over the heads of the gang. Jakob probably could have shot any one of them at this distance, but with open sights, combined with the fact that he was not the most accurate long-distance shooter, they had decided that Sarah would pepper them with the shotgun and hopefully get their full attention. The .00 buckshot wouldn't kill them at this distance, but it would hurt pretty bad, and hopefully blind them with rage so they'd come in recklessly, giving Sarah and Jakob an advantage to add to their elevated position.

Sarah made eye contact with Jakob and nodded slightly. He returned the nod. She shouted, "We're down here in the barn!"

As her words trailed off, she squeezed the front trigger of the shotgun. The three men dove to the ground. A split second later, the lead pellets rained down on top of them. Small puffs of dust burst into the air as the pellets that didn't hit the men buried themselves into the dirt road. The leader, Randy, jumped up and ran toward the barn, flanked by his men. The elders that had been kneeling in the dirt jumped up and ran toward the safety of her house.

Sarah quickly opened the action on her shotgun and inserted a fresh round. Randy slowed seventy-five yards from the barn and let his two men go past. When he was fifty yards out, he stopped altogether and knelt in the middle of the road while the other two advanced slowly. Sarah's heart sank. She knew they wouldn't be able to get all three as easily as she'd hoped. She lowered her gun a few inches. If they shot the two, what would stop Randy from going back to her house and killing her family? She wasn't sure they could take care of the two and still have time to catch Randy before he reached her house again. It didn't matter, she decided. This was the best chance they had.

She raised her shotgun, settled it on the face of the man on the left, and whispered a countdown to Jakob: "Three, two, one."

They shot at the same time, both hitting their targets perfectly. Sarah's man stopped cold, stood motionless for a moment, then slowly fell to the ground. The one Jakob had shot took a few steps sideways, dropped his rifle, and turned toward Randy before he too fell into the dirt and was still.

Randy jumped up and began running back toward her house. Jakob shot two more times, completely missing the fast-moving target. Sarah grabbed the rope hanging from the pulley on the outside of the barn just above the loft door and swung down to the ground. She had to catch Randy before he got to the house, or at least get close enough for the shotgun to do its work. He had a seventy-yard head start, but Sarah was fast. Her dress snapped in the wind as she quickly closed the distance.

Randy reached the gate to the yard. Sarah had reduced the gap to thirty yards. He grabbed the latch to open the gate. Sarah raised the shotgun and fired the second barrel on a dead run. Her aim was off. The full load of buckshot exploded into the board fence two feet from the man's back.

Randy turned away from the gate and fired over his shoulder as he ran toward the cover of the tree line. Sarah dove to the ground and covered her head. She rolled into the irrigation ditch and lay motionless, not daring to look up until Jakob ran up beside her.

"We need to go after him," Jakob said.

Sarah stood and brushed the dust from her chest. "What if there's more of them?" she asked. "What's to stop them from picking up where these left off? I think we need to go after him, but I think we need to follow him wherever he goes, and if there are more, we need to get every one of them."

They walked back up the road and collected the weapons the men they'd shot had carried. Both had full magazines. Sarah looked back toward the church and the rest of the village, took a mental picture, and almost smiled. She'd been raised here. It had been such a peaceful place. But she would not pass this way again.

She walked past her house. The front door opened. Her father came out, followed by the elders who had run in a few minutes earlier. They began picking up the bodies in the dirt road, not looking at Sarah and Jakob or even acknowledging the fact that they had just killed two more gang members and saved more of their people's lives.

Sarah's anger erupted. She stomped up to her father and pushed her face next to his. "Why won't you look at me?" she shouted. "I am your daughter!"

Her father put down his end of the body he'd been lifting, and slowly raised his head. The look on his face was the saddest Sarah had ever seen.

"I have no daughter," he said. "Any daughter of mine would not have taken this path. She would not have murdered in cold blood, and she would not have caused such hardship and danger to her friends and family."

He bent down, picked up his end of the body again, turned his back on her, and walked away. Sarah knew those were the last words he would ever speak to her. She turned her back on her village for the last time and ran into the woods, her only remaining friend right behind her.

CHAPTER 10

Lexington Avenue
Pittsburgh
1:45 P.M., Tuesday, September 30

RANDY JACKSON SAT in the doorway of the apartment building he'd grown up in and stared down at the bottle of cheap whiskey in his hands. He took a long drink, wiped his mouth, and mumbled a string of cusswords. He hadn't eaten anything for days. All he'd had to drink was whiskey and a few swallows of water he'd found in toilet tanks. The effects of the thick brown booze mixed with the lack of food had begun to show. His ribs were nearly pushing through the thin layer of skin on his sides. His face was drawn, his cheeks sunk in to the point that the outline of his teeth was visible.

He had returned to the city after fleeing the Amish village. His home on Silent Run was gone. There were no supplies left on the property. With no other options, he had wandered back to familiar surroundings, hoping to find something to eat that others might have missed after the collapse, or to find someone who was still in the city. If he did find anyone, he knew he could feed on them for a short time.

But the entire city was abandoned. He found no food anywhere. He had shot a few dogs and cats, but soon his ammunition had run out, and he didn't have any other skills for killing them. He gave up, found some booze in a back room of the neighborhood liquor store, and drank himself into a stupor. He had the constant feeling that someone was following him. But when he turned around, there was never anyone there. He thought about jumping off the roof of a building, hanging himself, putting a gun in his mouth and pulling the trigger, or maybe slitting his wrists. But he couldn't do it. No matter how desperate things got or how much he was suffering, he just didn't have the guts. He knew it made him a coward, but he didn't care. He knew he was afraid of death and what came after, and had accepted it a long time ago.

He had been king of his neighborhood before the collapse. He hadn't been afraid of anything. In fact, people were afraid of him. He had been cold blooded and killed without remorse. If anyone so much as looked at him in a way he didn't like, he'd walked up to them, stuck a pistol in their face, and laughed as he pulled the trigger, splattering their brains out the back of their exploding heads. Even before he took his first life, people had feared him. His own mother had feared him before he'd killed her boyfriend on his twelfth birthday.

Randy looked through the open door of his childhood apartment building, took another long swig from the bottle, and closed his eyes. Blurry memories settled behind his eyelids. They came slowly at first, but soon the images exploded into his mind, faster and faster, until one memory pushed out all the others and became crystal clear. A memory of the day he had become a man.

His mother had planned a birthday party for him and invited all of the kids in their neighborhood. She had worked overtime and entertained as many as five men a night for a week to come up with the extra money for a cake and a shiny new bicycle. Randy had been so excited about being the only kid in the neighborhood that would have a new bike. He already had a bicycle, but it was a hand-me-down from his older brother, Mike, who'd given it to him when he'd stolen a better one. People in their world didn't waste money on things like toys and bicycles. They barely had enough money for food, booze, and their next hit of crack. Randy's mom had done the best she could, but she'd been a victim of circumstance. She had dropped out of school at fourteen. Her parents kicked her out of their apartment shortly after, so she'd been forced to live on the streets. She stayed with friends but was never welcome for long. She bounced around until she was eighteen, then got on the system and was provided with an apartment on Lexington, food stamps, and eleven hundred dollars a month from welfare. Soon after she moved into the apartment, Randy was born.

From the beginning, his life was filled with danger. Different men came into his mom's life and lived with them. They took what they could from her welfare check and spent it on drugs. Sometimes they beat up his mom. If Randy and Mike tried to protect her, the men turned their fists on her children.

The man who lived with them the day Randy turned twelve was the worst of the lot. Randy never knew what his real name was; he knew him only as Barber. He'd been the warlord of the Hilltop Boys, and had a reputation of killing rival gang members by cutting their throats with a barber's straight razor. The brutality of his life didn't end when he came home each morning. Randy's mom was regularly admitted to the hospital with broken bones and head injuries. Whenever his mom was in the hospital, Randy and Mike hid in the basement of their apartment building until his mom came home to again provide a thin buffer between them and Barber.

The morning of Randy's birthday, Barber had beaten up his mom, taken all of the money from her purse, worked over Randy for fifteen minutes straight with his belt, and stormed out of the apartment. His mom left shortly after and was gone until early afternoon. She came home completely blown out on crack and crashed face down on the couch. As soon as Randy's friends started showing up for his special birthday party, Barber had returned and chased them out of the apartment. He turned on Mike and punched him until he was unconscious. Then he went for Randy's shiny new bike in the hallway. He took out his razor and laughed as he slashed the tires and scraped the paint.

Randy felt as if he were outside of his body, watching himself in a movie. He went to his mom's room and grabbed a pistol Barber kept in the nightstand next to the mattress on the floor. He slowly walked back to the front of the apartment and pointed the gun at the man who had ruined his birthday and his family's life.

Barber laughed at him. "Whatch you gonna do with that? Did mama's boy grow a pair?"

Barber rushed at him. Randy pulled the trigger. The bullet hit Barber in the face. He fell to the floor, a shocked expression on what was left of his features.

Randy stood over the body and stared at the thick blood pouring out and puddling on the dirty yellow linoleum of the kitchen floor. He smelled the blood through the smoke from the gun. He calmly walked into the living room where his mother was still passed out on the couch. He leaned down and kissed her on the cheek. Then he dropped the gun, sat on the floor, and everything went blank. The next thing Randy remembered was his brother dragging him out the door and them running down the street while his friends stared after them. It was the last time he ever saw his mother. She was convicted of Barber's murder and sent to prison. Randy and Mike spent the next few years on the street until they both joined the Hilltop Boys. Two years after their initiation into the gang, Randy's brother was shot in a drive-by shooting. From then on, his only family was the crew he ran with.

Back in the old apartment on Lexington, Randy opened his eyes and laughed. He never imagined then that he would one day lead the Hilltop Boys. The world was certainly a strange and funny place. He briefly wondered about his mother. He hadn't thought of her for years, but after his trip down memory lane, he wondered if she'd died in Camp Hill Penitentiary after the power went out or if she'd somehow escaped and was in the same situation as him.

He loudly swallowed the last of the whiskey, threw the empty bottle into the street, and got up. His head spun and his eyes temporarily lost focus. He leaned on the railing of the stoop until his head cleared, then staggered down the street. He wasn't sure where he was going. He knew only that there was nothing on Lexington Avenue for him anymore. He walked for hours. He stopped walking and looked around. The sun had set. He was in a part of the city he hadn't been in for a long time. There were malls, restaurants, and hotels on every street corner. Most of the abandoned cars were newer models. The buildings that hadn't burned were fairly well kept and decorated. This was definitely a place Randy would not have spent time in before the collapse.

He walked through the broken front doors of a Hampton Inn and looked around. The lobby was filled with garbage. All of the furniture had been ripped or broken. There were empty fruit and vegetable cans everywhere, along with several bones. Blankets and pillows were scattered around and empty shell casings littered the floor. He walked past the front desk and into a hallway. More empty cans and bones covered the floor. Most of the doors to the rooms stood open. He took the stairs to the fifth floor and walked into a hallway that was a mirror image of the bottom floor. He turned into the first room, lay on top of a blood-stained mattress, and closed his eyes. Sleep came quickly, but was accompanied almost immediately by nightmares and hellish visions of his past—and possible future.

The television preacher shouted to his viewers, "There's no liquor in Hell! There's no crack cocaine in Hell! There will be no sex in Hell! There's craving and desire in Hell, but there is no peace! There's just an eternity of torment and pain. Your flesh will burn forever. You must repent! You must be forgiven. Just pick up that phone right now. Call the 1-800 number at the bottom of your screen. People are standing by to help you get right with God."

Randy held his middle finger up to the TV screen and laughed. "Hell!" he said. "People are so stupid."

The vision changed. Randy stood on the corner of Lexington and Carter with his back to the red-bricked community center. Several of his boys loitered nearby. This was his office, the place he ran his kingdom from. People would come there several times a day and give him money in exchange for the escape from reality he provided. A black Escalade rounded the corner and slowly drove up the street toward him and his security detail. Randy nodded toward the Escalade, but it had turned into a small, horse-drawn buggy. His boys came from the shadows and converged on the vehicle. The buggy rolled to a stop. Several young boys dressed in black coats and white shirts emerged, followed by a girl in a long gray dress, wearing a white bonnet. When the girl spoke, fire shot from her mouth, burning his men to ashes. "It's time, Randy," she said.

He tried to run, but he couldn't get traction. He was standing in a river of blood. Boney hands reached out, trying to pull him down. They got a firm grasp on his legs, and he went under. He gasped for air. Warm blood filled his lungs.

"NO!" he shouted.

Randy sat straight up in the bed and gulped air. The dream had been so real, so terrifying. Beads of sweat exploded from his face. He shivered. He reached up with a corner of the dirty bed sheet and wiped his face. He pulled the sheet from the bed and wrapped it around his shoulders.

"There's still time, Randy."

Randy jumped from the bed and scanned the room, looking for the man who had spoken to him. No one was there. Had he imagined it? Maybe he was losing his mind. Maybe the steady diet of whiskey had caused him to hallucinate. Randy shook his head to clear away the cobwebs and started for the door.

"You are running out of time," the voice said in a flat tone.

Randy was starting to panic now. The voice was definitely there.

"Who are you?" he shouted. "What do you want?"

"You can change," the voice said. "All you need to do is ask me for forgiveness and invite me into your life, and you will be saved. If you don't, there is no hope for you."

Randy grew angry. He lifted the middle finger of his right hand and waved it around the room. "Leave me alone!" he shouted and headed toward the door. His legs barely held him up. He had to lean on the wall as he walked out of the room and down the stairs.

He emerged from the front door of the hotel and stepped into the evening darkness. The air had cooled, and he wrapped the sheet tighter around him. He didn't know where he was going or why. He just needed to walk, to clear his head. Maybe he had missed something before, there had to be something left to eat in the city. He turned and saw a flash of someone ducking into a gas station across the street from the hotel. He wasn't sure if it was real or if he'd imagined it, like he'd imagined being followed, or imagined the voice that had just spoken his name. He closed his eyes and tried to shake the vision from his head. When he opened his eyes, two people filled the doorway of the gas station. One was a tall, muscular, bearded man in black suspenders. Deep blue eyes bored into him from beneath a wide-brimmed black hat. The other was a girl in a gray dress with a simple bonnet on her head. The girl left the gas station and moved toward him. He knew she wasn't real.

Terror took hold of Randy's mind. It was the girl from his nightmare. This demon was trying to push her way into his consciousness. "You're not real!" he shouted. He fell to the sidewalk in the fetal position. Heavy sobs racked his body. Deep moans of fear and torment burst from his throat as she walked up to him, raised a shotgun, and pointed it at his face.

"You're not real." He whispered it this time. "Leave me alone. You don't belong here."

The girl stared down at him. He could see his reflection in her tear-filled eyes. It struck him how pathetic and weak he had become. He set his jaw firmly and spit in her face.

"You don't matter," he hissed.

Randy Jackson raised his hands in front of his face and closed his eyes.

CHAPTER 11

Logans Ferry Heights
Pittsburgh
8:00 A.M., Thursday, October 2

Tom Dixon lightly tapped on the bedroom door.

"Come in," a voice called out.

Tom removed his Pittsburgh Penguins ball cap and slowly opened the door. Julia Lapp sat upright in bed, a breakfast tray resting on her thighs. She set the tray and its half-eaten toast and bacon on the nightstand near the bed and smiled as Tom came in. Tom smiled back.

"How are you feeling today?" Tom asked.

"Pretty good," she said. "But I'm tired of being treated like an invalid."

Julia had taken longer to recover than anyone had expected. The injuries she'd sustained at Jackson's house on Silent Run were worse than they realized when Tom brought her back to his group. She had a severe concussion, a punctured lung, a bruised kidney, several broken ribs, and a broken arm. Nurse Green had managed to fix her lung and her kidney, and the ribs had healed well. Without the ability to do surgery on her arm, it had healed less than perfectly. She could still use it, but her wrist didn't bend anymore.

Tom was about to speak again when another knock came through the door. He opened it and was greeted by the leathery face of Nicole Green. Nicole was the only member of their little family who had medical training. She'd been a nurse at Allegheny General Hospital before the collapse. Her parents had owned a farm a few miles from the compound. She had wandered in looking for food and help a few months after the collapse. Tom had instantly liked Nicole. She was sarcastic and built like a mixed martial arts fighter. She was always calm in a crisis. Tom and a few others had started calling her Nurse Ratchet behind her back.

"How's my patient?" Nicole asked.

"I'm fine, but I was just telling Tom, I need to get out of the house and get some fresh air. I can't stand being cooped up any more."

"Well, that all depends on how you're progressing."

Nicole stuck a thermometer in Julia's mouth and placed a blood pressure cuff on her forearm. She checked her pulse and temperature, then looked up at Tom and cleared her throat.

"I need to listen to her lungs now if you don't mind."

"Not at all," Tom said, turning a little red. He looked down at the floor and twirled his Penguins cap in his hands.

"If everything checks out," Tom said, "I was gonna invite Julia to go for a little ride with me later. I need to go down to the warehouse district and look for a few supplies."

"Yes!" Julia shouted, spitting out the thermometer and throwing the covers back.

Nicole placed a firm hand on her shoulder and held her down while examining the slobbery thermometer. "Not so fast," she said. "Your temperature and blood pressure are all right, but I need to listen to those lungs."

"I'll be in the kitchen," Tom said, "when you're ready."

Nurse Ratchet glared at him as he backed out the door and closed it.

Forty-five minutes later, Tom was driving his Ranger down the hillside toward the warehouse district, with Julia Lapp sitting in the passenger seat looking like an eager puppy going for its first car ride. It was a warm Indian summer morning, so Tom had taken the top off the UTV. Julia squealed with delight as her dark-brown hair blew in the wind.

Tom had grown fond of Julia since she'd joined their group. He'd spent many hours at her bedside learning about Amish culture, her family, and the dreams she had before the collapse. Julia had confided that it had always been her dream to one day leave the Amish and join the Englishmen's world. She'd always been fascinated with modern technology and envious of the fast-paced life in urban America. She had already been through more grief and torment than anyone deserved in a lifetime, but had managed to retain a childlike innocence. She reminded Tom a little of his own daughter. Putting aside the torture and brutality of her existence, Julia was similar to his Abigail in so many ways. Her hair was almost the same color, she had a level of sarcasm that rivaled Abigail's, and when she laughed, her face scrunched up, small wrinkle lines forming around her eyes. The similarities brought Tom both pleasure and pain.

"How far are we going?" Julia asked.

"It's about five miles to the warehouses. We should be there and back before dinner."

Tom hadn't been back to the warehouse district since shortly after the collapse, when he'd discovered the truckload of crated ATVs that had no doubt been headed to the Polaris dealership. The semi-truck that hauled them was abandoned in the middle of Logans Ferry Road just three blocks from the port. Tom had fled the city with Mary after they'd come out of the basement at Carl's Tavern shortly after the collapse. They had ended up in the warehouse district.

He'd been excited when he opened the steel shipping container and found the crates wrapped in chicken wire. The terrorists had apparently knocked out the nation's power with an electromagnetic pulse. Tom didn't know much about the effects of an EMP, but he figured that if an ATV was surrounded by metal, the pulse probably wouldn't reach the electronics. He had been right. When he unloaded the first ATV, put gas he'd siphoned from a nearby car into the tank, and turned the key, the engine had come alive. Then he and Mary found the farm on Farneth Road, complete with three hundred–gallon gas and diesel tanks. Over the next few months, they made several trips to the truck and rode nearly all of the ATVs back, with the exception of two smaller children's models. These, Tom had disabled by removing the electronic control modules. They stored the vehicles out of sight in the barn.

Up to now, there hadn't been much need to explore the warehouse district beyond the immediate area of the ATVs. But their group had grown in size and their canned food stores were running low, as well as their supply of toilet paper and other personal hygiene items. Tom hoped that the Wegmans grocery distribution warehouse hadn't been completely emptied by other survivors and that he could find some items they could use. He wouldn't be able to carry much on this trip, but once he learned what they had and determined it was safe, he would return with others from the farm and load all they could.

Tom and Julia turned onto Logans Ferry and headed downriver toward the port. Tom drove slowly past the warehouses, stopping several times to explore some of the buildings. They found a few useful items, but none of the food or sanitary supplies they really needed. The stops took a little more time than he'd anticipated. As evening approached, he ignored the other buildings and went straight to the Wegmans warehouse. He didn't expect trouble, but he was cautious anyway. He wanted to be in and out before dark. Since the collapse, he'd seen only a few people in this part of the city, and those he had come across had ended up joining his group. He'd never encountered any of the Hilltop Boys on this side of the river and wasn't sure why they hadn't thought to search here for supplies. Even if they had come here unnoticed, Tom didn't think they would have been able to take much back to their Silent Run house without motorized transportation. The distance was over twelve miles. From what Tom had observed, they'd been solely focused on ruling their part of the city and living off the people and supplies within that area. Tom was pretty sure the warehouse still had supplies in it.

As they neared the end of Logans Ferry, Tom pulled the Ranger over next to a dumpster and turned off the motor.

"The warehouse is two blocks ahead," he said. "I think I should go in on foot at first to make sure it's safe. Do you mind waiting here for me?"

"I don't mind," Julia said. "But do you think it's dangerous at the warehouse?"

"I don't think we'll have any problems. I just feel it's smarter to check it out without the noise of the Ranger alerting anyone who might be there that we're coming."

Tom reached into the glove box, removed a 9 millimeter pistol, checked the load, and handed it to Julia. "You know how to use that?"

Julia held the weapon awkwardly and frowned. "Not really. I watched Randy and the others handle guns, but I was never allowed near them. When I was left alone, the room where they were kept was always locked. We never had them in our home growing up. Even though many in our village did, my papa was against having any weapons."

Tom spent a couple of minutes showing her how to hold the pistol, how to take the safety off, and how to reload the magazine if she emptied it. He gave her an extra box of ammunition and told her to wait for him. He grabbed his Blackout from the backseat, smiled and winked at Julia, then trotted toward the warehouse.

He moved cautiously, jogging fifty to seventy-five yards at a time, then pausing next to whatever cover he could find to scan the area before moving forward again. When he was within a hundred yards of the warehouse, he ducked behind a forklift to survey his destination. Someone had piled pallets, bricks, and other debris in front of the chain-link roller gate, completely blocking the entrance. This was something Tom hadn't expected. The warehouse looked abandoned, and there was no sign of activity on the grounds around the building. But the gate had definitely been barricaded from the inside.

Tom crouched behind the forklift for the next half hour. Should he move closer and actually get inside the fence, or wait until dark and come back with more people? If it was dark, they'd likely see any light coming from the warehouse. If there were people occupying it, the next problem would be getting close enough to talk to them without starting a firefight. Tom and his people needed the supplies that were most likely inside. If someone else had claimed the warehouse, was it worth the risk to try and negotiate for the supplies? Or should he look for what he needed somewhere else? He hadn't passed any stores on his trips into the city that didn't look completely picked through already. Most of the stores and houses inside the city were in ruins. This warehouse might be the only place left with any supplies for miles.

Tom decided to move closer and try to see if there was anyone in the warehouse. He jogged in a crouch toward the back of the building. The backside didn't show much sign of human activity either, with the exception of the few windows next to the back door. They'd been spray-painted black. Someone had definitely been here, and might still be here.

Tom scaled the chain-link fence as quietly as he could and ran in a crouch to the metal staircase that led up to the back door. He slowly climbed the stairs, leaned with his back to the wall next to the door, and listened for several minutes. Nothing. He knelt in front of the door and placed his ear against it. Still no sound other than his own heartbeat and steady breathing. Tom reached up and rubbed one of the window panes. No good—they'd been painted from the inside. He gently curled his fingers around the doorknob and slowly turned it.

The sound of a glass bottle breaking on the concrete floor on the other side made him jump. He ran down the stairs and made for the fence. He was halfway over when the backdoor of the warehouse flew open and slammed into the steel railing on the porch. Tom climbed faster and flung himself over the top. His feet were moving as soon as he hit the ground.

"Stop!" someone shouted behind him.

Tom kicked into high gear and sprinted for the cover of the forklift. He dove behind it just as a burst of automatic gunfire shredded the pavement where he'd been a split second before.

"I just came to talk!" Tom shouted.

Another burst of gunfire filled the air. Bullets ricocheted off the cab of the forklift. Tom put his rifle up to his shoulder, raised his eyes above his cover, and pointed the weapon downrange. Four men, all carrying automatic rifles, were opening the gate. A fifth man was scaling the fence in the same place Tom had. He cursed himself for coming to the warehouse without backup and again ducked behind the forklift.

Where had these people come from? The city had been mostly abandoned for at least a year. His community really needed the supplies, but Tom didn't want to kill these men to get them. He would much rather negotiate for what they needed, but it seemed these people were in no mood to barter. He knew if he didn't act soon, he might not get the chance to decide. He could lay down his weapon, put his hands up, and hope he could get them to listen to reason. But by doing so, he would throw away any means he had of defense. He also needed to think about Julia. She wasn't proficient with the gun he'd left her. If he was neutralized and these men explored further, she would be virtually helpless. He had begun to think of Julia like his own daughter, and he was not about to let anything happen to her. Not only would Julia be in danger, but his whole community could face danger from this group. If they found his Ranger, they would have the ability to explore farther from their warehouse. The chances were good they could discover the farm.

Tom crawled to the back of the forklift and tried one more time to reason with them. "If we can just talk, I'm sure I have something I could offer you in exchange for a few supplies!"

The air erupted in gunfire again, this time from all of them at once. He ducked low and covered his head while hugging the back tire of the forklift. When the gunfire stopped, he immediately leaned around the forklift, took aim at the man who'd climbed the fence, and lined up his sights on center mass. He squeezed the trigger of the Blackout in a double tap. The man fell to the ground, squirmed on the pavement for a few moments, then tried to get to his knees. When he began to raise his rifle, Tom shot him in the throat.

The other four men had ducked back through the gate and were running for the safety of the building. Tom crawled out from behind the forklift, took a knee, lined up his iron sights in the middle of the last man's back, and fired one shot. The poor fellow was dead before he hit the ground. His head made a loud crack as his face bounced off the pavement. The last man cleared the stairs and dove through the door before Tom could bring his sights to bear on him.

"I just wanted to talk!" Tom yelled. "Now two of you are dead! This wasn't necessary!"

"Tom?"

He whirled and pointed his weapon at a figure running his direction, now just twenty yards away. Her face was white, her eyes wild. It was Julia.

"Stay back!" he shouted at her. He turned again toward the backdoor of the warehouse, in time to see a black barrel emerge and point toward his friend. He raised his weapon yet again and went full pray and spray, emptying his entire thirty-round magazine in a few seconds.

Julia was now sprinting back toward the Ranger. Tom ejected the spent mag from his Blackout, inserted a fresh one, and quickly unloaded half of its contents into the warehouse door. Then he sprinted after Julia. Just before rounding the corner and losing sight of the building, he stopped and emptied the rest of his mag. He continued running toward the Ranger and almost overtook Julia. They reached the vehicle at the same time and jumped in. Tom fired it up, stomped on the gas pedal, and turned toward the farm.

CHAPTER 12

Pittsburgh
8:30 A.M.

SARAH AND JAKOB took their time moving through Pittsburgh. It was a beautiful morning, and they had never been to this part of the city. Sarah tried hard to focus on the wondrous things they were seeing. She wanted desperately to erase the memory of the evening before.

As they walked between the abandoned cars, Sarah daydreamed about what it would be like to sit behind the wheel of one and drive with the window down through the countryside on a summer afternoon. She looked at mannequins through broken store windows and imagined how she would look in the latest fashion. She dreamt about wearing such clothes to a night on the town, maybe a movie or fancy restaurant. Even though she had never done any of these things and didn't know what she was missing, it still made her sad to think she would never be able to now. Her best chance to experience at least some of what the Englishmen's world supposedly offered was in the West. A man had travelled through her village in the spring and told of places in Oregon and Washington where there was at least partial electricity.

There were even a few cars on the roads, and people were working to restore modern conveniences.

The man also told tales of war. A reduced army remained of those who had invaded and ruled America just after the collapse. The invaders still sought to control the country. But people were fighting back, working to restore the American government to the way it was before. Sarah knew nothing of American government or its history. She had never been taught any history other than biblical history and the history of the Amish people. Her world had always been separate. They had followed the Amish rule of law; the American system of justice rarely crossed over into her world. She had no desire to be involved in war or more killing. She had killed, but only in the name of protecting her loved ones.

Until last night. The memory made her shudder. Once again she pushed it out of her mind, replacing it with thoughts of their journey.

The idea of visiting the West had stirred a nearly forgotten desire. On one of her trips out of the village as a child, Sarah had found a picture book in a thrift store her mother frequented. She'd hidden it in her dress pocket and never revealed its existence to her father. During the weeks that followed, after bedtime, she'd light a candle, read about the West, and pore over images of wildlife and scenery. Then she'd stow the book under her mattress and fall asleep dreaming of the snowcapped Cascade Mountains in Oregon, the stark, warm deserts of Arizona, and the sandy beaches of California. Her father might not have even objected to the book, but it was a part of her own dreams and desires. She hadn't wanted to share that part of her with anyone else.

Each step brought Sarah and Jakob a little closer to her dream. As they neared the edge of the city, the landscape began to change. Shopping malls were replaced by mechanic shops, car dealerships, and other industrial buildings. They crossed a four-lane bridge over a lazy river and walked to the water's edge to rest in the shade. They hadn't spoken more than three words to each other since the night before. The desire and passion Sarah still felt for Jakob had been shoved into a corner of her heart.

Sarah excused herself and walked up the riverbank, out of Jakob's line of sight. Her clothes were torn, dirty, and bloodstained. Her hands and face were grimy. Dried blood was caked under her fingernails. She needed a bath and fresh clothes. Sarah stripped, walked into the river, and dove under the water. The shock of the cold took her breath away. She quickly broke the surface and filled her lungs with air.

Sarah waded out of the river, rubbed herself down with sand and mud, then gingerly waded back in to rinse. Once she was clean, she put on the extra underwear, tights, and dress from her pack. She scrubbed her dirty garments, including her bonnet, on a rock and laid them in the sun to dry. She put her wet bonnet back on, pulled her Bible from the pack, and began to read and pray. Sarah hadn't opened God's Word for over a week. The peace and stability she normally felt after her daily devotion and study of the Bible had started to slip away.

After a few minutes, the words on the pages began to swirl in and out of focus. The warm sunshine and exhausting days of travel were catching up to her. Sarah placed the Bible on the ground, lay back in the grass, and shut her eyes.

Abram Beiler's beard rose slightly as he smiled at his daughter over the hind end of the cow he was milking. His dark brown eyes twinkled above his bulbous red nose. Sarah grinned back.

The vision shifted. Sarah now sat in the driver's seat of a horse-drawn buggy. She was next to a man who held the reins. The buggy rolled to a stop. Behind her, Jakob and several other boys from the village got out of the buggy. Sarah looked at the driver. He stared straight ahead. Sarah tugged on his sleeve. The driver still refused to acknowledge her. A sharp pain sliced into her heart.

"Father?" she said.

Still nothing. Sarah found she couldn't breathe.

"Father!" she yelled. "What did I do? Papa?"

Her father still would not turn her way. Instead, he thrust his right arm out in front of her nose, pointing at the ground beside them.

"You did this!" he shouted.

Sarah turned and began to cry. Her mother was laying in the dirt in a pool of blood. The leader of the gang stood over her, his eyes wild. He was so thin he was almost a skeleton. In his hand was a bottle of liquor.

Sarah's anguish transformed into a burning anger that engulfed her. She jumped off the buggy. Suddenly a shotgun was in her hands. She held it up to the gang leader's fear-struck face and began putting pressure on the trigger. The ground around her began to shake and move like a river. Small, black demons with red eyes and tiny talons crawled from the waves and reached for her as she pulled the trigger.

"No!" she screamed as their talons tore her dress and scratched chunks of flesh from her legs.

"Jakob!" she shouted. He ran toward her. She stretched out her arms to him.

"Sarah!" he shouted! "Hold on! Sarah! Sarah!"

Sarah bolted upright, looked down at her legs, and gulped air. Gone were the demons. Gone was the leader of the gang. Gone was her dead mother. And gone was the man she had once called Papa.

Jakob's voice floated over the sound of the river.

"Sarah, you all right?"

She shivered, put her Bible back in the pack, wadded up her damp underthings, and put them out of sight in the pocket of her dress.

"I'm...I'm fine," she said. "I just needed to clean up. I'll be back down in a minute."

She gathered the rest of her clothes, took the damp unmentionables from her pocket, and stowed them in her pack. They weren't completely dry, but she would lay them out while they slept. Her bonnet went in the pack as well. She didn't have an extra, and she was not enjoying the wet cloth on her head. Sarah realized Jakob had never seen her without the covering. She worried about how he might react. She knew her father wouldn't approve.

"Father," she said aloud, and shook her head. "I no longer have one."

She put on the backpack, picked up her shotgun, and walked downstream. She found Jakob sitting on a rock and chewing on a piece of grass. When he looked up at her, the piece of grass fell from his mouth. His face froze in a boyish grin. Sarah suddenly felt exposed and vulnerable. With her left hand, she absently twirled her hair with trembling fingers.

"What are you looking at?" she snapped. "Haven't you ever seen a girl without a bonnet?"

Jakob quickly looked down, his face red. "I'm sorry" he stammered "I just wasn't expecting—"

The sound of gunfire in the distance interrupted their conversation. They both snapped their heads downriver and listened intently. After a few seconds, more shots rang out.

"Come on!" Sarah shouted. Her feet barely touched the ground as she bounded over river rocks, up the bank, and into the roadway. Jakob was right behind her. After they'd run several blocks, the shooting stopped. Sarah slowed and began looking for cover. The last shots were close. They moved to the side of the road and walked slowly behind parked cars and trucks. When they rounded a corner, Sarah dropped to her stomach on the asphalt, dragging Jakob down with her. A small vehicle with two people in it was moving down the road toward them at a high rate of speed. It passed by not twenty feet away. All of Sarah's breath escaped her body at once when she realized who was in the passenger seat: Julia Lapp.

Sarah rose up on her elbows and watched the vehicle disappear around the corner. She fought the urge to run into the road and call after her friend. She wasn't sure if the man in the vehicle was part of Randy's gang or not. He was black, but he didn't have the same look as the others she'd seen. He was well fed, and something about the man's eyes was softer. Also, as far as she knew, the gang had no vehicles. If they had, they would have used them in their village raids.

Sarah and Jakob lay flat for several more minutes. Suddenly, three white men wearing black, military-style clothing and carrying military rifles came into view, running down the road. Sarah pointed her shotgun at them and held her breath. Her finger twitched over the trigger as they ran by. When the men were halfway to the corner, they stopped. Sarah could no longer hear the motor from the buggy over her hammering heartbeat. The men turned and began walking back the way they'd come. When they were just twenty feet away, they stopped. Sarah was terrified they would hear her breathing, or look over and see them lying there. She knew she could get off at least one shot, but also knew that with the types of weapons they were carrying, she wouldn't live to fire a second.

"We need to post guards tonight," one of the men said. "We also need to find out who they are and where they came from. I'd really like to get my hands on the UTV they were in. We'll wait till morning, then see if we can't find some tracks."

The men continued on, leaving Sarah and Jakob with their thoughts. She needed to know who the man with Julia was. If he was friendly, he might be able to help them. Their food was running low. Even if they rationed what they had, if they didn't hunt or find something else to eat, they would be out in three days' time. If the man wasn't friendly, why was Julia riding with him? She hadn't looked as though she was a prisoner.

Sarah rose from the pavement and brushed oily dirt off the dress that had been clean a half hour earlier. It wouldn't be dark for at least an hour. If they moved quickly, they might be able to pick up the tracks before they needed to camp for the night. Even if they didn't find the tracks, she wanted to be out of the city and in the woods, where she felt less vulnerable.

She and Jakob walked slowly back up the road, scanning the soft dirt of the bank on either side. As they neared the bridge, they found what they were looking for. The vehicle had left the road, climbed the bank, and driven into the forest. Sarah followed the tracks into the tree line and paused to listen before continuing on. Satisfied that the vehicle was gone, they moved further into the forest. After fifteen minutes, Jakob reached out and tugged on the sleeve of Sarah's dress.

"I've been thinking," he said. "If we found those tracks as easy as we did, what's to stop the other men from finding them and following? If the man Julia is with is good and someone who can help us, we probably shouldn't let those men find the spot they drove off the road."

Sarah agreed. They went back to brush away the tracks. By the time they finished, the sun had dropped and darkness was settling in. They followed the tracks back into the forest as quickly as they could and made it at least quarter mile from the road before it was pitch black.

They built a small fire and ate some of their dwindling food supplies.

After supper, Jakob put his bedroll next to Sarah's. She briefly glared at him, moved her bedroll ten feet away, and settled in for the night. Fifteen minutes later, when she was flat on her back and just on the edge of sleep, Jakob picked up his bedroll and moved it next to hers again. Sarah smiled in spite of the irritation she felt. She rolled onto her side and turned her back to him. After a few minutes, Sarah rolled back toward Jakob and leaned in close. Her hair fell onto his face as she kissed him tenderly. He reached his hand behind her head, pulled her closer, and kissed her back forcefully. Sarah pulled back a few inches and smiled down at him.

"I do love you," she whispered. "But you must give me some time. There are some things that must take place before we can be together. I have faith that if God wants us to be together, he will make a way. Now let's get some sleep. I want to be up and have the fire completely out before we head off." She rolled over, closed her eyes, and fell into a deep sleep.

The next morning, they were on their way before sunrise. Sarah didn't know how far they would have to travel to find Julia. She wanted to cover as much ground as possible the first day.

The tracks were easy to follow and they made good time. By mid-morning, they had travelled at least four miles. At a gravel road, Sarah stopped in the tree line. She scanned the road in both directions and the hillside across the road for several minutes. Satisfied that it was safe, she moved across the road, found the tracks again, and started up the hill. Two hundred yards later, a man's voice from above them stopped her in her tracks.

"Don't move," he said. "You're surrounded."

Sarah slowly raised her head. At first she couldn't see anyone, and she wondered if everything that had happened was causing her to hear things. But when she saw Jakob frozen and intently scanning the trees above them, she pushed the thought aside.

"We don't mean any harm," she said. "We don't have any food or many supplies. We just want to continue on the way we're going. We're looking for our friend Julia. We saw her come this way last night. She was riding in a vehicle with someone else. We're just following the tracks."

The man didn't answer. Sarah caught movement from the branches of an oak tree twenty-five feet up. Finally, the man who had spoken came into view. He stood on a platform tree stand wearing full camouflage, his face painted black and green. He had a rifle trained on them, and he looked as though he knew how to shoot it. He pulled a radio from his belt and spoke.

"Tom, this is tower six. Over."

A few seconds later the radio crackled and another man's voice floated across the air waves. "I'm here tower six. What's up?"

"I've got two people here. A girl and a boy. They seem to be following your tracks. Please advise, over."

The radio crackled again. "Are they armed?"

"Yes, sir. One has an old rusty shotgun, and the other a Winchester."

"Be advised six, I'm coming down. Hold them there, please."

Sarah wasn't sure what she should do. So far the only aggression the man in the tree had shown was to point his rifle at them and ask them to stop. If this man was one of the people Julia was living with, she didn't want to fight. But if he was not and he meant them harm, they were in a bad position. From where he was, he could easily shoot them both before she could react. She moved her eyes and almost impercep-tibly turned her head. A four-foot tree lay on the ground ten yards to their left. Sarah wondered if they could reach the tree before the man could react. If they were at least behind the tree, their position would be a little stronger. Sarah shoved the notion aside as she recalled the first words the man had spoken. He had said they were surrounded. So far she hadn't spotted anyone else, but she wasn't willing to take the chance that other guns might be trained on them. Sarah gave herself over to fate. They would have to let this play out.

The sound of a motor coming down the hill reached her ears. A couple of minutes later, the same vehicle they'd seen the evening before came into view. The man rolled to a stop in front of them, turned off the motor, and raised a short, black pump shotgun.

"Who are you?" he said. "Where did you come from?"

Sarah swallowed and stiffened as she spoke: "My name is Sarah, and this is Jakob. We just came from the city yesterday, and saw you by the river. We thought we may have seen someone we knew riding with you, so we followed your tracks. Her name is Julia, and she was taken from our village over a year ago by—"

"You know Julia?"

"Yes. We grew up in the same village, and we haven't seen her since she was taken by the gangs. If she—"

The man didn't let her finish. He spoke into his radio. "Mary, is Julia with you?"

The radio crackled and a woman's voice came through. "Yeah, do you need her?"

"No, just ask her if she knows someone named Sarah or Jakob."

There was a long pause before the response came back.

"I think she must. When she heard the names, she shrieked, got a huge smile on her face, ran out of the house, and headed down the hill toward you. I couldn't stop her."

The man smiled at Sarah. "It seems you are telling the truth."

Sarah released the chest full of air she hadn't realized she'd been holding and loosened her grip on the shotgun.

The man spoke into the radio again. "Stand down towers."

He got out of the vehicle, walked over to Sarah and Jakob, and shook their hands. They spoke for a few more minutes, then they all got into the vehicle. Sarah grabbed onto the roll bar, and began to jump out when the motor started and the machine vibrated. Tom put a hand on her arm and smiled.

"It's okay," he said. "I promise. It's perfectly safe, and I won't go fast."

Sarah relaxed and let herself enjoy the ride. It was much smoother than riding in the Mercer Buggies her people used, but also a lot louder than the horses and their jingling harnesses. It amazed her how well the machine climbed hills and navigated rough, brushy terrain.

She filled Tom in on the men they'd seen following them the night before, and how they had heard their plans to follow. Near the top of the hill, Tom stopped and turned off the motor. He pointed up the hill. Sarah's breath caught in her throat. Julia Lapp was running down to meet them. Sarah jumped out and ran to her. They came together at a full run. Tears rolled down both their faces as they fell to the ground, laughing. Sarah was overcome with joy. She'd regretted not going after Julia when she's been taken and thought she'd never see her again. Each time Sarah had rescued someone else, her feelings of regret and guilt had grown. Now, here she was. Julia had survived. Sarah would have someone else to talk to and lean on besides Jakob. Someone who could understand her as only another Amish girl could.

Tom walked up, followed by Jakob. He cleared his throat and smiled down at them. "I hate to interrupt, but we're almost back to the house, and I'm going to let you walk the rest of the way. I need to go back to the edge of the property and make sure we're ready in case we have any unwanted company."

Sarah and Jakob got their weapons and packs from the UTV, then walked up the hill as Tom drove away. They each had an arm around Julia's shoulders. This was the happiest Sarah had been since the gangs first appeared. The excitement of heading West burned in her with a renewed enthusiasm. Sarah had no doubt that her life would change for the better and she would have her happy ending. Nothing could change that.

CHAPTER 13

Lowellville Road
Outskirts of Struthers, Ohio
6:20 P.M., Friday, April 18

JULIA JERKED THE handlebars hard to the left, leaned over the outside edge of the Polaris Sportsman 500, and gunned the throttle, nearly losing Sarah. She felt Sarah's arms grip tight around her waist as another bullet struck the vehicle, this time taking out one of their taillights.

"Hang on!" Julia yelled as they bounced into the narrow ditch, up the other side, and into thick brush. She plowed through the undergrowth without slowing down. Tree limbs scratched her face and arms. The springtime pollen flew off the vegetation, making her eyes water and nearly choking her. Julia wasn't sure how far ahead Tom and the others in the Ranger were, but she was beyond irritated at him for leaving her and Sarah behind.

She turned the ATV to the right. Soon they were again in the roadway, where she could fully open the throttle. She pushed her thumb on the gas as hard as she could. The quad shot forward, now going 50 mph. At a sharp corner, Julia glanced over her shoulder. Three men were in the roadway several hundred yards back. One was taking a knee.

"Duck!" Julia yelled.

She leaned low over the handlebars, and Sarah laid her chin in the small of her back. They roared into the corner. Hot sparks shot into Julia's face as a bullet tore through trim plastic on the side of the vehicle and glanced off the steel handlebars. They emerged from the corner in time to see Tom and the rest of their group in the Ranger disappear around the corner ahead. Julia didn't let up on the throttle until they'd started into the next corner. As they came out, she went full bore again, closing the two hundred–yard gap between her and her friends. She rode up next to the Ranger and waved her arm. When Tom looked over, she pointed behind her, then motioned for him to follow. She left the roadway again and crashed through the brush.

A hundred yards from the road, Julia stopped in a small clearing and turned off the motor. Tom, Jakob, and Mary pulled up beside the Sportsman, and Tom jumped out.

"What happened?" he asked as he reached into the Ranger, grabbed his Blackout, and began scanning their back trail.

Julia hadn't realized she'd been holding her breath. Now she needed a few seconds to get her wind before she could answer.

"We were driving kind of slow," she said, "enjoying the scenery, and you pulled away. When we came around a corner, there were three men in the middle of the road pointing rifles at us. I hit the throttle and they jumped out of the way. Before we got to the next corner, they were shooting at us."

"We need to get back to the road before they get to where we took off," Tom said.

"Why don't we just ride off?" Sarah asked. "We left them behind. The longer we stay here, the more chance they have to catch up."

"Exactly," Tom said.

He turned and took off on foot down the hill. Julia looked at Sarah, Mary, and Jakob and shrugged her shoulders. They left the ATVs parked in the brush and also ran down the hill. Tom had stopped ten yards from the pavement and was studying the roadway through the brush.

"I don't understand," Julia said. "I agree with Sarah. We've already outrun them. Why don't we just ride off?"

"Because I need some answers," Tom said. "I'd like to know who they are and if there are more up ahead before we continue down the middle of a wide-open highway."

Tom pointed at Julia, then Jakob and Sarah. "You three stay on this side and cover the roadway. Watch the hill behind you as well, and listen in case they're coming through the brush. If they were willing to shoot at you, I'm assuming they really want our vehicles. They'll be coming. Since we didn't shoot back, I'm also assuming they aren't aware of how well armed we are. When they come, don't shoot until I do. "

Tom and Mary took up a position directly across the road. Two minutes later, a pair of young men in camouflage fatigues and carrying black rifles came into view. They jogged up the road toward Julia's position. She took several deep breaths and gripped the handle of the semiautomatic pistol Tom had given her at the farm. Tom had spent several days with her, teaching her how the weapon functioned and how to shoot accurately.

Julia had never fired a gun before. She'd never needed to. Some of her friends in the village had hunted with their fathers since they were old enough to walk. Julia had always envied them, wishing she had that type of relationship with her father. But she and her father were anything but close. He always seemed more concerned with his day-to-day role in the church and his own farm than he was about his relationship with his only daughter.

The two men coming toward them were thirty yards out when Tom shouted from the brush: "Stop! We have you covered!"

The two looked at each other, shock on their faces.

"Put down the guns and step back."

The two men complied. Tom walked out of the brush pointing his weapon at them, Mary right on his heels.

"We just wanted a ride," one of the men said. "We see now that's probably not possible, and that's okay. We'll just go and leave you alone now."

The one who spoke took a step backwards. Tom pointed his rifle at his feet and squeezed off a round. The man jumped into the air.

"Okay!" the man yelled. "We don't want trouble."

Tom raised his rifle to the man's chest and gritted his teeth. "If you didn't want trouble," he said, "you shouldn't have shot at—"

The sound of an ATV starting somewhere above them on the hill caused everyone to snap their heads toward the sound. The two men bolted from the road and plowed into the brush. Julia ran toward where they had parked the ATVs. Shots rang out behind her. She heard a man scream.

Julia made it to the clearing and broke out of the brush just as a third man drove the Sportsman right at her. She dove to the ground, rolled twice, and got to her knees. She pointed her pistol at the middle of his back and fired just as he disappeared into the brush. Sarah's shotgun roared behind her. Julia scrambled to her feet and ran for the Ranger. She jumped in, turned the key, and slammed it into gear. Jakob and Sarah jumped in, and she tore off after the thief. They needed that other ATV.

Julia followed the Sportsman's tracks, plowing through the brush like it wasn't there. They hit the roadway fifty yards below Tom and Mary. The Sportsman disappeared around a corner two hundred yards away. Julia stomped on the throttle and gave chase. The man had a head start, but the 500 was no match for the Ranger 800. Soon they were just fifty yards behind. The man pointed a pistol behind him and filled the air with lead, but it was impossible for him to shoot accurately and steer. Julia quickly overtook him and pulled alongside him. Sarah stood up in the back, hung onto the roll bar with her left hand, and raised the shotgun with her right. She fired.

The lead pellets tore into the man's back, shredding his jacket and knocking him off the quad and into the road. He hit the pavement and bounced several times before rolling into the path of the Ranger. Julia hit the brakes, but the front tires bounced over his body, throwing the vehicle out of control. Sarah bounced out of the back, landing hard on her side. The rider-less Sportsman veered into the ditch and flipped end over end into the brush.

Jakob jumped out of the Ranger before they came to a full stop and rushed back to Sarah. She lay face down in the road. Jakob fell to his knees and rolled her over. Julia was relieved when Sarah opened her eyes and pulled away from Jakob.

"I'm fine," she said. She stood and brushed dirt from her dress. She had a bloody knee and several scrapes on her arms and face, but she seemed okay.

Sarah pointed to the man she'd shot. "Check on him, and somebody should check on the other ATV."

Jakob walked over to the man and checked his pulse. "He's dead," he said flatly.

Julia walked into the brush and found the other ATV. It sat upright, the motor still running. The Sportsman had taking a beating. The left handlebar was bent all the way down to the gas tank, the front brake handle hung by a cable, most of the plastic was either missing or broken, and the seat was ripped to shreds. Julia climbed on and managed to turn the handlebars enough to get it back to the road. She rode up next to the Ranger and left the motor running as Tom and Mary jogged up to the group.

"Is everyone okay?" Tom asked.

"I think so," said Julia. "Sarah fell out, but I think she's fine. What about the other two?"

Tom let out a long breath and leaned against the Ranger. "One's dead," he said. "But the other one got away. He dropped his gun, though, so I'm pretty sure we've seen the last of him. We still don't have any answers, so we may need to get off the highway for a while and try some back roads, at least until we get out of this part of Ohio."

They spent the next half hour bandaging Sarah's scrapes and patching up the Sportsman the best they could, bending the handlebar close to its original position and tying a coat over the ripped seat. They rode back slowly on the pavement and took the first dirt road they came to. After riding for an hour, they pulled up to a wide spot under a towering oak tree and made camp. After a small supper, they spread out bed rolls.

Just as darkness fell, Sarah and Jakob walked away from the group and into the brush, holding hands. Julia chuckled. Since their group had left the farm and Pittsburgh two months earlier, the two newlyweds hadn't wasted any opportunity to go off by themselves. They'd been married by Pastor Ken two weeks after coming to the farm. Sarah had wanted a traditional Amish ceremony, but their new group was fresh out of Amish clergy, so she'd settled for a Presbyterian wedding. She might have tried waiting until they ran across more of the Amish on their journey, but Julia knew Sarah couldn't wait even if she'd wanted to. Julia had seen the longing on her face each time she was near Jakob, and sensed Jakob's anguish each time Sarah pushed him away. Julia was happy for them and had, like everyone else in their village, always known the two would be together one day. Yet their wedding also made her a little sad. She had given in to the fact that she might never meet someone to share her life with intimately. Even if she met someone she was attracted to, how could they want her after what she had been through? The fact that Tom and Mary were hopelessly in love and acted like teenagers added to Julia's sadness.

Julia lay in her bed roll and thought back to the day they'd left Pennsylvania. Tom had decided to head west shortly after his run-in with the men at the warehouse. With Randy Jackson dead and his city in ruins with no sign of ever recovering, there was nothing keeping him around. Tom had invited along anyone who wanted to make the journey, but only Mary and the Amish youth were interested. So after many tearful goodbyes to the people who had become like family, the five of them had left the hilltop refuge for adventure. They took two of the ATVs, some weapons, ammunition, and canned food. Julia had been excited and full of anticipation for the first time since she had escaped the horrors on Silent Run Road.

Forty-five minutes after sneaking away, Sarah and Jakob returned to camp. Dried sticks and leaves stuck in the folds of Sarah's dress. Jakob's shirt was only partially tucked in, and was buttoned unevenly. Julia covered her mouth and laughed.

When Julia awoke the next morning, the smell of wood smoke hung in the air. No one in their camp had lit a fire. Tom had an uneasy look in his eyes.

They stashed the ATVs in the trees and covered them with brush. Tom decided they should investigate the source of the smoke before they started the motors and alerted anyone else to their presence. They walked near the road, concealed in the brush with the wind and smoke in their face. Julia hoped that the smoke came from far away and had carried to them when the evening breezes tended to fall with the dew.

After more than a mile of walking, Tom held up his hand, stopping the group. The sound of a man's voice—he was shouting—reached their ears.

They were definitely not alone in these woods.

CHAPTER 14

Lowellville Road
Saturday, April 19

ALLEN KASDEN BLINKED rapidly in the predawn light. His conscious mind was in a tug of war with the unconscious. The dream he'd been having was so warm and comforting. Memories of a simpler past and the days of his youth.

He stretched, yawned, and threw back his blankets. The cold hit his bare chest like a freight train. He quickly pulled the warm covers back under his chin. A few more minutes in bed wouldn't hurt. Spring had descended on Ohio, but the nights still brought near-freezing temperatures. He couldn't wait until hot summer days rolled into warm summer evenings. He let his eyelids settle back over bloodshot eyes and decided to try to return to his dream.

Sunlight danced across the waves, caressing his face like soft, warm fingertips. His father's voice boomed over the noise of the water slapping against the hull. The tip of his fishing rod bounced up and down furiously, his reel singing like a siren as the big lake trout stripped line. "Keep your rod tip up! Don't horse it in!" his father shouted.

The fishing boat faded, floating up and away through a mist. Like late morning fog fleeing from the piercing sun, the dream swirled and was replaced by the front room of his childhood home.

"Allen, don't go out without your coat," said his mother. Her gentle voice wafted through the house.

Allen pulled on his winter boots and buttoned his coat to keep out the winter wind and the lake-effect snow that was coming down sideways. Outside, he pulled his sled runner hard to the left, hit a bare patch of frozen earth, tumbled off his sled, and rolled down the hill. He came to a stop with his face planted in a snowbank and his gloves, hat, and boots filled with snow.

The scene swirled and shifted again. He was in a wet suit, a scuba tank strapped to his back, sliding through the cobalt waters of the South Pacific. A Coast Guard helicopter hovered overhead as Allen broke the surface of the clear, warm water. He removed his mask and gloves and waved his hands. A cable from the helicopter lowered a survivor strop toward him. The rhythmic slap of the bird's blades was nearly deafening. He felt the sound waves as they vibrated against his newly exposed skin.

The slapping of the blades grew louder. Something was tugging him away. He kicked his fins and pulled at the water with his cupped hands. He rose into the air, separated from his body in the waves, but he couldn't get back. The distance grew. Soon he could barely make out the figure that was bobbing in the waves.

Alllen's eyes snapped open and he pushed himself upright. The thumping sound lasted a few more seconds and suddenly stopped. Allen reached for his clothes and slippers on the nightstand next to his bed and quickly dressed. He gripped the handle of his chair with one hand and used his other to swing his legs over the edge of the bed. He settled into the chair, released the brake, and wheeled himself toward his bedroom door, pausing to take hold of the metal-tipped spear that leaned against the door jam. The thumping began again as he wheeled across the house and out the front door.

He rolled down a ramp and navigated the paver path to the back of the house. The thumping grew louder. By the time he reached the edge of his garden, it had risen to a feverish pitch. Allen's muscles trembled as adrenaline surged through his veins. He slowly approached the pit trap and peered over the side, making eye contact with and startling the eight-point whitetail buck that had fallen in. The buck jumped and kicked, trying to find traction on the oil-covered, steel-lined floor and walls. The harder the buck fought, the more it lost its footing. Finally it gave up and cowered in the corner of the six-foot pit. Allen worked his wheelchair into position and raised his spear. He made eye contact with the buck again and felt a stab of remorse when he saw the terror reflected in its big brown eyes. His biceps rippled as he aimed the spear behind the buck's shoulder and thrust it forward. The spear sank into the buck's rib cage with a hollow thud. It kicked and struggled, its breath coming in short, ragged gasps. Soon the struggle was over. The buck bled out. Its chest rose and fell slowly until it could no longer draw a breath.

Allen sat in his chair for several minutes, allowing the adrenaline to subside and his breathing to return to a normal rhythm.

"Holy crap! Backstrap tonight!" Allen shouted, a smile on his face.

He hadn't eaten meat in months. The woods had teamed with deer before the collapse, but they had all but disappeared since. After two years, he had begun to run out of his supply of canned venison. It several more months before he could harvest and can the vegetables he would grow. The animal tracks and sign he had recently begun to notice were a most welcome sight. The deer were beginning to return, which meant other, less cautious game might also return.

Allen hoisted the buck out of the hole with a come-along winch and hung it in the barn. As he began to dress and skin the buck, he thought back to when the world had changed. He still wasn't sure who was responsible for the attack on America or exactly what had happened, though he'd heard rumors from the occasional traveler that wandered across his property and set off his proximity alarms. All he knew for certain was that nuclear weapons were detonated and the ensuing EMP had fried everything with an electrical circuit. One traveler had come through in the spring with a tale of the American president turned dictator, and a group of ex-military and citizens who had fought a war in the West to remove the tyrant and set up a basic government based on the U.S. Constitution. The traveler had said there might even be areas in the West near hydroelectric dams where partial power had been restored. The thought of restored electricity was particularly exciting to Allen. It was the simple, everyday things that he missed the most: hot showers, refrigerator and freezer, his electric razor. Not to mention the biggest one of all, having a power wheelchair again.

He finished skinning the buck and closed the barn door. He would let it hang for a few days before he processed it. The temperatures were still cool enough at night, but he wouldn't be able to hang it any longer than a few days due to the risk of spoiling. He wheeled himself back to the house to make some breakfast, and clean the blood, hair, and deer smell off his hands.

Once he'd prepared some hot cereal and two eggs sunny side up, he sat at the kitchen table and looked toward the garden and his property beyond. He had called this place home for the last fifteen years. The house wasn't large house by anybody's standards, but the lack of square footage was trumped by the twenty acres of hilltop hardwood forest he owned. Beyond his property line, he was surrounded by state forest on two sides and lush farmland on the remaining two. Before the collapse, his property had been a favorite bedding ground for whitetail deer. He'd never had any trouble filling a buck tag. He owned an Action Track all-terrain vehicle and could cover every inch of his property.

But when the electricity went, so did the electronics that powered his vehicle. Now Allen was limited to the areas where he'd installed paver paths. He'd bought the home and land within six months of his forced retirement from the Coast Guard. The location of the property also provided a certain amount of security. It was on a hilltop, with only one road up the steep grade, giving him the chance to see or hear anyone approaching from the valley floor. The woods around him were thick, brushy, and nearly impenetrable. He'd seldom had unwanted or uninvited guests before the collapse. Since then, only a handful had passed through, and only twice had he been forced to meet them with violence. None of these visitors surprised him. His series of proximity alarms around the perimeter did their job.

The lack of human company didn't bother Allen much. He'd always been a private person and had few close friends. His mates in the Coast Guard were the only ones he'd ever let into his personal world. He had always been the quiet one, the one who would eat his lunch at school, the one who felt more at ease in the wide open oceans or wilderness than in town. Since the collapse, he hadn't seen or heard from anyone he'd been close to. But he was happy now, or at least as happy as he could be stuck in his chair and his twenty-acre universe. When he thought about his time in the Coast Guard, though, he felt a sliver of loneliness. His former mates were the best friends he'd ever had. They faced their day-to-day hardships and drama of Coast Guard life together. After his accident, they'd stood by him. But when he'd moved away, the connection and closeness had drifted away. They still had their lives in the Coast Guard, but Allen was no longer part of that world. He didn't blame them for losing interest. If their roles had been reversed, he might have done the same thing.

Before he'd put down roots, Allen had been stationed at bases across the country, from Sector San Diego and Golden Gate on the West Coast to Station Clearwater and Station Cape Cod on the East Coast. He finished his time in the South Pacific at Integrated Support Command in Honolulu. Which was where the training accident had changed his life, paralyzing him from the waist down.

Allen took a bite of egg and shook his head. He broke the yoke of the second egg and stirred the thick, orange goo with his fork. The memory of that day was still fresh in his mind. It always would be.

In an instant, his mind took him back. He was breathing in the strong scent of salt air. Trade winds blew softly across his face as he floated motionless in the South Pacific. He knew he was hurt badly, but he didn't feel any pain.

Eighteen weeks of training recruits under his belt and only two weeks away from sending another group of young people into the life of a rescue swimmer. He really did love his job and his life. The fact that so many looked up to him and seemed to hang on his every word gave him the ultimate sense of purpose and fulfillment. He was tough on his recruits, but never hesitated to jump in and join in their rigorous training schedule. When they bent over to vomit in the middle of their sprints or pull-up training, Allen laughed inwardly and shouted encouragement, all while not skipping a single rep or step. He knew that no matter how tough the training was, it wouldn't be nearly as hard as the real application. Nothing could fully prepare them for an actual rescue or for the mental hardships that came with losing a victim to the sea.

After the afternoon classroom time, he'd joined his latest group in the bay for evening training. The first cadet was on the helicopter skids, preparing for a jump. Allen was treading water beneath the chopper while the boy was given final instructions. There was some confusion—for some reason the boy jumped from the chopper prematurely. Allen wasn't watching. He never had the chance to move out of the way before the young man's heels landed squarely on the top of his head, compressing his spine and fracturing his neck in three places.

He'd lain in a hospital bed for six weeks, mostly feeling sorry for himself and regretting not being able to complete his cadets' training and attend graduation. The boy who'd caused the injury had walked away from the Coast Guard and never visited Allen in the hospital. Allen didn't blame him for what had happened. He blamed himself, and it tore him up that the boy would not fulfill his dream. He didn't know whether he could have changed his mind about quitting, but he wished he'd had the chance to try.

After he left the hospital, Allen settled on his Ohio property. He had started his life in this part of Ohio, so it was only fitting that he live out the second half of it here. When he was still on duty, he'd dreamed of exploring the rest of the inland U.S., but he knew that would be impossible now. Even if he could get to the pine forests of the West, he wouldn't be able to do the things he most wanted.

Allen finished his breakfast, cleaned his dishes, and began the process of cleaning up his trap, spear, and other equipment. He was exhausted. Every muscle in his upper body screamed out in pain. Harvesting, hanging, and skinning a buck was a difficult task for anyone, but being stuck in a stupid wheelchair made it ten times more difficult. Now the task of clearing away the evidence of the kill had to be finished. A deer's nose was always its best defense against predators. Any blood or human sweat left in the area was the scent of death. If it wasn't washed away, no deer would come close to his pit trap again.

Allen wheeled himself down to the creek with an empty bucket and dipped it into the cool water. In the spring and winter, Mill Creek ran cold and clear. But through the summer and late into the fall, the sun warmed the creek and moss covered the rocks, making the water cloudy and unfit to drink without boiling.

He placed the bucket on his lap and began wheeling himself back up the path toward the garden and dirty pit trap. Though he hadn't completely filled the bucket, some water still splashed out and soaked his jeans.

He was halfway back when an alarm sounded—one of his proximity alarms had been triggered. Allen dropped his bucket and reached into the holster mounted on the side of his chair above the right wheel. He pulled out his Sig Sauer P250 and placed it in his lap. He quickly wheeled himself into his barn and watched from the shadows as five strangers walked out of the trees near his garden—a tall black man, a middle-aged woman, and three teenagers. The man leading the group carried a nice rifle. The others carried rusty-looking firearms. Allen waited until they had passed by, then slowly raised his Sig and pointed it at the back of the young girl bringing up the rear. The group stepped onto his porch and the man knocked on his door.

Allen wheeled himself from the shadows. "Don't turn around," he said, "and don't make any sudden moves. Put your guns down on the porch, back away, then slowly turn around."

The group stiffened, but made no move to comply. If they chose to turn and fight, Allen knew he wouldn't be able to take them all out.

"We have you surrounded, and we will not hesitate to shoot," Allen said, gambling on a bluff.

After several more seconds, the group placed their guns on the porch and slowly turned around. The shock on their faces was obvious. He knew they hadn't expected a man in a wheelchair.

"What do you want here?" Allen said.

The black man took a step forward and held out his hand. "My name is Tom Dix—"

"Far enough," Allen barked.

The man stopped and lowered his hand.

"We don't mean any harm" the man said. "We were camped just up the road and smelled your fire this morning, so we came to introduce ourselves. We were hoping we could barter with you for a few supplies if you have extra."

Allen wasn't sure what they had to barter with, and he already had everything he needed. He was hesitant to trust these people. The first few months after the collapse, others had come, but they were anything but friendly. He had killed a few, and managed to disarm and run off a few others. The few people he had seen since those early months had been less aggressive, and he'd managed to learn quite a bit from them. Still...it would be nice to have some company.

Allen decided to hear them out, but he'd keep his distance, and not let them into his home or barn. The less they knew about his supplies and armaments, the better. He made them unload their weapons, put the ammunition in their pockets, and place them on the porch rail.

They talked on his porch for over an hour. They seemed like genuinely nice people with no ill will projected, but he also felt they were holding something back. Certain things did not add up. When they told him the events of the evening before and the men that had attacked them, he knew they were leaving out several details. Allen thought it was impossible for them to have travelled from Lowellville Road all the way to the ridge above his house, camp out for the night, and walk up to his front door in a span of twelve hours. It was over eighteen miles to Lowellville Road.

He decided they must have either horses or a vehicle. He'd seen only one working vehicle since the collapse. It was an old pickup, devoid of modern electronics. If one person had figured out how to replace points and condenser in a truck and get it to run, others might have also. The more likely mode of conveyance, though, was horses.

"We're hoping to reach Oregon before winter," the man said. "We know it won't—"

"How many horses do you have?" Allen interrupted.

The two girls in the group looked at each other, then quickly turned their heads toward the woods. The boy with the beard looked down at his lap and brushed imaginary dirt from his pants. The man, on the other hand, looked Allen directly in the eye, and stared for at least thirty seconds before answering.

"We don't have horses," he said.

Allen sensed he was being sized up. He knew now that this group had a vehicle. He cleared his throat and spoke in the most reassuring tone he could muster.

"I don't have any desire to hurt any of you, or to try and take whatever vehicle you have. If I had ill intentions, don't you think I would have tried something by now, with your weapons over there?" He pointed at the porch railing. "I've been here since the collapse and have had no way to leave."

He gestured toward the rolling prison beneath him. "I was thinking the whole time we've been talking about how nice it is to have some company. I was also hoping that this meeting was divine intervention. I would like very much to leave my home and see the West. I have prayed to God daily that he would provide a way."

The youngest girl looked up at him then with a slight smile on her face. Allen couldn't tell if it was pity or if she now felt some sort of kinship with him because he'd revealed his relationship with God. Either way, Allen felt he was winning them over. What worried him was what these people might think of hauling around a cripple stuck in a chair. It would be like jumping into an ocean filled with sharks while having a boat anchor chained to an ankle.

No one spoke. Allen felt the awkward tension. He took his pistol from his lap, reholstered it, and wheeled himself toward the house. He knew if he had any chance at all of joining these people, he would need to open himself up completely. He hoped he wasn't making a fatal mistake.

"I'm hungry," he said, "and it's almost lunchtime. You're all welcome to join me. I have fresh venison backstrap and some Yukon gold potatoes."

Allen wheeled past the group and through the front door. He stopped just inside the door jam and looked back over his shoulder.

"You can wash up over at the creek," he said. "You'll find a bar of soap and a towel hanging from a tree branch. Come on in when you're ready. Lunch will take about thirty minutes to cook."

Allen looked each member of the group in the eye and smiled. His gaze lingered a little longer on the youngest girl, and his smile grew a little broader. Somehow he knew she was his best asset. He turned his back on the group, leaving them with their own thoughts, and closed the heavy wooden door—now unlocked—behind him.

CHAPTER 15

Independence, Missouri
10:30 A.M., Sunday, May 31

SARAH KNELT IN the soft mud of the creek bottom. She put 10x50 millimeter Zeiss binoculars up to her eyes and slowly raised her head above the bank. The camp was large. She estimated at least one hundred men, women, and children occupied the nearly sixty tents in the middle of the small clearing. A large fire pit in the center was tended by three women who slowly turned a spit with portions of meat hanging from it. Each time the spit made a full rotation, fat dripped onto the coals and burst into bright orange flame. Children ran through the camp playing a game of tag. Most of the rest of the men and women lay in the shade, trying to escape the hot morning sun. The entire scene was peaceful, almost welcoming—except for the well-armed sentries posted on the outskirts at each corner of the encampment. It looked to Sarah as if the group had been here quite a while. A row of latrines lay fifty yards from the fire pit, while a large pile of garbage and bones sat about two hundred yards from the opposite side. The only part of the camp she couldn't see was the space directly behind the tents.

She lowered herself to the creek bottom and crawled another three hundred yards. She rose up again and looked through the binoculars at a fifty-foot-wide corral filled with horses. A row of four wooden cages sat in a straight line just to the right of the corral. Each cage held at least ten adults, men and women of varying ages. Every prisoner seemed large, either muscular or overweight. An eight-foot-tall tripod made from stripped lodgepole pine trees stood to the left of the cages, a length of sturdy, bloodstained rope hanging from its center.

Sarah swept her binoculars to the right of the cages. She nearly dropped the optics when her mind registered what she was seeing. Two men with long butcher knives stood over a roughhewn wood table, slicing chunks off what had once been a very fat man. She looked back at the prisoners. A heavyset Hispanic man stared back at her. His eyes seemed to bore into her binoculars. Sarah quickly dropped below the bank. Vomit gushed from her mouth and covered the rocks at her knees, some of it splashing onto her face. Terror unlike any she had ever felt ensnared her waist and squeezed. She wanted to jump up and run back to Jakob, but fought the urge. Had she been seen? It felt as if the man in the cage looked right at her, but at that distance how could he have seen her?

Sarah lay on her back and tried to steady her breathing. The bubbling creek helped to drown out the nightmare she'd just witnessed. She crawled to the water's edge and put her lips in the cool brook, drinking deeply for several minutes. With her thirst quenched and the taste of vomit dulled, she took one more look at the camp before heading back. This time no one looked her way from between the bars. Satisfied she had imagined being seen, she made her way back down the creek. When she had crawled well out of sight of the camp, she left the creek and ran through the trees, back toward her companions. Seventy-five yards from the tangle of brush where they'd parked the ATVs, Sarah pulled the wing bone call from her pocket and yelped a series of hen calls. Once Jakob answered, she jogged the rest of the way in.

Jakob stood as she entered the brush. She slammed into him and buried her face in his chest. She took a deep breath, filling her nostrils with his scent.

"What's the matter?" he asked, gently pushing her back to arm's length. "You're white as a sheet."

Tom Dixon jumped out of the front seat of the Ranger where he'd been lounging, ran to the edge of the brush, and looked out.

"Were you followed?" he asked.

Sarah shook her head, walked over to the Ranger, and took Tom's seat. She sat for several minutes with her head between her knees. Jakob walked over and placed a gentle but firm hand on her shoulder.

"What happened?" he said.

Sarah took a few more long breaths, then looked up. "We need to leave," she said. "And we need to avoid the camp."

The image of the man on the table, half of his body sliced away, exploded back into her mind. She shuddered. "They're butchering people."

Tom walked over and knelt in front of her. He placed a hand on her knee and spoke in a soft voice: "Tell me what you saw, and try not to leave out any detail, no matter how small. It may be important."

Sarah recounted everything she had seen. When she got to the body on the table, she struggled for words. Finally, she finished the horrid tale and looked into the faces of her companions. The revulsion in their eyes reflected her own.

Tom decided they should stay until a few hours after dark and then slip away. They would set up a watch on the strange camp. If anyone there moved in their direction, they would have plenty of warning.

In the shade, Sarah lay on her side, facing Jakob's back. Her arm rested on his chest, which rose and fell in a steady rhythm. The hours passed, but Sarah couldn't sleep. Sometimes she envied Jakob and his ability to stay calm in dangerous situations. He seemed able to completely detach himself from the horrors of their new life and fall asleep at any time. Sarah needed to sleep and recharge her body, but her mind would not allow it. So many thoughts and emotions swirled in her head; there was no way to turn them off. So much had happened since they'd been forced to leave their village. They had plunged completely into the darkness of the outside world.

Even so, Sarah could point to a few bright spots of hope. Her childhood fantasy had turned into reality when she'd married the man of her dreams. Her relationship with Julia had grown into a bond even stronger than sisterhood. And she had begun to think of Tom Dixon as a second father. He was strong like her father, compassionate, and driven by love. Unlike her father, he would never betray his family. That was really what their group had become: family. Even Allen Kasden, whom she'd known for only a little while, was dear to her. He was strong and courageous. The fact that he didn't let his disability stand in the way of living his life made him quite noble in her eyes. He always tried to contribute in his areas of strength. His mechanical abilities had saved them all on a few occasions. When the banged-up Sportsman had died just outside of Ramey, Illinois, and Tom had given up on it, Allen had repaired it. Allen had also made a bow drill and taught the group how to build a fire after their last lighter had run out of fluid. His knowledge of wild plants had kept them fed when no other resources could be found. Sometimes, when both Sarah and Allen had trouble sleeping, they sat and talked. He'd been a great listener when she revealed how hurt she felt over being banished from the village. They couldn't travel as quickly with Allen in the group, but Sarah thought the extra "burden" was more than worth it.

Sarah leaned over and kissed Jakob on the cheek. He stirred, rolled onto his back, smacked his lips twice, and began to snore loudly. She chuckled, crawled out from under the bed roll, and stretched. They would be leaving in a couple of hours, so there was no point in lying here any longer.

She drank some water, ate a few bites of deer jerky, and decided to relieve Tom from guard duty a half hour early. He'd been pushing himself hard since their run-in with the men on the road in Ohio. He wanted to get to the West as quickly as possible. Tom believed that if the people there had restored power, they must have regained a certain amount of humanity and order. Once they got there, Tom said, their lives would change for the better.

Sarah grabbed her shotgun and walked out of the brush. Tom was leaning against a tree trunk, fast asleep. Sarah smiled, sat down, and gently shook him. Tom's eyes snapped open and he lifted the rifle lying across his lap. When he saw who it was, he relaxed and rubbed the sleep from his eyes.

"See anything?" Sarah asked with a certain amount of sarcasm in her voice.

Tom looked offended, and slightly embarrassed. He turned away from her and shook his head.

"Everybody else is still sleeping," she said. "I came to relieve you. It's getting close to when you said you wanted to head out, so I thought you could use a little sleep first." She laughed. "Unless, of course, you've already gotten enough rest."

Tom turned back and smiled, apparently giving in to the levity she was sporting at his expense. "I *would* like to lay down in a bed roll for a bit," he said. "After leaning against this tree, my back is killing me."

Sarah laughed again and patted Tom on the shoulder as he got up and walked back toward their temporary camp. She laid her shotgun across her lap and scanned the area in the direction of the stranger's camp. Nothing moved, and the normal sounds of a typical springtime evening were missing. Not even one cricket chirped. She thought it strange that nothing seemed to be alive around her. In spite of the warm temperature, Sarah shivered. She couldn't wait to leave this place.

A twig snapped behind her. She raised her shotgun and swung it around. Jakob and Julia ducked when they saw the muzzle pass across their chests.

"Watch that thing," Jakob hissed.

Sarah relaxed and lowered the weapon. When the two of them sat down beside her, Jakob reached over and took her hand. Sarah leaned in close and put her head on his shoulder. The fear and shivers she'd felt moments before suddenly fled. Whether he was holding her hand or making love to her in the moonlight, the tenderness of Jakob's touch and the love she felt flowing from his warm skin into hers always managed to make her world seem complete.

When it was time for them to leave, the trio walked back to their little hole in the brush and roused the others. Fifteen minutes later, her trusty 12-gauge bungeed on the front of her quad, they were rolling along cross country, backtracking the way they'd come earlier in the day. By the time they reached the roadway, the night was half gone, and the moon had begun to set in the west. Tom pulled the group over and off the roadway.

"I don't know how all of you feel, but I'm exhausted," Tom said. "I think we're probably far enough from the camp to rest up until the sun sets tomorrow."

Sarah was relieved. She would never admit it, but she could barely keep her eyes open. Several hours of deep sleep would help recharge her and chase away the demons that tormented her after what she'd seen.

There wasn't a lot of small talk as the group unloaded their sleeping gear and settled in. Within minutes, Sarah had her back pressed up against Jakob, his arms wrapped comfortably around her middle.

"Sarah!"

She craned her neck and tried to focus on Jakob's face through the slats of the cage. He jerked on the wooden bars, rattling the padlock that held the door closed.

"It will be okay," a strange unfamiliar voice said reassuringly. "Don't fight it. You have been given a special honor. You have been chosen so that we can live."

Sarah looked at the face of the man that was dragging her to the large, flat table. He smiled down at her through brown, rotting teeth.

"Noooo!" Sarah screamed.

"Should we wake her?" Julia asked. "I wouldn't want her to miss out on Allen's feast."

"I'll save her some," Allen said.

The voices interrupted Sarah's scream. She struggled to clear her mind and slowly opened her eyes. As her senses returned to her, she was overwhelmed by the aroma of fresh berries and frying meat. She sat upright and massaged her eyelids with her knuckles. The last wisps of her nightmare drifted away and were replaced by the face of her husband, who grinned at her through a mouthful of half-chewed meat and berries.

"Good morning," she said, smiling back at his boyish face. "That smells amazing."

"Sage-seasoned grouse with huckleberry sauce," Julia said. "Compliments of Chef Allen."

Sarah looked at Allen with a mixture of pity and admiration. To go through life confined to a chair was one of the most horrible things she could imagine. To go through it that way now that the world had turned wild and dark was even worse. In spite of his disability, Allen still took life on headfirst and at full speed. He was truly amazing, and she was growing to love him more with each day.

Sarah's stomach vibrated with a pang of emptiness. The group had not had a freshly prepared hot meal since they'd met Allen at his cabin. They'd been living on canned venison and the few greens he'd shown them along the way.

"My grandpa told me once to never look a free horse, or rather a gift horse, in the mouth," Sarah said. "And I'm not complaining, believe me. But where did we get grouse and huckleberries?"

Allen chuckled as he answered: "I woke just as the sun was coming up. I noticed a creek with a gravel road going up it as we came in last night, and I figured there might be a few grouse picking up gravel first thing in the morning. So I took the ATV and my slingshot. Forty-five minutes later, I had four fat birds. The berries were a bonus."

Julia grabbed the cast-iron pan from the fire and held it out to Sarah. She thanked her friend and wrapped her fingers around a sticky chunk of breast meat. As she chewed the bird and relished the flavor, she wondered about the people at the cannibal camp. Why had they turned to eating people instead of being resourceful and utilizing what nature had to offer? If a guy without the use of his legs could hunt and provide for himself and others, they had no excuse. It was true that she'd never experienced the kind of desperation that would drive someone to eat another human. Her father had always provided everything her family ever needed, and if he'd been injured or killed, someone else in the village would have stepped in and cared for them. Even so, resorting to cannibalism was difficult to comprehend.

Sarah took another large bite of the berry-covered grouse and surveyed her new family. Everyone was there, smiling, except Tom and Mary.

"Where did Tom and Mary run off to?" Sarah asked.

Julia answered quickly through a broad smile. "They wandered off about an hour ago, carrying Tom's bed roll."

Sarah grinned and shook her head.

After breakfast, Sarah and the rest talked into the late afternoon. Allen did most of the talking until Tom and Mary wandered back into the camp, but Sarah didn't mind. The more she learned about Allen, the more she rejoiced in the fact that God had brought them together. She had never known what it meant to be a patriot or to actually love America. She had been taught that man should be part of the Kingdom of God and should separate himself from the world. Allen and Tom both loved God with all their hearts, but they also loved America and what it stood for. For the first time in her life, she began to understand that the foundation America was built on was the love of God and freedom. This, she realized, was why her people were able to live the life they had. Now that the nation's foundation had eroded, her people were in danger of losing their way of life.

"Do you have any brothers or sisters, Allen?" Sarah asked.

Allen didn't answer right away. He looked down at a spot of dirt on his thigh and absently rubbed his fingers over the denim of his jeans. "I had a sister," he said finally. "But we lost her when I was a teenager."

"I...I'm sorry," Sarah said. "I didn't mean to pry."

"It's okay," Allen said. "It was a long time ago. I just haven't talked about her for years."

Allen looked away, seemingly lost in a memory. He started speaking again without looking back at the group. "She was two years older than me. We were the best of friends. I really looked up to her. The night of her graduation, we got together with several of her friends to celebrate with a bonfire and keg. On the way home, I lost control of my pickup, and we went off the road. Sheila was riding in the back. She was thrown out. When I woke up in the hospital four days later, my mom told me what had happened."

No one around the fire spoke. Sarah felt Allen's pain as if it were her own. She also felt guilty for making him talk about it. She wanted to apologize again but couldn't bring herself to do it. Why couldn't she have just kept her mouth shut?

Just when Sarah thought she wouldn't be able to bear the silence another moment, Allen looked Sarah in the eyes. "If not for my faith in God and his forgiveness," he said, "that one bad choice would have ended my life. I learned that no matter what we have done or who we have hurt, there is always forgiveness with God. All you need to do is ask, Sarah."

Sarah looked away, her face suddenly hot. In an instant, the sympathy and compassion she'd been feeling for Allen were replaced by her shame and guilt over the sins in her own life. She hadn't told Allen or Tom about what she'd done in Pennsylvania, but somehow, it seemed, Allen knew.

Mary rescued Sarah from her discomfort.

"I would like to say something," Mary said, glancing at Tom before continuing. "We weren't going to tell you until we were closer to the West, but I can't wait any longer."

Everyone sat and waited for Mary to make her announcement, but she paused for what seemed minutes before speaking again.

"As soon as we get to Oregon..." Mary paused again.

"Spit it out!" Sarah snapped.

Mary ignored Sarah's impatience and finally made her announcement. "As soon as we get to Oregon, Tom and I are getting married."

Sarah forgot her irritation and jumped up to hug Mary. There were tears and laughter from the whole group. A little joy was just what they all needed.

By early evening, everyone seemed more hopeful about the journey that lay ahead. As the sun set low on the horizon, they all separated to rest up for the night's journey—everyone but Tom and Mary. They once again took Tom's bed roll and walked into the trees, laughing and holding hands.

When it was dark and the moon had risen, the group started out again. Tom led the way in the Ranger with passengers Mary, Jakob, and Allen. Sarah drove the Sportsman with Julia hanging on behind her. Soon they were rolling down the highway at 30 miles per hour. After about an hour, Tom's UTV began to pull ahead. Sarah didn't feel comfortable enough behind the handlebars to go faster in the dark, so she kept her pace steady. If they got too far behind, she knew Tom would slow down and wait for her to catch up.

Julia leaned close and shouted in Sarah's ear: "I'm starting to get cold."

Sarah was also feeling the chill. The sun had set four hours earlier and the temperature had dropped at least thirty degrees. She stopped the ATV in the middle of the road and turned off the motor. Putting on their jackets sounded like a good idea. Stretching for a minute and taking a drink of water sounded even better.

The night was eerily quiet without the sound of their ATV. Sarah realized that she couldn't hear Tom's vehicle either. They had either stopped as well or were too far ahead for the sound of the motor to reach her.

Sarah and Julia put on their jackets, and rested and stretched for ten minutes, before starting out again. It had been over thirty minutes since Tom had pulled out of sight. Sarah was a little frustrated with him for not keeping the group together. This wasn't the first time that he'd pulled ahead, and she thought it probably wouldn't be the last.

The Sportsman was back up to thirty miles per hour when it rounded a sharp corner. Sarah nearly lost control when she saw the scene laid out before her. The Ranger was on its side in the middle of the road. Allen lay face down on the pavement. No one else was visible.

Sarah slid to a stop, jumped out, and checked Allen's pulse. Relief washed over her when she felt a steady heartbeat. She covered him with her jacket and ran to check the UTV.

Mary was the only person in the vehicle. Sarah knew she was dead even before she checked her pulse. A thin trickle of blood ran from the corner of her mouth, while her eyes stared into nothingness.

"Jakob!" Sarah shouted. She ran down the road while scanning the ditch, then ran up the other side. Where was Jakob? She couldn't lose him now. She'd just started her life as his wife. This couldn't be happening.

"Jakob!" she shouted again.

Sarah reached into the Ranger and retrieved a flashlight from the glovebox. She had to find Jakob. And where was Tom? She took a closer look at the Ranger. Blood covered the roll bar and the pavement near the front of the vehicle. Sarah used her flashlight to scan down the road as far as she could. Several drops of blood and pink foam led down the road and disappeared into the tree line. She followed the blood trail just as she'd done as a child while chasing a wounded deer. The blood trail ended in a small clearing fifty yards from the road. The ground had been freshly torn up.

Sarah walked slowly around the clearing, trying to read the sign. On the far side, several horse tracks led off through the trees down a small trail. She followed them for nearly a quarter mile. Then she saw a body lying on its side in the dirt ahead. It was Jakob.

She rushed to him and felt for his pulse. He was unconscious but alive. He had a four-inch purple goose egg on his forehead. Bits of gravel stuck to dried blood on his skinned-up face.

"Julia!" Sarah shouted. "I need help."

Sarah did her best to pull him from the trail, and was trying to stop the bleeding from his head wound when Julia came running down the trail holding a second flashlight.

"Over here!" Sarah shouted.

Julia ran over to them and knelt down.

The sound of the Sportsman motor coming to life caused them both to freeze.

That has to be Tom, Sarah thought. Except why didn't he say anything when she was shouting for Jakob?

Sarah ran back toward the road. She emerged from the tree line just in time to see the taillight of their ATV disappear around a corner, back the way they had come.

CHAPTER 16

Austin, Mexico
1:00 PM, Wednesday, June, 3

GENERAL EDZARD SCHEPER sat at a table in the Yacht Club Bistro looking out over Lake Travis on the outskirts of what was now called Austin, Mexico. A light lunch of tortillas, beans, and shredded beef sat on his plate, half eaten. He was tired of Mexican food and would have killed for a bratwurst and sauerkraut, washed down with a warm mug of stout, foamy bräu. Scheper had been back on what had once been U.S. soil for three months, assessing the progress made by the Mexican government. He was also back to broker a deal with the Mexican president to join forces against the Americans. As of yet, no one from the Mexican government had been on hand to negotiate a forces agreement. Today he would finally meet with the vice president and begin negotiations.

After the final battle in Colorado, where he had killed resistance army leader Levi Nirschell, he had returned to Germany to recover from severe injuries sustained at the former presidential palace. In his absence, the Mexican government had reached an agreement with the drug cartel armies, joining forces to reclaim portions of Texas, Oklahoma, and New Mexico. The few residents that still occupied the land had resisted, but the collapse had killed 80 percent of the people who had once called it home. The rednecks fought hard, but any help that could have come from the new U.S. Army did not. The army was, unfortunately for the backwoods Texas hillbillies, concentrated in the West, so the invaders were able to take over with only minor casualties. The people that remained were assimilated, unless they were considered to be a future threat. Those people were executed, which made controlling the remaining population much easier.

The fighting in the West had ceased after U.S. President Hartley was killed. All of the foreign troops that were on U.S. soil at the time, with the exception of Germany's, had pulled out. Russia was now fully entrenched in the Middle East and had laid claim to most of the sand and oil territories, except for Israel. The only Russian presence left in the U.S. was in Alaska, where they had reclaimed and now occupied their former territory. With the majority of the world's fossil fuels in the control of Russia, it was just a matter of time before they would be in a position to rule the entire globe. They would be able to set any price they wanted on oil and governments would be forced to pay it. The only place in the world not controlled by Russia where oil was accessible was in the United States.

The Israelis had struck a deal with the Russians, and now answered to them in exchange for being left alone. The Russians attacked in full force and completely took over the West Bank, killing nearly the entire population. The Israelis now fought alongside the Russians to eradicate the remaining Muslim populations.

The only place remaining where the Germans could expand their empire was in the United States. Great Britain controlled most of the smaller European countries and Germany wouldn't have stood a chance in claiming territories there, so it had gone all-in to claim the U.S. This, Scheper mused, was proving to be a monumental task. From the Midwest all the way to the Pacific Ocean, the resistance was deeply entrenched. Even though Germany had come in with superior firepower and weaponry, it had been unable to have much effect in the mountainous West.

To make the task even more difficult, a small number of Canadian troops were assisting the locals with rebuilding efforts. Citizens had begun repairing power-generating facilities at dams on the Columbia and Snake rivers, partially restoring the grid. Scheper had sent small strike teams that had taken out some of the larger high-capacity transmission lines, but his people were unable to get close enough to the dams to inflict damage. Each time they destroyed part of the powerline, the resistance had it back up within a week. Small manufacturing facilities had been constructed in the town of Hood River, but these were well protected. The resistance had a fairly large fleet of military vehicles, and their people had begun repairing civilian automobiles for use as well. The only chance Germany had of defeating the troops in the West was to put a stop to their rebuilding of the infrastructure. Even then, it would take time to starve them out with the wild resources that were at their disposal.

The other factor in Scheper's favor was the Americans' inability to access fuel. Russia controlled the oil fields and pipeline in Alaska. Shipping oil across the ocean from the Middle East was also impossible, as Russia owned all of those resources as well. The only fuel resources the Americans had were those in the Midwest and mountain states. So far, oil from the Sydney, Montana, area, Wyoming, and the Dakotas had been enough. Their main refinery was near Cheyenne, Wyoming, but it could crank out only so much gasoline and diesel. Scheper knew the quickest way to victory was to take out his enemy's fuel production facilities, but like the dams, these were heavily fortified and protected.

The only path forward was a multi-front attack, and the only way this could succeed was with the help of the Mexicans and a group of eco-purists that was gaining a large following in the West. Germany could not afford to send more troops and resources to the U.S. or they would be left vulnerable to attack by Great Britain. To achieve their objective, they needed to partner with Mexican President Ramos and split the final spoils of war. This needed to happen soon, or Russia would be back in full force when all of its other fronts were secure and stable. If Germany did not secure the American territory and its vast oil reserves and weaponry before Russia reorganized, it would badly lose the battle and be forced to abandon everything it had gained. The hated Russians would take the final piece of the global puzzle.

Scheper absentmindedly stirred a puddle of red sauce on his plate with his fork and grumbled. He was homesick. He didn't have any family left alive and had never been married. He had a few friends at his favorite pub back home, but he missed the pub and country more than its people. He desperately wanted nothing more than to walk into Altdeutsche Bierstube, find his favorite stool, and let the aroma of bräu fill his nostrils. That, and perhaps take a walk along the Frankische Rezat with a fishing pole and catch a few fat brown trout. He hated everything about this new frontier he was stuck in. The air was too dry, the mountains and rivers too foreign, and the food was abysmal. He would stick it out, though, and see his government's aspirations fulfilled, if only for the future wealth and status it would provide him. He was not much of a patriot, but war was the only thing he was good at, so he'd volunteered for the U.S. assignment right after it had been attacked. His leaders weren't happy about his failure to stop the resistance forces in Colorado, but they were giving him another chance. The only thing that had saved him from a lifetime of shame was the fact that he had managed to kill the leader of the Americans before he left. The death of the Collective's President Hartley was seen as a bonus. It saved them from having to dispose of him later, and also eliminated the task of assimilating the former U.S. military forces that had fought for the Collective. The United Collective troops that survived the war now fought willingly for Scheper. If everything he would propose to the Mexicans was agreed to and they finished their planning within a week, it could all be over as quickly as six months.

Maybe when it's all over, he thought, I will go back to Ansbach. Maybe find a lady who likes rich war heroes and settle down. Maybe I'll take one of the young American girls back with me.

Scheper did like American women. There was such a variety to choose from. It was like a world department store of beauties, all there for his pleasure. Black ones, Asians, Latinas, redheads, blondes. And those accents. He did love to hear them talk. He also loved the fact that he could have the kind of fun with them here that would not be allowed in his home-land. So-called decency laws did not apply in this brutal new frontier.

"Maybe I'll take several," he said aloud, and laughed.

The sound of a chopper approaching the restaurant pulled Scheper away from his mental smorgasbord of flesh. He walked to the window in time to see Mexican Vice President Mendez touch down in the parking lot, barely missing a young girl on a bicycle riding by. Scheper stared at the helo until the blades stopped spinning. Mendez exited the chopper, flanked by his security team. Scheper thought the show of security was pointless. They were safe in Austin. There hadn't been any violence here for months. Anyone still living in the area was loyal to Germany and/or Mexico. Perhaps the show of security was for his benefit.

Scheper turned from the window and walked toward the front of the restaurant to greet Mendez. He paused in front of the ornately carved doors, straightened his uniform, and reached for the handles.

An explosion rocked the building, throwing open the three-hundred-pound doors and knocking Scheper to the ground. He lay on his back for several seconds, unable to focus. His ears were ringing and his vision was cloudy.

The sound of rifle fire snapped Scheper back to attention. He jumped to his feet and staggered outside. The chopper was in pieces. Chunks of twisted metal and burning debris were scattered in a hundred-yard circle. Vice President Mendez lay on the tarmac in three pieces. Scheper screamed in frustration and looked toward the lake. The girl on the bicycle was just disappearing over the hill. Three of Scheper's men were in pursuit, firing at her as they ran. He waved at two more of his men near the legs of the former vice president, ran to his Hum-V, jumped in, and started to turn the key. A voice inside his head screamed, "Wait!"

Scheper got out, dropped to his knees, and looked under his vehicle. A small parcel wrapped in duct tape hung from the frame near the fuel tank. He jumped to his feet and ran from the vehicle, waving his arms in an attempt to turn his men around. He was two hundred feet away when the earth shook again, knocking him to the pavement. His face slammed against the asphalt. He screamed once again in frustration and pain. More gunfire came from the lakeshore. He got to his feet a third time and tried to run for another truck, but his legs wouldn't cooperate. The most he could do was a slow stagger. His eyes stung and his vision blurred as blood poured from a gash on his forehead. Scheper pulled a handkerchief from his breast pocket and put pressure on his wound as some of his men pulled up in another truck.

"Did you check it for explosives?" he asked.

"Yes, sir."

He jumped into a backseat and rode with them to the lake shore. Scheper was angry with himself for letting security slide. He'd become comfortable away from the fighting, and his comfort and complacency had nearly cost him his life. Regardless of his own failure as a commander, his men should never have allowed this to happen. If they'd done their jobs, it wouldn't have.

"Who was on duty outside the restaurant?" Scheper asked.

A passenger cleared his throat and stuttered his response: "Corporal Beltz, and, um, I was, sir. We didn't think she, what I mean is, she's been hanging around for a few days now. She was kinda sweet on Beltz. She spent the night in his quarters last night. I'm sorry, sir. If I thought there was any chance—"

Scheper was fully engulfed in anger. "This will not happen again!" he shouted. He pulled his 9 millimeter from its holster, put the barrel an inch from the back of the soldier's head, and pulled the trigger. The man slumped forward in his seat, head resting on the dashboard. Scheper climbed over the seat and pushed the man out onto the pavement. The driver never slowed down or gave any indication that he'd noticed what had just happened. This pleased Scheper. At least some of his men still feared him and respected his authority.

Scheper took his handkerchief from his own wound and tried to wipe the blood and brain matter from the front window, but all he managed to do was smear it. They rode in silence the last quarter-mile as Scheper stared ahead through the pink-fogged window. By the time they reached the lakeshore, Beltz and the other soldier were kneeling near the abandoned bicycle and going through the contents of the basket attached to its front. The truck rolled to a stop and Scheper stepped out.

"Beltz!" he shouted.

They walked toward each other. When Beltz was only four feet away, Scheper pulled his pistol from its holster a second time and shot him through the center of the forehead. Scheper never broke stride. He stepped over the body that had fallen face first in the sand and continued toward the bicycle.

"Where's the girl?" he asked the soldier who remained.

"She went into the water, sir," the soldier said quickly. "By the time we got here, she had gone under."

"What do you mean, gone under?"

"She just walked out and dove under the water. She never came up."

Scheper walked to the water's edge and strained his eyes, looking across the dancing waves. He didn't like this at all. The one thing they had feared, but had avoided until now, was civilians carrying out terrorist-type attacks on their forces. Scheper had seen this over and over again in the various theaters where he'd been engaged in combat. Those doing the killing looked like every other civilian, and before you knew it even a seemingly innocent young girl became a threat. By then it was too late. Many of his comrades had died from such attacks, and many more had lost limbs. From now on, Scheper knew, they would need to treat the civilian population differently. They would need to be searched, and any threats would need to be dealt with publically. These people possessed one thing that Islamic terrorists didn't. They valued their own lives. The attacks they would attempt to carry out would not involve suicide, Scheper was sure of it. By publically torturing or executing the perpetrators, it would spread fear among the population, and possibly prevent future attacks. Scheper was especially disappointed that the girl had not been captured. He wouldn't be able to make an example out of her. He really did need an example.

A new thought popped into his mind. He addressed his men.

"Take the bicycle back to the restaurant and find the little blonde waitress that works in the mornings. Bring her and the bicycle to the hangar in a half hour. I'll meet you there after I talk to the former vice president's security team."

Scheper went back to the restaurant, cleaned the blood off his face, and bandaged his forehead. He changed into his dress uniform and went to look for the vice president's men. He found them sitting in the restaurant passing around a half-empty bottle of Mescal. Scheper could see they were shaken. They hadn't bothered to clean up or change clothes, and they didn't look up when Scheper approached the table and sat down.

The guard directly across from him tilted his head back and took several noisy swallows of the rancid alcohol. Scheper cringed. He had never liked tequila, and couldn't understand what the Mexican people liked about it.

"I have to say, Scheper, you're not starting your negotiations off well," the guard said in broken English . The man slid the bottle across to Scheper. He picked it up and held his breath as he took a drink. He fought down a shudder before he responded.

"Don't forget," Scheper said, "we are on Mexican soil. If this is what happens where your government has taken over, I'm not sure that the German people want to deal with you after all." Scheper took a couple more long pulls from the tequila and slid the bottle back across the table. He stood up quickly, sliding his chair six feet across the hardwood behind him.

"I need to take care of a few things," Scheper said. "I will join you for dinner at six and we can begin our discussion. That is if you are now allowed to speak for your government without the vice president."

Scheper turned his back on the table, smiled, and walked out, leaving them to the rest of the Mescal and their own thoughts.

Round one, he thought, to Scheper.

He needed them to feel partially responsible for the bombing, and needed to give the impression that he didn't care whether or not he worked out a deal with the Mexicans. If they thought they needed the Germans' help at all, it would definitely strengthen his bargaining position.

Scheper walked to the hangar. He was already feeling the effects of the distilled cactus juice. By the time he walked in the door, he had a nice buzz going, which would make his upcoming task a little easier. The waitress, wearing a light-blue uniform, sat in a chair surrounded by his men. She stood as he approached.

"Is everything all right?" she asked. "Did I do something wrong?"

Scheper smiled at the pretty young girl. "No, my dear," he said. "I just wanted to talk to you about what happened earlier."

Scheper addressed his men: "Leave us."

When he and the girl were alone, he walked over and hugged her tightly. She squirmed in his arms. He squeezed tighter. He felt her struggling for breath. This excited him. He relaxed his grip. Then, with his left hand, he grabbed a handful of her soft blonde hair. She screamed as he dragged her across the hangar and threw her onto a workbench. He held her down and tore open her shirt, licking his lips while staring down at her heaving bare chest.

Scheper leaned down and tenderly kissed the girl on the cheek. Then he reached into a sheath at his waist and pulled free a long, wicked knife. He leaned back slightly and stared into the girl's green eyes. She begged him to let her go. Scheper's hand flashed from behind his back. He thrust the knife up under her ribs into her heart. The girl gasped and tried to pull away as he stabbed her several more times. When she stopped moving, he gently laid her on the floor and cut her throat from ear to ear. He leaned down, kissed her softly on her red lips, and dragged her across the floor before leaning her body against the legs of a chair. Her hot blood spilled down her chest, soaking her uniform. When the girl had completely bled out, Scheper made several deep slices across her cheek, and removed part of her scalp and an ear. He stood back, put the ear in a pocket of his uniform, and examined his handiwork. She definitely looked hideous.

He called his men back in. "Tie her bicycle upright in the back of a pickup, and tie her onto the seat," he said.

His men hesitated. Some had turned away from the sight of the girl.

"Now!" Scheper barked. "And make sure her face points outward."

He walked to a steel cabinet in the corner of the hangar and whistled while he searched the contents. He removed a small can of red paint and a medium-sized paint brush. He searched the rest of the garage and found a two-by-three-meter piece of plywood. The same German folk song that had played in his head the day he had killed Levi Nirschell popped into his mind. He sang loudly and slightly off key as he painted big red letters across the board. It read:

VIOLENCE AGAINST US BRINGS SWIFT JUSTICE

His men mounted the sign on top of the truck's cab and climbed in as Scheper started the motor. He drove slowly through the once-gated neighborhoods of Lakeway, covering every street. Some people rushed into their houses as he drove by. Some stopped what they were doing and stared, opened mouthed. After forty-five minutes of driving the billboard around, he pulled back up to the entrance of the gated community and removed the sign. A crowd gathered to watch as he tied the girl on the bicycle and the sign to the gate post. When he was finished, he stood in the back of the truck and shouted to the crowd.

"This girl thought it would be a good idea to attack us at the restaurant today. She was wrong. Let this serve as your one and only warning. If you attack us or even look at us in a way we don't like, this will be you. We will not hesitate to come in with all of our troops and kill every man, woman, and child."

Scheper unholstered his pistol, lined up his sights on a small child clinging to his mother's leg, and pulled the trigger, blowing a fist-sized hole in the toddler's chest.

The child's mother screamed and scooped up the body of her son, holding him to her chest. The rest of the crowd panicked and trampled each other in a stampede, trying to melt back into the afternoon shadows. Scheper climbed into the truck cab and laughed deeply as he drove, windows down, back to the restaurant.

All in all, he thought, this had turned out to be a pretty good day.

CHAPTER 17

Independence, Missouri
7 P.M., Friday, June, 5

SARAH CRAWLED ALONG the bottom of the familiar creek again, this time followed by Julia, and tried to keep the guilt out of her mind. It was men from the butchers' camp that had attacked the Ranger two days before, striking without warning and killing Mary within seconds. Both Tom and Allen had been taken captive. Jakob would've been taken also if he hadn't been thrown clear and ended up in the narrow ditch, out of sight of the attackers. The cannibals had stretched a rusty logging cable across the road at the perfect level above the ATV's tires. Tom hadn't seen it until it was too late. The cable had cleared the tires and wrapped around the front axle, causing him to lose control and roll the vehicle.

Sarah felt completely responsible for the attack. She speculated that she must have been seen by the captive in the cage, and he had obviously alerted the people in the camp. She could only assume he had tried to trade the information for freedom. There was no other reason to help his captors. Sarah was also angry with herself for not riding faster and keeping up with the group. If she hadn't stopped to put on her jacket, she could have been there to help fight off the attackers. Jakob had come to just as men on horseback grabbed Tom and rode off. Jakob had followed until he lost consciousness again and was discovered by Sarah. Of course, Jakob had tried to convince her that it was a blessing she hadn't been with them at the time of the attack. But she wasn't buying it. This was her fault. Nothing anyone said would convince her otherwise.

They had lost both of their ATVs and most of their weapons. All they had left was the 9 millimeter pistol Jakob had been carrying and the .45 pistol that was still tucked in Allen's wheelchair. They had about seventy-five rounds for the 9 and close to a hundred for the .45, as well as fifty 12-gauge shells that would do little good without her shotgun. Sarah knew they needed transportation and more weapons. She also knew there was no way she was going to leave Missouri without rescuing Tom and Allen.

The cannibals had horses. If Sarah and her friends could get a few of these, their trip westward would be easier. The ATVs were the best way to travel, but they were already having trouble finding enough fuel. Even if they could get the Sportsman back, it would be difficult for all three of them to ride it, and impossible once they rescued the other two. Horses were by far the best choice, and Sarah knew just where to find some.

They reached the spot where Sarah had been two afternoons earlier and waited for Jakob to initiate their plan. She didn't look at the camp. She would wait till it was time to attack. The cannibals might have people watching more closely now, and she didn't want to risk being seen again. She and Julia had left Jakob in the spot they'd camped before with a box of the .45 ammo and some of the shotgun shells. The plan was to wait for darkness, then for Jakob to build a fire and feed several rounds into the flames. When the ammo started going off, this would hopefully create a diversion and give Sarah and Julia a chance to grab a few horses and get away with their friends before the campers knew what was happening. Jakob had wanted in on the raid at first, but Sarah had convinced him that with the bump on his head and a possible concussion, he wasn't in shape to move quickly. They would only get one shot at a rescue, and they couldn't afford to chance him possibly blacking out. They would meet Jakob at a designated location when it was all over.

Sarah looked over her shoulder at Julia. She returned the look with tear-filled eyes. Sarah crawled over and wrapped her arms tightly around her friend.

"I still can't believe they were taken," Julia said. Sarah softly caressed the back of Julia's head. "And Mary," Julia continued. "She was so kind to me. How? What am I supposed to…? It's not fair. I'm just so tired of everything. Where is God when we need him? I'm not even sure that there is a God anymore."

Sarah cringed at this last statement. The one thing she had left of her humanity and the girl she had been was her unwavering faith in God. Her world had become cruel and dark, but that didn't mean God had forsaken them. He said in his Word that "Weapons would form." He never said they would prosper, even though it seemed like there was plenty of prospering happening around them. Now more than ever, they needed to have unshakeable faith. Sarah knew it was the only way they would make it. She had struggled herself with her faith along this journey. It felt like every time she killed, a little piece of her relationship with God died also. She could have easily sat and waited for the world to take her out, but Sarah had never been a victim. She hated injustice and those who preyed on others. She had been told all her life to turn the other cheek and ignore the cruelty of others, but she could not. Even on the few occasions her father had taken them into the Englishmen's world, she had tried to fight back against the jeers and insults directed toward their way of life. Each time, her father had held her back. "They are part of a lost world," he would say. "We must treat them with love and show them a better way."

Sarah hugged Julia tighter, kissed her on the cheek, and lay back against the creek bank. It was still at least two hours until dark and she needed to sleep. They had pushed hard for two days, only stopping for four hours one night. They needed to be rested for what was coming.

Sarah snapped her eyes open and bolted upright, knocking Julia aside and causing her to roll into the creek. Julia gasped and crawled from the water, panting. She glared at Sarah, removed her coat, and wrung the water out. Sarah's laughter infected Julia. They laughed hysterically for several minutes, all the while trying to keep their voices down. Finally they calmed down and caught their breath.

"Sorry," Sarah said. "I thought we'd overslept."

"What time do you think it is?" said Julia.

"Not sure, but it can't be more than forty-five minutes until dark."

Sarah crawled to the top of the bank and put the binoculars up to her eyes. The camp appeared the same as before, except that the number of sentries had doubled and there was now a Sportsman 500 ATV parked next to the horse corral. Sarah looked intently at the cages. She didn't see Tom or Allen in any of them, though a few of the cages were so crowded that she couldn't see every head. Her heart sank. She was sure they would be there. Had they died on the way back to the camp? Were they being held in one of the tents? Had they already escaped and were now searching for their friends?

She scanned the cages again. Sarah wished she knew for sure. If they were roaming the woods somewhere, she and Julia might never be able to find them. If they were in one of the tents and she and Julia attacked, it would guarantee they would die at these monsters' hands. Were they doing the right thing? She fought the urge to rush back to Jakob and call the attack off.

Still monitoring the cages, Sarah started kneeling to get in position for Jakob's signal. Then she froze. Two men in aprons had walked to one of the cages and pulled it open. One went in. He emerged a second later, dragging by the feet the squirming body of Allen. Sarah watched in horror as they hung him upside down from the tripod and began sharpening a nasty-looking cleaver. Allen yelled and cussed at them. He tried to bend at the waist and reach the rope around his ankles, but he couldn't make his paralyzed lower body work. Sarah rose and was about to run into the camp when Julia grabbed her by the ankles and held fast.

"Not yet!" Julia hissed. "We won't survive."

Choking back a sob, Sarah watched one of the men reach up with the cleaver and chop into the back of Allen's neck, nearly removing his head. Sarah's scream was covered up by Jakob's first exploding round of ammunition. The sentries converged in the center of the camp, then ran toward the gunfire. When they'd disappeared into the woods, Julia let go. Sarah and Julia broke cover and sprinted for the corral and cages.

"Get the horses," Sarah hissed.

Julia reached the corral, grabbed three hackamores hanging from a post, and slipped into the pen. Sarah hurried to the cages and looked inside each one. Tom was definitely not there. She rushed over to the butcher table and avoided looking at Allen as she grabbed the bloody meat clever off the ground. She chopped through the wood bar holding the lock of each cage in place. The captives poured out. Sarah dropped the cleaver and grabbed the arm of an elderly, plump woman as she tried to rush past.

"Where is the big black man they brought in yesterday?" she said.

The women didn't answer. Instead, she locked eyes with Sarah, a forlorn expression on her face, then glanced at the butcher table and Allen's lifeless, swinging body. The woman shook her head.

Sarah's heart sank lower than ever before. She screamed in rage. She let go of the woman, who hurried off. In the next instant, a boy about ten years old ran from the area of the tents directly at Sarah. He carried a 12-gauge shotgun—Sarah's shotgun, the one that had belonged to her grandfather—and was pointing it at her head. A few feet behind him, a dark-haired woman in her thirties ran toward the boy.

"Darin, no!" the woman screamed.

Sarah reacted without thinking. She yanked her pistol out of her belt and shot the boy in the center of his chest.

The boy fell forward and skidded through the bloodstained dirt by the butcher table. The woman screamed again and picked up speed while pulling a knife from her belt. Sarah shot her twice. The woman dropped the knife, fell beside the boy, and crawled over to him as if she hadn't felt the bullets ripping into her. She grabbed the body of the lifeless boy and began rocking him back and forth, sobbing, as blood poured from her wounds, covering his face and chest.

"Darin! Darin! Why?"

Sarah blinked and dropped her pistol. What had she done?

She sat down hard in the dirt, hung her head between her knees, and heaved. She removed her bonnet, wiped her mouth with it, and looked up just in time to see the woman rushing toward her with the 12-gauge. Sarah reached for her pistol but knew she wouldn't be fast enough.

The woman raised the shotgun at Sarah, then grunted and dropped to the ground, dead. Julia stood behind her, the bloody meat clever in her hands. Julia dropped the cleaver, picked up the shotgun, and pulled Sarah to her feet.

"We need to move! Now!"

Men had started to flood back into the far end of the camp. Julia pulled Sarah along to where their new horses were tied. In the commotion, Sarah's bonnet dropped to the ground. Before she could pick it up, Julia roughly pushed her onto one of the mare's backs, then jumped on another. They galloped hard for the tree line, the other fifteen horses following. Bullets filled the air all around them. Sarah's ears rang and her arms and legs felt like weights. Her mind barely registered what was happening around her. She hung onto the reins with all the strength she had left as they rode into a nightmare that seemed to have no end.

CHAPTER 18

The Dalles Dam
Columbia River, Oregon
10:30 A.M., Wednesday, September 9

LARRY COLLINS GRUNTED as he pulled the flopping twenty-five-pound Chinook salmon from the dip net, knocked it on the head, and threw it onto the fish pile. After two hours of netting salmon, his muscles ached, but his mind was clearing. A little fishing would help him unwind and change his demeanor before he returned home to the ranch in Seneca in two days. He always tried to leave the stresses and horrors of war on the battlefield and save the best of himself for his wife, Amanda. He also felt obligated to be a positive male influence to fifteen-year-old Adam Nirschell. Since the death of his dad in the battle for freedom in Colorado, Adam had lived on the ranch surrounded by women, along with the old codger Bill. The old man was tough enough and could teach the boy about the value of hard work and how to be independent, but he was not the most nurturing of fellows. Larry tried to bring the more tender aspects of fathering to the boy. He and Amanda didn't have children, though they'd tried. Since her accident on the trail during those harrowing days after the first nuclear attack, Amanda had been unable to conceive. Larry felt like a second father to the boy, and he took that role seriously.

The dip net shook violently, and Larry nearly dropped it. He regained control and braced his feet against the concrete bank of the fish ladder. He leaned back and pulled for all he was worth. When the net cleared the water, he was surprised to see three salmon occupying the space. He pulled the quivering fish out one at a time, and again knocked each on the head before throwing them on the pile. The man just downstream whooped and pumped his fist in the air as he watched Larry's successful dip.

The number of fish going through the fish ladder at The Dalles Dam had been increasing daily since the first of August, and was not up to an estimated fifty thousand a day. Thirty men and women with nets like Larry's were spread out fifteen yards apart up the whole length of the ladder. The crew at the dam needed the extra protein to supplement the beef, deer, elk, and vegetables that had just been harvested. A crew of 650 was in charge of power restoration, spread out from Bonneville Dam in Oregon all the way up to McNary in Washington. The Dalles Dam was the only place generating power, and they'd had to rob parts from other facilities to keep the dam generating. They currently had five of the twenty-two turbines going, but the others were nearly ready to bring online as the demand for electricity grew. A crew of three hundred men led by Chad Ellison was repairing power lines from The Dalles Dam all the way to the oil refinery in Cheyenne, Wyoming, and to towns all across Eastern Oregon, Idaho, and Washington.

Chad had joined the resistance at the outset of the conflict to remove President Hartley from power and had stayed on and volunteered to lead the power line restoration efforts due to his background as a lineman with Idaho Power. The biggest challenge for Chad's crew was the lack of transformers. When the power first went out, they'd repaired and used older diesel pickups. When the service station storage tanks ran out of fuel, people began removing residential transformers from the power poles and draining them of the mineral oil used to keep them cool. Each transformer contained thirty gallons of mineral oil, which burned as well as diesel. The sudden necessity had outweighed future power restoration. Larry and his men were collecting transformers from closer to Portland, but the biggest supply in the urban area was untouchable. The radiation levels were still too high to risk trips into the metropolis, so they settled for harvesting the ones at abandoned or destroyed homes.

Unfortunately, someone had been systematically trying to destroy entire sections of the line. It was most likely the Germans. They had remained in the U.S. after the battle to defeat the Collective and its allies in Colorado. The Russians had pulled out, but Germany's military leaders had kept the basic structure of the United Collective together and were still working to claim at least some U.S. territory. The attacks in the West had all but ceased, as their forces were concentrated in the South. But Larry knew that once they gained enough ground, troops, and weapons, they would attempt to claim the West and its vast resources.

The other possibility was that the power lines were being targeted by a radical environmental group that had formed after the initial collapse. Several surviving members of the ERB—the "Earth Restoration Brigade"—had gotten together and declared war on rebuilding efforts. They saw the destruction of modern technology during the attacks as a gift for Mother Earth. The reduction in population had been a great step in reducing mankind's impact on the ecosystem. The fact that man was once again trying to reclaim his previous advances in technology was seen by the environmentalists as a direct attack on their philosophy and the earth itself. Before the collapse, the group was fairly harmless, aside from the occasional protest, such as hanging themselves from a bridge to fight against fossil fuel or chaining themselves across a logging road to save trees. The average person was mostly unaffected by their actions. Since the collapse, however, that had changed. Those in their ranks who had once been opposed to guns and violence now embraced both with vigor. They were well armed and very motivated. At first the group had attacked towns and the power crews, but people didn't take too well to being attacked, and met violence with violence. The group's losses were great, so now they mostly engaged in sabotage of the infrastructure in remote areas.

A former member of the group named Carlson had been captured a year earlier. He was half starved and living on bugs near the town of Millican when they found him. His group had been caught blowing down a section of high transmission line. A firefight broke out. Several of the environmentalists were killed, and the rest fled into the badlands. Carlson had hidden in a cave when the fight broke out. By the time he came out, his group had fled and the power crew had gone back to The Dalles to get supplies to re- stand the towers. After Carlson was found, he spent a month in the town of Bend, where he had eaten rich food and slept in a soft, warm bed with a roof over his head. He decided at that point that his own comfort was more important than his ideology, so he had turned on his group. Now he did his best to educate Larry's troops on the environmentalists, and tried to help anticipate where the attacks would happen next.

Larry caught another fish and began carrying them one by one to a small trailer on the back of an ATV. He really didn't need to be personally dipping salmon out of the river. There were plenty of more important things he could be doing, but dangit, he didn't want to. He'd always loved to fish and he needed a break. He had been coordinating defenses all over the West, and had been more or less in command of the new U.S. troops since his friend Nirsch had been killed three years earlier. He was tired, stressed, and war weary, but the conflict was still not resolved. He knew there would be much more killing before it was over.

The sound of a train whistle grabbed Larry's attention. He laid his dip net on the concrete path next to the fish ladder and ran toward the opposite end of the powerhouse, where the train was pulling in. Larry had loved trains since he was a boy. His grandfather had bought him a Lionel set on his eighth birthday, and for the next four years he had been obsessed with locomotives. He had an engineer cap, engineer pajamas, and a hand-carved train whistle. The old steam locomotives were his favorite, so the day the power crew came rattling up the tracks in the old Southern Pacific 4449, Larry experienced the same excitement he'd felt on his eighth birthday.

As soon as work had begun on the dam, the power crew had been searching for a better way to get the heavy equipment—some parts weighing over seventy-five tons—from one dam to another. It wasn't possible to haul such large loads by semi-truck. One member of the crew recalled going on a school field trip when he was a child to Portland's Union Station, where the 4449 was on display. The same crew member also remembered reading in the newspaper, just a few days before the nuclear attack, that the locomotive was in Pasco, Washington, for the grand opening of the Eastern Washington Railway Heritage Museum. He had planned on taking his children to see it.

The train was three days overdue. If it hadn't arrived that day, Larry would have taken a small team out to search for it. The train crew had travelled upriver to McNary Dam a week earlier to get another Kaplin turbine and to pick up a load of harvested transformers from the Washington crew. Once the power was fully restored to Eastern Oregon and up into Southern Washington, they would be able to begin manufacturing parts again.

Larry climbed into the engine cab to talk to the engineer and soon discovered why the train was late. The ERB had pulled up nearly a hundred yards of track and attacked the train crew while they were trying to repair it. Three of Larry's men had been killed, and two others wounded. But his men had also killed several of the radicals and run them off before continuing on.

Larry was growing very tired of this group. At first they had been the subject of jokes and ridicule, but now they were beginning to piss him off. He knew they would need to be dealt with sooner than later. Winter was fast approaching, and there were still over one hundred and fifty miles of line to repair in order to connect to the town of John Day, and seventy beyond that to reach Burns. He had hoped Chad would already be to Burns by now, but knew there was no way to make it before winter unless the crews were able to work overtime and not worry about attacks.

While the train crew unloaded the new turbine and transformers, Larry went off to find Chad and make plans to locate the ERB. It amazed Larry that anyone who had lived through the brutality of the world after the collapse could be fighting so hard to stop them from rebuilding and return to some sort of civility. He hoped to end their interruptions once and for all.

Larry found Chad in the powerhouse cafeteria, just finishing up a salmon dinner. "Ready for a little trip and change of pace?" he asked, smiling down at Chad.

Chad smiled back through a mouthful of mushy pink meat.

Larry had grown fond of Chad since their first meeting in Nirsch's living room at the ranch in Seneca. They'd fought together during the campaign to remove President Hartley, and had saved each other's bacon on more than one occasion. Chad had proven to be strong and a loyal friend. Like Larry, he was driven by a passion to see America restored. His faith in what they were trying to accomplish was unshakeable. Even when he lost one of his sons during the battle in Colorado, he never stopped fighting. He seemed to understand that what they were doing was more important than any one man, and that if they were successful, history would record the sacrifice of his boy. His son would be immortalized and honored forever.

They spent the rest of the evening in Larry's room planning the upcoming hunt. The environmentalists had attacked the train from the cliffs just outside of Boardman. If Larry's team could pick up the trail, they should be able to find the radicals and finish the fight. Chad had a man on his crew that had travelled across the country before the collapse, training search and rescue units in the finer points of "man tracking." Even though the trail would be cold by the time they found it, Chad indicated his faith that their tracker would pick it up and they'd be able to follow.

The next morning before sunrise, Larry, Chad, and thirty men loaded their horses and gear onto a box car and chugged up the tracks toward Boardman. They got to the spot of the attack and unloaded just as the sun was coming up and dancing off the waters of the Columbia. The ERB had removed the train tracks, then stationed themselves in the steep cliffs above the river. When the train had stopped, they'd attacked from an elevated position.

Larry studied the spot of the ambush. It's a good thing the eco nuts aren't better shots, he thought, or they'd have picked off every one of the train crew.

Larry's men skirted the cliffs until they found a way up, then carefully picked their way through the rocks to the top of the plateau, dismounting and leading their horses the last hundred yards. Larry paused at the top and marveled at the seemingly endless rows of giant wind turbines. He had flown over them several times, and had seen them from a distance while driving on Highway 197, but this was the first time he'd observed them up close. When they'd started planning the restoration of the electrical grid, someone had suggested repairing the wind generators first, but this plan was abandoned due to the relatively small amount of electricity they produced in comparison to the hydroelectric dams. The windmills were also a fairly new fad, and were almost entirely regulated with computers and electrical circuitry. For now, they would sit unrepaired. Larry wondered if they'd ever be brought back on line.

It didn't take the tracker long to pick up the trail, and in a few short minutes they had a general direction to follow. It was slow going through the large patches of lava rocks. The only sign in those sections was an occasional boot scrape through the dry lichens covering the stones, a rock that had been kicked over, or dirt scattered across the surface of a rock. Once they were a mile from the cliffs, the rocks thinned and gave way to orchards, wheat fields, and rolling prairies. Here the sign was easier to follow; even those without tracking experience could easily spot the trail of broken-down grass. They picked up the pace, and Larry sent the tracker on ahead a few miles to scout.

By noon, the hunters had gone at least fifteen miles. The scout had reported back twice, and the trail up ahead was getting fresher. The ERB had a forty-eight hour head start, but they were on foot. Larry knew that if his men could keep up the pace, factoring in that the ERB would need to rest and sleep, that two-day lead would be cut to no more than half a day by sundown.

By the time the shadows grew long and the scout returned for the final time, they had traveled over thirty miles. Larry had a good idea of where the group may have been holed up, but it was pure speculation on his part. They had been travelling in nearly a straight line since leaving the river and they were on the edge of the town of Antelope.

If his hunch was correct, they would find the group at the site of the old Rajneesh compound. In the early eighties, a cult leader had bought the property and created a compound for his followers. They had pretty much taken over the town of Antelope and had poisoned some of the townspeople before the U.S. government raided the ranch and deported the religious leader back to India. It was big news and had garnered national media attention. Larry and his wife had followed the story from Washington D.C.

Since the drama had played out, the ranch had changed hands several times, and was being run by a Christian group as a youth retreat just before the attacks. Situated in a long narrow valley, with high buttes on each side, it was a fairly defensible space. If the ERB had lookouts on the tops of the rims, they would be able to see anyone approaching from several miles out and have time to warn everyone before they could be reached. He would follow the trail where it led, but he would be shocked if it didn't end at the Rajneesh ranch.

They camped at an abandoned farmhouse for the night, where Larry shared his theory about the Rajneesh ranch with the others. They decided that the scout would ride ahead in the morning and go straight to the ranch without worrying about following the trail. Larry and the rest would stay on the trail in case it led somewhere other than where his gut told him it would. Larry wasn't a great tracker, but he thought he'd be able to follow the path of the ERB.

He wasn't completely used to his new life out west, even though he'd now lived here for over five years. He still got saddle sore when he spent more than a couple days on horseback. Much of the landscape and vegetation were still foreign to him. Life on the streets of D.C. was all he had known. Aside from the occasional trip to the Nirschell ranch before the collapse, and the few times his father had taken him fishing and camping in the Blue Ridge Mountains of Virginia, he hadn't spent much time away from the concrete, steel, and crowds of the city. He'd often dreamed of being a cowboy or living as a mountain man when he was a boy. But like all childhood fantasies, that was put away with other boyhood foolishness when he left home and became a man.

Larry lay in the dark after everyone had bedded down for the night and thought of Amanda and their new home on the Seneca ranch. He hadn't been home for over five months, and he missed his green-eyed girl terribly. They talked every other day or so by radio, but Larry ached to hold her in his arms and actually look into her eyes. Their romance and subsequent marriage before the collapse had been one for the storybooks. Since Amanda had lost one of her legs and they'd faced many other hardships together, their bond and passion had grown even stronger. They were both now in their forties, but still managed to make love like ravenous teenagers. Larry still looked at Amanda with the same desire he had the first time they'd met. Sure, they were both a little grayer on top, had a few more wrinkle lines on their faces and around the eyes, not to mention a little less stamina. But age had definitely not slowed them down.

Larry smiled in the dark, rolled over on his side, pulled the sleeping bag tighter around him, and fell into one of the most restful sleeps he'd enjoyed in recent memory.

The next morning, just as the warm, fall sun peeked over the top of the prairie grass, they started on the trail again. The tracker had left two hours before daylight and would check in with them after he scouted the Rajneesh ranch.

They made decent time and had covered close to eleven miles by noon. It was a pretty good pace considering Larry's poor tracking skills and the fact that he'd lost the trail on several occasions. Whenever the sign disappeared, the group would fan out until one of them picked it up again.

They had just stopped for a break and a little lunch when the tracker rode back in among them. Larry's hunch had been correct. The ERB was definitely at the ranch, and their numbers had grown. The scout had left his horse in a shallow draw and snuck between two sentries up to the rim overlooking the compound. From what the scout could tell, there were over a hundred people at the ranch, and at least fifteen on the rocks above.

Larry decided the only way they could get close and have any chance of hitting the compound was at night. They would need to quietly take out the spotters and slip down the steep cliffs from all four sides. Once in among them, they would need to hit them from all sides simultaneously. If they had air support, they could take out the sentries, take positions in the rocks, and wait for the chopper to strike a few of the buildings. Then Larry's team could snipe them as they exited the structures. The only drawback to that plan was that none of them had night scopes, and visibility would be poor. There were only thirty men with Larry, so each one would need to take out anywhere between two and four radicals.

Larry had faith in his men. Some of them had been fighting with him since his initial battle in Boise, Idaho, four years earlier. He knew they were all better shots and more tactically aware than the eco-terrorists. The wildcard was the new group that had joined with the ERB. They could have been members that had been temporarily separated, or they could be opportunists that saw the group and compound as a solution to hunger and wandering the wilderness alone. If they were outsiders, Larry hoped they would not want any part of the hell that he was going to unleash, and would flee as soon as the first shots were fired.

Everyone agreed that a night attack utilizing a chopper was their best option. Larry radioed for one of their Black Hawks to hit the ranch two hours after dark. The team continued on. They moved slower now, with the scout leading the way.

When the sun had set, and there was barely enough light to walk into the cliffs, they tied their horses in the draw the scout had found earlier in the day. Larry and five men would hit the sentries closest to their position, so they knelt near the horses and waited until the moon was up to move in. The rest of the group spread out across the prairie and got into position to hit the rest of the sentries.

The air had started to chill. Larry's muscles tensed in anticipation of the upcoming battle. He had never liked killing, even though he had become very good at it since the collapse. While he was still a police officer in D.C., he had been in some scrapes and had pulled his service weapon on several occasions, but he'd had to fire it only a few times. He remembered the first time he'd been in a firefight with a gang. He was scared almost to the point of paralysis, but was also excited and charged up from the surge of adrenaline. Now as he knelt in the darkness, that same adrenaline surged through him. The only thing missing was the fear.

The moon finally peeked over the horizon, seeming to touch the prairie grass. Larry motioned for all thirty of his companions to move out. They silently slipped across the prairie and slowly made their way into the juniper trees at the top of the cliffs. Thirty yards out, one of the sentries stood. Larry held up his hand, stopping his men. The sentry stretched, leaned his rifle against a tree trunk, and lit a cigarette. When he'd finished his smoke, the man sat against a rock, his back to Larry's group. Larry motioned for his companions to split and move to his left and right. Larry removed his K-Bar knife, the blade glinting dimly in the moonlight. The knife had belonged to Nirsch. Larry had retrieved it from his body after the battle in Colorado. It was one of Larry's most treasured possessions. The blade had gotten Nirsch out of countless scrapes around the world. Larry hoped now that the magic of the blade hadn't worn off.

He crawled up behind the sentry until he was ten feet away. He could smell the man's body odor and hear and see his breath as it floated into the cool night, misty in the silver moonlight. Larry took a few deep breaths to calm himself. Then, nearly in one motion, he rose up behind the man, reached a hand around his mouth, and pulled him back into the blade that Larry was thrusting toward his kidney. Larry pulled the knife free and thrust it forward several more times. He felt the man's warm blood on his hand. When the sentry stopped squirming and his screams no longer pushed against the hand over his mouth, Larry gently lowered him to the ground. He took the man's jacket off and put it on. The stench of the tattered coat burned his eyes and nearly made him gag. He wiped his bloody hand off on the coat tail and walked to the edge of the cliff, offering him his first look at the compound below. Several buildings covered the valley floor, including a large airplane hangar next to a mile-long runway.

A few people sat around a large fire pit, but overall the camp looked quiet. Larry turned to one side and then the other, waving his hand in the air. When he saw the return waves from his companions, he scouted around and found the perfect cradle for his rifle. He sat down, put his own jacket in the crevice between two rocks, and cleaned the scope with a handkerchief from his shirt pocket. He checked the load and placed several rounds on a flat rock just to the right of the rifle's forestock. Satisfied that he was as ready as he could be, he leaned back against the rocks, closed his eyes, and waited for the chopper.

CHAPTER 19

Wellington, Colorado
10 A.M., Saturday, September 12

ENERAL SCHEPER SAT in the passenger seat of his M-ATV—a fortified Humvee with a .240-caliber machine gun mounted on top—
watching the fence posts go by and thinking about home. He'd been on
American soil off and on for over four years, directing a war he was not
sure was even winnable. He had not been given the resources or manpower needed to completely take the United States. If he had, the conflict
would've been over the first time he had been in Colorado. His government had relied on the Russians, and a joke of a former U.S. president, to
win against an enemy that didn't follow typical military strategy. When
Scheper had killed the leader of the resistance army, he'd thought the
resistance might fold. He didn't realize that there were multitudes in rural
America just like the late Levi Nirschell. When the battle ended in Colorado, these men didn't stop fighting. They continued to engage the U.C.
troops and managed to push them all the way back to Texas.

The Russians' thirst for American resources had died along with
24,000 of their bravest comrades. They licked their wounds, counted

their losses, and returned to the motherland to join in the conquest of the Middle East. The Mexican drug cartel army also had proven to be worthless. They were no match for the good old boys of the American West, and disappeared after the Presidential Palace fell. Until the Mexican government joined forces with the Germans, the cartels had stayed underground. Now that they had competent leadership and a fresh supply of the latest weaponry, they were once again in the fight.

Scheper was leading an armored column and 450 Mexican and German troops. They would attack the oil refinery at Cheyenne, Wyoming, in ten days. The only way to win the big prize was to stop the flow of fuel to the American troops and crews rebuilding the country's infrastructure. The main source of that fuel flowed from Cheyenne. Scheper's plan hinged on cooperation from an anti-technology environmental group living on the High Desert of Oregon. Scheper didn't have enough troops to launch a multi-front attack. But he needed the Americans divided. He was not very confident that the environmentalists would do much damage to those they attacked, but they just needed to be a distraction. Scheper had provided them with explosives, RPGs, and shiny new AK-47s, along with several thousand rounds of ammunition. If they could pester the work crews enough, the Americans would need to concentrate a certain amount of troops and weaponry near The Dalles Dam to protect the power generators.

If Scheper attacked the refinery at the same time as the dam, the Americans would not be able to get resources to Wyoming in time. Even if the enviros didn't damage the hydropower facility, it wouldn't matter. Scheper would destroy the refinery, then turn his army toward The Dalles. Once both sites were destroyed, the war would be over. Without fuel, the Americans' vehicles and armaments would be useless. Without power, they would not be able to rebuild. Scheper would starve them into submission, much like the European colonists had done to the Indians that once roamed the wilds of North America.

The column rolled into Wellington, Colorado, late in the evening. They avoided the main part of town and hid themselves in an abandoned feed and farm supply center. Before leaving Austin, Scheper had sent a chopper here to scout the route they would take to Cheyenne. The chopper team had reported a decent-sized population in Wellington, but there didn't seem to be any U.S. troops anywhere along the route. Scheper had learned the value of discretion during his initial battles, especially in rural communities. Even if there were no troops with a clear command and support structure, average citizens could cause tremendous damage if they perceived that their homes were threatened. Scheper had found out the hard way that most people in America owned at least one firearm, and most of the population in the rural parts of the country had multiple weapons. When his troops had first rolled into the U.S. with the Russians and formed the United Collective under President Hartley's leadership, there had been a major push to confiscate as many privately owned firearms as possible. The tactic had not been very successful in disarming the population. They managed to get only about thirty million weapons. At the height of Hartley's presidency, U.S. gun manufacturers were producing nearly eleven million units a year for sale to the private market. If the number of guns purchased in the decades prior to Hartley's term of service was added to the ones made while he was in office, the total was astounding. The German government estimated that there were over one hundred million firearms unaccounted for.

Scheper's driver pulled the M-ATV to the side of the entry gate into the feed and farm compound. Scheper stood beside the vehicle and watched as the convoy drove into the largest warehouse. Most of the buildings in the compound were empty. Any usable fencing, animal feed, or building materials had been removed by the locals. There was more than enough room to house the four Leopard tanks and the rest of their vehicles.

They had made good time from Texas and were now ahead of schedule. Scheper had estimated the first leg of the journey from Austin to Wellington would take four days if they moved only at night. After the first night passed, he had decided to move during the day also. There were few people between Austin and here, so the risk of being seen was marginal. Once they left Colorado and moved closer to Wyoming and the U.S. troops charged with securing the refinery, they would need to be more cautious.

Scheper knew the extra time would be beneficial. They could stay here for a few days and send a small team to the refinery for a recon mission, then plan their attack accordingly. He had chosen not to utilize the limited air power they had in Texas. The Americans could possibly have radar stations up and running, and Scheper couldn't risk being spotted. The crew at the refinery might also have antiaircraft weaponry. He hadn't been too worried about being spotted from the air, as the Americans' air power was also limited. They had a few Black Hawks, but couldn't really afford the extra fuel needed for recon missions. He was confident that most of the enemy's aircraft were in Oregon.

Scheper supervised as all of the weaponry and equipment was tucked away. Satisfied that everything was under control, he changed into civilian clothes, splashed a little cologne on his face, put a handful of one-tenth-ounce gold coins and a hundred rounds of 9 millimeter ammunition into his pockets, and walked toward downtown Wellington. He needed to blow off a little steam, and a young, healthy girl would be just the thing to make that happen.

Most of the small- and medium-sized communities in the West that were not abandoned had managed to recover a certain amount of normalcy. Most towns had markets where people could barter goods and services, some had held elections for mayors and sheriffs, and almost all of them had a community pub or gathering place where people could drink homemade liquor and gossip about their neighbors. Scheper's English was pretty good, and if he concentrated, he could speak with only a trace of his normally thick accent. A soldier in uniform was one thing, but most people wouldn't question the occasional traveler passing through.

The sun had set, and it was nearly dark when he strolled into town. Most of the houses he passed showed signs of life. Candles glowed in the windows, smoke curled from the chimneys, and the smells of family meals tickled his nose. Scheper's stomach growled. He fought the urge to burst into one of the houses, kill the occupants, and take their hot meal. He had lived on nothing but military rations for three days since leaving Austin, and before that had choked down a steady diet of beans, ground meat, rice, and tortillas. He really hoped to find a pub and get a decent meal.

He walked for another fifteen minutes. The houses gave way to abandoned retail stores, and some abandoned bars and restaurants. Scheper began to question whether or not these people had any sort of gathering place, and was a block away from turning around and heading back to the warehouse, when piano music and people's laughter floated to him on the evening breeze. He followed the sounds to a small bar tucked between a hardware store and a bait and tackle shop. Several people loitered on the sidewalk. Through the front window, he saw that the inside was crowded. Most of the men had handguns hanging at their sides. Scheper unconsciously patted the Berretta hanging under his left arm and strolled into the bar like he'd been there before.

He found a small, empty table in a dark corner and sat down to observe how things worked. Most towns these days accepted small amounts of gold or common-caliber ammunition for currency. The only variation from town to town was the amount needed for services. An attractive, dark-haired waitress carrying a tray loaded with two platefuls of roasted meat and potatoes walked by. She set the plates in front of seated customers and retreated to the kitchen. A short time later, she returned to the same table with two foamy mugs of dark beer. Scheper's stomach rumbled and he smacked his lips. He wasn't sure if he had enough to barter with for a full meal, but he had to have enough for at least a beer or two.

The waitress came over to him to take his order. He hadn't seen anyone pay yet, so he told her he was waiting for someone and asked her to come back in a few minutes. Four women seated at a nearby table were preparing to leave. By the looks of their empty plates and empty beer mugs, he assumed they'd enjoyed a full meal and at least one beer apiece. The waitress walked to their table and leaned on the back of one of the chairs. One of the women, a redhead about twenty years old with a fit body and blue eyes, leaned in close to the waitress, who also leaned down and let the girl whisper in her ear. The waitress obviously enjoyed the private joke. She tilted her head back and laughed. The other women around the table joined in, then stood to leave. The waitress hugged each one, set a small metal bowl on the table, and went to tend to other customers. The redhead reached into her pocket, counted out forty or fifty rounds of ammunition, and placed them in the bowl. Scheper was too far away to know exactly what caliber was counted out, but it looked to him to be pistol rounds, 9 millimeter or .38 caliber. If all four women ate a meal and had beverages for fifty rounds, he could be in for a great feast with the hundred rounds he carried.

The waitress returned to his table. "It doesn't look like my friend is gonna show, so what's for dinner?" he asked.

The waitress smiled at him, and Scheper sensed a spark of attraction. She was about thirty years old, about five feet eight inches and 130 pounds, with long, jet-black hair and a nice, wide set of hips, as well as just the right amount of baggage on her backside.

He smiled back and winked as she answered.

"Elk roast and fried potatoes," she said. "We had some bread, but were busier than expected. We're out. I could bring you a flour tortilla with a little butter and jam if you'd like."

Scheper scrunched his face into a frown and shook his head. The last thing he wanted was a tortilla. "Roast and potatoes would be great," he said. "Could I get one of those beers too?"

The waitress put her hand on his shoulder and let it rest there. Scheper's face grew warm. This girl was definitely attracted to him.

She answered him without removing her hand. "Coming right up. I haven't seen you around here before. Have you been in town long?"

"I'm just passing through," he said. "What's your name?"

"Kate."

Scheper reached up with his left hand, placed it on top of the girl's hand, and slowly squeezed her fingers.

I think I'll call you Katie, Scheper thought. You look like a Katie.

Scheper grinned, flicked the tip of his tongue across his top lip, and put more pressure on her fingers. The waitress quickly removed her hand, smiled awkwardly, and backed away from the table. Scheper knew he had made her nervous. This girl was obviously someone who liked to be in control. He had only been with a few strong women, but they were his favorite type. The moment they realized they were no longer in control and were powerless was like a drug to Scheper. The harder they tried to fight him off, the more pleasurable the experience. This was one girl he couldn't resist. Before the night was over, he would have her.

So begins our date, Ms. Katie.

A few minutes later, she brought his meal out and set it in front of him without saying anything.

"Thank you, darling," Scheper said.

She quickly turned and retreated to the kitchen. A short time later, the kitchen door opened a crack, and a rather large gentleman in a greasy apron peeked out. Scheper raised his mug toward the man, smiled, and took a long drink. He set the mug down and wiped the foam from his upper lip with the back of his hand as the man came out of the kitchen and up to his table.

"Is everything okay?" he asked. "How's the roast?"

"Delicious," Scheper said.

"I haven't seen you before. Have you been on the road long?"

Scheper smiled and laughed in his head. This fool, he thought, is trying to be intimidating. He has no idea who he's addressing.

Scheper knew he could kill this man and everyone in the restaurant before his food got cold. But no matter how pleasurable it would be, he needed to think about his mission and long-term goals. He decided he would play along, project a little weakness, and not draw any more attention to himself. He would wait in the shadows outside the pub, and when his Katie left for the night, he would have his fun.

"I've been traveling a couple of weeks," Scheper said. "I lived in a cabin in Missouri the last couple of years, but wanted to make a change. I heard they needed help out west restoring electricity. I figure the three square meals a day and soft bunk they were offering was a fair wage. Sure beats not knowing where my next meal is coming from."

Apparently satisfied with his story, the cook went back to the kitchen. Scheper laughed out loud when he saw the waitress through the open door waiting for an explanation from her brave boss.

Scheper finished his meal without any more interaction with the waitress. In spite of the excitement bubbles that were swirling around in his stomach, and the overwhelming anticipation of what he was about to do to this smoking-hot woman, he took his time and thoroughly enjoyed the food. Until now, he had never tried elk meat. He had eaten stag in Germany, but elk was different. The flesh was a little gamier, and not quite as tough.

When he had finished and it was time to pay, the cook brought the metal bowl out for him. He was pleased that he had made the waitress so nervous that she couldn't face him now.

"What do I owe you?" Scheper said.

"Fifteen in 9 millimeter or twenty-five in any other pistol round. If you have any .223 or other rifle rounds, it's ten."

Scheper counted out twenty-five of the 9 millimeter and smiled at the cook. "Keep the change."

He walked out into the cool night air and looked for a shadowy place nearby to watch the restaurant. He tucked himself into the doorway of a craft store across the street, pulled his collar up to block out the chill, and waited. He wondered how long it would be until people went home and the waitress left for the night. It was only 9:00 P.M., but the flow of new customers had stopped while he was eating. He decided he would wait until 11. If his date didn't show by then, he would head back to the warehouse. The fantasy about what was to come nearly overwhelmed him. He could hear her screams and feel her warm body beneath his. He would take his time and enjoy it. It might be a long while before he found another as strong as this one. He didn't want to waste a second.

At 10:15, the cook exited the restaurant and walked down the street. Scheper felt a stab of panic—he hadn't seen the girl leave.

Maybe she slipped out the back, he thought. Or maybe she lives in the pub.

He dismissed both notions when he saw candlelight shining through the windows. She was still in there. He also thought she'd been too well-dressed and too clean to be living in a pub that likely had no apartment in it. There was no upstairs, and the single story wasn't big enough for living quarters. He wondered if he should go back inside and begin their date, but quickly thought better of it. There was a chance that the cook would come back and interrupt them, in which case he would need to kill him, and that would raise questions in the community when he didn't show up for work along with the black-haired girl. If anyone started searching, they might discover the troops at the warehouse. If he did everything right, he could enjoy his time with her and make sure she wasn't found until long after he had left Wellington.

At 10:45, the flicker of candlelight disappeared and the girl walked out, carrying a small, brown paper bag. She locked the door behind her. Scheper licked his lips and stared at her hips as she swayed down the street. He waited until she rounded a corner, then slipped from the shadows. He followed her for several blocks, moving from shadow to shadow. Twice, the girl stopped and looked behind her.

You are a cagey little thing, aren't you? Scheper thought.

He followed her to the edge of town and beyond. When they were at least two miles from town, she turned into a long gravel driveway and stopped again. Scheper ducked under a pine tree. He was nearly fifty feet from her, but the look of fear on her face in the moonlight was clear. A little moan escaped his throat. He slowly pulled his knife from under his coat. He reached down and grabbed a small rock. When she turned and began walking again, he threw it as hard as he could over her head. It landed in the bushes twenty feet in front of her. She jumped high into the air, flinging the bag she'd been carrying. Several fatty chunks of left-over roast landed in the driveway.

The color of the girl's skin had changed to a ghostly white. She looked all around. Scheper tensed in the shadows. He was wound up like a bow string ready to break. The girl turned and began running up the driveway. Scheper leapt from the shadows and sprinted into the cover of the brush next to the driveway. He ran much faster than she did and soon passed her by. When the two-story house came into view, he was over a hundred yards in front of her.

Scheper ran to an old Chevy pickup and crouched behind a front wheel. His breath came in short gasps, and his heart pounded in his chest. He smiled and tried to calm his noisy breathing as she came into view. She ran past him and took the front porch stairs two at a time. He watched her fumble with her keys. She dropped them twice before she managed to get the front door open and slip inside, slamming the door behind her. Scheper could have grabbed her at any time since leaving the restaurant, but the longer he waited, the more fear she would feel. It was also getting colder out, and he wanted to take her where it was warm and cozy. He didn't perform as well in the cold.

He stayed next to the pickup for several minutes. The girl lit a few candles and closed the curtains. He tiptoed to the front door, put his ear against the wood, and listened. The girl was talking to someone. He had a sudden urge to abandon his fun and leave. When no other voices drifted out, he relaxed. Perhaps she'd been talking to a dog or cat. This would explain the bag of dropped goodies at the beginning of the driveway. Scheper hoped it was a cat and not a dog. He had never liked dogs, and the feeling had always been mutual. He had never encountered a mutt that didn't growl or bare its teeth at him.

Scheper took the point of his knife and scraped the backside across the metal door handle. It made a loud, screeching noise, like fingernails on a chalk board. The girl quit talking to the animal that Scheper was now sure had to be a cat. A dog would've barked.

He heard the girl's footsteps as she retreated further into the house. He really was having a good time. He crept off the porch and made his way toward the back of the house. He got to the back door, reached for the knob, and turned it slowly. It stopped halfway around. Locked. He continued to a window, stuck the blade of his knife under the frame, and pried. Also locked.

Though he was enjoying his date, he was also getting frustrated that he couldn't get into the house. Scheper stepped back and looked up toward the second story. He laughed out loud and rubbed his hands together excitedly when he saw white, sheer curtains hanging out a window, dancing in the breeze. He climbed a gutter downspout at the corner and hoisted himself to the roof. Slowly, he moved along the roof above the window, laid on his belly, and looked upside down over the edge into the opening. It was completely dark inside. He couldn't hear the girl. He dangled his legs over the edge of the roof and felt for the window sill with his feet. Once he found a solid foothold, he quietly slipped inside.

Scheper pulled a flashlight from his coat pocket and looked around. He thought he must be in the main bedroom. A king-size bed sat against a wall. An old patchwork quilt covered the mattress and several teddy bears were scattered across the pillows. A white, antique dresser lined the wall opposite. Scheper slowly opened the top drawer. Several sets of lacy under-garments lay neatly folded inside. Scheper picked up a red bra and white silk stockings. He rubbed the soft material against his cheek and breathed in deeply. He wadded the lingerie up and put it in his coat pocket. Next, he played his flashlight beam across a large, silver picture frame above the bed. He studied the picture. A much-younger version of his date stood next to a jeep on a rocky mountain top. Behind her was a man, his arms wrapped across her chest. Both were smiling and looked very much in love.

A pang of jealousy stabbed at Scheper. He removed the picture and stashed it in the bottom drawer of the dresser. He took one more look around, slowly opened the door, and stepped into a dark hallway. The floorboards creaked slightly as he made his way to the end of the hall. He crept to the stairwell and looked down. Candlelight still flickered on the first floor. He started down the stairs and was halfway to the bottom when a shadow moved below. He crouched and put his back against the wall. He had definitely seen movement on the first floor, but wasn't sure if it was his date or the cat.

A single drop of sweat slid down the side of his face. He reached up a trembling finger and wiped it away. He felt very alive. Every muscle in his body was tense. He was truly made for the hunt.

Scheper slowly stood and started down the stairs. A step creaked loudly. He froze. Anyone in the house would have heard it. He waited a full two minutes before starting down again.

Five steps from the bottom, from around the corner of the stairwell, he saw the end of a black shotgun barrel come into view. He turned and sprinted back up the stairs. He reached the second floor and dove onto the landing as the banister exploded where his head had been a split second before.

Scheper rolled into a crouch and reached for his pistol. If he had to shoot his date to save himself, he would, but that would be a last resort. If she was dead, his fun would be over.

He took his hand off the butt of his pistol and smiled. "Are you mad at me?" he yelled. "Did I do something wrong or say something I shouldn't have at the pub? We should make up. I really don't want to fight. Let's sit and talk. You can make us some tea or coffee and we can work it out."

Scheper listened intently and waited for a response.

"Katie? Sugar? You still there?"

He heard a door open. Scheper leapt to his feet and took the stairs down three at a time. He turned the corner into the living room in time to see his date disappear through the front door. He chased after her and nearly tripped over a hefty orange tabby cat that ran from the kitchen, between his legs, and also out the front door. Scheper followed the cat outside into the moonlight. Katie stood square-shouldered in the driveway with the shotgun raised. She fired. Scheper dove to the floor of the long porch and belly slid under a swing, driving splinters into his chest. It felt wonderful.

He looked up just as she entered a small shed near the Chevy pickup.

"Katie? You're being a little unreasonable."

Scheper tiptoed off the porch and to the side of the shed, carefully avoiding the small window at face level. He got on his hands and knees, re-sheathed his knife, and crawled to the side of the shed door. Slowly, he reached his arm around the corner, jiggled the knob, and quickly pulled his arm back to his side. The center of the shed door exploded. Though he hadn't been hit by the shotgun blast, he screamed and got to his feet. He stomped hard on the ground, then waited, staring at the doorknob, ready to pounce.

After a couple of minutes, the knob began to turn. The door opened a crack. The end of the shotgun barrel poked out, then Katie's head. Scheper grabbed the barrel and wrenched the gun from her hands, pulling her halfway out of the shed in the process. Katie screamed. He grabbed a handful of her hair and dragged her into the moonlight. She kicked, clawed, and scratched the side of his cheek with her sexy red fingernails. Scheper laughed and pushed her to the ground. He wrapped his arms and legs around her and held her tightly.

"Please don't fight me," he said. "This is going to happen, but I want us both to enjoy ourselves."

He felt Katie relax a little, so he released some of the pressure. As soon as he did, Katie drove an elbow hard into his groin, kicked her legs free, and squirmed out of his hands. Scheper reacted quickly and kicked her behind the right knee. She fell onto the driveway. Her head bounced when her face crunched into the gravel. She stopped moving.

Scheper lay on his back panting for several minutes, letting his adrenaline subside. Once his groin stopped throbbing and he'd caught his breath, he got up and looked down at his prize.

"You really are quite a catch," he said.

He picked her up, threw her over his shoulder, and returned to the house, making sure to lock the front door behind him. He made his way up the stairs and gently laid the girl on the bed. With the silk stocking he'd collected earlier, he tied her arms and legs to the bedposts. He walked over to the dresser and rummaged around in the top drawer until his fingers latched onto a pair of heavy wool socks. He stuffed one of the socks into her mouth. Satisfied with his work, he went back downstairs. A few minutes later, he returned with a pan of water and a washcloth. He carefully cleaned the blood and gravel from her face, then sat on the edge of the bed to take in her beauty. Gently, he ran his fingers through her hair. He leaned down and kissed her tenderly on the cheek.

She moaned and started to stir. Her eyes snapped open. She screamed into her gag and thrashed in her restraints.

"Hi, sleepyhead," Scheper said. "I wondered if you were going to sleep all night."

Katie thrashed even harder. The bed squeaked and the legs bounced on the hardwood.

"You got anything sweet to eat? I didn't have desert at the pub and I've got a terrible sweet tooth."

Scheper left her to think about her situation and went to the kitchen to look for a treat. By the time he returned, Katie had stopped struggling. She just lay there staring at the ceiling. Her face was soaked with tears and her lower lip quivered as he walked back to the edge of the bed.

"Don't cry," he said. "Everything is fine now."

She stared up at his face with red, moist eyes. Her gazed paused on his left cheek. He sensed her fear.

"You like it?" Scheper asked as he traced his finger along the nasty red scar that ran the full length of his face. "This was a gift from a *dummkopf* who thought he could take back this country and send me back to mine. I think it gives me a handsome, rugged look."

He grabbed a corner of the bedsheet and gently dried the tears from her face. "This is what we've both been waiting for. Someone to come along and drive the loneliness away. I know you've been lonely since he was taken from you."

Katie's eyes grew wide. She tilted her head back and glanced at the spot the picture had been hanging above the bed. Scheper followed her eyes.

"It's okay," he said. "I think he would want you to move on."

Katie's eyes filled with tears again. A large drop slipped from the corner of an eye and slid down her cheek, coming to rest just under her chin. Scheper bent down and kissed the tear from her neck. He slowly licked his lips. The sweet, salty teardrop tasted delicious. With his hand, he cupped the back of her head. He worked his way up the side of her face with his lips, pausing at her hairline. The smell of sweat, fear, and blood caused a slight moan to escape his lips. Katie struggled again. She shook her head from side to side. Her forehead connected with Scheper's upper lip, splitting it open. Scheper grunted in pain, drew his right hand back, and slapped her hard across the cheek. Katie screamed against the gag again. Scheper got to his feet and swore.

"Now look what you did," he said, pointing at his throbbing lip. "And just when everything was going so well." He slapped her again, then returned to the kitchen to clean the blood from his lip.

Scheper found a roll of duct tape in a kitchen drawer. He tore a small piece of paper towel from a roll and taped it over his cut. He glanced at his watch: almost 12:45. He would have to wrap up his date soon and get back to the warehouse. He needed to finalize plans for his recon team, and he needed to rest before the attack.

Scheper smiled and began to hum as he walked back toward the stairs. As his foot landed on the third step, a knock at the front door echoed through the empty house. He froze.

"Kate?" A man's deep voice shouted out from the front porch. "Kate! It's Jim Baxter. Are you in there? We brought your cat back. He came to the house earlier."

"Jim! Over here," another man called.

Scheper began to panic when he heard Katie's muffled screams. He ran up to the room. Her gag was half out of her mouth and she was bouncing up and down furiously, banging the legs of the bed against the floor again. He jumped on top of her and clamped a hand over her mouth. He was unsure what to do. He didn't know who these men were or if they were skilled fighters. If he hunted them it would be fun, but there was a chance that he would be the prey. He really wanted to finish his date. The thought of ending it early made him angry. He had worked so hard to get to this point, and he was nearly ready to fully commit to her. She was perfect. He doubted he would ever find another who possessed all of her qualities.

When both men began banging on the door and shouting, Scheper made his decision. He removed his knife from its sheath and placed the blade flat against Katie's cheek.

"Shhh," he hissed.

Her eyes grew wide and filled with terror. Scheper leaned down and nibbled on her bottom lip. He raised his head a couple of inches and stared into her eyes.

"I'm sorry," he said. "I felt like we really made a solid connection. I could have loved someone like you."

He turned the knife and sliced deeply across her throat, cutting clear through her windpipe. Blood gurgled in her lungs as she tried to scream out. He lay on top of her, staring into her eyes until the last breath hissed out and her stare went blank. He kissed her on the lips one last time, just as the front door splintered and crashed open.

Scheper reopened the bedroom window and slipped out into the pale moonlight.

CHAPTER 20

Rajneesh Ranch
Antelope, Oregon
8:40 P.M., Saturday, September, 12

LARRY COLLINS HAD just dozed off when the distant sound of Black Hawk rotors echoed across the prairie. He rubbed the tiredness from his eyes and leaned into his rifle scope. Still no movement from those at the ranch—the sound apparently hadn't reached them yet.

He took a few deep breaths, stretched his arms over his head and cracked his knuckles. He leaned into the scope again and watched the first signs of activity in the compound. The people around the fire pit stood and stared into the sky. One of the men ran to a large building and jerked the door open. Several people carrying guns poured from the doorway. Larry lined up on the first chest and squeezed the trigger. The man fell and rolled, tripping two others. Shots rang out from the rocks all around Larry. Several more men in the compound fell. Larry lined up on another chest and fired. The camp was in total chaos now. People ran everywhere. Larry scanned the faces he could see in the dim moonlight, but it was too dark to recognize Yates Asante, the leader of the ERB. Larry knew if they could end his life here, the eco-terrorist threat would be over.

The Black Hawk flew over Larry's head at treetop level and dropped into the valley. The first sidewinder flew from the bird, an orange flame trailing behind. The missile struck the first building. The explosion illuminated the compound in a sun-like flash, giving the group in the rocks clearer targets. As more missiles struck, the snipers increased their fire rate and accuracy. Larry took out eleven targets himself. Its missiles spent, the chopper banked at the end of the valley and strafed the remaining men that ran between the buildings that still stood. At the opposite end of the valley, the Black Hawk turned to make another run.

Larry looked through his scope again, searching for another target. Several eco-terrorists had dropped their guns and were breaking for the hillside behind a large barn. Larry let them go and searched for a more hostile target. He scanned the grounds in a fluid motion, stopping on a man kneeling in the dirt and holding a large weapon on his shoulder. It was Asante. Larry steadied himself, lined the crosshairs up just under the man's left shoulder, and squeezed the trigger. His rifle bucked again and Asante fell, but not before he triggered the weapon he'd been holding. A fireball streaked across the sky and struck the Black Hawk. The chopper went down in a burning ball of twisted metal and the bodies of its crew.

A loud cheer went up from the ERB members who remained fighting, and from those who'd been fleeing. Apparently, the downing of the chopper had renewed the bravery of those who wanted to escape just moments before. They ran back down the hill, picked up weapons, and joined the rest of the eco-terrorists in running for a large hangar near the airstrip. Larry lined up on three more and took them down before the rest disappeared into the hangar. He jumped up and shouted to his men: "Get down in the valley! Move! Now!"

Larry carefully picked his way down the rocks. They needed to get into the valley before the terrorists regrouped. He was also worried that there might be more weaponry in the building, including more RPGs like the one that took out the chopper. Up till now, the ERB had not possessed heavy weaponry. Larry wondered how such a weapon was in the camp. He also wondered how Yates had gained the knowledge to operate the RPG.

Halfway down to the valley, Larry had to slow as the slope became steeper and the foot and handholds became less available. He felt below him with his left foot, stretching his leg to the maximum to find the next solid spot to stand. His toe made contact just as a flash of light blinded him and the rocks he was climbing down shook. He let go of his handholds and settled on a narrow ledge just as rocks began rolling down from above. He tucked in tight to the wall and put his arms over his head. Basketball-sized boulders hit all around but somehow missed him. When the rocks quit rolling, he uncovered and looked to his left and right. The rock face a hundred yards to his right was nearly half blown out. There was no sign of the men who moments before had been scaling down.

Larry started down again, moving faster than before. He hit the ground running. Others from his team had also made it down and were converging on the hangar. The hangar door slammed shut as he and his remaining team members spread out around the structure, weapons raised. Larry searched his men's faces for Chad. He hadn't seen his friend since they'd started down the cliff face. Larry hoped he wasn't on the section that had blown.

The hangar door opened a crack and the barrel of an AK-47 emerged. Larry and his men dove to the ground as the rifle sprayed full auto over their heads. The door closed again. Larry rose to one knee, threw the rifle on his shoulder, and went through an entire mag, sweeping back and forth through the aluminum door. His men followed suit. Soon the entire hangar was riddled with bullet holes.

Larry wasn't sure how many men were in the hangar, but from the looks of the bodies littering the compound, he estimated it couldn't be more than fifteen or twenty. He needed to figure out a way to get them out on open ground or make them surrender. If he didn't, they could be locked in a standoff for days.

He knew they couldn't breach the door. If they tried it, they'd be caught in a pinch point at the doorway and be easy prey. There was a large airplane door, but that would be too heavy to open quickly enough. Tunneling in was a ridiculous idea since the concrete hangar floor was probably several inches thick. Another way in was the windows that surrounded the building just under the roofline, but this would also be impossible—they wouldn't be able to scale the building without making noise. They also didn't have enough ropes and gear needed to drop in to the floor if they breached the windows. If they hadn't lost the chopper or if they'd brought explosives, their entry would be easy.

Larry looked more closely at the windows. An idea began forming in his mind. He waved one of his men over.

"Bennett, go back to the top of the prairie," Larry said, "and get our horses. You'll need to come in at the head of the valley. It'll be several miles farther than the way we came down the rocks. You need to get back here before daylight."

Bennett rushed off toward the cliff. Larry returned his attention to the hangar. "You need to come out and give yourselves up!" he shouted. "There's no way out. We've got you completely surrounded, and there are more of us than you. It's time to give it up."

Their answer was the door cracking open again and more AK rounds filling the air.

These people were pissing Larry off. He got up from the dirt again and brushed dust from his chest. "Listen!" he yelled. "You have no chance. Asante is dead. No one is going to come and rescue you. It's just us. If you come out now, we'll let you walk away."

Larry waited for several minutes. No response. He made his way to each of his men and shared his new plan with them. Larry was now very worried about Chad. None of the men remembered seeing him after the chopper went down.

Larry walked back to his original spot outside the hangar, lay on his belly with his rifle on the ground in front of him, and closed his eyes for a few minutes. It was still nine hours until daylight. He and his team would rest in shifts until he could put his plan into motion.

An hour before daylight, Bennett approached and knelt in the dirt. "I've got 'em," he said.

Larry followed Bennett to the edge of the valley and found their horses there. He and Bennett worked quickly. First they chose five of the strongest-looking horses. Then swapped saddles with some of the other horses to make sure each of the five had the sturdiest saddle tree possible. They took a hundred-foot length of rope, folded it in half, and braided it. When they'd finished, Larry inspected the braids, looking for any frayed or weak spots. Satisfied that it was strong enough, he looped one end of the rope twice around each saddle tree, tied it off, walked in front of the animals, and pulled the rope's other end tight. He quietly led the five horses to within fifty feet of the hangar, removed a hatchet from the saddlebag of his own horse, and knelt in the dirt.

As soon as it was light enough to see, well before the sun actually made an appearance, Larry crept to the side of the hundred-foot-long hangar. He hefted the hatchet in his right hand and raised his left hand in the air. He took a few deep breaths while staring intently at the wall of sheet metal and the line of screws that ran horizontally, chest high, the length of the building in front of him. Most of his men—all but four who stood with weapons in front of the door on the side of the hangar—lined up behind and to the side of him.

Larry dropped his hand. The four men began firing at the door. He chopped into the sheet metal above and below the line of screws, exposing the two-by-six-foot steel beam the sheet metal was attached to. He chopped two holes, four inches around and four feet apart, and attached the braided rope around the beam. While Bennett walked the horses back, Larry ran to join the rest of his men. The creaking of metal and leather and the ripping of steel away from the rest of the frame could be heard over the gunfire. The entire wall gave way in a cloud of dust.

Larry and his men rushed into the hangar. Larry dove through the opening first and rolled into a crouch while bringing his weapon to his shoulder. The light was dim inside—it took his eyes a split second to adjust. Several shots came from the group in the hangar, and two of his men fell. He turned toward the shooters, found a target, and fired. The man fell. Larry found another and took him out. By now his men had fully breached the building and fully engaged the enemy. Eco-terrorists started dropping like flies. In a matter of no more than two to three minutes, it was over. The remaining members of the ERB threw their hands up in surrender.

The six remaining prisoners that were conscious and able to walk were quickly tied up. Larry radioed The Dalles to send two more choppers and some medical supplies for the wounded. He walked around the base of the cliff, looking at the faces of his dead and wounded men. A hundred yards from where he'd started, he found a man lying face down, several stones atop his back and legs. It was Chad.

Larry carefully removed the rocks, dragged Chad clear of the cliff, and checked his pulse. He was alive but badly beaten up. His right cheek was split the full length of his face. His nose was broken, and gashed badly enough that Larry could see all the way into his sinus cavities. His left arm was broken in a compound fracture and he'd lost some of his front teeth.

After placing the dirty jacket he'd taken from the sentry beneath Chad's head, Larry worked on trying to stop the bleeding from the broken arm and nose. With Chad stabilized, Larry returned to the hangar to survey the supplies stored there. Several crates of new AK-47s lined one wall. Larry examined one of the crates more closely and swore—the side revealed German writing. In addition to the automatic weapons, he found several thousand rounds of ammunition, several crates of RPGs, and hand grenades. Somehow, the Germans had gotten to the ERB and had been supplying them with weapons. Larry shook his head and cussed again. The scarred face of General Scheper popped into his memory. Larry was still cursing as he walked back into the light of sunrise.

Twenty minutes later, the two choppers set down near the hangar, medics with supplies pouring out. Everyone worked together, tending to the wounded that had a chance of survival. All in all, their losses could have been worse. Larry had lost six men, most of whom had been on the wall where the RPG struck it. Eleven were wounded, but only four severely enough to require major medical attention. The ERB had it much worse. Eighty-five had been killed, seven had minor injuries, and three were injured badly enough to necessitate further attention.

Chad was the first to be loaded onto a helo. After an hour, they were ready to evac the rest of the injured. The closest medical facility that could treat injuries this severe was at the oil refinery in Cheyenne. The makeshift hospital at The Dalles was closer, but no one there could provide everything the injured needed. Due to job accidents at the refinery, they'd set up the Cheyenne hospital soon after bringing the facility back on line. They would restore more hospitals across the West as soon as the grid was working again.

Larry decided to ride in the chopper with Chad. His men would return to The Dalles with the horses and the eleven healthy prisoners. They would hold them in the old fallout shelter under the powerhouse until they figured out what to do with them. Larry was tempted to just execute them and leave them in the prairie, but couldn't bring himself to give that order. He also believed they might have valuable information on Scheper and the German forces. After Larry had Chad secure in the hospital, he would fly back to Seneca for a week, then return to The Dalles to interrogate the prisoners and resume his work.

The choppers lifted above the valley walls and banked toward the east, heading directly into the sun. Larry looked out the side window at the endless rolling prairies and yawned. He leaned back in his seat, closed his eyes, and let the whir of the rotors sing him to sleep.

CHAPTER 21

Greeley, Colorado
6:00 A.M., Sunday, September 13

SARAH SAT STRAIGHT up in bed and threw her covers off, knocking her pillow to the floor. For a minute she couldn't remember where she was or how she'd gotten there. Jakob stirred next to her and slowly opened his eyes.

"What is it?" he asked.

"Nothing," she said. "I just couldn't remember where I was for a minute."

"Well, if you're done giving me pneumonia, lay back down and give me some covers."

Jakob grabbed her around the waist and pulled her down next to him, then pulled the covers back over them both. He kissed her between the shoulder blades, then worked his way down her body with his lips. Sarah lay with her back to him and didn't react until he kissed her on her hip. Then she quickly threw the covers off again and jumped out of bed. She lit a candle, retrieved her dirty, tattered dress from a chair in the corner of the room, and quickly put it on. The garment made her feel dirty and worn on the inside. She looked down at her grimy arms and tried to wipe the smudges off.

Jakob pulled the covers up to his chin, sunk back down into the soft pillow, and sighed. Sarah finished buttoning her dress, slipped on her holy stockings and boots, then walked out of the room, closing the door behind her.

In the hallway, she leaned against the wall and slid to the floor. She laid her head in her hands and began to cry. How could she go on in this unfamiliar, violent world she was now a part of? Everything she thought she knew about herself was now in question. Her life as an Amish girl had been stable and comforting. Even when she'd stepped outside of her convictions and killed the men that had threatened her way of life, she had always been able to go home. Her father, her faith, and her community had been the solid rock that held her life together. But something dark had entered her. She hadn't even hesitated about shooting that boy in Missouri. She'd just raised her pistol and fired, like he was merely an obstacle to be removed. By killing him, she'd destroyed a place deep inside herself. Now she felt the evil struggling with whatever good remained within her.

Without her Amish foundation to turn back to, she wasn't sure if she would ever recover, and that hurt even more than seeing the terror in the boy's eyes as she pulled the trigger, or seeing the pain and anguish on his mother's face just before Julia had struck her down.

Sarah had thought that when she married Jakob, she would never want for anything. He was supposed to be a familiar island in the storms of life. She thought he would be her connection to her old life, but he was separating himself from their past more with each passing day. He had tried to comfort her after the incident in Missouri, but she had rejected any affection he showed. He was still trying, but she refused to accept it. She knew now, as sure as she had ever known anything, that she no longer deserved the love of anyone.

A door down the hallway opened, and Julia stepped out, holding a flashlight. She wore a clean set of blue jeans and a red button-down shirt, and carried a thick blanket. Sarah wondered where the new outfit had come from. Julia had disappeared the afternoon before. Sarah hadn't seen her since.

In the dark, Julia didn't seem to see Sarah sitting on the floor feeling sorry for herself. Julia walked down the hallway and out of sight. A few seconds later, Sarah heard the front door close. She was once again sitting alone in the darkness.

It seemed so easy for Julia. As far as Sarah could tell, the fact that none of them could ever go back to their village didn't bother her friend at all. In fact, Julia seemed to revel in her newfound freedom and welcomed each new adventure with excitement and anticipation. Even the struggles and dark things the trio had done weren't enough to break the girl's spirit. She faced each new day with hope.

Sarah stood, wiped her eyes dry with a corner of her dirty dress, and followed Julia outside. The sky had begun to grow gray in the east, and the air was cold. Sarah wished she would've put on a jacket. She found her friend sitting on the ground, her back to the trunk of an Aspen tree, the blanket wrapped around her shoulders. She was reading her Bible and waiting for the sunrise. Sarah sat down beside her. Julia wrapped her arm around her friend and shared the blanket.

"How can you read God's Word, or even talk to him, without a head covering?" Sarah asked, pointing at the tattered Bible on her friend's lap.

"I just do," Julia said. "Do you really believe that God is so easily offended that he can't hear from his daughters unless their heads are covered? He hears from men, and their heads aren't covered. Aren't we loved by him the same as men? We didn't have a choice to be in the situation we're in right now. I believe that when things become the darkest for his children, he is more offended if they don't come to him for help."

They sat together and watched the sun come up. When the sun was fully risen and the warmth had filled them both, Sarah felt a little less somber. Julia stood, grabbed her by the hand, and pulled her to her feet. She looked Sarah up and down and shook her head.

"Come on," Julia said.

"Where?" asked Sarah.

Julia pointed at Sarah's outfit and shook her head. "We've got to do something about that."

Sarah reluctantly let Julia lead her off. Where, she wasn't sure.

They walked for nearly fifteen minutes past rows of abandoned houses and into a retail section of town. Sarah had the same eerie feeling she got each time they moved through an abandoned community. She wondered where everyone had gone, and what horrors they must have endured to make them leave their homes and all of their belongings.

Julia led Sarah to the Greeley Mall. Once there, they walked directly to a store with a sign that said "Buckle," but didn't go inside. On the sidewalk was a large aluminum water trough set on cinder blocks, the half-burned remnants of a recent fire underneath. Julia dumped the dirty water from the trough onto the sidewalk.

"Get out of that dress," she said. "I'll be right back."

"It's cold," Sarah protested. "Why do I need to get undressed?"

"Just do as I ask, please."

"Where did all of this come from?" Sarah said, waving her hand at the trough and bricks holding it up.

Julia pointed up the road to a Wilco Farm store, grabbed two empty, five-gallon plastic buckets that sat next to the trough, and walked across the road and down the bank of a canal.

Sarah did as she was told and stood next to the trough shivering in the blanket, while Julia made several more trips to the water. Ten trips later, the tub was nearly half full. Julia relit the fire, grabbed some wooden shelves from the store, and fed the flames. After twenty minutes the water began to steam.

"Get in," Julia said.

Sarah protested again while looking around the area. "We're right out in the open. What if someone sees me?"

"There's no one else around. Now would you just please get in the tub?"

Sarah dropped her blanket just as a slight breeze blew across her bare skin. She shivered and gingerly stepped into the water. In spite of the embarrassment of Julia seeing her completely naked, she let herself relax and lay back. The hot water felt amazing and instantly warmed her to the core. Goosebumps popped up on her arms and legs. It had been months since she had a hot bath. The few times she'd tried to clean up in whatever creek or river she came across, she had instantly felt dirty again once she put on her dress.

Julia walked off and entered a Bath and Body Works store. She returned holding a bottle of sweet-smelling shampoo and some gardenia body wash. Sarah tried both, feeling a little ashamed at using such alluringly scented hygiene products. Yet they did stir her senses. Such things had always been forbidden. She had grown up on homemade unscented soaps.

When Sarah was thoroughly washed and dried with the soft cotton towel Julia provided, Julia led her into Buckle. Julia looked her friend up and down, then selected a crisp new pair of blue jeans and a bright green button-down blouse. Sarah had never worn anything but a dress. If her family could see her wearing this, they would be even more ashamed of who she had become.

Nevertheless, Sarah put on the outfit and admired herself in a full-length mirror. They both laughed when Sarah poked her butt out and looked over her shoulder, winking and fluttering her eyelashes at her reflection. She instantly felt guilty, but it was the first bit of joy she'd experienced since Missouri. Sarah quickly looked away and frowned.

"I can't wear these clothes," she said. "And there is no way I'm going to let Jakob see me looking like...like Delilah."

Julia grabbed Sarah by the hand and led her back to the tub in front of the store. She pointed at the tattered dress wadded up on the sidewalk. "That hideous thing," she said, "needs to be burned."

Sarah lifted the garment and stared at the holy gray fabric. This dress symbolized the last remaining connection to her former life. She knew that once it was gone, the last piece of her that was Amish would go with it. Julia stood next to her, not saying a word. She couldn't destroy the dress. Sarah turned back toward the store. She wanted to put it back on and hide away in the familiarity again. Julia grabbed her by the arm and turned her around.

"You have to do this," Julia said. "Burn it."

Sarah thrust the dress toward her friend. Julia lifted her hand and pushed it away.

"You need to do this yourself, Sarah."

Sarah stood there a few minutes and silently asked God for forgiveness. Then she gritted her teeth and tossed the dress onto the fire. Her eyes filled with tears. She choked down a sob as the flames licked at the soft cotton fabric. A full five minutes after the garment had turned to ash, Julia gently took hold of Sarah's hand and led her back into the clothing store to pick out a few more outfits.

The duo spent the next two hours going from store to store. They went into an REI and loaded up backpacks with camping gear. They returned to the Bath and Body Works for some more smell-good items, picked out some comfortable sunglasses at the Sunglass Hut, and finally ended up in a Victoria's Secret. That store proved to be too much of an assault on Sarah's modesty, so they called an end to their shopping spree and returned to the house they'd stayed in the night before.

Jakob was waiting for them on the porch when they walked into the front yard. He stomped down the stairs to meet them, waving his arms in the air. "Where have you been?" he said. "I was starting to get worried…"

He stopped mid-lecture, dropped his arms to his sides, and stared at his bride.

"Do you like it?" Sarah asked. She turned in a circle, modeling her new outfit for him. "I have to say, it's pretty unfair that you men get to wear pants and we do not. These are so darn comfortable."

Jakob walked up to her, grabbed her around the middle, and hugged her tightly. He buried his face in her hair and inhaled deeply. "You…you smell amazing," he managed to say without removing his nose. He squeezed her even tighter, moved his hands to her hips, and pulled her lower body to his.

"Maybe we should take a little nap before we go on," he whispered.

Sarah giggled and playfully pushed him away. "Later," she said. "Now let's get going. I want to find some more elk and actually enjoy the journey." She started to turn away, then stopped and slowly turned back to face her husband.

"I'm sorry," she said. "You haven't deserved to be treated the way you have."

Jakob cupped Sarah's face in his hands. "You have nothing to apologize to me for," he said. "I'm sorry you've had to endure all that you have."

They saddled the horses, stowed their gear, and mounted up. Sarah turned to Julia, smiled, and mouthed "Thank you."

Julia returned the smile and nodded.

They rode out of Greeley at midday. The sun was shining and the rays felt warmer and more comforting than Sarah could ever remember. Her mind was clearer. Once again she had hope and a taste for adventure. The dark memories still lingered just beneath the surface of her mind. She could still hear the woman in Missouri calling out to her son, Darin. But her Amish convictions had been buried deeper, almost out of reach of her memory. Those convictions, she realized, were among the sources of her self-torment. She would always feel sadness and regret over the lives she had taken, especially the little boy's. But the self-hatred was now dulled, as if covered by the ashes of her burned, tattered gray dress.

CHAPTER 22

Nirschell Ranch
Seneca, Oregon
8:30 A.M., Sunday, September 13

MICHELLE NIRSCHELL ROLLED over and reached for her husband. Her hand made contact with the bottom bedsheet where Levi had slept for twenty-three years. Her eyes snapped open, the realization that his pillow was the only thing next to her slamming into her consciousness. She pulled his pillow close and held it tight, imagining that his scent still lingered on the pillowcase. Michelle drew as much as she could into her nostrils, held her breath, and shut her eyes. An image of Levi on horseback formed in her mind. The sun lit up his face. She heard his booming laugh as he watched their son, Adam, try to wrestle a Hereford steer to the ground that was lassoed and attached to Levi's saddle. She squeezed her eyes tighter. A tear slid out, rolled down to the end of her nose, hung briefly, and fell onto his pillow. More images of Levi flashed in her mind, each forming and disappearing quicker than the last, until finally the images came so fast that they became a swirling, unintelligible blob.

Michelle practically smothered herself in his pillow and released the rest of the tears and moans of anguish that had been fighting to burst from deep within her.

"Why God...why?"

Those three words had been the extent of Michelle's prayer life since Levi was taken from her. He was consumed by a country that didn't deserve his love. Americans had allowed evil men to take over and rule their country. In spite of all the warning signs from history, they'd voted for these men to rule them time and again. When the evil was fully realized, Levi had left his family, led the fight against their tyranny, and paid the ultimate price.

Michelle had always been someone who prayed without ceasing. She'd made no important decision or move that was not first prefaced by a conversation with her Lord. Now that Levi was gone, she couldn't bring herself to speak to a God who had allowed him to be killed. She had felt nearly instant bitterness and anger toward him, and as the days, weeks, months, and finally years passed, that bitterness and anger had nearly turned to hate. It churned in her soul like a black, angry cloud. Some days she didn't even get out of bed. She would lie there all day and cry until her very soul was raw and wrung out. Fatigue would eventually overtake her and she would drift off to another night of fitful sleep.

Michelle pulled the pillow down to her stomach and wrapped her arms and legs around it in a death grip. Her sobbing grew louder, and her stomach burned with the pain of loss and emptiness. She lay this way for several minutes, engulfed in the blackness, until a faint tapping at her doorway brought her back.

"Mom?" It was Adam calling from the hallway, a tremble in his voice. "You okay?"

Michelle released Levi's pillow, wiped her eyes with a corner of the bedsheet, and compose herself before answering. "I'm fine, buddy. What's up?"

There was a long pause before Adam answered. "Um, I uh, um, thought... Were you crying?"

Now it was Michelle's turn to pause. "I'm fine, sweetie. You can come in."

Adam slowly opened the door and peeked around the corner with his big blue eyes. Michelle's breath caught a little as she looked at him. It had been over three years since Levi was taken, and in that time Adam had nearly become a man. He had grown two heads taller, his once spindly legs had bulked up, he had broadened across the chest, and for the first time Michelle noticed a slight layer of peach fuzz on his upper lip. It struck her just how much he was beginning to look like his father.

Michelle hadn't been there for her children like she should have after Levi died. She was too consumed with her own sorrow and torment. After Larry Collins had returned to the ranch with the news, Adam had retreated to the comfort of the barn and Levi's workshop, where he had spent countless hours with his dad building bows and fletching arrows. Adam had been looking forward to elk hunting with his father, an adventure that would never be. He'd dragged a sleeping bag and his pillow out of the house and slept on the sawdust-covered floor of the shop for weeks.

Michelle's nineteen-year-old daughter, Jillian, took Levi's death even harder. She had lost her new husband, Brett, just a few months earlier. Levi was supposed to be there for them forever. He was supposed to be the constant, supportive rock. The shoulder to cry on, the man who would always wipe Michelle's tears away when life got rough, who was supposed to fix all of her problems. After Brett's death, and again after Levi's, the family had rallied around Jillian and Michelle. Her friend Debbie became the main shoulder to lean on, with help from Amanda Collins. Everything was just beginning to normalize when Debbie made the decision to move closer to The Dalles to be with her husband, Sam. He was charged with leading the defense of the resistance rebuilding efforts, and needed to be on site. After Debbie left with her son, Jake, Jillian stayed holed up in her home up the canyon for weeks at a time. Michelle didn't know what to say to her daughter anyway. She still wasn't ready to talk to her about what had happened.

Adam walked to the edge of the bed, his eyes seemingly transfixed by his feet. Michelle pulled the covers back and patted the bed beside her. Adam climbed in and allowed his mother to snuggle up to him and pull the covers over them both. Neither of them spoke for several minutes.

"Mom?" Adam whispered. "I'm tired of being sad. I don't want to be angry anymore, and I don't think Dad would want me to either. Can we go see Jillian today, and maybe have a picnic in Kelly Meadow?"

Michelle swallowed the lump in her throat that was threatening to choke her. Kelly Meadow was the last place Levi had taken his son turkey hunting. It was the first place he had taken her for a picnic when they were dating. It was where Levi had proposed to her on bended knee, and where Brett Hanson had proposed to Jillian.

"I suppose we could get out of the house for a bit," Michelle said. "But are you sure you want to go to Kelly Meadow? It's a little far. I'm not sure I feel much like a long horseback ride."

"I'm sure, Mom," Adam said. "There's something I need to take up there for Dad."

Adam's words split Michelle's emotional dam wide open once again. The tears flowed. Her son reached up with a man-sized finger and touched Michelle's cheek. "Don't cry Mom, it's really cool, and I know Dad would love it. Wait here, I'll be right back."

Adam jumped out of the bed and ran from the room. Michelle closed her eyes and was transported back to the day Larry Collins had returned to their ranch with the news. The whirring blades of the Black Hawk helicopter had echoed across Bear Valley. The excitement at the approaching aircraft nearly overwhelmed her. She was cooking bacon and eggs, Adam was out doing chores, and Amanda Collins was standing in the open front door of the guest house, sipping the day's first cup of coffee and immersing herself in the warm spring morning.

Michelle had run onto the front porch and squinted into the sun, trying to make out the face of Levi as the Black Hawk touched down in the pasture. Swirls of excitement and anticipation bounced around in her stomach. She felt like she had when he'd picked her up for their first date. The anticipation of him stepping off the helicopter, holding her in his arms, and lying with her that evening caused her skin to tingle. The door of the chopper opened, Larry Collins emerged, and the hollow thud of Amanda's wooden leg could be heard over the whir of the blades as she hurried across her porch and down the lane. Michelle stood, unblinking, as Amanda jumped into the waiting arms of her husband. She watched the two slam together, arms locked tightly around each other. She looked intently at Larry's face as he gently broke his embrace and pushed Amanda aside. He turned toward Michelle. His eyes connected with hers and she knew. She didn't need to look at the open door of the empty helicopter to know that Levi was not coming home. She fell to her knees, bowed her head, and moaned deep, primal sounds of anguish. The blood pounded in her ears and her face burned. She felt as though a blade had pierced her abdomen, thrust upward, and sliced into her heart. The world began to swirl, moving in and out of focus. Then everything went black.

The sound of Adam's bare feet running across hardwood floors yanked Michelle back to the present. She quickly used the corner of the bed-sheet to again dry her eyes, finishing just as Adam entered the bedroom.

"It's pretty cool, huh Mom?" Adam held up a large wooden cross. It was painted in a camo pattern complete with sticks and leaves. Two fir arrows were attached to the front, complete with two bladed-razor broadheads. The word "Dad" was painted a little sloppily with blocky letters across the middle, and an American flag was painted at the top.

"I fletched the arrows with the feathers from the last turkey I got with Dad, just like he taught me," Adam said, a big grin on his face. "I used Predator for the camo. It was his favorite."

Michelle threw back the covers, jumped out of bed, and grabbed Adam in a bear hug. "Careful, Mom!" Adam yelled as he pulled away and held the cross behind him. Michelle again swallowed the tears that were trying to claw their way out and forced a smile.

"I think it's beautiful, son, and I think your Dad would love it and be proud of your craftsmanship."

"Beautiful?" Adam asked, seeming a little offended. "I was kind of expecting cool, or maybe awesome."

"It's very cool indeed," said Michelle.

Adam smiled again, trotted out of the bedroom, and yelled over his shoulder: "I'm gonna go do my chores, then saddle the horses so we can go. You want to ride Matilda or Gracie?"

Michelle stood unmoving for several seconds. "Gracie," she finally said.

Adam smiled and disappeared down the hallway. A few minutes later she heard the front door close. Michelle sat back down on the edge of the bed and reopened the floodgates.

By the time Adam had finished his chores and saddled the horses, Michelle had gotten dressed and managed to fix her son some eggs, bacon, and toast. Adam sat down at the table.

"I think I'll see if Amanda wants to go with us," Michelle said.

"Okay, Mom."

Amanda Collins had not been the best company the last few days. She'd stopped speaking to Larry when her husband had told her he was going on a trip to take care of some delays in their progress on the powerlines. Michelle and Amanda both knew that meant he was going to be in danger, and most likely involved in some sort of combat.

Michelle had been close with Amanda before Levi had died, but as the loss of her husband set in, the two women had grown apart. Michelle had avoided Amanda after Levi had died. In some small way, Michelle had blamed Larry for Levi not coming home. She was also jealous of Larry and Amanda's relationship. In an unfair world, the fact that Levi was killed while others continued on as before was the king of crappy outcomes. Levi had fought harder than anyone against Hartley's evil, yet he was the only one from their ranch community that had paid the ultimate price. In time, Michelle forgave Amanda for the perceived sin, and more importantly had forgiven herself for the misdirected anger and blame toward her friend.

Michelle walked onto the porch and lightly knocked on the door. She heard the steady clumps of Amanda's wooden leg striking the hardwood floors as she came to the door.

"Good morning," Michelle said.

"Hi."

Michelle shifted her weight and didn't look Amanda in the eye as she spoke: "Adam and I are going to ride up to Kelly Meadow and have a picnic after we stop and get Jillian. You want to come along?"

Amanda shocked Michelle by answering with no hesitation: "Yes."

Michelle returned to her house and pulled out the old wicker picnic basket from under the sink. She fixed sandwiches, wrapped up chicken left over from dinner the night before, and dished some potato salad into a Tupperware container. After gathering paper plates, plastic silverware, and napkins, she opened the basket and began packing. A happy memory from another day in the meadow settled into her mind and she closed her eyes.

"Is there any more chicken?" Levi asked while standing there with an empty paper plate. "I swear, nobody fries a bird as good as you. Not even the colonel can fry chicken like that."

Michelle stood and laughed. "Is it better than your mother's?" she asked.

Levi looked around, ducked his head low, and whispered: "Way better, but if she asks me I'll deny it." He grabbed her around the waist and pulled her down onto the red checkered blanket. She struggled, trying to get away, and he squeezed her tighter. She gave up and lay in his arms, laughing. He leaned in close and kissed her. She kissed him back, raised a trembling hand, and ran her fingers through his hair. He grinned, rolled onto his side, and pulled her closer. The smell of green meadow grass and wild roses caressed her nostrils. The songs of birds singing in the tops of giant Ponderosa Pines was one of the most beautiful things she'd ever heard.

"What kind of bird is that singing?" she asked.

"That is the Oregon state bird," said Levi. "Western Meadowlark."

"They're so pretty. We have nothing like that in Florida."

Levi got up from the blanket, went to his horse, and fished around in his saddlebag. He put something in his front pocket and walked back to their picnic. "I love you, Michelle," he said. "I love you like I've never loved before. This past year has been the happiest time in my life. I love everything about you. I love your family."

"Even my dad?" Michelle asked with a big smile on her face.

"Even him," Levi answered. "I saw your dad when I was at Fort Bliss last month, and we were able to have some time to just talk and get to know each other a little better."

Levi got on one knee and continued. "I have never been someone who jumps without thinking. One thing my military service has taught me is to look at all things carefully before deciding anything. Well, I have looked up, down, and sideways, and I see no other way forward than this."

He reached into his front pocket and pulled out a small box covered in red velvet. Michelle's breath caught. Her vision turned blurry when he opened it, revealing the gold engagement ring. "Michelle Marie Nelson, I want to spend the rest of my life with you. Will you marry me?"

"Mom?"

Adam walked into the kitchen wearing blue and green flannel and hiking boots, as well as, strapped to his hip, his father's Sig .40. Michelle noticed again just how much her son looked like Levi on the day he'd proposed. She smiled through tear-filled eyes and they walked out the front door together.

CHAPTER 23

Ten miles east of Wellington, Colorado
5:40 P.M., Tuesday, September 15

SARAH SHIFTED HER position on her horse, glanced over her shoulder at Jakob, and offered him a hint of a smile. Jakob, a few feet behind, smiled back and blew her a kiss. She rolled her eyes and turned away, not letting him see the full smile that had formed on her lips.

Since leaving Greeley two days earlier, she had felt like a different person. The anger at herself, at her father, and at God had pulled back like an outgoing tide. There were still feelings of guilt and shame over some of the things she had done. But now that some of her other burdens had lightened, she could smile once in a while and try to enjoy the world God had created. She had prayed nearly continuously since leaving Greeley. She wondered how she could have gone so long without talking to God. It was as natural to her as breathing.

Jakob rode up beside her and held out his hand. She locked her fingers in his and they rode side by side for several miles, neither speaking. Finally, Sarah shifted her weight and let go of Jakob's hand. She was

getting tired of riding bareback. Even though it was much more comfortable in her jeans, she desperately wanted a saddle.

"I think we should try and find some saddles in the next town," she
said. "Maybe poke around in some of the abandoned ranches. This bareback stuff is getting old."

"Sounds good to me," Jakob said. "I've never been much good at
riding bareback. I like the feel of a solid chunk of leather between my
legs, and a nice sturdy tree to rest my hands on."

Julia rode up beside her friends. "How far you wanting to go before
we stop for the night?" she asked.

Sarah shrugged her shoulders. "I don't know. But we passed a sign a
few miles back saying a town called Wellington was fourteen miles. I
think we'll make that before dark, and I would sure like to find a soft
bed to sleep in. My back is killing me after the last couple nights."

"You're not getting soft on me are you?" Jakob asked.

Sarah playfully punched him in the arm. "You wanna see soft? Get
down off that horse, and I'll show you who's soft."

"No, ma'am," he said. "I hear you fight dirty."

Jakob and Julia had a good laugh at her expense. Sarah shook her
head and grinned wider than she had in a long time.

An hour before dark, they rode into an industrial area. It was the outskirts of Wellington.

Most of the buildings they passed were small, single story, and metal
framed. All of them looked abandoned—except for the biggest one, which
appeared to be a warehouse. A ten-foot chain link fence surrounded it
and several smaller buildings scattered on the grounds. The main entry
gate was closed. A large sign on it read: "Ag Co Farm & Feed."

As they rode past, Sarah saw movement through a partially open
door of the warehouse. She studied the surroundings carefully, and soon
noticed men peering out at them from the shadows around the building.
They all had rifles hanging across their chests.

"Let's go," she said, and kicked her horse into a trot. Jakob and Julia
followed suit.

"What's the hurry?" Jakob asked.

"Nothing," she said. "I just want to get into town and have time to look around before dark."

The trio had gone a few hundred yards when Jakob reined up. "Look," he said. "It's a saddle shop."

Sure enough, there was a small building with a wood carving of a horse on top. Big red letters above the broken front windows spelled out "Wellington Leather Works and Saddlery."

"We'll come back," Sarah said without slowing her horse.

"What's the matter with you?" Jakob yelled after her.

Sarah still didn't slow or turn around. She hoped he would follow. A few seconds later he rode up on her left side. Julia rejoined the group on her right.

"That big gated area we just passed had several armed men around it watching us," Sarah said.

Jakob looked over his shoulder. "I didn't see anybody."

"Don't turn around," Sarah hissed.

The trio rode for another ten minutes and reached a residential area. It looked like a typical town. Neat houses with white picket fences lined the streets. Some had vegetable gardens planted where lawns most likely had once been. A group of about ten children were kicking a red rubber ball in the middle of the street. They stopped and stared as the trio rode past. Several more people came out of their houses and stared at the teenagers on horseback.

Sarah suddenly felt uneasy. They hadn't seen other people since they'd left Missouri. With the cannibals' camp still fresh in her mind, these strangers made her nervous. Everything seemed peaceful. No one seemed aggressive or angry about their arrival. But she knew she'd have been a lot happier to find Wellington deserted.

They rode on into the middle of town. Most of the stores and restaurants were abandoned, with the exception of a small brick building between hardware and fishing stores. The place looked cozy and inviting, but Sarah hesitated. They might be able to get a meal and find out where to get a bed for the night, but they also might be walking into danger. They pulled their horses next to the others tied in front of the building and dismounted. A young couple exited the front door, laughing. They paid no attention to the newcomers and walked down the street.

Sarah shrugged her shoulders at her companions. They tied the horses up and cautiously walked in, stopping in the middle of the doorway. The room was crowded. The smell of cigarette smoke and roasting meat hung heavy in the stale air. None of them had ever been in a restaurant, and they weren't sure how it worked. Sarah felt panicky and fought the urge to run back outside.

"Excuse me," someone said behind her. They stepped aside and allowed an older gentleman to shuffle past. He chose an empty table and sat down. A few minutes later, a teenage girl much younger than Sarah brought the man a glass and a pitcher of water. She poured the man some water and they talked for a couple of minutes. Two more minutes passed and the girl returned to the table with a plate of meat and potatoes.

"Come on," Sarah said, tugging on Jakob's coat sleeve.

She led the group to an empty table in a corner. They sat down and watched the other tables. The young girl came over with water and glasses.

"We're out of elk roast," the girl said, "but we have deer burger left, and plenty of potatoes."

Sarah and her companions sat stiff and silent.

"Cat got your tongues?"

"Cat?" Sarah asked.

The girl laughed. "Do you want me to bring you food or did you come for the beer?"

"I'm sorry," Sarah said. "We've, um, never been in a restaurant before. We're not sure exactly how this all works."

The girl squinted her eyes. "Okay," she said. "You tell me what you want, I bring it to you, and when you're finished, you pay for it. A meal will cost you fifteen 9 millimeter rounds, or twenty-five other pistol rounds, or ten rounds of any caliber rifle ammunition."

Sarah looked at her companions, then back to the girl. "Can you come back in a few minutes?"

The girl shrugged her shoulders, turned on her heels, and walked into the kitchen. The trio talked it over and decided they could spare some of their 9 millimeter rounds for a hot meal.

Sarah sent Jakob out to get the ammunition and relaxed. She realized they hadn't had a good meal since they'd left Allen's house in Ohio. His smiling face flashed into her mind, and the familiar darkness returned. She really did miss him.

The group got their meal and wolfed it down, barely taking a breath and not speaking a word. When they had finished, they all leaned back in their chairs. Sarah giggled when Jakob reached down and loosened his pants just like her father used to do after a hearty meal.

The restaurant started to empty out. The waitress returned with a small metal bowl and asked for payment. Jakob counted out forty-five 9 millimeter rounds and smiled at the girl. They talked with her for several minutes and learned what they needed. Not many people in town rode horses. Most of the animals had been butchered a few years earlier in the wake of the collapse, so there was no need for a working saddle shop. The girl did mention the shop they'd passed on the way in, and that it was likely the group's best hope of finding saddles and tack. They asked her about the men at the big warehouse, but she knew nothing about them. Most people thought the place was abandoned. They had everything they needed in their community, so few people ventured out that far.

The girl gave them directions to some empty houses on the far end of town where they might stay for the night. They thanked her and got up to leave.

"If you're going to stay in town," the girl said, "make sure you get to a house before dark, and lock the doors. The people in these parts are wary of strangers, especially now. The waitress that used to work here disappeared a few days ago after a stranger came in and gave her a hard time."

It was dark and the moon had started to rise when they found the houses the girl had told them about. Sarah had been jumpy since leaving the restaurant, and was relieved when they picked out a small, single-story home and moved their things inside. They picked out their rooms, unpacked, bundled up in heavy jackets, and headed for the saddle shop. Sarah was reluctant to go back into the night after the warning, but they did need saddles for the rest of the journey, and the darkness was their best chance of getting what they needed. If they were quiet, they had less chance of being seen by those at the warehouse.

At the saddle shop, they peered in the front windows. Judging by the mess inside, it had already been ransacked, but some merchandise still sat on the shelves. Several saddles lined one wall. On the back wall hung a few bridles and bits. It was all the tack they would need.

While Jakob crawled through one of the broken windows to open the locked door, Sarah walked to the edge of the building and looked toward the big warehouse. Light shone through the upper windows. Faintly, she could hear people talking. Who were these men? Why were they holed up in a warehouse? Curiosity tugged at her.

Sarah slipped away from her companions and jogged down the road toward the building, keeping to the shadows. She got to the compound fence and slowly walked around the chain-link perimeter, looking for an opening. At last, she found a small, loose section of fence that was a few inches off the ground. She wormed her way under, crept to the edge of the warehouse, and put her ear to the wall. The talking was louder now, though she still couldn't make out any words.

She walked to the back of the building and looked for a window. The only windows she could see were about twenty feet off the ground. She turned a corner and nearly ran into a giant stack of wooden crates and pallets leaning against the wall. The tower ended a few feet below the window line. Twenty feet from the wall stood two plastic silos the size of a small house, mounted above a truck loading ramp. The tallest silo was almost as high as the windows.

Sarah climbed the ladder on the side of the hopper at the bottom of the silo, pulled herself onto a steel platform above the fill hole, and tried to peer into the warehouse. Even when she stood tiptoes, it was still impossible to see inside. She climbed back down and looked again at the stack of pallets. She studied the shaky tower for a minute, then committed herself to climb it. She was nearly to the top of the stack when it swayed underneath her. She froze as dizziness threatened to knock her off balance. When the movement stopped, she continued up.

Near the top, Sarah raised her head around the corner of a pallet. With satisfaction, she saw that she was a couple of feet above the window. When she took in the view through the window, however, she gasped and nearly fell. As many as two hundred, maybe more, men in military uniforms lounged in the facility. The warehouse was also filled with military vehicles, including tanks on trailers hooked to semi-trucks. It all seemed so out of place. They hadn't seen anything military during their entire journey from Pittsburgh. Why now? Why here? She had been told about a war in the West three years earlier, but as far as she knew, that war had ended. She wondered if coming out west was such a good idea. If she'd thought she was heading into a war zone, she would have never left Pennsylvania. She and Jakob would have been happy building a small cabin in the forest and growing old in the land they were born in.

"Sarah!" Jakob hissed.

Startled, Sarah flinched, and jerked her eyes away from the window. The tower started to wobble again. She silently cursed her husband. Hadn't he learned his lesson the night she was shot?

Sarah quickly climbed down and sprinted for the opening in the fence. Jakob was just starting to crawl under when she reached it.

"Go back to the horses," she hissed. "Run!"

Sarah crawled under the fence, jumped to her feet, and started to run just as the wooden tower of pallets gave way, crashing down and bouncing off the side of the building. Sarah didn't turn around, instead picking up speed and overtaking Jakob. At the saddle shop, Julia had all three horses saddled and outfitted. They jumped on their backs and galloped off.

Sarah looked over her shoulder. Several men with flashlights were searching the compound. She kicked her horse into high gear and tore back toward town.

CHAPTER 24

Cheyenne, Wyoming
9:00 A.M., Thursday, September 17

LARRY COLLINS LOADED his rifle and his duffle bag into the side of the Black Hawk. He paused, unzipped the bag, and removed a turquoise and gold bracelet. He turned it in his hands and smiled. Amanda would be so happy to see him when he flew in that afternoon, and to see the new bauble. It had cost him an AR-15, a new knife, and three hundred rounds of .223 ammo, but he would have paid twice that much for whatever happiness it would give to the bride of his youth. She had sacrificed so much since leaving their old life.

A group of Native Americans had ridden by the refinery a few days earlier, just after he'd gotten Chad checked into the hospital. Larry's men had fed the visitors and talked with them for hours. Their group had been travelling since a few months after the collapse, just as their ancestors had done hundreds of years earlier. In the summer months, they moved to the high mountain peaks and rich meadows of Yellowstone, and in the fall they made for the plains to wait out the cold winters. They lived on migrating buffalo, deer, elk, and native plants.

Larry was a little jealous of their way of life, and how they seemed to be living one hundred fifty years in the past. He had always been fascinated by tales of life out west in the 1800s. If he could pick one time period to travel back to, that would be it. Larry closed his eyes and imagined himself as a mountain man, trapping beaver, living off the land, and raising a family in a one-room cabin.

"Sir?" One of his men had walked up to the helicopter.

"What is it?" Larry asked.

"Three people just rode in, and I think you'll want to hear what they have to say."

Larry followed him to the cafeteria.

Three teenagers—two girls and one boy—sat at a table, loudly smacking their lips as they chewed on bacon and eggs. He smiled, shook each one's hand, and sat down. The boy and oldest girl looked to be eighteen or nineteen years old, while the youngest couldn't have been more than fifteen or sixteen. They all appeared to be in pretty good health, not overly skinny.

Larry sat and hung on their every word as Sarah, Jakob, and Julia recalled their journey from Pennsylvania. When they told him of the group of men and military equipment in Wellington, he knew his trip home to see Amanda would have to wait. The trio agreed to go back to the town and show him where the warehouse was.

While the three friends finished their breakfast, Larry left to gather up gear and a few men for the trip. The soldiers had to be German. Larry knew exactly where all of his troops were, and if any had made a move to Wellington, he would have known about it. The only reason for the Germans to be this close to Cheyenne had to be a planned attack on the refinery. He recalled the weapons they'd found at the Rajneesh ranch with the ERB. On one hand, it made perfect sense that Scheper would utilize the enviro army to distract his men from their efforts at the dam, but something told him the ERB had not completely executed the plan. It didn't seem likely that Scheper would instruct them to only attack the train and not directly assault the power plant. The firepower that had been provided for the group was wasted on the locomotive.

A full hour past the time Larry was supposed to be heading home to see his wife, he was reluctantly travelling down I-25 with five of his men and three teenage strangers in a mine-resistant military truck, or MRAP. He hoped they would get to the warehouse before the Germans left. A convoy as large as the teenager had described would take at least two hours to travel the forty-five miles between Wellington and Cheyenne. He and his team would make the journey in forty minutes. If the Germans planned to attack that day, they would already be on the road, and Larry knew they would run into them. Larry assumed that Scheper would want to mount an attack under the cover of darkness. That meant his forces would likely move either three hours before sunrise or two hours before dark.

The front window of the MRAP suddenly exploded, covering Larry's face with shards of glass. His driver turned hard to the right and crashed through a barbed wire fence. The vehicle bounced across a shallow creek and over a steep bank before sliding to a stop behind a stand of juniper trees. Everyone bailed out. Larry grabbed his rifle and a pair of binoculars and ran to the top of the hill. He lay on his belly and scanned the highway. Five hundred yards out, a Humvee sat sideways in the middle of the road. Larry pointed his rifle downrange and scanned for targets. The vehicle looked empty. There was no sign of a driver or anyone else.

The sniper was well hidden. Larry knew that unless he could take him out, they would be pinned down until the rest of the Germans arrived. He scanned the terrain above the vehicle a little more carefully. There he was. The barrel of a rifle shifted almost imperceptibly a hundred yards from the Humvee on top of a ridge, nestled snugly between two granite boulders.

Larry pushed the range button on his scope: 587 yards. This man was good. He'd hit their moving vehicle from quite a distance. He calmed his breathing and focused on slowing his heart rate. He adjusted the scope, settled in, and started to apply pressure to the trigger. Just as the trigger was nearly depressed enough to send his bullet downrange, he caught a glint of sunlight out of the corner of his left eye.

Dirt flew up into his face as a bullet hit the ground right below his trigger guard. Larry rolled backwards off the mound below the second shooter's sightline and hurried back down to the stand of junipers.

"There's at least two of them," he said "I need another shooter. Any volunteers?"

"How far are they?" one of his men asked.

Larry smiled. "Nearly six hundred yards."

At that statement, a few of his men put their hands in their pockets and looked down at their feet. To Larry's surprise, the young boy stepped forward. "I think I could make that shot."

The boy looked down at his old .30-.30. Larry also looked down and shook his head. It was a difficult shot for anyone, but it would be an impossible shot for the old saddle gun the boy carried. Larry reached into the back of the MRAP and grabbed a rifle that was nearly identical to the one he carried. He adjusted the elevation and tossed it to the boy.

"This one will make things a little easier," Larry said. "If you actually make the shot, the gun is yours."

The boy shifted his feet. "I've, um, never used a scope before."

"It's easy," Larry said. "It's a lot like using the sights on your old Winchester there. Just hold it steady, center the two black lines in the middle on your target, and squeeze the trigger. The trigger won't be as stiff as you're used to, so avoid any pressure on it until you're ready to shoot."

They returned to the mound overlooking the highway. Five feet from cresting the hill, Larry offered final instructions. The duo crawled to the top of the mound and quickly settled in. When Larry found his target, he looked over at the boy. "You ready?" he asked.

"Yup."

"Okay," Larry said. "One...two...three."

They fired at the same instant. Larry's man didn't move after his bullet found the center of his target's forehead. Larry swung his rifle to the left in time to see the other target roll down the hill in a cloud of dust toward the sideways Hummer.

"Moederneuker!" the boy shouted.

Larry held back the laughter that was bouncing around inside of him. He wasn't exactly sure what the cussword the boy used meant, but knew the lad had good reason for being upset. A perfect, half-circle-shaped wound had formed just above his right eye. The scope had pushed back from the recoil of the rifle and popped him in the forehead. A thin trickle of blood flowed from the wound and streaked down the side of the boy's cheek.

"I forgot to tell you," Larry said, a slight grin on his face. "Don't hold your face close to the scope or you'll get scope eye."

Larry looked back through his scope and scanned for the man the boy had shot. He spotted him just in time to see him jump up and stagger toward the Hummer.

"Come on!" Larry shouted.

They ran back to the rest of their group. Larry jumped into the driver's seat of the MRAP while the rest of the group found seats. He tore down the hill and bounced onto the road in time to see the other vehicle disappear around a corner. He stomped on the gas. By the time they got to where the sniper's rig had parked, he was doing 87 miles per hour. He slowed to 50 and roared into a 30-miles-per-hour corner. A quarter of the way through, he again hit the gas. When they came out of the curve, he was nearing 80 miles per hour again. The other vehicle was nearly a quarter mile ahead of them. Larry knew he wouldn't be able to catch him on the straight stretches, but if the road had enough curves, he would draw even well before they reached Wellington.

Three miles later the road did become curvy. One 30-miles-per-hour curve after another greeted them. By the fifth curve, Larry could see the other truck in front of them.

He yelled at the blonde girl in the backseat: "What type of shot do you have in that double barrel?"

"Double O."

"I'm gonna try and get up next to him. When I do, shoot him."

The girl reluctantly agreed. Larry could sense her fear. He gunned the motor, and the distance quickly lessened. He pulled alongside the other vehicle just as they came out of a corner and into a long straightaway. The sniper stomped on the accelerator and started to pull away. Larry turned the wheel hard to the right and bumped into the rear quarter panel of the Humvee. It began to lose traction and slide sideways. Larry pushed down harder on the gas and followed the driver into the skid. The sniper overcorrected and slid back in the opposite direction. Larry backed off. The other vehicle went completely sideways and flipped over. It rolled several times and came to rest on its tires in the middle of the road.

Larry slammed on the brakes and the MRAP slid to a stop. He jumped out, pistol in hand, ran to the Humvee's driver-side door, and jerked it open.

The sniper was a middle-aged Mexican in a U.C. uniform. He was curled up in a ball on top of the center console. A bullet hole in his right shoulder and a few broken bones had messed him up pretty good, but he was alive. Larry looked at the U.C. logo on the man's sleeve and cursed. He never thought he would see that uniform again after they'd killed President Hartley and destroyed the United Collective army, yet here it was.

He grabbed the sniper by the shirt collar and dragged him into the road. The man groaned and slowly opened his eyes. "Puto americana estúpida!" the sniper yelled. "No tienes idea de lo que viene!" He spit at Larry.

Larry put his foot on the bullet wound and ground down with the toe of his boot. The man screamed out in pain. Larry removed his foot.

"English, please. You, sir, are in America."

The sniper grabbed his injured shoulder and wrapped his other arm tightly around his injured ribs. He gasped for air. Larry grabbed him by the hair and dragged him to the side of the road. The man kicked and tried to get to his feet. Larry slapped him across the face and put a knee in his chest.

"Hold his arms and legs!" Larry shouted to his companions. "Bring me a couple bottles of water and a T-shirt."

The prisoner's eyes, as well as those of Larry's teenage companions, grew wide when Larry soaked the shirt with water and held it just above the man's face. "I'm going to give you one more chance to tell me what you know." Larry said. "You'll find I'm a pretty nice guy. My mama taught me manners, and to always say please and thank you. So I am going to ask you again. Please tell me what you know."

The man's eyes narrowed. A thin smile opened on his cracked lips, revealing yellow teeth. "No hablo Ingles," he said slowly with a slight growl.

"Well, then," Larry said. "Consider this your first English lesson."

Larry shoved the shirt across the man's face and began to slowly pour water over the fabric. The prisoner held his breath for several seconds. Then, unable to control his body's need for air, he breathed in deeply, taking several ounces of water into his lungs. He coughed and hacked for several more seconds. Larry stood, held the shirt above the man's face, and let it drip onto his whiskered chin.

"You know," Larry said with a lilt in his voice, "there was a time in my life that I actually considered being a teacher. I really think I have a knack for it."

Larry knelt down again. Terror filled the prisoner's eyes when the shirt was again placed over his mouth and nose. Larry slowly started to pour the water again. The sniper shouted out with a thick accent, "I tell you all I know!"

Larry stood, threw the wet shirt on the ground near the man's head, and smiled down at him. "Now, see? That wasn't too hard, was it?"

Fifteen minutes later, after leaving the U.C. sniper tied up in the ditch to think about things, Larry's team was again on the road toward Wellington. Larry was trying to process what the soldier had told him.

The forces in Wellington were set to attack the refinery. The ERB was going to attack the dam. When the attack on the refinery was finished, the U.C. would meet up with another small force waiting in the desert near the town of McDermitt, Nevada. From there, the combined forces would march to The Dalles and finish what the ERB had started.

Larry knew the timing was going to be tight. They would need to deal with the Wellington troops, then quickly regroup in time to mount a defense at the dam.

A mile and a half from the warehouse, Sarah had Larry pull off the road. They hid their vehicle in a ditch and covered it with brush. Sarah led them toward the saddle shop, where they slipped inside to wait for dark.

From the shop, the observed some activity at the warehouse, but those inside were keeping a fairly low profile. There was a sentry stationed at each corner of the building, and one seated at the top of the fertilizer silos. Even under the cover of darkness, Larry knew it would be difficult to get close enough to do a thorough recon. If he could draw the closest sentry away from the building and take him out quietly, he might be able to slip under the fence where the girl had the night before. The sniper had said the attack would begin in two days. If the enemy commander decided to move the timetable up, Larry would have to retreat quickly and get back to the refinery in time to mount some sort of defense. Considering the heavy artillery the girl had described, Larry didn't think they would have much chance of saving the refinery if those guns were allowed to get into position. He could call in their few remaining Black Hawks, but knew he would risk losing them. His best hope was to somehow take out the artillery before the U.C. reached the refinery.

He had another concern—if they were discovered, there was no way that he, five of his men, and three kids could fight off over a hundred well-trained troops. He could go back to the refinery and gather more of his men, but that would leave the precious gasoline exposed.

Larry turned to the oldest girl. "How many people do you think live in town?"

"I'm not sure," she said. "Maybe five hundred."

"I need to go into town. Since you've been there, would you mind going with me?"

"Sure," she said, "if my friends can come with us."

Her two companions followed them to the front door.

"We can't all go," Larry said to his men. "Eight strangers walking into town would probably make the townspeople uncomfortable. Since these three know the area, I'll take just them along. The rest of you should stay here and keep watch until we return. It's at least three hours until dark. We should be back by then."

Larry and the teens slipped outside and headed into town. Larry knew it was a longshot to get the people of Wellington to fight. But he'd begun to think it was their only option.

CHAPTER 25

Nirschell Ranch
Seneca, Oregon
7:15 A.M., Thursday, September 17

ADAM STARED AT the boyish face in the mirror, raised a finger, and felt one of the seven strands of black stubble sticking out from the bottom of his chin. He had never shaved before and wasn't very excited about starting now, but the thick little hairs were starting to itch. His dad had never taught him how to shave and had died before there was a need, but Adam had spent many a morning talking to his father in front of the same mirror. He was pretty sure he could figure it out.

He put a fist-sized glob of shaving cream in his hand and awkwardly rubbed it across his cheeks and chin. Thoroughly lathered, he carefully placed the disposable blade against the flesh just above his Adam's apple and pulled the razer up to his bottom lip, cutting a chunk out of the point of his chin in the process. In ten minutes, nearly all of the shaving cream had been swiped away, and what little remained he wiped off along with what seemed like several ounces of his own blood.

He opened the bottle of Aqua Velva in the medicine cabinet and poured a quarter-sized puddle into his hand. Every muscle in his body contracted when he splashed the burning liquid on his freshly scraped skin.

"Shaving sucks," he said as he tore small bits of very valuable toilette paper from the roll and stuck them to his bloodied face.

"Adam! Breakfast," his mother called from the kitchen. He took one last look in the mirror and trotted toward the kitchen.

His mom put a plate of bacon, eggs, and hash browns in front of him and sat down across the table. He rested an elbow on the table and did his best to cover his face by leaning on his left hand.

"I'm going into John Day today," his mom said. "I want to get some wool and some Winter Wheat seed. You want to come along?"

"Sure," he said.

Either his mom hadn't noticed the butcher job on his face or she was just being nice and pretending not to notice. Either way, Adam relaxed a bit and enjoyed his breakfast.

At midday, Adam and his mom rode their horses into John Day. They could have driven, but his mother thought it would be a waste of precious fuel to drive anywhere they could just as easily ride. The rebuilding efforts and defense took precedence over a personal pleasure trip.

As the pair rode through town, Adam thought it was odd that more people weren't out and about. Usually at noon on any given day, people would be busy outside doing chores or visiting with their neighbors across white picket fences. Today however, it seemed like the town was completely abandoned.

"Where do you think everybody is?" asked Adam.

His mom looked concerned. Adam had to repeat the question before she answered. "I'm not sure. Maybe we should check at the fairgrounds."

As they rode closer to the fairgrounds, the sound of a crowd reached their ears. The rodeo arena was full of townspeople, and Mayor Harshem was addressing them from the announcer's tower. Adam and his mother rode through the gate and reined up at the edge of the crowd.

"...may not be any trouble," the mayor was saying. "I for one would rather be safe than sorry. Any extra defensive support we can provide will help ensure their success in restoring power. The latest report I received has the U.C. in southern Nevada, moving north. It's not a large number of troops, but if any of you that can join the linemen at The Dalles, I know they would appreciate the help. Without the extra manpower, they may not be able to finish the repairs. Jesse Williams is waiting at the south entrance. If you can go, please stop on your way out so he can get a head count and let those at the dam know what kind of support is coming."

At the mayor's last words, a spark ignited in Adam's spirit. The more he thought about his father and others who had fought at the beginning of the country's crisis, the more that spark began to burn. He'd regretted the fact that he was too young to go with his dad and fight for America at the start of the war. Now that Adam was fifteen, he believed his father would be disappointed if he didn't do his part for their country. The way he saw it, he had no choice in the matter. He had to go.

Adam turned and looked at his mother. She sat in her saddle, unblinking and staring up at the mayor. Her skin had grown several shades paler and her lips were pressed tightly together. He turned away and walked his horse toward the south entrance.

"Adam, stop!" his mom yelled after him.

Adam reined up and looked back over his shoulder. "What's wrong, Mom?"

She didn't answer, but Adam knew what was causing her fear. The war to remove the U.C. had started in the same place, in nearly the same manner. The dirty war that had gotten Adam's father killed.

"We're going home," his mother said. "Come on." She turned her horse and started to trot off without looking back.

"Mom, wait," Adam called after her. "I need to do this. I am not a child anymore. If Dad was here, he would expect—"

"No!" his mother snapped. She'd reined up and turned around. "I don't care what your father would do. I said no, and I meant it! We are going home."

Without waiting for him to answer, she turned again and trotted toward home. Adam reluctantly followed. He really did want to help. It frustrated him when his mom treated him like a child. He'd tried to be the man of his household since his father had been killed. He'd worked hard. He knew he worked harder than two of most men, but no matter how hard he tried, she just didn't see him as anything other than a child. Even with old Bill slowing down and not able to do most of the difficult chores, she didn't seem to notice or acknowledge how much he did to keep the ranch running.

Adam scowled and pulled the collar of his coat up around his ears. "You'd realize how much I do if I wasn't around," he muttered at her back as the pair rode out of town and up Canyon Creek.

His mom didn't speak again until they'd ridden into the ranch just before dark. "Turn the horses out and wash up," she said. "I'm going to fix supper."

Adam did as he was told. When he was finished, he joined her in the kitchen. "Smells good," he said. "How much longer?"

She answered without looking up from the pot she was stirring on the wood stove. "Fifteen minutes."

"I'm gonna go change clothes," he said.

He slipped from the kitchen and walked down the hall toward his room. He paused in front of his door and looked back over his shoulder. Satisfied that his mom was busy in the kitchen, he tiptoed past his door and slipped into her room. He opened his dad's gun safe and grabbed the SCAR rifle and Sig pistol. He also removed several boxes of ammo. Then he quietly opened the bedroom window, leaned out, and lowered the weapons and ammunition to the cold ground. He slipped from her room back to his own to change clothes.

When dinner was finished and the dishes had been put away, Adam excused himself and went to bed. It had been a quiet evening. Neither he nor his mother had much to say.

Adam lay in the dark thinking about what he was about to do and feeling guilty about it. He had never defied his mother, and had been her main support system since his father's death. He knew she would worry about him and might even try to find him. But he also knew he had to help. His dad had been passionate about his country and had sacrificed everything to defend it. That passion and patriotism was handed down to Adam. When the first conflict broke out after the collapse, Adam had been too young to join in the fight. Now there was no way he could resist the call.

He slipped out of bed, lit the candle on his desk, took out a piece of paper and a pen, and began to write.

> *Mom,*
>
> *First of all, I am sorry. I know you don't want me to go and help those at the dam, and I know you think I will get hurt. But I have to do this. I have faith that God will protect me, and will honor my desire to help in the rebuilding efforts. You and Dad taught me to help those who need it, regardless of the sacrifice. Right now, the people working to restore power need my help. Whether you acknowledge it or not, I am no longer a little boy. I wouldn't be much of a man if I sat by and did nothing. I hope you understand. Please don't try to find me. There are things that need doing on the ranch that Bill can't do. He will need you and Jillian both to help him. People depend on our family for the beef we provide. Please don't let them down. I will be home when the dam is safe.*
>
> *I love you.*
> *Adam*

Satisfied with his note, he laid it on his bed and packed supplies for the journey. He hoped she wouldn't come after him. Whether or not she wanted to admit it, he was a man. He refused to let her continue to treat him like a child.

With his pack nearly full and his sleeping bag strapped on, he tiptoed to the kitchen and filled what space was left with food and water. Excitement and apprehension danced across the hairs on his arms. He swallowed hard, took a long look around the pale kitchen, and smiled.

I can do this.

He started out the front door and into the night, then stopped. His dad had always emphasized preparedness. If he got stranded in the mountains, he might need to hunt for survival. The elk rut was at its peak, and he knew he could kill one if needed. He went back to his room and got a couple of his favorite Glen Berry elk calls and his hunting knife. Back at the front door, he paused and took a mental snapshot of his living room, then walked out, gently closing the door behind him. After saddling his horse and tying down his supplies, he tiptoed under his mom's open window. He quietly picked up the weapons, started to turn away, and froze. The soft sounds of sobbing drifted through the open window.

Adam fought the urge to run back into the house and hug his mom. She had been through more heartache than anyone should experience in two lifetimes, and he was about to pile on more pain and fear. No matter how much it would disappoint her, he just had no choice but to go to the dam. He knew he had to do it. He set his jaw firmly, turned his back on the house, mounted his horse, and rode off into the darkness.

The farther he got from home, the more the guilt retreated. By the time the sky had started turning grey in the east and he could see more than a few feet in front of him, he'd made it over Fall Mountain and nearly down to Hanscomb Creek. He reined up on a low ridge overlooking the creek, drank a bottle of water, and put the empty bottle in his coat pocket. He dug into his pack for breakfast and had just taken a bite of dry biscuit when a bull elk bugled from the creek bottom. His horse perked up his ears and tossed his head. Adam patted his mount on the neck and dug into a side pocket of his pack. His fingers found the diaphragm game calls, and he smiled.

Adam had learned how to call elk from his father, but had never hunted elk with him before his death. He had bow hunted elk a few times since, but had actually killed only one with his bow. Usually his frustration had taken over and he'd used a rifle instead. Tonight he would use neither. This would be just for fun.

He needed to get to the dam, but a half-hour detour wouldn't hurt. It was true that he was older and ready to fully embrace his newfound responsibility, but he would always retain the best parts of his youth. His love of wildlife and the thrill of the chase would always make him feel childlike.

Adam ran down the hill for a hundred yards, sat with his back to a bushy fir tree, and placed the "Sleazy" cow call reed in his mouth. He blew out a series of mews and calf chirps. Adam grinned when the bull answered almost immediately. He repeated the cow and calf sounds, and the bull answered again from the same place. A single cow call sounded just beyond the bull. Adam replaced his cow call with a "Triple Deceiver" bull call. He didn't have a grunt tube with him, so he unsheathed his knife, pulled the empty water bottle from his coat pocket, and cut out the bottom. Satisfied with his makeshift tube, he ran another fifty yards downhill and picked up a heavy, four-foot tree branch. He then found a tree with several feet of dead limbs hanging from its trunk. He clubbed his tree branch against the dead branches. The sound of breaking tree limbs echoed into the shaded canyon.

The bull bugled again, and did his best to intimidate Adam by finding his own tree to crash his antlers into. Adam smiled again and moved closer, stomping and rolling rocks as he went. After another fifty yards, he tucked in behind a fallen log. If he'd been hunting, he would have set up with the cover at his back so he could draw his bow. He placed the small end of the tube to his lips and sounded the most intimidating bugle he could muster through the short, skinny water bottle. He followed it up with several breathy grunts and waited. This time the bull didn't answer, and the woods all around him grew eerily quiet. A yellow jacket warmed by the morning buzzed around Adam's face. He for a large rock and rolled it down the steep bank. He watched it as it crashed down and bounced off a tree trunk.

The bull bugled again, causing the fine hairs on the back of Adam's neck to stand straight. The sound was louder this time. Adam switched calls again, blew out a sequence of three cow calls, and waited. Ten minutes passed. He was thinking of closing the distance again when the crack of a dry tree limb below broke the stillness. Adam strained his eyes as he peered into the shadows. A flash of movement in his peripheral vision caused him to snap his head around.

The bull had worked his way up the ridge and was now parallel with Adam, seventy-five yards away. A branch from below snapped again. Adam spun his head. A fat cow stood in an opening eighty yards directly below him. He heard the bull's hooves scrape on a patch of shale and slowly looked back. He could see the bull now. He was a big six-point.

The bull had stopped forty yards away and was looking from side to side, trying to spot the bull that had encroached on his territory. Drool dripped from his bottom lip, and Adam caught a strong whiff of his pungent odor. The bull tilted his head back and bugled directly at Adam. Adam froze and tried to control the shaking that threatened to take over his muscles. This was the most alive he'd felt in quite some time.

The bull walked past him at fifteen yards. As the bull's head disappeared behind a Ponderosa Pine, Adam pretended to draw a bow. Once the front shoulder had cleared the tree, Adam sounded a single cow call. The bull stopped, as if running into a brick wall, and craned its neck backwards, searching for the cow that had just called to him. This caused his vitals to turn nearly broadside. Adam settled into his pretend bow and took a deep breath. He let a little air out and held it as his fingers slowly opened and the imaginary bow string slipped from his grasp. He made a hissing sound as the pretend arrow flew through the air and sunk behind the bull's front shoulder, burying into both lungs all the way to the fletching.

"Gotcha," Adam said.

The bull immediately spun and plowed down the hill, nearly running over his cow. She followed him out of sight. Adam could still hear them crashing through the brush below, him long after the dust had settled.

He lay back. His breath came in short puffs, and his muscles twitched as the adrenaline began to subside.

"Why can't it work like that when I'm actually hunting?"

He rested a few more minutes. When the shaking finally stopped, he trudged back up the hill to his horse. He re-stowed his gear and climbed back into the saddle, just as the sun rose above the treetops. He looked down the hill again, waved goodbye to the elk, and trotted down the ridge toward The Dalles.

CHAPTER 26

Wellington, Colorado
9:00 P.M., Thursday, September 17

SARAH KNELT IN the dark on a small hill that sat eighty feet from the fence surrounding the warehouse. There was no moon, and the faint light from the stars gave her only about fifty feet of visibility. A breeze blew across the back of her neck. She shivered and pulled her stocking hat low around her ears. Her nose hairs had begun to freeze—she estimated it was less than 20 degrees. It seemed too early to be this cold, but winter was pushing its way in regardless of what the calendar said.

In spite of her newfound freedom to roam, and her desire to fully experience the Englishmen's world with its electricity and modern conveniences, she truly did miss her childhood home. She pictured her family and everyone in her village working nearly around the clock to put up the harvest for the winter. The wheat would be stacked in bundles and ready for the threshing floor and grist mill. The smell of smoked meat would be heavy in the air as the winter's supply of beef and pork were cured in the smokehouses. Her mother and the other women in the village would be making pickles and canning fruit and vegetables.

Sarah smiled as she realized the harvest would be safe from those who had taken from her people and brutalized them. But her smile turned to a frown and the familiar pain in her chest returned when she pictured the gang leader on his knees, broken and beaten, as she ended his life.

Julia crawled up beside her. "Everyone's in place. When Larry starts the attack, we'll be ready," Julia said.

"Are we doing the right thing, Julia? I mean, what do we really have to do with this conflict between the Englishmen and their enemies? When we fought off the gangs, we were doing so to protect the innocence of our people. I haven't seen the men in this warehouse do anything to threaten or hurt anyone. Who's to say what they really want or believe?"

Julia shook her head and squared her jaw. "You're right. You did what had to be done back home to protect our people. But the Amish are no longer our people."

There it was. Someone had finally voiced what Sarah had known since her father had walked away from her for the last time. She was no longer Amish, and would never be again.

"We are part of the Englishmen's world now," Julia contnued. "They are our people. If they say that this U.C. is a threat, we have no choice but to stand with them and fight. You heard the stories from the people in this town about what they had to endure at the hands of these invaders during the war. If the things they suffered are not just cause to join in the fight, then nothing is."

The big rollup door at the front of the warehouse squeaked and whined as one of the soldiers pulled on a heavy pulley chain. Sarah snapped her head around to watch as the giant door slid upward and headlights from a small vehicle shot outward, piercing the darkness.

"Everybody down!" Sarah hissed. "Hide in the ditch!"

She sprinted down the hill and dove into the dense weeds in the bottom of the narrow ditch. Julia dove in next to her and they both lay flat on the ground, panting. Sarah parted the weeds to peer out. The jeep exited the building and stopped at the front gate. A soldier opened it. The jeep was halfway through the opening when it stopped. The driver got out and spoke to the soldier: "I shouldn't be gone more than an

hour. I'm going to look for Melendez and Fritz. You need to have everything ready to move out before I get back. We leave at 4:30."

The man got back in the vehicle and turned onto the road, passing
Sarah from no more than fifteen feet away, giving her a good view at
his face. He had a truly wicked look about him: narrow eyes set above a
hawk-like nose, thin, pale lips, and a red scar that ran the full length of his
cheek, down his neck, and disappeared under his shirt collar. Sarah shuddered as the jeep drove out of sight.

The soldier closed the gate and walked back into the warehouse,
leaving the rollup door open. Sarah looked skyward and thanked God
for the carelessness of the soldier. An open door gave her and the townspeople clearer targets for their part of the operation. The disadvantage of
not being in an elevated position now that they were stuck in the ditch
was also lessened. Everything hinged on them providing the distraction
needed for Larry Collins to fulfill his mission.

Sarah looked at the watch Larry had given her: 1:00 A.M. She had
fifteen minutes to get to the loose spot in the fence and—

"Einfrieren! Auf deinen knien."

The shout came from the side of the warehouse near the fertilizer silos.

"Larry!" she yelled as several soldiers ran from the warehouse toward
the shouting. She knew they had to attack now or risk failure. "Fire!"

The townspeople rose up from the ditch and opened fire into the
exiting troops, easily cutting them down. The inside of the warehouse
came alive with men rushing into action. Several men got behind the
wheels of the troop transport trucks and began moving them out of the
way of the heavy artillery. Sarah sprinted for the fence, ducking as bullets whistled overhead. She got to the loose spot, crawled under, and ran
toward the tower. When she rounded the building, she skidded to a stop
and froze in terror. Larry was on his knees. Two soldiers stood over him,
their weapons pointed at his head. Sarah fought the urge to turn and
run. She knew if she did, Larry would die.

She quickly ducked behind a pile of empty pallets. She lay her head
between her knees. A spark of panic began to consume what little courage
remained in her. After everything she had been through, all of the pain

and torment for the lives she had taken, all of the self-loathing and bitterness, she had little bravery left to give. When she'd made it to Colorado and decided to embrace life without the Amish and burn the last symbol of her past in the fire on the sidewalk, she had changed. At the moment her dress had turned to ashes, she was certain that her life would be free of violence. She could love her husband and enjoy their new adventures in the West. Yet here she was, again faced with the choice: kill or let live. She didn't owe these people that kind of sacrifice. She didn't have a close relationship with Larry. Would coming to his aid and more bloodshed really make a lasting difference in the world? She could justify, even if it was a stretch to get there, the loss of life she had arranged. She had done so to protect the ones she loved. It had been her duty to shield them from evil.

"Ahhhh!" Larry screamed out.

Sarah jumped from her hiding place and rushed the two men standing over Larry. When she was fifteen yards away, she raised her shotgun and fired the first barrel, hitting the closest man in the center of his neck. His head flopped backwards. He staggered for a few steps, turning his back to her. His eyes stared into hers as he fell to the ground. The other man began to turn and raise his rifle. Sarah fired the second barrel into the center of his ribcage, knocking him off his feet and into the dirt.

She knelt next to Larry and cradled his head in her trembling hands. Blood slid between her fingers and dripped onto the red clay dust.

"I'm sorry," she said. "I . . . I should have been here."

Larry coughed. His lips turned bright pink as blood and bits of lung sprayed from his throat. He reached under his coat, pulled a bundle of dynamite, and thrust it toward her.

Sarah let go of his head, threw her hands up, and scooted backwards. "No. I can't."

Larry coughed again and managed to speak. "You have to do it. This needs to end here. Whether you know it or not, you are part of America now. You are the only one who can do this."

His hand fell to the ground. The bundle rolled from his grasp. Sarah crawled back up beside him.

"If you don't do it," Larry whispered, "everyone will suffer. Not just the people here, but everyone. Even the ones you left behind in Pennsylvania."

Sarah picked up the bundle like it was a rattlesnake and stared down at it.

"Just light the fuse and...drop it into one of the silos," Larry choked out.

Sarah reached into his coat pocket, grabbed a lighter, and stood. She turned and took one step toward the tower. A weak hand closer around her ankle.

"When it's done," Larry said, "go back to the refinery. Tell them the dam is in danger. They need to get there. Please find my wife, Amanda, in Seneca. Tell her I'm sorry. Tell her..."

Larry's face relaxed. His eyes stared blankly into the night sky. Sarah reached with trembling fingers and closed them. She knew it was her fault he was dead. If she hadn't hesitated, he would still be there.

She walked to the silos, leaned her 12-gague against a support, and looked up at the platform above the loading ramp that held the silos through tear-filled eyes. She fought the urge to turn and run, to leave it all behind and hide away with Jakob. Surely someone else would do what needed to be done for America without the help of an Amish girl. She shook her head, squared her shoulders, and climbed to the top. She opened one of the silos, lit the fuse, and dropped the bundle in.

Sarah clumsily scrambled back down the ladder. Ten feet from the bottom, one of her feet missed a rung and she fell, landing on her back and knocking the wind from her lungs. She gasped for air, but no matter how much her mind willed her to breathe in, she could not. She looked up at the silo and could see the orange glow of the burning fuse through the dirty white plastic.

Get Up! her mind screamed. *Run!* But she couldn't move. With her brain starved of oxygen, she began to lose focus. Two arms reached under her and lifted her into the air. She looked into the sweet face of Jakob. Her body convulsed and air rushed back into her lungs. She bounced in his arms as he sprinted toward the chain-link fence. He lay her on the ground and lifted the fence.

"I'm fine," she said, and crawled under the wire.

Jakob crawled through and ran two steps behind her as she sprinted for the saddle shop. Halfway there, she reached into her coat pocket. Her fingers closed around the flare gun Larry had given her. Without breaking stride, she pointed it into the air and sent the red flare blazing across the night sky. The sounds of gunfire ceased as she dove behind the building and covered her ears. Jakob lay across her body and wrapped his sinewy arms around her head. Thirty seconds later, the ground rumbled and shook from the force of the explosion, and the darkness was swallowed by a blinding white light.

They lay perfectly still for a full two minutes before Sarah rolled out from under Jakob. Smoke hung heavy in the air, burning Sarah's eyes. They slowly made their way down the street to where the front of the warehouse had stood. Burning debris helped light their way. Sarah stepped over a stump-sized lump and realized it was someone's mid-section, with no arms and legs attached. She turned her head to the side and heaved what was left of the breakfast she had eaten eighteen hours earlier. She wiped her mouth with the back of her hand and looked around. The scene before her was straight out of a nightmare. She imagined that the depths of Hell could not be more gruesome than what her eyes were taking in. The fence around the building was in pieces. Some of the tall metal posts had melted into shiny puddles on the ground. Bits of bone, blood, and torn clothing covered everything. Townspeople with bloodied faces and torn clothing stumbled through bodies. The sounds of people screaming and crying pounded on her eardrums, boring into her mind.

Julia! What about Julia? Sarah's mind screamed.

"Julia!" Sarah began walking faster, weaving in and out of the dying and injured.

"Sarah! Wait!" Jakob called after her.

She stopped and turned to face him. She couldn't look him in the eye. The shame of what she had just done pressed in on her, making it nearly impossible to breathe. Jakob placed a gentle hand on her shoulder. She jerked back like he had struck her.

"We need to find Julia," she whispered. "We need to find her, and we need to leave."

Sarah turned her back on Jakob again and jogged toward the other side of the road. Panic began to set in. She got to the ditch, leapt across, and began searching the faces of the bodies that were stacked across the hillside like freshly swathed hay.

"Sarah."

She whipped her head around and stared into the dirty face of Julia. They embraced, and Sarah began to cry. The tears flowed slowly at first, but soon were pouring down her face while her body convulsed with deep sobs. They fell to the ground. Sarah buried her face into the delicate shoulder of her friend. They lay unmoving until Jakob's strong arms lifted Sarah into the air.

Sarah's grew dizzy. Jakob's voice sounded faint, dreamlike, as he spoke to Julia: "We need to get her away from here."

Sarah had the sensation of floating. The screams and cries began to grow distant. Soon the only sounds she heard were Jakob's steady steps and her own shallow breathing as they moved away from Wellington and back toward Wyoming.

CHAPTER 27

Dale, Oregon
2:50 P.M., Sunday, September 20

ADAM PATTED HIS horse on the neck and stared down at the barbed-wire fence that stretched across the highway, blocking his path. A hand-painted, four-foot sign hung from a T-post and read:

KEEP OUT
TOWN OF DALE
NO RESOURCES

Adam looked for a gate or opening in the fence line, which ran in both directions as far as he could see . The wire was tight and the posts were driven deep in a perfectly straight line. His dad would have been impressed.

Adam sat a few minutes longer and weighed his options. If he rode along the perimeter, he would get around the boundary eventually, but that would take him away from the easy travel on the highway. He wasn't sure how far the fence went in either direction. Looking both ways, there didn't seem to be an end. Another problem with going around was

231

that he wasn't sure he could find his way to The Dalles moving cross country. He knew it was downhill and he would eventually run into the Columbia River, but there might be cliffs or other obstacles that would prevent him from reaching the bottomland. His trip had already taken him two days longer than he'd expected. Going around the fence might add another day.

Adam made up his mind to go straight through. He would be cautious and avoid people until he reached the other side. The few people he'd seen since leaving Seneca had been friendly, with the exception of the guy outside of Long Creek that tried to steal his horse and gear while he napped under a tree. If he hadn't woken up and hadn't been sleeping with his pistol by his side, he would've been on foot for the rest of his journey.

Adam dismounted and walked up to the fence. The wire was continuous, with no splices. He didn't want to cut the fence, so he settled on trying to jump it. His horse was a decent jumper, but it was too high in this spot to attempt it. He walked up the hill until he found a spot low enough to make the jump. The fence crossed a shallow ditch, just under a short rise in the terrain. If he had enough of a run at it, he was pretty sure he could make the jump.

He reached up and rubbed his horse's nose. "Whatcha think, Moe? Can you make that?"

He remounted and walked Moe back fifty yards. He dismounted again, checked the cinch, and made sure his load was secure. Then he gave Moe a last-minute pep talk: "You can do this, boy. This ain't no higher than Becker's split rail meadow fence, and I'm pretty sure I saw some really tasty grass on the other side. You know it's gonna be greener over there."

Adam climbed onto Moe's back, tightened his grip on the reins, and stood slightly in the stirrups. "Hup!" he shouted and kicked Moe's flanks.

Moe shot forward. Adam squeezed his legs against the horse's ribs. By the time they got to the fence, Moe was in full gallop. His hooves left the ground and tucked under his belly. The pair easily flew over the fence and landed gently on the other side. Adam reined Moe in and smiled.

"Atta boy," he said. "I knew you could do it."

In response, Moe tossed his head and whinnied. His nostrils were flared and his breathing was heavy, so Adam dismounted and led him back to the highway. They rested in a small meadow, where Adam ate his last dry biscuit while Moe gorged on lush grass. Forty-five minutes later, they were moving back down the road. Adam wasn't sure how many people lived in Dale or how far it was, but he decided to take his time, and if at all possible avoid the town itself. The trees were thick enough that they could leave the road when they got closer and quietly pass the town without being seen. Adam would've liked to trade with someone for more food, but the people within this boundary obviously did not want to be bothered, otherwise they wouldn't have so clearly said as much with their sign. If the trip dragged out any longer than another day or two, Adam knew he could shoot a few squirrels or grouse and feed himself.

Since he'd entered the Blue Mountains, he had seen numerous grouse, squirrels, and rabbits, as well as several mule deer. He would shoot a deer if he had to, but this would be a last resort. His dad taught him at a young age to eat every bit of what you kill. He knew there was no way he could eat a whole deer before reaching the dam.

A loud, melodic whistle sounded from the thick trees to Adam's left. He reined Moe in. A few seconds later, an identical answer sounded from the other side of the road. Adam had spent his whole life in the forest, and something about this whistle seemed out of place. It was unlike any bird he'd ever heard. Suddenly uneasy, he had the strange sensation he was being watched. Another whistle sounded down the road and around the corner. The back of his neck started to tingle. Moe was also nervous. His ears stuck up and his breathing had quickened.

Adam dismounted and quickly led Moe off the road and into the dense cover, thinking, I guess we must be getting close to Dale.

He slowly picked his way through the trees while carefully scanning the terrain on both sides of him. A dog barked in the distance. Adam froze. The dog was answered by another, and soon, several more echoed through the trees.

He turned and led Moe deeper into the forest, farther from the road. After a mile, he turned again, and was once again paralleling the highway. They walked for fifteen minutes. Adam stopped when they came to the edge of a gravel road. He tied Moe to a tree, unholstered his pistol, and crept into the roadway. The road led several hundred yards in both directions before disappearing around corners. He still had the sensation of being watched, but no more bird calls echoed through the trees. The sun had set, and he estimated he didn't have more than an hour left until it was pitch black. He walked back into the brush and contemplated his next move. It would be better if he could travel at night, but he knew that would be impossible due to the rough terrain and thick vegetation. He could pull it off if he travelled the highway, but that would surely put him to close to the town. He decided to camp for the night and start out again at first light. Hopefully he could be beyond the town before sunrise.

You should have gone around, idiot.

Adam knew the voice in his head was right. But he could also picture his Dad standing there, scowling at him for second guessing his choice. "Hindsight always has twenty-twenty vision, son," he would say.

He camped on a clear spot at the top of a small ridge overlooking the dirt road. He tethered Moe, unpacked his bedroll, and settled in for the night. His stomach rumbled and his mouth watered as he lay there and watched a fat gray squirrel chatter down at him from the top of a fir tree. He could easily take out the rifle and make a clean shot, but couldn't risk the noise. Even if he managed to kill a squirrel, he had no fire for cooking, and couldn't risk lighting one for fear of being discovered. There was no other option than to go hungry until he could get away from Dale.

He tossed and turned for over an hour before his eyes finally grew heavy and he slipped into a restless sleep.

Adam bolted upright and stared into the darkness, straining his eyes. His mind had registered the sound of a breaking twig below him. He listened intently for a full two minutes. All sounds had ceased, including the natural sounds of a nighttime forest. No crickets chirped, and no frogs croaked from the creek.

Adam crawled from his bedroll as quietly as he could and quickly stowed the gear back on Moe. He had slept in his clothes, hadn't removed his boots, and hadn't taken Moe's saddle off for his customary evening rubdown. He thanked God for his foresight, jumped into the saddle, and plowed down the hill, crashing through the brush. He hadn't seen anyone since entering the Dale boundary, but everything was telling him he wasn't alone. The fact that no one had tried to talk to him also told him that these people were anything but friendly.

As he neared the gravel road, a shadow jumped from the brush, blocking his way. Another shadow jumped into his path. His mind registered that one of the shadows held a rifle. Adam spurred Moe forward and crashed into the two, knocking them to the ground. He reached the gravel road and turned away from the highway. Adam spurred Moe again, and the horse jumped into another gear. Adam could hear men yelling behind him as he tore down the road. Just as they entered the corner, several shots sounded over Moe's hoof beats. They galloped full speed for fifteen minutes, putting at least five miles between them and the mysterious strangers. Adam slowed to let Moe walk and catch his breath. The old horse was lathered up from his head to his flanks. Adam felt bad that he hadn't taken the time to rub him down and give him a break from the saddle and stinky old saddle blanket, but he was very glad he hadn't.

"I'm sorry, buddy," Adam said as he patted Moe on the neck. "As soon as we get away from here and we're sure we aren't being followed, I'll make sure you get some rest."

The pair walked until daylight began to brighten the edges of the night sky and snuff out the stars. By the time the last star was swallowed up by the dawn, they'd come to a fence blocking the road. It was identical to the one they'd seen on the highway.

Adam dismounted and pulled his Leatherman multi-tool from his pocket. He hadn't wanted to cut the fence before, but now he relished the thought of damaging it. These people had made his life miserable for a day, and would make his trip more difficult now that he would be forced to travel cross country. He smiled as he cut the first strand of barbed wire. By the time he'd severed the bottom strand, he was in a pretty fair mood.

As soon as enough wire was cut, he wiggled the T-posts back and forth until they broke free and he could pull them up. He pulled up five posts in both directions, bending them beyond repair in the process. He randomly cut more wire every few feet. He finished his sabotage and looked at his handiwork.

"What do you think, Moe? That oughta tick 'em off a bit, huh?"

Adam remounted, rode through the opening, and turned around for one last look. He was about to continue up the road when he noticed a fat paper nest halfway up a fir tree. It contained, no doubt, a family of very ill-tempered baldfaced hornets. The air was still cold enough that the aggressive insects had probably not yet ventured out of their cozy nest for the day.

Adam dismounted again and laughed as he went to work. He cut a thirty-foot strand of the wire and attached one end to a bent T-Post. He walked Moe under the nest, climbed up, and stood on top of the saddle. Carefully, he wrapped the other end of the wire over the branch that held the nest and twisted it tight. Satisfied that it was tight enough, he climbed back down, hid the wire leading up to the nest on the opposite side of the tree, and laughed out loud.

"Boy, is that gonna suck?"

With his surprise complete, they continued on. He followed the road until the sun had fully cleared the treetops. He turned north and started to leave the gravel road when he noticed a large patch of shaggy mane mushrooms poking out of the deep dust of the road bank. He dismounted, pulled out his knife, and cut one of the short, white 'shrooms. He turned it over to examine the bottom. It was still closed and hadn't started to ink out yet. His stomach rumbled as he picked several pounds of the delicious fungus. He stowed them in his saddlebags and continued on toward the Columbia River.

At midmorning, Adam estimated he'd travelled at least ten miles. The landscape had started to change and the temperature had begun to rise as evergreen forest transitioned into juniper and sagebrush high desert. Moe was winded and starting to stumble in the rough terrain.

"Just a little farther, my friend, and we'll take a break."

They came to a spring bubbling out of the rocks. Adam decided they probably wouldn't find a better place to rest and recharge, so he reined up and dismounted. The horse drank deeply from the spring while Adam removed the saddle and rubbed him down with a handful of sagebrush. He tied him to a juniper and let him graze while he took his rifle and wandered off to find something to eat.

A quarter mile from camp, Adam began to grow frustrated. The only wildlife he'd seen was an occasional starling or meadowlark. He was too far below the timberline to find any squirrels, and so far he hadn't seen a rabbit. He wanted some protein to go with his mushrooms, but if he had to, he knew he could fill up on the fungus.

He started back to the spring. A fat cottontail rabbit burst from a clump of sage at his feet, sprinted across the rocky ground, and hid himself in a brush pile. Adam tiptoed up to the pile and peered into the tangle. The bunny was tucked in tight, with just its tail stuck out between a couple of branches. Adam could shoot it, but there wouldn't be much left if he put a .223 round into its body at that distance. He decided he would try and grab it, and if it broke cover and ran into the open, he would try a running shot. He wasn't very confident he could hit a moving target freehand, but it would be his only option.

He gently lay his rifle on the ground and slowly knelt down. The rabbit's head was out of sight, and as far as the bunny was concerned, it was hidden and safe. Adam slowly reached out a trembling hand and cautiously moved it in among the brush, careful not to touch anything that would vibrate and cause the rabbit to flee. His hand directly over the hind end, Adam paused and took a deep breath.

His hand flashed forward and his fingers closed over the back of the rabbit. It kicked and squealed as he pulled it from the brush. When he had it pulled free, it turned and tried to bite him. Adam swung it in a high arc and slammed its head down on a sharp rock. The bunny lay still. Adam fell back, panting, while the adrenaline slowly left his limbs.

Adam had never liked butchering the rabbits his family had raised when he was a child. He always got a little sad on butcher day, but the sadness was quickly forgotten when they sat down for their first meal of fried rabbit and potatoes from the garden.

Adam made his way back to the spring, stopping a few times to dig wild onions from the clay. He dressed the rabbit, broke it into quarters, and laid it on a flat rock. He dug his cast-iron pan from his saddlebags and lit a small fire. He had no oil or grease, but there was enough of a fat layer on the rich meat to melt and fully coat the bottom of the pan. Once the rabbit was fully cooked, he removed it and sliced up the mushrooms. He sautéed them in the fat with the wild onions and mixed everything together.

All in all, the meal wasn't bad. It needed a little salt, but that was something he had forgotten to pack in the haste of leaving the ranch. He finished off his lunch with cold, clear water from the spring. Once he'd stowed his gear back in the saddlebags, the events of the night before, combined with a full stomach, began to take their toll. His eyes grew heavy and he yawned deeply.

"Moe, my friend," he said, "I believe I need a nap. Wake me if somebody comes."

CHAPTER 28

Cheyenne, Wyoming
8:00 P.M., Tuesday, September 22

SARAH, JAKOB, AND Julia walked into the oil refinery at sundown, four days after fleeing Wellington and the destruction Sarah had caused. The trio had spoken barely a word since turning their backs on the dead and dying. They would have used the vehicle that Larry had driven to Wellington, but the keys had been blown to pieces along with Larry's body. So they took off on foot, traveling around ten miles a day.

Sarah hadn't eaten anything since leaving for Wellington, but she wouldn't have been able to keep it down if she had. The little water they had on their journey was barely enough for one person, let alone three people walking for four days. By the time they entered the refinery, Sarah was weak and dizzy, and her hands shook. Jakob had to have been in worse shape. He had carried her for miles after the explosion. She'd been passed out for hours, and been disoriented when she woke. They stopped for ten to fifteen minutes every three hours, but had pushed on with every bit of strength they had, trying to reach Larry's friends in time for them to get to the dam and defend against the attack that was surely coming.

The trio stumbled to the cafeteria and loudly slurped down nearly a gallon of water each. When they were finished, they lay on the floor near the water barrel and passed out.

"Sarah? Sarah?"

Sarah opened her eyes and looked into the face of the man gently shaking her. He took a step back as she rubbed her eyes and shook her head to clear the cobwebs. "Are you all right?" he asked.

She sat up and rubbed her eyes more forcefully. They felt as though they had sand in them. She opened her mouth and tried to speak. Her voice cracked and the back of her throat burned, as if she'd swallowed shards of broken glass. Her words came out in a raspy whisper: "Yes, I'm fine. Could I get some water, please?"

The man complied. Sarah drank an entire glass without taking a breath, then handed it to him again: "More, please." This time her words came a little easier.

After finishing a third and then a fourth glass of water, Sarah got up and walked to a cafeteria table. She sat down hard and leaned her back against the wall.

The man sat across from her. "My name is Josh McDowell," he said. "I was here when you left with Larry a few days ago. Can you tell me what happened in Wellington and why Larry hasn't come back yet?"

Sarah looked away. Tears began to fill her eyes. A sharp pain moved upward from her stomach and pressed in over her heart. She forced the tears back inside and looked back at Josh.

"I...we were at the warehouse...Larry. Larry is dead."

Sarah laid her head in her hands and began to shake. Sobs escaped her throat. She clenched every muscle in her body to stop the tears from escaping.

"Start at the beginning," Josh said.

Sarah composed herself the best she could as she recalled the events in Wellington, including Larry's dying wish that she go to Seneca and find his wife. When she was finished, Josh helped her wake her companions and brought them all some food. In spite of not eating for days, Sarah had no appetite. At Jakob's insistence, she managed to swallow a few bites of meat and a slice of warm bread smothered in butter. When they'd finished eating, they were led to a room with several bunks. They all curled up and quickly found sleep again.

The next morning, Sarah woke before her companions and went to the shower room. The morning refinery shift had already started its work day, so the showers were empty. Even though no one was around, Sarah still felt uncomfortable at the thought of showering in a place that anyone could walk into at any time. She looked around carefully before slipping out of her jeans and shirt. She placed them on a bench in front of a row of lockers, tiptoed back to the entry door in her bra and panties, and cautiously peeked out. The hallway was empty in both directions. She went back to the showers and stripped the rest of the way. Being clean had become a rare luxury since leaving her home. The only hot water she'd felt on her skin since the beginning of her journey had been the bath Julia had prepared on the sidewalk at Greeley.

She started the shower, stepped in, and let the warm water flood over her face and body. Instantly the dirt flowed down to her feet, turning the water swirling into the drain a dark brown. She reached up and slowly increased the hot water. Soon the dirt inside her began to work its way out as well. By the time her skin had turned a bright red, the inner blackness was rushing out in agonizing waves. She wrapped her arms around her stomach, closed her eyes, and bent over. The horror story that was her life after she'd left her home began to play out in her mind. The images that settled behind her eyelids became more vivid with each agonizing second: The cold, lifeless eyes of her first victim, staring up accusingly. The tormented face of her daddy as he turned his back on his little girl. The hoarse, pleading whisper of the gang leader. The young boy, Darin, falling forward and bouncing across the ground after the bullet tore through his chest.

The image of the face of her love, Jakob, filled Sarah's head. She quickly pushed it aside. It was replaced by the shining meat cleaver cutting into Allen's neck, then the burning bodies in Wellington.

"Sarah? Are you...um, is everything...?"

Her eyes snapped open and stared into Jakob's freshly shaven face.

241

Without answering his question, she ran from the shower and fell into his arms, knocking him off balance. His feet slipped on the wet floor and he stumbled backwards before sitting down. She laid her head in his lap. The tears she had bottled up began rushing out as he rocked her gently. They stayed that way for several minutes, until goosebumps covered Sarah's arms and legs and she began to shiver.

Sarah walked over to a stack of towels, dried herself, wrapped the soft cotton around her waist, and turned back to Jakob. She stared at his clean-shaven face, then slowly walked across the locker room, picked up her jeans and underwear, and stood in front of him. He rubbed the smooth skin where his beard had been. Sarah gently pushed his hand from his face. He looked so different, so much younger and innocent. She stretched trembling fingers toward him. Jakob smiled as her fingertips caressed his skin.

"Do you like it?" he asked.

"I think I do," Sarah whispered. She reached behind his head, grabbed a handful of hair, and roughly pulled his face down toward hers. She kissed him deeply and pressed herself against him.

Someone whistled a tune from the hallway outside the lockers. Sarah pulled away, wiped her mouth with one hand, and started to put on her underwear with the other. "We need to go to Oregon," she said. "I made a promise to Larry that I would go to the town of Seneca and deliver a message to his wife, and I intend to follow through."

"Josh asked me if we would go to the dam in Oregon," Jakob said. "And tell the men defending it what happened in Wellington, and what the soldier Larry captured had said. We'd be riding in the helicopter." There was no mistaking Jakob's childlike joy and excitement over his last sentence.

"What about our horses?" Sarah asked. She'd become quite fond of her horse and felt responsible for his wellbeing since rescuing him from the cannibals in Missouri. She also didn't care about the men at the dam, or care to be involved in their conflict any longer. She had only reluctantly become a part of America and the war to reclaim its independence. On the other hand, Seneca represented a place of hope for her. A place to start fresh with Jakob. According to what Larry had shared with her on their way to Wellington, it was peaceful there, and far from violence.

"We can leave the horses here at the refinery," Jakob said. "They have other horses and livestock, and Josh has assured me they'll be cared for. We could come back in the spring if you'd like and get them."

Sarah thought about it carefully before answering. If they went in the helicopter, they would reach Oregon much sooner than continuing cross country. It would take over a month, maybe two, before they could reach Oregon on horseback. The temperature was dropping, and the unmistakable chill of the coming winter had set in. There was a good chance they wouldn't get there in time to beat the snow. The chopper would definitely be quicker. Even if they stopped at the dam and had to travel on foot from there, they would still make it to Seneca at least three weeks earlier than they would riding the horses.

"Do you think we did the right thing, helping Larry?" Sarah asked.

Without hesitation, Jakob answered her. "Yes I do. I don't completely understand what everyone who is not Amish lost when everything collapsed, but I am beginning to understand that all of our lives are woven together by the idea of America. I feel like we're making things easier for our families, even though they'll never know what we did to protect them."

"I'm in," Sarah said after a pause. "Let's go for a helicopter ride."

Jakob smiled and let out a long breath. "I'll go tell Josh." Without waiting for her to respond, he turned and rushed from the showers.

A smile played at the corners of her mouth. She loved everything about her husband, but two of the things she loved most were his child-like heart and the way he looked at life. No matter how dark things got or how much pain she felt, he always managed to bring her back from the edge and keep a spark of joy burning in her.

An hour later, Sarah was seated between Julia and her husband in the backseat of a helicopter. The vibration of the blades spinning just a few feet above her head caused her to grip the pilot's seat in front of her, shut her eyes tight, and pray. As the skids left the ground and they began to rise into the air, her fingernails speared into the vinyl seat. The higher they rose, the heavier her insides felt. When they were well above the treetops and moving forward, she opened her eyes to a slit and took a quick glance out the side window. When she saw the ground and trees flowing by underneath, it was all she could do to keep from fainting. Jakob, meanwhile, bounced up and down like a toddler in a high chair waiting for a piece of birthday cake. Julia wasn't acting much more like an adult than Jakob. She had a full-toothed smile on her face, and she clapped her hands with delight as they roared over each landmark.

Sarah thought they were both being ridiculous, and wondered how they couldn't see the danger they were all in. Riding on the ATVs and in the other cars was bad enough, but this? This was just stupid. People were not supposed to fly. At least if they wrecked in a car, they wouldn't have far to fall in order to reach the ground.

Sarah snapped her eyelids shut again and threw more urgency and pleading into her prayers. Fifteen minutes passed before she dared another glance outside. The ground was at least twenty times farther away and the trees below looked like toothpicks. Directly ahead, the snow-covered tips of the Rocky Mountains glowed fiery orange in the morning sunlight. Sarah's breath caught. In spite of her consuming terror, she couldn't help but feel an equal amount of joy at seeing the beauty of creation in a way few other Amish had experienced.

Sarah let go of the seat in front of her and reached for Jakob's hand. He clasped his fingers in hers, turned his head briefly in her direction, and smiled. Just as quickly, he turned away again to stare out of the window. Sarah smiled and stretched her other hand to Julia. Her friend smiled and mouthed, "I love you." Sarah squeezed her friend's hand tighter and smiled back, just as the chopper cleared the Rockies and the ground suddenly dropped several thousand feet below them. Sarah let go of her companions, re-gripped the seat in front of her, and shouted a fresh series of prayers.

Four hours after Sarah's first trip in a helicopter began, and shortly after she'd started to actually enjoy it, they touched down on top of The Dalles Dam amid a flurry of activity. Men were rushing in and out of the powerhouse. Large guns were being mounted on top of the dam. Everyone seemed tense yet moved with a sense of purpose. Sarah felt fear begin to tug at the corners of her mind again. It made her angry. She had wanted to walk away from violence and death. She'd made a promise to

God in Wellington that she was finished with killing. Yet here she was, right in the middle of an upcoming battle.

"We need to find the man Josh sent us to talk to," Sarah said. "Even though they obviously already know what's coming. What was his name?"

"Sam. I think," said Jakob.

Sarah didn't respond. She turned her back on Jakob and Julia and rushed toward a large building to the side of the dam.

"Sarah!" Jakob yelled after her. "Wait!" He and Julia jogged after her. "Wait!" he yelled again.

Sarah stopped and slowly turned around. She could feel her face getting hot. Jakob and Julia caught up to her.

"What's the hurry?" Jakob asked. "I was looking forward to seeing the inside of the dam and learning a little about where the electricity comes from."

Sarah relaxed a little and forced a smile. There it was again, the child-like enthusiasm she loved so much. "I know you want to see the dam," she said, "and I was looking forward to it myself. But I don't think this is somewhere we want to be when these men start using those for what they are intended." She pointed at the row of big guns on top of the dam. "I want to be gone from here as soon as I can deliver our message and get our packs supplied for our journey to Seneca. We can always come back and see the dam another time."

"You want us to walk to Seneca?" Jakob asked. "I'm not sure exactly how far it is, but picture the map Josh showed us back at the refinery." Jakob pointed up at an imaginary map in front of his face. "If you remember, The Dalles is here, and Seneca is here," he said, pointing down about twelve inches. "It will take us at least a month to walk that far. If we had horses, we could probably do it in a couple of weeks, but we left those at the refinery. Think about what you're saying. Wouldn't it be safer to stay here until this is over? I'm sure someone could take us there in the helicopter after that."

Sarah considered Jakob's statement. She could see the logic in it. But if they stayed, there was a chance they would get pulled into the violence again.

"I'm not sure what the right thing is," she said. "Let's first find this Sam guy, do what we came here to do, and then we can decide what's next."

She turned her back on her companions and walked into the building.

CHAPTER 29

Banks of the Columbia River
9:00 A.M., Friday, September 25

MOE TROTTED ACROSS the freeway and walked along the railroad tracks that paralleled the riverbank. Adam sat tall in the saddle and turned his head rapidly from side to side, not wanting to miss any of the breathtaking scenery. He had never been to the Columbia River, but his dad had described it to him in reverent detail. From what Adam could see, his dad hadn't left anything out. The canyon walls were as tall as he'd imagined, and the wind blew hard and straight to the west. The willow bushes on the banks of the river swayed with the weight of red-winged blackbirds, brightly colored swallows, and mourning doves. He passed several groups of bighorn sheep sunning themselves among the rocks of the canyon wall. As far as Adam was concerned, this was by far the best part of his journey. He had always enjoyed being near the water, and some of his fondest memories of being with his dad were made on the banks of the John Day River, catching steelhead or rainbow trout. In spite of his time on the small river that flowed through Grant County, he was unprepared for the grandeur of the big river. Seeing it now made him a little sad. He had always hoped to view it for the first time with his dad.

He kept a steady pace throughout the day, stopping only occasionally to let Moe get a drink or nibble the tender grass at the water's edge. By late evening, he began looking for a place to camp. He had hoped to make it to the dam by now, but hadn't realized just how far from the Pendleton junction it was. He'd passed a road sign two hours earlier that said The Dalles was fifty-six miles farther. He was sure that after a good night's sleep and with an early start, he could make it there by midday.

He made camp near the water under a railroad trestle. After his experience near the town of Dale, he was a lot more careful about choosing a campsite. The sheltered location would hide him from anyone passing by on the freeway above. It would also help to mask the light of his campfire.

He unpacked his bedroll, unsaddled Moe, and gave him a thorough rubdown. Once his responsibilities were out of the way, he quickly dug through his pack and removed his telescoping fishing rod. He smiled at the memory of his uncle giving it to him on his seventh birthday, a week before his first trip through the Strawberry Mountains with his dad, where they'd fished the high lakes. The excitement he'd felt the moment he made his first cast into Slide Lake coursed through his veins once again. He definitely loved to fish. The fact that he'd eaten only a few bites of cold rabbit leftovers over the last few days helped explain why his stomach was in a state of permanent cramps.

This part of the Columbia was supposed to have large numbers of smallmouth bass. Adam had been looking forward to catching some since he'd left home. He rigged up with a number one hook and a couple of medium-sized, split-shot sinkers a foot up the line. After taking off his boots and rolling up his pants legs, he gingerly tiptoed to the water's edge. He hadn't brought any lures with him and had only a few hooks and sinkers, but this was his favorite way to fish. His dad and grandpa had taught him how to turn over rocks on the bank to find worms, catch grasshoppers in the dry grass, or turn rocks in the water to find crawfish or periwinkles. Natural bait always worked the best.

After turning over several rocks, he found what he was looking for:

a fat, juicy nightcrawler that tried to squirm back down his hole when the light touched its slimy body. Adam's hand shot out, and his thumb and forefinger latched onto the back of the worm before it could escape. He carefully pulled and jerked on the tasty bait until it cleared the hole and lay squirming in the palm of his hand. He threaded it on the hook, leaving about an inch hanging off. After creeping down to the edge of the water, close enough to dip his toes in, he tossed the bait into the middle of several boulders sticking out of the water. The sinker hadn't even hit the sandy bottom before his rod tip jerked down. He let the fish tug on it a few times, then snapped the rod tip back, completely hooking it.

He repeated the process several more times. After twenty minutes and six worms, he had a half dozen twelve-to-fifteen-inch bass. Adam skinned and filleted the fish on a flat rock, then gathered a few pieces of sagebrush. He sprinkled the sage over the fish and seared them in his cast-iron pan. It wasn't as fancy or tasty a meal as the rabbit, but it was nearly dark, and he wanted to sleep so he could start out before daylight.

When it was pitch black, he stripped down to his skivvies and crawled into the bedroll. There was no moon, and the flickering light from his small fire barely illuminated the creosoted timbers of the trestle. Camping by himself always made him a little nervous, and being someplace other than the familiar forest near his home added to his unease. He crawled out of his bedroll and retrieved his pistol from the saddlebags. He crawled back in and laid the gun at his side. Feeling a little braver now that he was armed, it only took a few minutes for sleep to come.

Adam bolted upright. At the same time, his fingers found the grip of his pistol. Twenty feet away, Moe whinnied and stomped his hooves. Adam wasn't sure what had woken him, but he sensed that something was out of place. He strained his eyes trying to slice through the darkness and listened for danger.

Was I followed from Dale? Is someone else close by?

He quickly dismissed the first notion, and then the second. There was no reason for anybody to follow him from Dale, and he hadn't passed any houses or farms since he'd entered the canyon. It was also too dark for anyone to travel. Nevertheless, he crawled from the bedroll, grabbed his pants, and leaned a hand on the trestle for support so he could put them on.

The trestle was vibrating. He pulled his hand away and wriggled his fingers. Had his hand gone to sleep? He touched the trestle again. The oily wood was definitely vibrating. He quickly dressed and scrambled up the bank. When he reached the edge of the railroad tracks, he lay on his side in the dirt and put his ear against the cold steel rails, just like they did in the western movies he used to watch with his grandpa. A low humming sound rose from the tracks.

He half ran, half slid back down the bank and scrambled to saddle Moe. He threw everything back into the saddlebags, not bothering to organize any of it, and pulled the horse up the bank behind him. By the time he reached the top, he could hear the distant sound of a train whistle echoing off the canyon walls.

"Looks like we may have company, Moe."

He'd heard from Chad Ellison that a train ran between the dams shuttling parts. As far as Adam knew, that would be the only working train in the gorge.

He looked up and down the tracks several times before the train came into view. A single white light pierced the darkness at least a mile upriver. The beams sparkled and danced off the water, filling him with anticipation.

"What do you think, boy? Shall we do a little hitchhiking?" Adam asked the old horse. Moe didn't seem to be listening. He stood stiff legged on tensed muscles, staring straight at the approaching light.

When the train was several hundred yards out, Adam stepped closer to the tracks and held his thumb out in a classic hitchhiker pose. As the train got closer, Moe stepped back and pulled on the reins held firmly in Adam's hand.

"It's all right, buddy" Adam said. "It's just a train, and if we're lucky, we can catch a ride."

Adam waved one arm over his head as the engine approached. The engineer locked eyes with him and had a bewildered look on his face as he hit the brakes. By the time the train came to a complete stop, the engine was nearly three quarters of a mile away. Adam jumped up in the saddle and trotted alongside the boxcars to the engineer who now stood on the ground holding a flashlight.

Adam dismounted, held out his hand, and squinted as the man shone the light in his face. "Hi. I'm Adam Nir, uhh, Nelson. I heard you were expecting trouble at the dam, and I'm on my way to help."

The engineer removed his hat and shook Adam's hand. "Pete Carter," he said. "We weren't sure if anyone else was coming. We picked up all the work crews from McNary and all points in between, and a group came in from Grant County earlier today. If you go back three cars, there's room for you and your horse, but make it quick. I'm already about five hours later than I wanted to be, and we need to have everything set as soon as possible."

The engineer turned his back on Adam, scrambled up metal stairs, and disappeared into the engine cab. Adam jogged down the tracks and pounded on the side of the third car. The door slid open and three men jumped out. They pulled a wooden ramp down so Adam and Moe could scramble up. The men were still closing the door when the locomotive jerked on the boxcars and started back down the tracks.

The boxcar was dark, but Adam could smell horse manure and unwashed men. His eyes stung at the stench. He stood unmoving next to Moe, not wanting to step on anyone. No one spoke. The only sound was that of steel on steel, and the occasional jingle of a bit in another horse's mouth. The ride was surprisingly rough. Adam had to hold onto the tree of his saddle to keep from falling down.

Soon Adam's legs began to tire, and he fought to keep his eyes open. By the time a sliver of light from the approaching dawn filtered in between the dirty wooden slats of the car, Adam could barely stand. When it was light enough to see well, he chose an open space against the opposite side of the car and lay down between two older men who were sound asleep. He closed his eyes and curled up in a ball.

"You gonna stay in here all day?"

Adam slowly opened his eyes and stared into the face of a green-eyed, dark-haired girl who looked to be close to his own age. He sat up quickly. A piece of dried horse manure fell from his face. He felt drool drying on his neck. He turned his eyes downward as he wiped off the slobber with dirty fingers.

The pretty girl laughed. "I'm Julia," she said. "Come on, I'll show you where they keep the horses."

Adam stared after her as she walked out of the dimly lit, completely empty boxcar. He rubbed his eyes, yawned, and stretched. They had obviously made it to The Dalles and everyone had left the train but him. The fact that he hadn't awakened while everyone de-boarded was embarrassing. The fact that this incredibly beautiful girl was the one who came to wake him made things even worse.

He got up and walked over to Moe, who was also obviously still tired. The horse stood with his head down and eyes closed. Adam picked up the reins that lay on the floor and gently stroked the silky soft hair on the side of Moe's neck.

"Why didn't you wake me up?" Adam asked his horse. "I'll remember this the next time you want to show off for some new filly we meet."

Adam led Moe down the ramp and into the midmorning sun. The girl waited with her back to him at the bottom of a grassy hill, next to a group of apple trees. Adam quickly ran his filthy digits through his hair in a feeble attempt to hide the fact that he'd been on the road for a week with no shower.

The girl turned around as he approached. "What's his name?" she asked.

"Uh, um, Moe," Adam said. He looked down at his feet.

The girl picked up a half-rotten apple from the ground and walked over. She scratched Moe on the top of the nose and held out the apple to him. Moe sniffed the overripe fruit, gingerly took it from her hands, and chomped it loudly.

"It's very nice to meet you, Uh Um Moe," she said with a wink at Adam. "You are a pretty boy."

Moe tossed his head slightly, and nuzzled her neck in response.

Her sarcasm wasn't lost on Adam. He felt his cheeks begin to warm. He'd always been a little awkward around girls other than his mother or sister, especially Amanda Collins. Amanda was very pretty, and he'd often thought about her. He knew it was silly, that nothing would come from such a childish fantasy. Now that he was around this Julia girl, he felt some of those same desires. There was something about this girl that caused his heart to race and his skin to tingle. It could be because she was the first girl he'd interacted with that was his own age, or it could be because he found her extremely cute. Whatever it was, he found it hard to speak to her or even look her in the eye.

She showed him the stables and helped him rub down Moe. Adam's discomfort was multiplied by ten when her arm brushed across his while they worked on the horse. He quickly pulled his arm away and walked to the opposite side of Moe. Julia giggled. When Adam shot a quick glance in her direction, Julia laughed a little louder and smiled at him.

"You are a funny boy," she said. "I still don't know what to call you."

Adam snapped his eyes downward, bent over, and pretended to examine a front hoof. Julia walked around the horse and stood over him. She was so close that he could feel heat from her and smell her perfume.

"What's your name?" she asked. "I told you mine. Now it's your turn."

"Adam," he said without looking at her.

"It's nice to meet you, Adam." She mussed the hair on top of his head.

Adam tried to stand up and step back at the same time. His feet became tangled. He fell back and landed ungracefully on the ground. This caused Julia to laugh as hard as she could, which in turn caused the heat in Adam's cheeks to burn with renewed intensity. He stood and rushed for the door of the stable.

"Thanks for the help," he said as he burst into the open air and breathed deeply.

"Where are you going?" she called after him. "I haven't shown you where you can bunk."

Adam kept walking. "It's okay," he said without turning around. "I'll find my way."

Her laughter floated over the roaring waters of the Columbia as he walked to the dam.

CHAPTER 30

The Dalles Dam
10:00 A.M., Sunday, October 4

Sarah sat with her back against the clammy, cold concrete wall in the corner of the dam's powerhouse control room. The sounds of the battle outside were muffled by twelve feet of cement and steel. Jakob wrapped his arms tightly around her and squeezed each time the big guns on top of the dam sounded and sent deep vibrations through their bodies. She had been praying and recalling different scriptures since the first shot rang out, but her mind kept coming back to Nehemiah 4:17: "Those who carried materials did their work with one hand and held a weapon in the other." She saw those fighting and trying to rebuild America like the men in Nehemiah's day who rebuilt the walls of Jerusalem, a sword in one hand and tools in the other.

Sarah looked over at Adam and Julia, smiled, and shook her head. They sat against the opposite wall, holding hands and staring into each other's eyes. The pair had been nearly inseparable since just a few days after Adam had shown up. In spite of the fact that Adam had used a false last name and had tried to avoid Sam Carson, his plan had failed. Sam had insisted that Adam hide inside the dam with those who weren't joining in the fight. Sarah thought he somehow didn't mind his banishment.

It wasn't that Sarah didn't want to fight alongside the people at the dam, or that she didn't understand what they were fighting for. She knew that if she and Jakob were ever going to live a life of peace outside of the Amish world, the United Collective troops would have to be driven from the land. She just didn't have the will to fight any longer. Since they'd left Pennsylvania, she had changed. With every violent situation she had been forced into and every life she had been forced to take, a small piece of who she had been was burned away. She was terrified of losing herself completely. All she had left to keep her grounded were her prayers, the love and strength of Jakob, and the hope of a normal life.

The gunfire ceased. Sarah let out the deep breath she hadn't realized she'd been holding. Jakob let go of her and walked to the door just as it opened and Sam Carson walked through.

"I think it's safe to come out now," Sam said. "The U.C. is retreating back down the river. We could use everyone's help cleaning up and tending the wounded."

Sarah followed Sam to the door. She paused in the entryway and looked back toward Adam and Julia. Neither had made a move to get up. Sarah smiled, turned on her heel, and followed Jakob into the bright sunlight.

When her vision had adjusted, the grisly scene before Sarah snapped into sharp focus. Several men on top of the dam had severe bullet wounds. Nearly every inch of the flat top of the dam was red and shiny. Sarah's hands began to shake. Bile filled her mouth with burning liquid. She swallowed the vomit and forced herself to take deep breaths.

"What can I do?" she asked.

Sam handed both Sarah and Jakob a toolbox filled with bandages and peroxide. "Help those you can," he said, "and let him know the ones who are injured the most severely." Sam pointed at a tall, skinny man in camo fatigues who had a stethoscope hanging from his neck. "That's Doc Harris."

Sarah and Jakob walked in opposite directions and got to work. Sarah had a difficult time keeping a firm footing as she slipped and slid through pools of blood among the dead and wounded. She crudely bandaged the ones she could and reported to the doctor the ones who were most likely beyond repair.

Neared the end of the dam, Sarah knelt by a man with a large wound in the center of his chest. He struggled to breathe and his face was twisted in pain. "Did we win?" the man asked in a hoarse whisper.

Sarah forced a slight smile, reached down, and grasped his hand firmly in hers. "Yes," she said. "Now lay still and wait for the doctor. You're going to be fine."

It struck her just how easy it had become to lie, and just how much the world had changed her. Before the chaos of their new existence sucked her in, she had been diffident, modest in her dress and mannerisms. Her life had a set order and she'd been sure of her place in it. Now she was someone new. Very little of who she had been remained. She easily embraced anger, she had killed, and she had felt pure hatred of her fellow man.

She looked down at the front of her bloodstained jeans and tried to wipe away the evidence of her transgressions.

The dam shook. Sarah felt herself moving through the air in a somersault—something had exploded fifty feet from where she'd been kneeling. She landed hard on her side, pushing all of the air from her lungs. It felt as if she'd cracked her ribs. She screamed out in pain as her body fought to suck in a breath. Gunfire erupted all around her. Men ran to the upriver side of the dam, shouting orders at each other. She got up and looked for a weapon as the familiar feeling of anger and hatred took over her mind. Her eyes locked onto a bloody rifle clutched by the hands of a very dead soldier. She took a step toward it and fell to the ground. Her left leg failed to support her weight. She looked down—her foot was turned sideways. Blood slowly seeped around the bone sticking through her pants leg and pooled on the cold concrete.

An RPG hit the top of the dam near the powerhouse door and exploded, leaving a four-foot crater behind. Sarah crawled to the dead soldier and picked up his rifle. She inched her way to the edge of the dam, dragging her leg behind her, and lay prone. She brought the rifle to her shoulder and searched for a target among the thick willow bushes on either side of the river, but the enemy was well hidden. The men on either side of her were firing wildly into the tangle of brush, shredding leaves and willow sticks but failing to actually hit anyone.

Sarah took a deep breath, looked through her rifle scope, and focused on a small section of willows two hundred yards upriver. A gun barrel emerged and pointed to her right. Flames and wispy tendrils of smoke curled from the barrel as the enemy soldier fired one shot, hitting a man fifteen feet from her position. Sarah controlled her breathing, shut out all the noise and chaos, and carefully aimed at the spot. Soon the barrel emerged again. She set her crosshairs a foot above the end of the weapon and slowly put pressure on the trigger.

The rifle bucked in her hands just as the enemy's rifle fired. A man tumbled from the brush and rolled into the river. Sarah stared at his body bobbing in the ripples and watched as it floated downstream and bumped into the face of the dam. The churning water rolled him over and over, eventually sucking him into the undertow and beneath the surface.

Sarah forced herself to refocus and managed to repeat her performance, killing five more of the enemy soldiers before the men on top of the dam repositioned the big guns and began filling the air upriver with lead. The cover of brush was no match for the heavy .50-caliber rounds. Soon the water of the Columbia was filled with floating corpses.

Gunfire filled the air from downriver again. Several of the men on top of the dam turned and ran for the other side just as a new wave of shots came from upriver.

Sarah held her position and concentrated her gaze on the shredded willows. A bullet struck the concrete just below her chin, sending sharp, stony fragments into the soft flesh of her cheek. She yelled in pain and touched the wound. When she pulled her hand away, she stared at the blood and chunks of skin plastered to her fingertips. Another shot barely missed her. She slid her body around to face the threat. A man emerged a hundred yards away and ran down the bank toward the top of the dam, followed by two others. Sarah focused on the first one and shot him in the center of the chest. He fell to the ground, dropping his rifle and a small duffle bag. The second man never broke stride as he charged past his fallen comrade and picked up the bag, just as Sarah's mind registered what he was carrying.

"BOMB!" she shouted.

She aimed at the second man and fired, missing him completely. She tried to calm herself, and took steady aim. She squeezed the trigger again. Nothing happened. She held the rifle in front of her and cursed at the sight of the open bolt and empty magazine.

Two of the men from the dam hurdled over her, dropped to one knee, and aimed their rifles. They got off a couple of shots each at the approaching threat before they both collapsed to the concrete, one with a bullet hole in the forehead and the other with a fist-sized hole in his back where his spine had been.

The enemy carrying the bag, now just fifty yards from the smooth concrete, continued toward the dam. His companion stopped and waited twenty yards behind him. More shots came from a sniper hidden in the brush on top of the hill. Sarah crawled to the fallen men and grabbed another rifle. She used one soldier's body as a shield and rest, raising her weapon and bringing the sights to her eye. A bullet struck the body she was hiding behind. Bits of clothing and a stream of blood splattered into her eyes just as she squeezed the trigger. She missed.

Sarah wiped the blood from her eyes and looked through her scope. She blinked rapidly, trying to clear her blurry pink vision, and focused on her target. She fired and missed. Another shot, another miss.

The man was only thirty yards from the dam. Sarah knew that if she didn't stop him now, everyone she loved would die. Twenty yards from the dam, one of her bullets found its mark. The enemy died on his feet, falling to the ground and sliding through the dirt. The last of the three men got to his feet and ran for the package in a zigzag pattern. Sarah fired several more times, missing completely. Thirty feet from the package, the last enemy soldier stopped running and brought his rifle up. Sarah steadied her aim and slowly put pressure on the trigger.

A blinding flash of light blocked her vision. At the same time, a sharp cracking sound pounded her left eardrum. The sniper's bullet tore through the cartilage of her ear. She rolled onto her side and grabbed for the side of her head. Searing pain scorched her nerve endings as her dirty fingers found the wound. She was already beginning to lose consciousness. She forced her mind back to the threat of the enemy with the bomb. She shook the cobwebs from her mind and reached for the rifle again, just as Jakob streaked past her.

"Jakob!" she yelled after him.

He didn't slow or look back. Sarah watched as if everything was in slow motion. Jakob charged toward the man with the duffle. Ten feet from him, Jakob leapt into the air, throwing his arms wide. He tackled the man at the waist. They fell to the ground, punching and kicking. They rolled around as bullets struck the dirt all around them, miraculously missing the mark.

Jakob wrapped his arms around the man from behind in a bear hug. The man kicked and squirmed. Jakob squeezed him tighter. The man thrust his elbow into Jakob's ribs, kicked himself free, and scrambled to his feet. Jakob recovered and kicked the man's legs out from under him. He fell face first to the dirt. Jakob was on him before he could roll onto his back. He grabbed a handful of the man's hair, yanked up, and slammed his face to the ground. More bullets hit near Jakob's knees.

Sarah raised her rifle and began randomly firing into the brush at the top of the hill. When her mag was spent, she looked for another rifle. She started to crawl to another dropped weapon. Fifty-caliber rounds whizzed over her head, causing her to lay flat and throw her arms over the back of her neck. A few seconds later all gunfire ceased, and a total silence fell over the smoke-filled air.

Sarah got up on her elbows and looked toward her husband. He had his back to her and was dragging the man away from the dam by his hair. She felt a surge of pride in the love of her life. After everything they had been through, he had stayed true to himself and had managed to be strong enough for both of them. More than anything, he was the reason she kept going.

Jakob and the man were now forty yards away. Sarah started to get to her knees and froze. A level of terror she had never known snapped her sanity in two. The ragdoll her husband was dragging reached out and grabbed the duffle bag as he slid by.

Sarah tried to scream as the man's hand reached inside the package, but no sound escaped her lips. She breathed deeply and tried to yell again, but it was as if a noose had tightened around her neck. She stood and hopped toward them, panting in short, ragged gasps. Tears filled her eyes. Desperation consumed her. She had to warn him, she had to get to him.

She took a final deep breath and exhaled in a guttural scream: "Jakob!"

Her strong, indestructible man turned to look at her. Their eyes locked. He smiled and lifted his free hand to wave at her just as the bomb exploded. The shockwave from the explosion slammed into her, throwing her backwards several feet, and knocking the wind she had just managed to regain from her lungs once again.

Sarah lay unmoving. Her mind floated in and out of reality. She felt as though she had dreamt everything. All of the trials and hardships that she and Jakob had been through together flashed through her mind in scattered, blurry images, bringing the pain of each event back to the surface as if it had just happened. After each scene played out, a clear picture of his face came into focus. It was all there. Her whole life since Jakob. Right up to this moment.

The scene of her husband dragging the man on the dam started to play out, then swirled and moved out of focus. It was replaced with the memory of the first time they had made love, in a pile of leaves under a towering elm tree. Sarah smiled and allowed her mind to leave the land of the living, dragging the last of her sanity deep into the world of dreams.

CHAPTER 31

The Dalles Dam
3:00 P.M., Sunday, October 4

ADAM AND JULIA emerged from the darkness of the powerhouse into dirty sunlight that pushed its way through dust and smoke, casting a mustard-yellow haze over the destruction. Nearly all of the gunfire had ceased except for an occasional shot or two from downriver as the enemy retreated.

Adam was stunned by all that his eyes were taking in. Bodies were scattered across the top of the dam. Some were missing limbs and some were shredded from head to foot. Nearly all were dead. Men moved among the bodies, looking for survivors and helping those that they could.

Adam turned away from the carnage, walked to the edge of the dam, and looked upriver. His stomach muscles tightened and dizziness clouded his mind when he saw the river running red with blood and bodies bobbing in the waves. He'd heard stories about the battle in Colorado and the aftermath, but nothing could have prepared him mentally for the reality of war. He was suddenly very glad that Sam had caught him and locked him away before the battle.

He felt a tear slip from the corner of his eye and slide down his cheek. Julia walked up behind him and placed a delicate hand on his shoulder. He quickly wiped away the tear and squared his shoulders.

"You okay?" she asked.

He turned and looked into Julia's eyes. She didn't seem to be affected the way he was. She seemed calm, almost relaxed. They hadn't talked about the things she had been through. Now Adam wondered if he wanted to know.

"I'm fine," he said. "I just...I didn't...I've never seen anything like this."

He turned away and glanced down at the churning water again. Most of the bodies and blood had moved downstream. The lifeless mounds of flesh were beginning to push together and stack up like a logjam.

Julia gently turned him back around. "We should help if we can," she said. "And I want to find Jakob and Sarah."

Adam smiled at her. "Go ahead," he said. "I'll follow you in a minute."

Julia smiled back, then walked toward the men who were tending the injured.

Adam stared at the bodies in the river for a few more minutes before turning away. He started off in the direction Julia had gone, but made it only a few steps before running into Sam Carson.

"How you holdin' up?" Sam asked.

"I'm all right," Adam replied. "What can I do to help?"

"We need to check on the wounded and assess the severity of their injuries. You'll most likely be needed to help carry the wounded to the infirmary. If you could get with Doc Harris, he can line you out. He's the guy over there with the stethoscope hanging around his neck."

Adam was about to reply when a man jogged up to Sam and excitedly gave a report. "We stopped them just below the lower lock," the man said, "but Scheper wasn't with them. One of the men saw him slip through right after the explosion. He's pretty sure he was wounded. Should we go after him?"

Sam cursed, then paused before answering. "Let him go," he said finally. "We need to take care of the wounded."

Adam walked off the dam and into the brush at the end of the large parking area. He sat down with his back to an oak tree, bowed his head, and began to cry. Anger, hate, and sadness swirled through his soul. Each emotion fought a battle for control over him. An image of his father settled behind his moistened eyelids and shoved aside the storm of emotions. It was by far his favorite memory of time spent with his dad.

Adam and his dad sat side by side on the edge of a grassy green meadow, shotguns to their shoulders and at the ready. The sound of a cold mountain stream bubbling over the rocks was muted by the gobble of a long-bearded Tom Turkey. His dad looked over and grinned, the sun softening the leathery wrinkles around his eyes. Adam smiled back, and his heart swelled with pride.

The image faded and was replaced by one of his mother and sister, Jillian.

Their arms were locked around one another, faces buried in each other's shoulders. Adam stood helpless, ten feet away. He wanted to stop their pain. He wanted walk to over and wrap his arms around them. He wanted to tell them that everything would be fine. But he couldn't move, couldn't find the words.

Adam stood and wiped his eyes with a dirty shirtsleeve. The images of his family were gone. Now the only vision left was the faceless form of General Edzard Scheper. More than ever before, Adam felt a burning hatred for the man who had taken his father. He wasn't sure what the monster looked like, but he had imagined a giant, seven feet tall, narrow red eyes set over a blank face, with blood-covered fangs jutting out over cracked and bleeding lips, and two horns poking straight out of the top of his head.

Adam walked to the corral, saddled Moe, and led him away from the dam. He tied him out of sight in thick brush and cautiously worked his way back toward the powerhouse. He retrieved his rifle, some water, and food. He also changed into full "predator" camouflage and painted his face and hands.

Forty minutes later, Adam knelt in the soft mud of the riverbank and studied a tangle of boot tracks. Several tracks of varying brands of boots led upriver. One track on top of the others led down. Adam walked into the brush above the trail and bent over, closely examining the tall grass and poison oak leaves. Satisfied that there were signs of only one person going downriver, he walked across the trail to the river side and repeated his examination all the way to the water's edge. Back at the trail, he took his time, inching forward while studying the tracks. He had to force himself to think about each step. It had been only an hour since the final explosion. Scheper couldn't be that far ahead of him, assuming he was still on foot. His dad had always told him while tracking an animal that "slow and steady wins the race." He wasn't tracking a deer or an elk, but the same principles ought to apply to tracking a man, especially if he was wounded.

For the next hour, Adam followed the trail downriver. So far he hadn't noticed any blood on the trail, but that didn't necessarily mean that Scheper wasn't wounded. The first elk he'd helped his father track was hit only a foot below the backstrap. The arrow had clipped the top of one lung, but the animal travelled nearly a half mile before his dad found the first drop of blood. After that, the amount of blood on the trail increased. They'd found the bull, dead, a short time later, just above an old logging road. If Scheper had been shot high in the chest cavity or through the stomach, it would take time for his body to fill with blood and leak from the wound.

The sound of gunfire from downriver echoed off the canyon walls. Adam raised his rifle and jumped into cover, leaving Moe standing in the open next to the trail. He cursed himself and ran out to grab the horse. When he reached for the reins, another volley of shots cut through the air. He could tell now that the shots came from a long ways downriver, at least a half mile.

Adam put his left foot in the stirrup, then froze. Every instinct was telling him to saddle up and ride hard for the shots. He took a couple of deep breaths, put his foot back on solid ground, and forced himself to calm down and think carefully about his next action. If he rode at a trot, he could be where the shots originated in just a few minutes, but he would be moving too quickly to study the terrain in front of him. This would leave him open to ambush. If he took his time and stayed focused on the tracks, he would also reach the place the shots came from. It would take longer, but would leave him more aware of potential threats.

The main drawback to following the tracks and not rushing down-river was that Scheper might find a vehicle and leave Adam with no more trail to follow. Adam didn't want to lose him. Still uncertain, Adam put his foot back in the stirrup and was ready to sling his other leg over the saddle. Then his father's voice sounded clearly in his mind.

Slow and steady wins the race, son. Take your time.

Adam smiled, took his foot out of the stirrup, and bent over again to study the tracks. He followed them for another fifty yards, where he found his first drop of blood on top of a smooth, gray river rock. It was no bigger than the head of a straight pin, but stood out like the long red neck of a mountain gobbler in a green meadow.

He moved a little quicker now but stayed focused. The size and fre-quency of the drops increased. Soon he was able to follow them without bending down. Adam also noticed that Scheper seemed to be slowing down. The tracks were closer together, and he seemed to be putting less weight on his left leg than his right.

Adam wondered how critically the monster was wounded. He also wondered why there hadn't been more blood on the ground in the begin-ning if he'd been shot in the leg. The only explanation seemed to be that the blood must have run down his leg and filled his boot before finally dripping onto the ground. If that was the case, it would explain the depth difference in the recent tracks compared to the earlier ones. If his boot was filling with blood, Adam hoped Scheper would stop soon and empty it. In an hour or two it would be too dark to see. Adam didn't relish the thought of spending the night alone in the woods on the trail of a wounded animal.

The blood trail was large enough now that Adam could see it sev-eral yards ahead. He mounted Moe and the pair moved steadily down the trail. After a quarter mile, the tracks left the trail and veered away from the tall cottonwood trees and through underbrush toward railroad tracks. The trail became faint again. Adam had to dismount and move slowly in order to follow it. By the time he reached the bank just below the railroad tracks, it was nearly dark.

Adam let go of Moe's reins and crawled up the bank, pausing just below the tracks. He reached into his pack, pulled out his father's Swarovski binoculars, and slithered to the top of the tracks. He scanned the terrain in both directions—no sign of Scheper. He had either been through here at least an hour earlier or he hadn't followed the railroad tracks. Either way, Adam knew he would have to wait out the night before picking up the trail again. He had a flashlight, but couldn't risk being seen. There was a good chance that Scheper had no idea he was being followed, and Adam was not about to tip him off.

He crawled forty yards down the tracks on his hands and knees, carefully studying every pebble in the railroad bed. He was about to give it up for the night when he found his next spot of blood. Even the most inexperienced tracker would've noticed the three-foot puddle next to the tracks. Adam's suspicion that Scheper was hit in the leg was now confirmed. He had obviously stopped here and dumped the blood from his boot. Adam decided the blood puddle would be a good starting point the next day. He removed a roll of orange ribbon from a jacket pocket and tied a long strand around one of the steel rails.

Adam slid back down the railroad grade and looked for a flat spot to camp for the night. An icy breeze blew across the back of his neck, sending a shiver down both arms and legs. Clouds had begun to gather overhead, and he could smell a hint of moisture in the air. He hadn't taken the time to pack his bedroll at the dam. If it rained, he would have no cover. He also couldn't risk lighting a fire. Even if Scheper didn't see the glow from the flames, the smell of smoke would likely give him away. He knew his best chance to be somewhat sheltered from potential rain and the Columbia Gorge winds was back at the river among the cottonwoods.

A light rain began to fall around two in the morning. By daylight it had turned into a downpour, and Adam was soaked clear through his clothes and shivering by the time he made it back to the ribbon he'd tied the night before. He walked to the top of the railroad bed and knelt down. The rain had completely washed away the tracks. Even more disappointing, the blood that had accompanied them was barely discernable from the rain-soaked mud. Now there was no way to tell which direction Scheper had gone. Adam knew he could start making circles from that point, gradually widening them in hopes of picking up the trail again, but it could take him all day. If Scheper wasn't injured as badly as Adam thought, he could be so far ahead in just a few short hours that Adam would never catch him.

He grumbled out his grandfather's favorite four-letter word and sat down hard in the mud. He felt helpless, totally beaten by the man who had taken his father from him. He had thought it would be easy to track Scheper. He thought by now he would have found him and killed him.

That's what I'm doing here, isn't it? I'm tracking someone in order to kill him. Is that who I am? Is this what I was raised to do?

Adam had killed a man once before to save his sister's life, but that had been an act of necessity, not a premeditated hunt. He wondered if he could live with himself or if he would be the same person if he killed Scheper. He knew he *could* do it, but he wondered if he should. He'd never been afraid of a fight. His dad had taught him that a man must stand up for himself and what he believes, and that sometimes the only thing a bully understood was a punch in the face. Violence was justified to protect yourself or others.

Am I trying to protect someone? Or am I just seeking revenge?

As soon as the question popped into Adam's mind, the answer rushed in behind it. He knew he was motivated by revenge. He quickly pushed the thought away. His pursuit was necessary to prevent Scheper from harming anyone else. He knew it was a weak justification, but he grabbed hold of it and vowed to hang on tightly.

He stood, studied the terrain again in both directions, and started to work out his options. If Scheper was having trouble walking well, as the tracks had indicated, he would most likely take the path of least resistance. When elk or deer were wounded and trying to evade a hunter, they always took the easiest route. Adam was almost certain Scheper would walk along the railroad tracks. But which way? Scheper had been travelling steadily downriver since leaving the dam. He probably wasn't aware anyone was hunting him, so there would be no reason for him to double back. Adam also knew that Scheper would likely head southeast, back in the direction of Texas and whatever compatriots he had left. This meant he would stay on the Oregon side of the Columbia and head west until he came to a southerly road away from the river. If he wasn't injured, he could leave the river at any point and travel cross country. But Adam guessed that wasn't what Scheper would do. According to the map Adam had studied at the dam, the next road that turned south was at least thirty miles west, near the town of Hood River. The easiest route.

He made up his mind and jumped into the saddle. He turned Moe south, toward I-84, and tore off through the brush. Three hours later, he reached the outskirts of Hood River, then turned back toward the railroad tracks. He wanted to avoid people, and couldn't afford the time it would take to explain who he was and where he came from. He had to catch Scheper before he made it to the town. A few vehicles ran on the streets and at the manufacturing plant. It would be easy for Scheper to steal one. If that happened, Adam knew he would lose him.

Adam rode to the riverbank and skirted the edge of town all the way to the bridge. He tied Moe underneath the bridge so he could reach the water's edge, then threw in all the supplies his pack would hold and patted his friend on the neck. He hated leaving Moe there, and hated not taking the time to rub him down. He had ridden pretty hard. The old horse was lathered up and rough looking.

"Sorry I can't give you a proper rubdown or take off that old smelly saddle," Adam said, "but we gotta be ready to ride as soon as I get back. I promise when this is over, you can have a couple days off back at the dam before we head home." Moe didn't seem to be listening or paying attention to anything but the tall moist grass under the bridge. Adam laughed, patted him on the neck one more time, and rubbed the end of his nose before heading back upriver.

He took his time on the railroad tracks. By early evening, he had travelled only four or five miles. At that pace, he figured there was no way he would catch Scheper until the next day. Assuming Scheper could cover ten to twelve miles a day with an injured leg, they would both have to spend another night on the trail.

By the time the sun had set and darkness was overtaking the landscape, Adam was exhausted. He hadn't rested enough or drank enough water. He started looking for a place to camp, and got excited at the prospect of taking his boots off and letting his feet breathe a little. He camped uphill from the river, seventy-five yards above the railroad tracks. From here he would have a good vantage point, and be far enough from the river that the noise of the water slapping against the rocks on the shoreline wouldn't mask any unnatural sounds.

He ate some smoked salmon and drank half of his water. He could've happily finished the water after the two pounds of salty fish he'd eaten, but without a fire there was no way to replenish his water supply until he got back to Hood River. He took his boots and socks off and moaned with delight when he rubbed his tired feet. Adam lay back and stared up at the stars that were visible from one end of the horizon to the other. At least it wasn't going to rain.

He had mostly dried out from his soaking the night before, with the exception of his under layers. These were still damp, due mostly to sweat. He had been taught to never sweat when hiking in cold weather and to dress in layers, but he couldn't help it. The temperature at night was still only in the low forties. He was pretty sure he would avoid hypothermia.

Adam rolled onto his side and tucked an arm under his head, exposing an armpit a few inches from his nose. He quickly regretted the decision. "Holy crap, I stink," he said. He hadn't had a shower for five days and was definitely ripe. If he'd have been hunting deer or elk and not a person, he would have taken the time to shower twice a day. His dad had taught him that the most important part of hunting was scent control. An animal's greatest defensive weapon was its nose.

He closed his eyes. The image of Julia settled behind his eyelids. She was unlike any girl he had ever met, not that he had met many. She was beautiful, confident, and very forward, yet she had a certain sadness about her. They hadn't talked much about her past. All Adam knew was she had been raised Amish and had travelled west with Sarah and Jakob from Pennsylvania. He had asked her about why she'd left and about her journey, but each time the conversation got close to her past, she'd quickly changed the subject or distracted him with a kiss.

Adam grew drowsy. Random thoughts flitted in and out of his mind. He thought about his mom and sister. He thought about how much he missed his dad, and about kissing Julia. The last thing he thought of was his first kiss. It had happened three days after meeting Julia. He'd been showing her how to catch bass in the river, and the line on her reel got a backlash. He reached out to take the fishing pole from her and their hands touched. He quickly pulled his back, and she slowly reached out and locked her fingers in his. When he tried to pull away, she grabbed the back of his head and pulled his lips to hers. He was terrified and embarrassed. He had never been kissed before, and he just knew he would make a mistake and she wouldn't like him. He had been wrong, of course, and realized very quickly that he liked kissing her, and that Julia was very good at it. He liked everything about kissing, and did it as much as he could. Even in moments when he didn't sense a closeness between them, he would cunningly steer the conversation to her past, and voila! Kissing. The thought of it was a pleasant way to fall asleep.

Adam sat straight up and reached for the rifle at his side. He fought to clear his mind. Something had woken him, but he wasn't sure what. He strained his ears and squinted into the darkness. There was no sound other than the river in the distance. The faint light from the stars only allowed him to see a few yards. He set the gun back down and reached for his jeans and boots. He was probably just being paranoid, but since the night in Dale, he had become extra cautious on the trail. He looked around for his horse, and felt a fresh infusion of paranoia and regret when he remembered he'd left Moe several miles downriver.

"Calm down, moron," Adam scolded himself. He closed his eyes and said a quick prayer to settle his nerves. He knew he needed to rest up to continue the hunt in the morning, but also knew he wouldn't rest until he'd discovered what had awakened him.

He crawled to the top of the railroad bed and gazed as far as he could in the blackness, sweeping his eyes slowly back and forth. He closed his mouth and breathed deeply through his nose. There it was. The faint smell of wood smoke tickled his nostrils. Someone had a campfire upriver. It had to be Scheper.

Adam slid back down the bank, put on his pack, and headed toward the low hill he'd spotted before dark. He decided he would go to the interstate, circle around, and come up the backside. He was fully awake now, his adrenaline surging as he jogged toward the freeway. His body tingled with a combination of excitement and fear.

At the base of the hill he startled several large animals that had been grazing under the oak trees. He froze in his tracks and listened as they retreated deeper into the brush. There was no rhythm to their hooves striking the ground and breaking branches. Adam decided they had to be either elk or cattle. If they had been deer, their hoof beats would be even and farther apart as they bounced away from danger.

Just after he started up, the long, shrill scream of a bull elk floated down from the top of the hill. Another bull answered the challenge behind him from the other side of the freeway. Several cows and calves began to chirp near the first. Adam continued slowly up the hill. By the time he could see the top of the hill a few yards in front of him, the sound of the elk talking was barely discernable. The herd had reached the river bottom and moved downstream, toward where he had camped.

Adam paused to take several deep breaths before crawling the last few feet to the top. By the time he'd settled in and looked for a fire below him, he was sweating profusely, in spite of the near-freezing temperature. The flickering light of a campfire bounced off vegetation at least a half mile up stream. Adam threw his rifle to his shoulder and squinted through the scope. Even with the firelight, it was still too dark to discern anything other than the dancing flames. He glanced at his watch and pondered his next move. It was 2:00 A.M. He had watched the three-quarter moon rise the night before at about 2:15 when he'd gotten up to pee. He decided to wait a half hour, then try and get a better line of sight.

By 3:00 A.M., there was enough ambient light to map the terrain below him. He moved down the hill twenty yards and looked back toward the top. Satisfied that his silhouette would not be visible in the dim light, he slowly moved diagonally down the hill. The farther down he got, the more the trees and bushes gave way to sagebrush and rock outcroppings. A hundred yards from the fire, he found a large boulder and crouched behind it.

He put the rifle scope to his eye again and settled his gaze on the dark figure on the ground. He could tell it was a person, but couldn't see any details. He wasn't even sure which end was the head and which was the tail, let alone if it was actually Scheper. He would need to get closer. He could easily hit the figure at that distance, but what if it wasn't the man that had caused so much destruction and suffering? What if it was just an innocent traveler? Even if it was Scheper, he might make a poor shot at this distance, only wounding him again. If that happened, Adam knew he might become the prey.

Adam kept his eyes on the figure and slowly moved closer, testing every step before putting down his full weight. Sixty yards from the fire, a loose rock rolled out from under his foot and crashed down the hill into a willow bush, shaking the dried leaves off the branches as it came to a stop.

In one motion, the figure by the campfire sat up, cast off his blanket, and threw it over the fire, extinguishing the flames and thrusting the riverbank back into darkness.

Adam held his breath. He heard movement below him and began to panic. If Scheper left now, it would be nearly impossible to track him without using a flashlight. Adam knew he needed to do something to keep the man from fleeing into the dark. He quickly and quietly removed his pack and dug out his cow elk call. He felt around in the dirt for a loose rock until his fingers wrapped around one. He picked it up and tossed it as hard as he could down the hillside.

The rock bounced down the hill, crashing off others. Adam put the cow call in his mouth, turned his head behind him, and blew out a few soft cow chirps. Over the next twenty seconds, he tossed more rocks and turned his head in every direction while making the elk sounds. As the last call drifted away, the bull that had been across the road earlier bugled from behind him, near the top of the hill.

Adam answered the bull with one long, whiney cow call. The bull bugled again. Adam could hear him charging down the hill. A man shouted out below him in German: "Mach weiter! Raus hier!"

Now there was no doubt. The man a few yards away was indeed Edzard Scheper.

Adam slowly exhaled, and began to relax when the fire flamed up below him once again. He looked around, chose another rock outcropping to hide behind, and settled in. He had a good vantage point now, and was close enough to make out Scheper's facial features. He was not what Adam expected. The man was only five-and-a-half feet tall and heavyset. No horns stuck out from the top of his head. Adam put the scope to his eye and studied him more closely. He didn't look like the ominous demon Adam had imagined. His eyes were blue, not red.

Scheper stood, limped over to the brush, and pulled several dead willow branches from the ground. His left leg was definitely injured. His pants were bloodstained from his thigh all the way down to where they disappeared into his boot. He stoked the fire and sat down.

Adam settled the crosshairs on the man's forehead and slipped his finger into the trigger guard. Just as he started to put pressure on the trigger, Scheper bent down to adjust the tourniquet around his thigh. Adam relaxed his trigger finger and took several deep breaths, trying to push away the nausea that was starting to twist his insides.

A sliver of doubt needled into Adam's mind and sank in deep. Could he actually kill someone in cold blood? Was it right to shoot someone who wasn't threatening anyone? When he'd left the dam, he had been so sure of himself. He had been focused on one thing: finding the man who killed his father, and killing him. If he shot Scheper, it would go against everything his father had taught him. The only time violence was justified was when you were protecting yourself or others. Adam had no doubt that Scheper would hurt innocent people again, but he wasn't hurting anyone now.

The minutes dragged on as Adam watched Scheper without making a move to shoot him. Several times he started to pull the trigger, but he couldn't commit the last sixteenth of an inch and complete the task.

He pulled his eye from the scope and let his thoughts wander. Several of those thoughts were focused on his dad. He knew he was ready to give up. It would be so easy to forget this man and melt back up the hill. He could go home and take Julia with him. Scheper was beaten. He would most likely leave America and return to Germany. But what if he didn't leave? What if he had another plan to destroy what had been built? Without Scheper gone, there would never be a guarantee that he wouldn't come back again and again until America was only a memory. Adam knew his mom would be so happy to see him. He also knew she had to be worried about him.

Adam's mind flashed back to a morning three weeks after they had learned about his dad's death. He'd stood outside his parents' bedroom in his pajamas, one eye peeking through a partially open door. His mom was squirming on the floor, her arms wrapped around a pillow, sobbing. Terror and helplessness filled him. He ran from the house and locked himself in his dad's workshop. Even there, he could still faintly hear her moans of anguish coming from the house as he sat in the dark with his knees pulled up to his chest, his head hanging down.

Adam began to cry as the pain of that morning returned fresh. His tears grew stronger. Soon his vision clouded and his nose ran. He wiped his eyes and swallowed his tears. The pain he and his family felt was not the only devastation caused by Scheper. Families all over America had gone through the same thing, all thanks to this man.

Adam settled in once again behind the rifle scope, lined up the crosshairs on the center of the man's chest, and slowly put pressure on the trigger.

The rifle bucked in his hands.

Scheper fell backwards into the dirt.

Adam let the rifle fall from his hands. He sat unmoving and shivered in the cold air. Only when the stars were slowly being snuffed out by the growing light in the east did he stand and slowly put his pack back on. Cautiously, he made his way to the body. He stood over the man, unsure what to do next.

Scheper moaned and moved his right arm. Adam was devoid of any emotion as he knelt down and gently rolled the body over. Scheper stared up into his eyes and tried to speak. Adam stood, folded his arms across his chest, and stared down at the man's face. Scheper coughed. Small flecks of blood and spittle flew from his mouth and settled on his lips.

"You," Scheper managed to whisper. "Who? Why? You're just a boy."

"I'm Adam," he said in a flat voice. "Adam Nirschell. Levi Nirschell was my dad."

Surprise and recognition flashed in Scheper's eyes. He began to laugh quietly. Adam turned his back to hide the tears that once again threatened to emerge. He walked downriver, the sound of Scheper's laughter growing weaker, yet following him. The soft morning rays of the rising autumn sun settled on his shoulders. Even as the chill on his skin melted away, the ice around his heart grew.

Staring straight ahead, Adam kept walking, until he could no longer hear the man. He stopped and looked back upriver. He was reminded suddenly of his seventh birthday. His grandfather had given him a Crossman BB gun, along with specific instructions to not kill anything he wasn't planning on eating. When a small sparrow landed on the fencepost outside his bedroom window, Adam forgot the words of his grandpa. He took careful aim and squeezed the trigger. The bird fell. He was so excited as he ran from the house to look at the bird. He knelt in the dirt near the fencepost and picked up the yellow-breasted sparrow. But the feeling of excitement turned to something else when he gently cradled the bird in the palm of his hand. Struggling for air, it looked up at him with tiny black eyes . A thin trickle of blood ran from the side of its beak and down the soft feathers of its breast. Adam began to cry. He held the bird gently and stroked the back of its head with a finger until it drew its last breath.

Adam turned again and started walking downriver. He looked up. White, puffy clouds drifted across a deep blue sky.

"I'm sorry, Dad," he whispered. "I'm sorry."

CHAPTER 32

Nirschell Ranch
Seneca, Oregon
7:45 P.M., Wednesday, June 30

SARAH MILLER STOOD on the porch of the Nirschell Ranch guest-house and leaned on the rail. It was her house. She had moved in a few weeks after arriving and delivering her message to Amanda Collins. Amanda had stood silently on that same porch, her arms folded, as Sarah had described all that had happened in Wellington, Colorado. When she'd finished, Amanda hobbled down the stairs and out to the end of the driveway. She'd stopped to look back over her shoulder. Then she slowly turned away and limped through the front gate. It was the last time anyone saw her.

The ranch had become Sarah's home, and in some ways her prison. Eight long months had come and gone since she lost Jakob, but the memory, and the burning pain of his death, had not healed. It festered in her like an open wound. The infection and fever coursed through every cell in her body. Some days she couldn't find the will to get out of bed. She just lay there with her eyes open, lost inside of herself, as the sun rose and fell. Joy-filled memories of Jakob would flood her mind, allowing her to escape the reality of consciousness, until her final memory of him on top of The Dalles Dam, smiling at her over his shoulder, rushed in. That was always where the memories ended. She tried to remember more, but each time his smile reached her, his image blurred and eventually broke apart, drifting away like a mist. Then the memories of him started at the beginning once again. She knew what had happened. Julia had told her, but somehow she couldn't see it.

She hadn't been able to go any farther outside the house than the porch since she'd settled in. Julia and Adam had tried to coax her out several times over the first few months, but she was afraid of what awaited her. She became uneasy and agitated when Julia visited and talked to her, almost to the point of hating their time together. Part of her even resented the relationship and love that had grown between Julia and Adam. She knew it was wrong. She knew she should feel joy for her friend, but she couldn't.

Adam's mom and sister had also visited in the beginning, but had given up on reaching her. The only interaction she had with any of them now was the occasional nod, wave, or friendly hello as they went about their day.

Sam Carson and his wife, Debbie, had visited the ranch five months after the battle at the dam, just as the power crews restored electricity to Seneca. They sat with Sarah in the house and told her in great detail, and with much satisfaction, all that had happened. After they'd cleaned up the destruction at the dam, they gathered all of their remaining forces and marched to Texas. With the help of the residents of Austin, they successfully took the land back and pushed the Mexican troops across the border into Mexico. Sarah didn't care. As she listened, all she could think was that she would trade every one of the people in her life to have Jakob back at her side.

The shadows grew long and the sound of crickets singing the world to sleep grew loud. Sarah walked back into the house and turned on the living room light. Her hand hovered over the switch as she looked around the room. She turned it off and on several more times.

"I wish you could see this," she said to Jakob.

She smiled. She could hear him as if he were standing next to her. "Lights at the flip of a switch is pretty great," he was saying. "But I want TV. I can't wait to watch TV. Do you think there will be cell phones again?"

Sarah sighed and walked into the kitchen to fix herself something to eat. Food no longer had much taste and she no longer had much of an appetite, but she forced herself to choke it down three times a day.

She carried a plate of bacon, eggs, and a slice of bread to the dining table, pulled out a chair, and carefully sat down. Her lower back cramped when she grabbed a piece of greasy bacon between her fingers, put it up to her lips, and paused. A familiar feeling of guilt washed over her. She dropped the strip of meat. Even though she hadn't bowed her head in prayer since The Dalles, she still felt conviction each time she ate a meal without first thanking God for it. Usually she could ignore the voice of conviction, but tonight it felt stronger, more insistent.

Sarah bowed her head, closed her eyes, and absently thanked God for the meal. She opened her eyes and reached for the food again. Before she could pick it up, the feeling of conviction intensified. A consuming warmth spread throughout her body. She tried to fight it. Tried to push it away. She could not. As if someone had flipped a light switch inside of her, words of prayer poured from her lips while tears poured from her eyes. Forty minutes later, she was still on the floor in the fetal position, crying out to a God she had tried to forget.

She opened her eyes, got to her knees, and reached for the napkin on the table by her plate of cold bacon and eggs. She dabbed at the corners of her eyes and stood as a flood of warm liquid poured from her body, covering her feet. At the same instant, an excruciating cramp started in the small of her back and moved to her stomach. She bent over and wrapped her arms around her middle. Another cramp slammed into her.

Sarah staggered across the house and out the front door. She made it to the bottom of the stairs and stopped, one foot suspended just above the gravel of the driveway. She looked out at the world beyond her porch, studying every shadow beneath the light. She turned to retreat up the stairs when the worst cramp yet enveloped her. She stumbled across the driveway, down the road, and up the stairs of the Nirschell home, where she opened the door and shuffled inside.

"Michelle!" Sarah yelled.

Michelle Nirschell rushed into the front room and caught Sarah just as she collapsed.

The distant sound of crying pulled Sarah back from the brink of unconsciousness. Her arms and legs burned, and her mind felt limp. Every ounce of strength had been squeezed from her. She could barely hold the squirming bundle Michelle had placed in her arms.

"Say hello to your son," Michelle said.

Sarah looked down at the face of her child and smiled.

"Hello little man," she said. "I'm your mommy."

The baby kicked and opened his eyes. Sarah smiled again.

A loud knocking on the door broke the tenderness of the moment. "Mom?" Adam said. "Is it okay to come in?"

Before Michelle could answer, the door flew open and Julia rushed into the room, knocking Adam aside. She hurried to the side of the bed, knelt down, and stared into the child's face.

"He's beautiful," she said. Julia reached for Sarah's hand. "He looks like his daddy."

Julia's words were a painful jab that tried to wedge its way into Sarah's joy.

Adam walked over, looked down at the child, and placed a finger in his tiny hand. The baby squeezed, causing Adam to smile. "He's strong," he said. "What's his name?"

Sarah smiled at her new family, started to answer, and then paused. The image of the Missouri child and his mother worked its way to the surface of her mind.

"Jakob" she finally said. "Jakob Darin Miller."

The End